Double
Lives

Also by Mary Monroe

The Lexington, Alabama Series
Mrs. Wiggins
Empty Vows
Love, Honor, Betray

The Neighbors Series
One House Over
Over the Fence
Across the Way

The Lonely Heart, Deadly Heart Series
Can You Keep a Secret?
Every Woman's Dream
Never Trust a Stranger
The Devil You Know

The God Series
God Don't Like Ugly
God Still Don't Like Ugly
God Don't Play
God Ain't Blind
God Ain't Through Yet
God Don't Make No Mistakes

The Mama Ruby Series
Mama Ruby
The Upper Room
Lost Daughters

Gonna Lay Down My Burdens
Red Light Wives
In Sheep's Clothing
Deliver Me From Evil
She Had It Coming
The Company We Keep
Family of Lies
Bad Blood
Remembrance
Right Beside You
The Gift of Family
Once in a Lifetime

"Nightmare in Paradise" in *Borrow Trouble*

Published by Kensington Publishing Corp.

Double Lives

MARY MONROE

www.kensingtonbooks.com

DAFINA BOOKS are published by

Kensington Publishing Corp.
900 Third Avenue
New York, NY 10022

All Kensington titles, imprints, and distributed lines are available at special quantity discounts for bulk purchases for sales promotion, premiums, fund-raising, educational, or institutional use. Special book excerpts or cus-tomized printings can also be created to fit specific needs. For details, write or phone the office of the Kensington Special Sales Manager: Attn. Special Sales Department. Kensington Publishing Corp, 900 Third Ave., New York, NY 10022. Phone: 1-800-221-2647.

The DAFINA logo is a trademark of Kensington Publishing Corp.

Library of Congress Control Number: 2023949925

ISBN: 978-1-4967-4315-2
First Kensington Hardcover Edition: April 2024

ISBN: 978-1-4967-4317-6 (e-book)

10 9 8 7 6 5 4 3 2 1

Printed in the United States of America

This book is dedicated to LuBertha and Otis Nicholson.

Acknowledgments

I am so blessed to be a member of the Kensington Books family. My new editor, Leticia Gomez, is so easy to work with! Thanks to Steven Zacharius, Adam Zacharius, Michelle Addo, Lauren Jernigan, Robin E. Cook, Stephanie Finnegan, the fabulous crew in the sales department, and everyone else at Kensington for working so hard for me.

Lauretta Pierce, you are amazing. Thanks to you, my website keeps getting better and better.

I am so lucky to be represented by Andrew Stuart, one of the best literary agents on the planet.

To the wonderful book clubs, bookstores, libraries, and my readers, thank you from the bottom of my heart for supporting me for so many years.

Please continue to email me at Authorauthor5409@aol.com, visit my website at www.Marymonroe.org, and my Facebook page.

Peace and blessings,

Mary Monroe

PART ONE

1901–1934

Chapter 1
Leona

*M*E AND MY IDENTICAL TWIN SISTER, FIONA, HAD STARTED SWITCH-
*ing identities when we was toddlers. It was fun fooling folks. If somebody
told her to do something she didn't like, I'd do it in her place and vice
versa.*

*Nobody ever caught on to what we was doing. Even when we ap-
proached middle age, we didn't stop. But I wish we had. Our last and
most elaborate switch was the reason somebody I loved got butchered to
death.*

*I wanted to help ease my guilt by telling my side of our story from the
beginning. And my twin wanted to tell her side.*

I only knew of three other sets of identical colored twins in
Lexington, Alabama. There was two elderly men who nobody
had trouble telling apart because one was real fat. Then there
was the Miller sisters at our church who was ten years older than
us. One had a purple birthmark the shape and size of a quarter
smack dab on the side of her right jaw. And then there was them
two boys who was three years behind us in school. One was cross-
eyed. They wasn't really twins, though. They'd started out as two
parts of a set of triplets. When they was a year old, a snake bit the
third boy on his rump and he died. After that, everybody re-
ferred to the other two boys as twins. Them other twins didn't
get along with each other like me and Fiona did. Me and her
was so close, we'd do anything for each other, even die.

Mama told us there had been a real bad storm the night me and Fiona was born in June 1901.

"The wind was so strong it blew part of the tin roof off our house and the rain flooded our living room. If that wasn't bad enough, it blew out every lamp in the house, *except* the one in my bedroom where I was giving birth. The midwife got so spooked, she left in such a hurry, she forgot to collect the dollar she charged for her service. And she never came back to get it. Folks said that was a bad omen, but I just laughed." Mama's words would come back to haunt her (and me) someday.

Our parents was old enough to be grandparents when me and Fiona was born. Daddy was forty-nine and Mama five years younger. Daddy had been married twice before. Both of his previous wives died before they could give him any children. Mama had never been married before Daddy.

"How come a pretty woman like you waited so long to get married when your friends—even the ugly ones—got married in their teens?" I asked her one day.

Mama looked nervous and started fidgeting before she answered. "I had a heap of boyfriends, but I was really particular about who I wanted to spend the rest of my life with. The right man didn't come along until I met your daddy. He was so good to me, I promised him that I'd stay with him for the rest of my life. And that if he died before I did, there'd never be another man for me."

Mama would keep the promise she'd made to Daddy. After his death, she would never keep company with another man for the rest of her life. He died in his sleep when me and Fiona was six-and-a-half years old. It was January 4, 1908. Mama took it so hard; she couldn't get out of bed for the next few days. Her best friend took care of the funeral arrangements and stayed at our house to look after me and Fiona. The same lady also packed up Daddy's things and gave them to anybody who wanted them. The things nobody wanted, like his underclothes, Mama made me and Fiona put the items in a pile in our backyard and set them on fire.

Like everybody else, Mama's friend couldn't tell me and Fiona apart. When one of us misbehaved behind her back, she took a switch and whupped us both to make sure she got the right culprit. Even at that young age, whuppings didn't faze me. The way Fiona screamed and bucked like a wild bronco you would have thought she was being tortured to death. I knew then that my sister was always going to be too "fragile" for her own good. I got tears in my eyes the day she told me, "I wish I could be more like you."

I missed my daddy. We all knew he'd been disappointed not to have a son, but I was a tomboy, so that was as close as he'd ever get. I spent a lot of time recalling some of the good times I'd had with him. While all Fiona wanted to do was sit around the house and read magazines and help Mama cook, I played ball with Daddy and we went fishing several times a week. There was times when he would get terribly sad about the way things was for colored folks. So he did something that made him feel better: He got drunk. When we went fishing, he'd stop at one of our neighborhood moonshiners' houses on the way to the lake and buy some moonshine. I noticed how "happy" he seemed when he drank and that made me happy. He would move quicker, his deep-set black eyes would shine like new coins, and a smile would spread across his dusky brown face and stay there until he sobered up.

Mama never allowed anybody to drink in our house. She didn't even know Daddy drank as often as he did, which was every time me and him went fishing.

"Clyde Dunbar, don't you never bring none of that unholy water into this house!" I heard her tell him one day when she smelled alcohol on his breath.

From that day on, Daddy would chew a plug of tobacco each time after he'd been drinking. It only made his breath stink more, but at least Mama couldn't smell the moonshine.

"Leona, I hope that by the time you get old enough to drink, things will be better for us and you won't need to drink," he told me one of the last times we went fishing. I usually did whatever Daddy wanted me to do. But I was so curious, I couldn't wait until I was old enough to do some drinking myself. I wanted to feel "happy" like Daddy and I planned to do it as often as I could.

On the second day in June the year Daddy died, Mama gave me and Fiona a party to celebrate our seventh birthday. While I was helping Mama clean up the mess we had made in the kitchen, she told me that when the midwife delivered me and Fiona, she named us right away.

"Leona was my grandmamma's name. She birthed eighteen babies. The first eight belonged to the white man who had owned her during slave days." Mama stopped wiping the counter and folded the dishrag. "Fiona was the name of a real nice old white lady I took care of until her family moved back to Ireland." There was a misty look in her eyes that I'd see almost every time she brought up my sister's name.

I propped up the broom in the corner next to the churn we used to turn milk into butter and plopped down in a chair at the table. I loved conversing with Mama. It seemed like every time she talked to me when Fiona wasn't around, I learned more things about her that I didn't know.

"I never would have guessed that you'd name a child after a white woman, especially because of the way they treat us," I said.

Mama raised her eyebrows. "Hush your mouth, girl. All white folks ain't bad. I done worked for some that treated me like family."

"Oh. Well, I hope I get to meet some like that when I get old enough to work for them. Fiona is a pretty name." I paused and gave Mama a thoughtful look. And then my tone turned harsh. "I wish you had named me that! Leona is a old lady's name!"

Mama didn't raise her voice the way she usually did when I sassed her. She continued to talk in a low, gentle tone. "Well, if you live by the Good Book, you'll be a 'old lady' someday."

Mama went on to tell me that she had the midwife tie a shoe-string around one of my ankles so she could tell us apart.

"The day after y'all was born, I told your daddy to give y'all a bath. I was still feeling poorly, so I had been lying down all that morning. That oaf took the shoestring off you and couldn't remember which one of y'all to put it back on! For all I know, you could really be Fiona and she could be you. That's why I never dressed y'all alike. And it's the reason I always made you wear a blue ribbon on one of your plaits and Fiona a red one, even when y'all go to bed for the night."

"I'm glad you don't want us to dress alike. I'd hate it if she ruined one of her frocks and switched it with one of mine."

Mama laughed. "Fiona wouldn't do nothing like that. Anyway, doing them ribbons every day got to be tedious real fast. But it was necessary. I never bathed y'all at the same time so I wouldn't get mixed up and put the wrong ribbon on the wrong head. I washed y'all's hair a day apart. I had hoped that by now one of y'all would have changed in some way so I could tell who was who without them colored ribbons." Mama heaved out a heavy sigh.

"Like how, Mama?"

"It would help if one of y'all gained some weight or lost some so y'all wouldn't be the same size no more. By y'all wearing them ribbons twenty-four hours a day, they get frayed real quick. If something was different about y'all, I could save money because then I wouldn't have to buy so many."

"What about that scar I got on my knee when I fell off the porch last summer? You could tell us apart then."

"Yeah, but after that scar healed up, y'all was exactly the same again. I never thought having twins as identical as you two would be so stressful. Sometimes I feel like I been blessed and cursed at the same time."

I snickered and stared at Mama from the corner of my eye. "If we wanted to play a trick on you, we could do it real easy. All we'd have to do is trade ribbons." I laughed, Mama didn't.

She gave me a hot look and wagged her finger in my face. "Oh, I ain't worried about that. Fiona is too virtuous to do something that deceitful. I declare, your sister is the kind of proper

little lady every mother would like to have. She can even play in
the yard without getting her clothes wrinkled or dirty. When you
come in from playing, you look like you've been rolling around
in a pigpen. You are so uncouth, you belch in church without
covering your mouth, you roll your eyes during the service, and
get into fights left and right. God bless your soul. I wish you
could be more like Fiona."

Hearing Mama praise my sister and berate me didn't bother
me at the time. It would someday, though. But I knew she loved
me and would even die for me, which had almost happened the
week before Christmas last year.

Me and Mama had gone to the only general store in Lexington that sold everything from clothes to household items. She
wanted to buy a wreath to put on our back door to replace the
one that a deer had chewed up. There was a heap of trees across
the dirt road behind our house. Every year we and our neighbors had to chase away all kinds of creatures that would mosey
up onto our porches and make a mess.

I was glad to go shopping with Mama, even when she didn't
buy me nothing. Colored folks was only allowed to shop in this
particular store for two hours a day, only on Friday and Saturday.
Fiona had been sick that Saturday afternoon and stayed home
so Daddy could tend to her.

Whenever we went shopping with Mama, she made us hold
on to the tail of her dress so we wouldn't stray off and get lost.
This particular day, I let go of her dress for a few seconds so I
could pull up my socks. When I attempted to grab hold of
Mama's dress again, I wasn't paying attention and I grabbed the
dress of a roly-poly, middle-aged white woman. She had on a gar-
ish hat that looked like a cross between a parasol and a bird's
nest. The way the woman reacted, you would have thought I had
pulled a gun on her. Her piggy blue eyes squeezed into slits and
her nostrils flared open like a bull.

"Don't you tetch my hem with your filthy black hands, little
nigger!" Before I knew what was happening, she kicked the side
of my leg like I was a mad dog. I got whuppings that caused me

more distress, so I didn't even flinch or stumble. Her calling me a nigger hurt more because no white person had ever called me that before.

Mama heard the commotion and stomped back down the aisle to where I was. My mama was a medium-sized woman at the time, and she looked so harmless and demure. Nobody would have ever thought that she was capable of violence. But she turned into a mama bear, a grizzly one at that, in a split second. The look on her face would have scared the devil himself. Her lips was quivering and her jaws twitched. Her eyes looked like they was trying to pop out of their sockets.

"Don't you ever kick my child again, you white devil!" Mama roared.

I had never seen her so mad. There wasn't too many other customers in the store, but I don't think Mama would have cared if there had been a hundred. She still would have risked her life to protect me.

The woman's mouth dropped open, and her eyes grew large as saucers. Before she could respond, Mama balled up her fist and socked her face so hard, her hat flew halfway down the aisle. The woman yelped and stumbled against a magazine rack and knocked it to the floor.

"Come on, sugar! Let's make tracks!" Mama hollered. She scooped me up in her arms and sprinted out the door before anybody could stop us. I was so proud of my mama that day. She ran with me in her arms all the way back to our house on the other side of town.

Mama made me promise not to tell anyone what had happened. She convinced me that if I did and the news got to the white folks, they would burn down our house with us in it. They had done that to another colored family last year.

She still shopped at that store. But every time she went, she wore a pair of old glasses that Daddy used to wear, a dollar bill–sized bandage on her jaw, and a floppy straw hat that covered so much of her face, she didn't look nothing like herself.

I chuckled to myself just thinking about that incident now. I chuckled even harder over what Mama had just said about Fiona being the kind of daughter every mother wanted.

"How do you know she ain't loud and rowdy when you ain't around? I can act like a 'proper little lady' and not get my clothes dirty if I wanted to and then you wouldn't know me from her."

Mama gazed at the ribbon tied around one of my braids. "That's why I still make y'all wear different colored ribbons."

Even with the hardships we had to face, we still managed to have fun from time to time. I had some fond memories. When we was in fourth grade, Fiona got picked to play Cinderella in our annual school play. I had been dreaming about playing one of the most beloved characters in fairy tales, but our teacher would only give me a role as one of her ugly stepsisters. I was so horrified I cried in front of the whole class. They laughed and that made me feel so much worse, I cussed at them and almost got kicked out of the play. Fiona begged our teacher to let me stay in. And then my wonderful sister consoled me the best way she knew how. She secretly played the ugly stepsister and I got to be Cinderella after all.

Everybody praised "Fiona" for playing her part so well. After we had switched back to our real selves, our teacher told me she was sorry she couldn't let me play Cinderella. Her excuse was that I wasn't "dainty, poised, and polished" like Fiona.

The following year, our teacher picked Fiona to play Sleeping Beauty. It was the only role I'd wanted more than Cinderella. Fiona let me play that one too and I got even more praises than I received for playing Cinderella.

Chapter 2
Leona

*T*HE NEW CENTURY HAD STARTED ONLY EIGHT YEARS AGO AND everybody from President Teddy Roosevelt to the elderly colored people who had been born into slavery and still living was predicting that the 1900s would be better for everybody. Even as young as I was, I knew it was only half-true. I'd overheard grown folks conversating about how things was going in the country, so I knew that white folks made all the rules, and they only benefited them. Colored folks had to do whatever they said. The same laws that they came up with to protect them and make their lives easier was made to keep us down.

I was sorry to see our birthday party come to an end. By the time me and Mama finished cleaning up the kitchen, all our guests had gone home. Fiona had claimed she was too "sluggish" to help clean up. She couldn't have been too sluggish because she was next door playing with one of the girls who lived there. Lazy was a better word in my book. I figured that was a privilege for girls who was too dainty, poised, and polished to do anything unpleasant. I didn't mind having to do extra work around the house when Fiona didn't want to. Something told me that I would also have to work much harder than she did for everything I wanted in life.

Me and Mama had left the kitchen and moved to our front porch steps where the flies and gnats was so bold, we had to swat the same ones two or three times. There was so many dark clouds in the sky, it looked like a dingy gray blanket.

"This smells like tornado weather. If it is, I hope it won't cause as much destruction as the one we had last June on your birthday," Mama said in a worried tone.

Our last tornado had demolished the homes of two families we knew, killed three people, uprooted the pecan tree we'd had in our front yard, and blew our next-door neighbors' mule into the next county. I was worried too, but I didn't want Mama to know that. "Aw, Mama. That little windstorm wasn't so bad. All it did to our house was blow out all the windows in our bedroom. We didn't get to have no party, but me and Fiona had fun helping you tack up the cardboard to cover our windows until you got enough money to get them fixed."

"Leona, I hope you will always look at bad things with a hopeful eye. You'll enjoy life better. But just in case we have another 'little windstorm' when we go in the house, get out the quilts so we can make pallets on the living room floor for us to sleep on tonight. If we huddle up together, we should be all right. I wouldn't want to live if something was to happen to one of y'all."

"Mama, I promise you, ain't nothing going to happen to me or Fiona . . ."

All of the colored folks lived in the same part of town. The houses on our street was small and shabby, but we all had decent-sized backyards and every single one had enough room for a small vegetable garden. There was a few colored folks in Lexington with money, like the folks who ran the colored clinic. They lived in the nicer, bigger houses two streets over from ours. Even though the doctors could afford to live in a better neighborhood, they couldn't because of the strict segregation laws. Mama said that them stupid laws had been made to protect the white folks from us. But they was the ones killing and tormenting colored folks, so how was segregation "protecting" them from us? I wondered.

On the other side of the trees behind our house was a street with more small shabby houses where the colored moonshiners did their business. There was a heap of white moonshiners too, but most of them lived in the more rural areas. Mama said the white folks with class like the ones she worked for bought their liquor from the few stores in Lexington that sold it, and from bootleggers. Most of the white-owned stores that sold alcohol and the bootleggers only dealt with white folks. So colored people made their own moonshine and made a good profit.

We had the party in our backyard, and one of the men in our neighborhood who went hunting a lot had gave us one of the squirrels he'd recently shot.

"Thanks for the party, Mama," I said. "We didn't get no nice store-bought gifts, and I wish we could have had something better to eat than squirrel sandwiches, but we still had fun."

Mama gave me a stern look. "In the first place, there is a heap of folks that would give anything in the world to have a squirrel sandwich. We ain't in no position to be so high and mighty. In the second place, don't thank me, thank God. If it wasn't for Him, we wouldn't be eating no meat at all." Mama leaned over and retied the ribbon on my braid. It had loosened up and was dangling in front of my face.

"Do you have to tie it so tight?" I complained with a grimace.

"If I don't, it might fall off."

I snickered. "And you wouldn't know if I was Fiona or me, huh?"

"Pffftt!" Mama waved her hand and gave me a mean look. "I ain't worried about that." And then she got real serious. "I know you and your sister better than I know myself, so I know y'all ain't got no reason to swap places just to pull a prank on me, right?"

"Right," I agreed. Poor Mama. She had eyes and a brain, but she couldn't see or think straight. She didn't know me and Fiona as well as she thought she did. We traded places all the time! How could we not when all we had to do was switch our hair ribbons? And we only switched when one, or both, of us had something to gain.

Because I was so tough and "unladylike," when Fiona did something bad, I took the blame for her. Like last month when she was playing with matches and caught the living room curtains on fire. When Mama confronted us, we both denied doing it. "I want y'all to go out in the yard yonder and each get a switch off that walnut tree so I can whup both of y'all. That way I know I'll get the right one."

By the time we got out to the yard, Fiona was already howling like a stuck pig. "Leona, I don't want to get a whupping. Can you trade ribbons with me and say you was the one playing with matches?" she sobbed. She had that pleading look in her eyes that always broke me down.

I couldn't say no to her even if I wanted to. I was strong and rarely got sick, but when we was younger she had one affliction after another. She had pneumonia twice within eight months when she was four and almost died. A year later, she had a five-day-long coughing spell. Right after she got over that, I woke up one night and seen her sitting on the floor in a corner. Fiona was scared of the dark, so Mama always set a kerosene lamp burning on top of a wooden crate by the door when we went to bed. "Fiona, why are you sitting on that hard floor?" I asked.

"I'm scared to go to sleep. If I sit up, I can stay awake."

"Why don't you want to go to sleep? Mama said you need as much rest as possible. What's the matter?"

"Last night and the night before I dreamed I went to sleep and never woke up."

"Oh. But the doctor at the clinic said you should be fine now."

She shook her head. "I didn't die from no sickness. Something just reached out and took me."

"You mean like the bogeyman?"

"I don't know. I couldn't see nothing but a dark shadow."

"Well, I ain't scared of the bogeyman or nothing else. Come get back in the bed. I'll make sure nothing happens to you." When Fiona got back in the bed, I wrapped her in my arms and held her the rest of the night. That was the position we would sleep in for several weeks, which was how long it had took for her not to be too scared. Sleeping like that was uncomfortable for me, but I didn't mind. Protecting my other half had become my mission.

Even though I was twenty minutes younger than Fiona, I felt

like I was obligated to protect her because she was such a scaredy-cat. She was terrified of dogs, cats, bats, horses, cows, every insect in the world, and even cute little creatures like ladybugs and butterflies. Just the threat of a whupping would paralyze her with fear.

I misbehaved way more than Fiona and Mama always chastised me with a switch. When she didn't feel like doing that, she would scold me so hard that one time she lost her voice.

We was still choosing our switches when Fiona got in front of me and asked, "Well, you going to take the whupping for me or not?"

"I guess so." I didn't mind making life easier for her, but it was nice when I got some benefit out of it. "What's in it for me?"

"I'll pay you a penny."

"Well, a penny don't go too far these days. If you make it two, I'll tell Mama I was the one playing with matches." Fiona stole the money to pay me from Mama's coin purse.

The next day, when Mama realized some of her change was missing, she confronted us. I took another whupping for Fiona.

Me and Fiona looking exactly alike had other advantages that didn't involve whuppings or scoldings, especially when we became teenagers. Fiona was smarter than me at school. Sometimes she did my homework so I'd get a good grade. Once she even posed as me and did a oral book report on a book I hadn't read, but she had. The teacher was so impressed, she gave me a A+.

One day at recess a older girl who liked to bully younger kids put a frog down the back of Fiona's blouse. Fiona was still terrified of small creatures, so she exploded and clobbered that girl like she had stole her candy. None of the colored folks we knew had telephones yet, but news traveled fast in Lexington. One person could tell ten others something and in no time, almost everybody in our neighborhood would know about it. Mama knew about Fiona's fight before we even got home from school that day. "Y'all get in that bedroom and get out of them school clothes. And then, Fiona, you go out in that yard yonder and get a switch."

As soon as we got to our room, Fiona looked at me and didn't even have to ask. "Don't worry, I got this one," I told her as we traded ribbons. Whupping her angelic Fiona must have really hurt Mama because she cried after she was done. To be more believable, I cried too.

When we went to school the next day, several of our class-mates told me that same bully had been laughing about Fiona getting a whupping. As soon as we went to the yard for our re-cess that morning, I gave that heifer a black eye and was glad to get another whupping when I got home.

Chapter 3
Fiona

ONE OF THE NICE WHITE LADIES THAT MAMA COOKED AND CLEANED for gave her a big boxy radio. It was one of the many "luxury" items we could never afford without letting something else go, like food and rent. Mama never turned down nothing somebody offered her, even things we didn't have no use for at the time, but eventually would. She set the radio on one of the end tables in our living room.

Our house wasn't no showplace, but we was proud of our mismatched furniture, curtains Mama had made by hand, and cheap pictures on the living-room wall of Jesus and his disciples. Despite all the tornadoes we had to deal with every year, most of the small, shabby, one-story houses in our neck of the woods was still intact. I told Mama it was because luck was on our side. She said it was because Jesus was on our side. One thing I knew not to do was argue with Mama when she brought the Lord into a conversation.

Me and Leona shared the smaller of our two bedrooms, as well as the bed. We had a itty-bitty closet, but we kept most of our clothes in a chifforobe facing the bed. It was another "gift" from one of the nice ladies Mama worked for.

Now that we owned a radio too, it seemed like we was really coming up in the world. Every evening after supper, we would sit in the living room for an hour or two and listen to it. The knob was missing, so we had to turn it on and off with a fork. Reception was so weak we could only pick up one station during the day, but at night around seven, we got two more stations. Some nights we'd listen to gospel music and laugh at the way them white folks sang. "That last soloist sounded like somebody stepping on a cat's tail," Mama laughed one warm night in May, a month before me and Leona's sixteenth birthday. "It's a shame them folks let us cook and clean for them, and raise their young'uns, but they won't let us show them how to sing proper."

"Listening to them sing is better than listening to one of President Woodrow Wilson's long-winded speeches. That man don't know when to hush," I said. "Especially after he got our country into that war last month with them folks in Germany."

Mama reared back on our fading brown couch and gave me a hot look. She narrowed her eyes at us so often, I was surprised they hadn't got stuck in that position. "Watch your mouth, girl. So long as there is a war going on, we need to listen to the president and all the news programs so we can stay up-to-date," she advised.

"Why come? That war ain't got nothing to do with colored folks," Leona piped in.

"That war affects us as much as it do them white folks! A lot of our young colored men done joined the military and some won't come back home alive, or in the shape they left here in. By the time y'all start looking for a husband, there will be five girls to every one man. And the cutest girls will get the best men."

The last part of Mama's comment made me feel good. People was always telling me and Leona we was cute. Mama liked to brag to her friends about the cinnamon-colored skin tone, big brown eyes, and high cheek bones we'd inherited from her. Even though we was teenagers now, she still wanted us to wear them doggone ribbons. But instead of them ugly plaits, we wore our shoulder-length jet-black hair in ponytails now. There was other ways for folks to tell us apart now, though. Leona wore face powder, rouge, and lipstick. Some of the ladies she babysat for gave her leftover makeup, but she bought most of them items with money she made running errands for neighbors and working on the farms when the crops was in season. For some reason, makeup made my face itch, so after wearing it a few times, I gave up. I didn't have that problem with lipstick, so I wore it when I wanted to get dolled up.

Boys gave us a lot of attention, but Mama said we couldn't start courting until we turned sixteen next month. We had the slip on her because we'd been sneaking out on dates since we was thirteen. The window in our bedroom was low to the ground so it was easy to jump out. And it was at the back of our house, so our nosy neighbors couldn't see us sneak out at night to go to get-togethers where there would be plenty of boys and moonshine.

Leona snuck out more often than I did, and she'd been caught climbing back in through the window a heap of times. But that didn't stop us from having a good time with our friends. We also let boys climb through our window to pay us late-night visits after Mama had gone to bed. Leona would only let her boyfriends feel her up and down and kiss her. I was too curious and hot to settle for something that unfulfilling. I was having so much fun, getting pregnant or catching the nasty-woman's disease never even crossed my mind.

On our sixteenth birthday, while we was sitting at the kitchen table eating the last of the cake Mama had made, she told us we could start dating. "I know most of y'all's friends been dating for a while, but I wanted y'all to be a little more mature first. Boys and men are like little puppies. A female needs to be at least sixteen because by then she's smart enough to know how to potty train them because they don't know their buttholes from rabbit holes." When Mama left the room, me and Leona snickered. I'd just been on a date the night before.

I always attracted boys that didn't have enough money to pay my way into the movies or buy me something often enough to suit me. Leona's luck was better. She was seeing a cute eighteen-year-old boy named Ernest Lee Royster, the son of a moonshiner. His puffy, chestnut-brown cheeks and itty-bitty black eyes made him look like a cuddly little chipmunk. Ernest Lee snuck alcohol out of his daddy's supply and shared it with his friends. He had dropped out of school in eighth grade and started working on a pig farm, so he had big money and he liked to spend some of it on Leona.

When I told Leona I was jealous because she landed the perfect boyfriend, she gave me a pitying look and then her eyes suddenly lit up. "I got a idea! Why don't you go up to Ernest Lee and pretend to be me sometime so he can treat you to movies and free meals at nice restaurants."

I looked at Leona with such awe you would have thought she'd just discovered a cure for every disease known to man. "Whoopy-doo! That is a good idea." My excitement didn't last long. "What if he wants to kiss me at the end of the date?"

Leona rolled her eyes. "Well, if he thinks you are me, what do you expect? Besides, you been kissed before—more than any girl I know."

"Well, if you don't mind, I'll go get him. I thought you really liked him, though."

Leona shrugged. "I do, but he's beginning to get on my nerves. He keeps hounding me to go at it with him and I keep telling him I ain't going to drop my bloomers for nobody until I'm good and ready."

I couldn't understand why a girl who liked to drink moonshine as much as Leona did could be such a prude. "Who you saving yourself for? You ain't no Queen of Sheba. What you trying to prove?"

"I ain't trying to prove nothing. I just don't want to be laying around with somebody just because they want me to. Besides, I ain't got that much interest in sex yet."

"If Ernest Lee keeps threatening to break up with you because you won't give him some, what do you want me to do when he asks me? It's hard for me to say no to a boy that cute. You know how much I like sex."

"You can let him have his way with you if you want to. Just remember, he'll think it's me. Don't do nothing so outlandish that you'll scare him off before I'm ready to cut him loose. I want to hang on to him until he takes me to see a few more movies."

Chapter 4

Fiona

*L*EONA CONTINUED TO SEE ERNEST LEE, BUT EACH TIME SHE DID, he got a little more impatient. I knew that if he didn't get what he wanted soon, she wouldn't have to worry about breaking up with him because he'd dump her first.

I would never admit it to Leona, but I wished I'd been the one to get with Ernest Lee first. It would have saved all three of us a lot of headaches. As far as I was concerned, sex was a function that was as normal as peeing, so I wouldn't have had no problem going at it with him. Shoot.

I hadn't been to the movies in a while, so me and Leona decided we'd trick Ernest Lee into taking me on the Fourth of July. The last time she'd seen him, he'd told her he'd take her. On holidays, the only movie theater we had in Lexington gave free candy bars to the first twenty people that paid to get in. What was so good about it was that if somebody colored was in that bunch, they got some candy too. But we was still only allowed to sit in the balcony where it was too hot in the summer and too cold in the winter. I figured if I got a free movie and free candy today, it would be worth sitting in the balcony. All I had to do was wait for Mama to leave the house so I could go meet up with Ernest Lee.

Leona thought it would be better for me to go to his house to pick him up because he was never on time. If I waited for him to come pick me up, we'd get to the movies too late and miss out on them candy bars for sure. I planned to be at his house by half past noon.

Almost everybody in our neighborhood celebrated the Fourth of July with a barbecue. Nobody I knew owned a grill, so some folks cooked their ribs and whatever other meat they had in their kitchen oven. "I don't see how folks can enjoy oven-baked barbecue," Mama said, right after we got up that morning. "Fiona, stack up some bricks in the backyard and take one of them racks out of the oven and set it on top. Leona, go chop enough wood for us to smoke them ribs with."

I didn't mind eating barbecue that had been cooked on a oven rack set on top of bricks. But when I got married, one of the first things I'd make my husband do was buy us a grill or make one.

Before it was even noon, we had cooked three slabs of ribs, a dozen chicken wings, and made a huge bowl of potato salad. Whether we had company coming or not, Mama insisted on preparing enough food for several guests every holiday. One reason she had wanted to get things done early today was because she had to go cook and serve at a party for her boss. Me and Leona could eat anytime we wanted during the day, but Mama expected us to sit down at the kitchen table and eat supper with her when she got back home later in the evening.

We was sitting on the couch and Mama was in her room getting ready for work. "Leona, what do you want me to talk about with Ernest Lee when I see him?" I whispered.

She glanced toward Mama's room before she answered. "He ain't that smart so you ain't got to worry about him conversating about nothing too deep. All he talks about is his job at the pig farm, how good his daddy's moonshine is compared to other moonshiners', and how bad he wants to have sex with me. After the movie, come up with a reason you have to go home right away. Or you can play like you suddenly got your monthly and cramps snuck up on you."

"What if I'm having such a good time, I want to spend more time with Ernest Lee?"

Leona shrugged. "That's fine with me. You can stay with him as long as you want to. Just remember that when you come home, if Mama is here, you need to keep up the act until she goes to bed."

"Ernest Lee is a nice boy. You don't feel bad about tricking him?"

"Nope. If you think you might feel bad about it, don't do it. We been tricking folks all our lives and I don't never want nobody to find out. We might want to switch places when something serious comes up someday."

Ernest Lee was sitting on the porch banister at his house when I got there. "It's about time you showed up," he griped. There was a pocketknife and a piece of wood in his hand that he'd been whittling. He heaved out a long loud sigh. "Sit down for a spell."

I just stood there, giving him a puzzled look. He dropped down off the banister and stood next to me. "Shouldn't we be heading to the movies?" I asked as he wrapped his arm around my waist. Him being so close to me for the first time made me nervous. "Um . . . we don't want to miss out on them free candy bars."

"Pffftt!" Ernest Lee waved his hand. "Girl, I can get you all the candy bars you want. My folks went to a barbecue at my auntie's house in Branson. Relax, sugar. We got the whole place to ourselves for at least two or three hours." He hauled off and kissed me long and hard and then he got right to the point. "Did you decide you was ready to fix me up? I ain't going to wait too much longer. All the damn tension you got me going through could cause me to develop something called the blue balls that I read about in a magazine last year."

"Well, I don't want no parts of you to change colors. I . . . I been thinking about it." Even though I wanted to jump right into it, I couldn't be too eager after Leona had put him off for so long.

"You might not realize it but you want to be pleasured as bad as I want to pleasure you. I got four sisters so I know how girls' minds work. Besides, I can see it in your eyes." Ernest Lee sucked in a deep breath and gave me a serious look. "It's now or never."

"Can we talk about it some more after the movies?" I asked in a meek tone.

"Dagnabbit! I hate sitting up in that dark balcony reading hundreds of words on the screen, half I don't even know. You know how seditty white folks talk, even in silent movies."

"But you said we'd go," I whined.

"I'll take you next week. Now get the spirit, sister. My folks might come back home early." Ernest Lee squeezed my hand and gave me a pleading look. "Let's go to my bedroom."

"Your bedroom?"

Ernest Lee clapped his hands and let out a howl. "What's wrong with you? You been in my room a heap of times. Why you acting like that's something new to you?" He reared back and looked at me with his eyes narrowed. "I figured it's the best place for us to go at it for the first time."

"It's just that . . ." I had to think fast. The last thing I wanted to do was cause Ernest Lee to get so impatient that he'd break up with Leona before she got him to pay her way to see a few more movies. "Okay. Let's go before I change my mind."

I held my breath as he led me by the hand to a room behind the kitchen. It didn't have no windows, but there was shelves on both sides with jars filled with everything from his mama's canned jelly to more than a dozen jars filled with the moonshine his daddy made in a still that was hid somewhere in the woods behind their house. Each jar had a slip of paper taped to the front with a date on it. I realized Ernest Lee's "bedroom" was actually the pantry. There was a pallet on the floor with a big fluffy pillow.

"Now you get naked and stretch out and get comfortable. I'll do the rest." Ernest Lee seemed surprised when I helped him tug off my bloomers. "You sure you ready? I don't want you to tell nobody I took advantage of you."

"I'm ready," I assured him. "I been ready for a long time."

It was over in less than five minutes. When he stood up and put his pants back on, he gave me a hot look. "Well now, *Miss Prudey Two-Shoes*, I ain't the first one." I didn't know if he was asking me a question or making a statement.

"What do you mean?" I got up and started getting dressed.

"You been holding me off all this time and all along somebody else been getting it."

The first thing that came to my mind was that the boys I'd been with had told him that they'd been with "Leona." I played dumb anyway. "I don't know what you mean." I patted my hair and straightened my dress because I didn't want to look at him.

"Girl, don't you know a man can tell when a female ain't a virgin?"

"I never said I was. And since you brought it up, you ain't no virgin yourself."

Ernest Lee gasped and glared at me like he wanted to punch me in the nose. "No, I ain't been a virgin since I was twelve. But I wasn't the one acting like a prude."

"Well, now that we done cleared the air and you know I ain't no prude, let's move on."

There was a smug look on his face. "So, I can get me some anytime I want?"

"Something like that." I didn't want to commit myself too deep, too soon.

"Who else you fooling around with?"

"Nobody since before me and you started courting. There was a boy I met at a fish fry. He was the only other one before you."

"What's his name? I don't want to run into him one day and have him coldcock me."

"His name ain't none of your business. But you ain't got to worry about getting coldcocked nohow. The day after I was with him, he moved to Mobile because all the rest of his family had already left Lexington." A lot of folks had moved away from Lexington, so I didn't expect Ernest Lee to ask more details. And he didn't. What he asked me to do was get back out of my clothes and lay back down on the pallet again. I enjoyed it so much the second time, I wanted to see him as much as I could before Leona dropped him.

Chapter 5
Fiona

*T*ODAY WAS A FOURTH OF JULY THAT I WOULD NEVER FORGET. I never thought I'd see the day when I would have sex with my sister's boyfriend with her blessing. I knew that some folks would have thought we was either crazy or straight-up floozies. But so long as me and Leona was the only ones who knew, we didn't have nothing to worry about.

I did like Ernest Lee, so that made what I'd done seem even more okay to me. If I didn't like him, or if he was ugly, there was no way I would have let him pester me. As much as I loved Leona and wanted to keep her contented, I should have advised her to drop that boy now and find one who wasn't so set on getting into her bloomers. I had stopped trying to figure out why Leona didn't want to do what every other girl we knew was doing. Shoot! People already thought she was a floozy because of all them parties she went to and all the moonshine she drunk.

When I got home from my "date" this evening with Ernest Lee a few minutes after 4:00 p.m., Leona was sitting on the living-room couch flipping through one of the mail-order catalogues Mama ordered stuff from. She did a double take when she looked up and seen me coming through the door. "Well, it took you long enough to come home!" she teased. "Your glassy-looking eyes and that Mona Lisa smile on your face must mean you had a good time."

I blew out a loud breath and flopped down next to her. "Yup. I sure did."

"How was the movie? Did y'all get there in time to get some of them candy bars?"

"Nope."

Leona shook her head. "I ain't surprised. I don't care what peckerwoods say, they ain't never going to do right by us. Even if they had enough candy for every kid in this town, they wouldn't give us none. Hmmm. I don't understand why they decided not to this year. We got some last year on Fourth of July and Memorial Day." My silence and the fact that I was wringing my hands made Leona curious. "Is there something you ain't telling me? You know we don't keep secrets from each other."

"The white folks ain't at fault this time. Me and Ernest Lee didn't get no candy bars because we didn't go to the movies. His folks was at a barbecue so he had the house to hisself. You never told me his bedroom was a glorified closet."

Leona gave me a confused look. "He shares a bedroom with his brothers. That was the pantry he took you to. Didn't you see all them canning and moonshine jars on the shelves? That's where me and him hide out when we want to take a few nips of his daddy's product. So, did y'all go in there to drink?"

"Not really." I couldn't look Leona in the eye when I said, "He was contented when we left that pantry . . ."

She stared at me with her eyes stretched wide open. "Y-you let him pester you on the *first* date?"

I rolled up my eyes. "Ain't that what you wanted me to do? Don't get jealous, because you knew what would happen if I got with him. I ain't a prude like you. Besides, it wasn't the 'first date' as far as he was concerned. You and him have been dating for weeks. Now when you go out with him, maybe he won't hound you so much to have sex." I gave Leona the most exasperated look I could manage. "Wipe that stupid look off your face. I did you a favor and now he is more in love with you than ever." I had to stop talking and catch my breath. "Now whenever he gets real frisky, rush home and let me know. If you want me to go take care of him, I will."

A wistful look crossed Leona's face. "As long as you don't have no problem with that, I guess I won't neither." We didn't say nothing for a few moments. And then Leona dipped her head and asked, "How was he?"

I took my time answering. What girl would want to hear the details about her boyfriend having sex with another girl—especially her twin sister? I didn't want to say nothing that would make Leona regret what she'd encouraged me to do. I had a feeling she already felt that way, though. "Well, he was clumsy, so it took a while for us to get really into it. And he had bad breath."

"Humph. His breath is always stinky."

"By the way, he brought up the fact that you wasn't no virgin. If he mentions it again, I made up a story about you being with a boy that moved to Mobile." While I was talking, we switched our ribbons back.

"Hmmm. Did you give him a name for the boy?"

"Naw. I told him it wasn't none of his business."

"Good! That's one less lie I'll have to be concerned about. Now that Ernest Lee is satisfied for a while, I might hold on to him until that new movie with Theda Bara playing Cleopatra makes it to our neck of the woods. The way the newspaper raves about that flick it's going to be a humdinger."

"I want to see it too. But mannish boys like him don't like them kind of movies, so I doubt if we can dupe him into going twice."

"You got a point. Oh well. But we'll keep him on the hook until one of us gets to see that movie. Do you think you can stand to be with him some more until then? I'll see him now and then and invite him to eat supper with us. I can hold him off by claiming I'm on my monthly each month until we decide he done served his purpose." Leona suddenly got a sad look on her face. "I like Ernest Lee, but I know he's doing stuff behind my back with other girls. I hear things about him. If he was being faithful, I wouldn't be taking advantage of him. His cheating is one of the reasons I don't want to let him have his way with me."

I exhaled and gave my sister a hopeless look. "Leona, sex ain't as bad as you think it is. So what if Ernest Lee ain't no angel? We ain't neither."

"I never said we was angels. But when I do decide to have sex, I don't know if I could do it with a boy that ain't being true to me."

"Look, girl. Sex ain't always about being faithful, it's about having a good time. Especially at our age. Being faithful is for married folks."

Leona threw up her hands and shook her head. "Whatever you say. I ain't ready to look for a new boyfriend yet, so enjoy him while you can. Now wipe off that makeup and put my clothes back in the chifforobe."

Two days after my date with Ernest Lee, he had supper with us. While Mama was in the kitchen putting away the leftovers, me, Leona, and Ernest Lee was in the living room. They was on the couch and I was in the chair facing them. He scooted closer to Leona and said in a low tone, "I got a itching to have some fun tonight. You want to go somewhere?"

Leona looked at me and I shook my head before she turned back to Ernest Lee. "I don't think so. I didn't do the ironing Mama told me to do yesterday, so she said I can't leave the house the rest of this week."

Ernest Lee waved his hand. "So? That ain't never stopped you from sneaking out before. Look-a-here, I'll tap on your bedroom window around midnight. Your mama will be asleep by then, so she ain't got to know nothing."

Leona looked at me again. This time I just hunched my shoulders. "All right, then," she told Ernest Lee. "Just don't tap on our window too hard and break it. Mama just replaced half of our windows after that last tornado blew them out."

When me and Leona went to our room to get ready for bed, as soon as she shut the door I said, "If you don't want to see him, I'll go in your place."

"I really would like to spend some time with Ernest Lee, I like the way he kisses. But he might want to go farther tonight, now that you done lit his fire."

"You sure you want to be with him tonight?" I didn't give Leona time to answer. "Since he's coming back and he said he wants to have some fun, I'll go in your place. He won a dollar in a card game yesterday so he's got money to burn. He said something about wanting to take you to supper at a nice restaurant this week. I can string him along long enough for you to get to enjoy a good meal. If we keep him on the hook long enough, maybe he'll win some more money and I'll be the one he takes to a nice restaurant next."

"Okay." Leona gave me a thoughtful look. "You better hurry up and put on some of my makeup and that flimsy red dress I wore to the last party I went to. He'll be pecking on the window before we know it."

Ernest Lee was at the window half a hour later. He was so frisky, he started groping me before I could even get all the way out the window. "Come on, sugar. I borrowed my daddy's car." He led me by my hand to the well-kept Ford his daddy had bought two years ago. During the ten-minute ride to a spot near Carson Lake, he kept one hand on the steering wheel and the other hand on my bosom.

This time I enjoyed having sex with him even more. But the backseat in his daddy's car wasn't as comfortable as that pallet at his house. Ernest Lee picked up a small canning jar off the floor. "Daddy just made this batch of moonshine today, so it's fresh and potent."

He unscrewed the jar lid and took a long pull. When he handed the jar to me, I only took a few sips. For a few seconds, it felt like a brick had gone upside my head. I got a buzz right away. I handed the jar back to him and he took another long pull. When he tried to hand it back to me, I shook my head. All I needed was to get sloppy drunk and pass out and not be able to climb back into my bedroom window.

After a loud belch he said, "I declare, Leona, I can't wait to see you again." We was still sitting in the car and the way he was pawing me, I had a feeling that if I didn't get away soon, he'd want me to pleasure him some more.

"I can't wait to see you again too. But I need to get back home now. I got to get up early in the morning. It's my turn to chop some firewood and go to the market for Mama."

"All right, sugar," he chuckled. "Anything you say. It took me long enough to get you this pliable and I don't want to mess up and be back where we started." Ernest Lee whistled all the way back to my street. He parked a block away in case Mama had woke up and found out "Leona" had snuck out. Before I could pile out of the car, he hugged and kissed me so long and hard, I had to pinch his hand to make him stop. He laughed as I scrambled out of the car and trotted all the way to my house.

When I slid the window open and hoisted myself up, my worst nightmare came true. Mama was waiting for me with a switch in her hand.

Leona was sitting on the bed looking as stiff as a plank. "Leona, where you been?" she yelled. "I told Mama I didn't know where you went because I was asleep when you left."

"Get your tail in here, *Jezebel*," Mama hollered as she rushed up to me and smelled my breath. "Just like I thought. You been drinking again. Didn't I tell you that you wasn't going nowhere for the rest of this week?"

"Yes, ma'am."

"What kind of example do you think you're setting for your poor little innocent sister by roaming at night like a hoot owl?" Mama turned to Leona and said, "Fiona, I hope none of this girl's bad behavior ever rubs off on you."

"It won't, Mama," Leona whimpered. I hated hearing Mama praise me and criticize Leona. She never complained about it, but I knew she was sick and tired of hearing it too. I could tell by the woeful look that crossed her face each time.

After Mama finished whupping me, she broke the switch in two, threw it on the floor, and stomped back out of our room. It had been so long since I'd actually got a whupping, I had almost forgot how unpleasant they was. But Leona still got at least one a month. Mama, and most of the other parents I knew, often reminded their kids that they was never too old for a whupping.

The mama and daddy of one of my used-to-be boyfriends who was eighteen was still whupping him with switches.

After I dried my tears, I rubbed my sore butt and legs. And then I washed off my makeup, got undressed, and crawled into bed. Leona wrapped her arm around my waist and squeezed me. "You all right?" she whispered.

"I guess I am. But I'm going to have welts on my legs for days."

"You can wear britches until they heal. We need to be more careful," Leona said in a low voice. "I don't want you to take no more punishments for me for a while. I'll see Ernest Lee the next couple of times."

"You going to let him have his way with you?"

"Nope."

"Then I'll have to keep seeing him too if you want him to pay your way to see that Cleopatra movie when it gets here."

"Okay. Good night, Fiona."

"Good night, Leona."

Chapter 6
Leona

I FELT BAD ABOUT DUPING ERNEST LEE, BUT NOT ENOUGH TO STOP. I figured he was getting the best end of the deal.

He came to eat supper with us a month after Fiona had fooled around with him that first time. They'd gone on three more dates since then. I'd gone to the movies with him last week and the week before. On both occasions, he'd tried his best to get me to have sex and I still said no. With Fiona contenting him in between our dates with him, he eventually stopped pressuring me so much when it was my turn.

I was glad Fiona was enjoying Ernest Lee's affection. Even though things had improved between me and him, I was still going to let him go after he'd supplied me with a little more free moonshine and paid for me to see a few more movies. I would miss him because I still liked his company. I was glad Mama did too. When she didn't like one of our boyfriends, she discouraged us from inviting them to have supper with us.

If Mama wasn't the best colored cook in Lexington, she was close to it. That was why people rarely turned down a invitation to eat with us. Ernest Lee's mouth was so full of food, it looked like he had the mumps. As soon as he swallowed, he wiped his lips with the back of his hand, even though there was a nice white cloth napkin next to his plate. "I declare, Sister Mavis, I ain't ate no greens and pig ears as good as yours since my grandmamma died."

"Thank you, son. I appreciate the compliment," Mama said, beaming like she'd just been praised by the president.

"Can you gather up some of your recipes for me to give to my mama?" he asked. "She could sure use some help in the kitchen." Ernest Lee reached for the tall glass of lemonade in front of him, guzzled every drop, and then he let out a loud burp.

I seen Fiona cover her mouth with her hand to keep from snickering. I coughed and fidgeted around in my seat to keep from laughing myself. Mama occupied the chair across from me. Fiona was in the chair next to her, and Ernest Lee was in the one right beside me. The boy was so frisky, he couldn't keep his hands off me. Even with my mama and sister sitting at the same table, he reached up under my dress and squeezed my thigh every few minutes. Each time, his hand got closer to my crotch.

Mama was still beaming. "Ernest Lee, I'd be glad to give your mama a few of my recipes."

"And your house is always so neat and clean," he went on. "That's why I look forward to coming over here."

"Well, no offense against your mama, but she got a big burden to bear trying to keep a clean house with a husband and you and all your brothers and sisters to look after." Mama paused and added in a dry tone, "Not to mention hosting all them rowdy folks that come to socialize and drink up your daddy's moonshine."

I took a deep breath and jumped into the conversation before Mama could say something that might offend Ernest Lee. "Ernest Lee, would you like to have some more lemonade?"

He swiped his mouth with his napkin. "Don't mind if I do."

"Leona, did you tell Ernest Lee you made the pecan pie?" Mama asked as she poured more lemonade into his empty glass.

"Yeah, I told him. He likes my cooking almost as much as he likes yours," I replied, gently kicking his foot under the table. Ever since Fiona had started having sex with him, his demeanor had changed. Now instead of being so energetic and flighty, he seemed almost docile. My only concern was how he was going to react when I broke up with him.

"I hope the girl I marry can make pies as good as yours," Ernest Lee said as he winked at me.

"So, you thinking about marriage, son?" Mama asked with a hopeful look on her sweaty face.

"I would like to settle down and start my family. But I ain't in no hurry," he replied. "Pass me them pig ears."

He had two more helpings of collard greens, another helping of pecan pie, three more pieces of corn bread, and he finished off the pig ears. If we hadn't run out of food when we did, he would have kept eating.

I was glad when Ernest Lee excused hisself to go home. I even walked him outside. The second we got on the porch, he started groping me. I slapped his hand. "You stop that! You want our neighbors to see you being nasty?" I snarled.

"All right, then. I wanted to do this in the house," he said with a sulky look on his face.

"Wasn't it enough for you to be touching and feeling me under the table?"

"No, I wanted to mount you right there in that kitchen." He snickered. "I wonder what your goody-two-shoes sister would have thought if she'd caught me?" He snickered again. "I declare, that girl is so prim and proper, she better look for a preacher when she decides to get married. She'd be a lot happier and more likeable if she was more like you."

I didn't like the first part of what Ernest Lee said, but the last part of his comment almost made me smile. This was the first time anybody ever said that Fiona should be more like me. I wondered what he would have thought about her if he had knew she was the one who'd been having sex with him all this time. "I don't think Fiona would want to be more like me." I hugged Ernest Lee's neck real quick and skittered back into the house before he could say or do anything else.

Less than a minute after I got back inside, somebody opened our front door and came in. It was Nadine Fisher, one of our neighbors. She was two years older than me and Fiona and had dropped out of school in seventh grade to get married. Her husband took off a year later when he found out she couldn't have kids. She had a lot of friends that she liked to socialize with. She threw parties all the time, and I went to almost all of them. Nadine had a cute bronze-toned face with big black eyes and high cheekbones, but she was so stout all she wore was long shapeless dresses, like some of the tents her mama and mine wore. For the last three years, she had been working as a chicken plucker at the factory where they slaughtered chickens. It was a steady job, so she was able to pay her bills and stay in the little brown-shingled house two blocks from ours that she'd shared with her used-to-be husband. "I seen Ernest Lee leaving," she said as she pranced over to the couch where me and Fiona was sitting and plopped down between us.

"He had supper with us," I said

"That's nice." Nadine paused and looked at me from the corner of her eye. "I wonder what he told that Davis girl? I seen her last night and she told me he was going to take her to the movies tonight. . . ."

Me and Fiona looked at each other. My face got hot; Fiona looked stunned.

"I didn't know he was seeing one of the Davis girls," I said.

"Yup. Big-booty Judy." Nadine cocked her head to the side and puffed out her chest, which usually meant she was about to deliver some news I didn't want to hear. "Then I guess you don't know he's fixing to marry her, huh?"

Me and Fiona looked at each other again. "He never said nothing about that to me." I could feel my blood heating up.

"How long he been seeing her?" Fiona asked.

"Oh, at least three or four months. His mama told me last week that she's fixing to have his baby. He done the manly thing and offered to marry her as soon as they can make the arrangements."

"That's nice," was all I could say. "I'll have to congratulate him the next time I see him." By now, my blood was boiling. I wondered what else Ernest Lee hadn't told me. "We need to get the kitchen cleaned up before Mama comes back out here. I'll come over tomorrow, Nadine." I stood up and opened the door. I could tell from the wounded look on her face that she wasn't happy about me dismissing her after she'd only been in the house a few minutes. She huffed out a loud breath and flounced back out the door.

Fiona looked at me with her jaw twitching. "Can you believe that boy? How could he carry on with me, I mean *you*, and not say nothing about him and Judy fixing to get married? And about her being pregnant!"

"I'm just as flabbergasted as you. Wait until I see that low-down, funky black dog again. I'm going to mean-mouth him so bad, he'll cry like a baby!"

After me and Fiona washed and dried the dishes, Mama came back into the living room. I had turned on the radio, but it was so rickety by now, it would play for several minutes, go off, and not come back on for a while. It had just gone silent.

Mama looked at me first with a confused expression on her face. Then she looked at Fiona. "I know, I know, so y'all ain't got to say it. I'm just as sick of this radio as y'all. But that ain't no reason for you two to be sitting here with them long faces. Especially after the nice evening we had with Ernest Lee."

I was the first one to speak. "I don't feel like dealing with this old radio tonight. I'm going to bed."

"Me too," Fiona said as she stretched her arms above her head and yawned.

"I guess I'll turn in myself. I have to be to work at eight tomorrow morning," Mama said. "Don't y'all forget to say your prayers."

Fiona followed me into our bedroom. We was as quiet as mice as we got into our nightgowns. She collapsed into the bed and slid up under the covers and pulled them up to her neck. I eased down on my side and stared at her. "Do you want to talk some more?"

She hunched her shoulders. "I don't care."

"I wonder when Ernest Lee was going to come clean?" I said as I crawled up under the covers and scooted closer to Fiona.

She was trembling. "I . . . why are you shaking like that?" I sat bolt upright and threw the covers back.

"Leona, I'm in a heap of trouble!"

I froze and held my breath as I mumbled, "Uh-oh. What did you do this time? I hope it ain't something I'll have to take the blame for. My butt is still stinging from that whupping Mama gave me yesterday for burning the corn bread."

The light from the kerosene lamp on our dresser was dim, but I could still see the scared look in Fiona's eyes. "I'm fixing to have a baby!"

"My Lord. That's going to kill Mama! Ernest Lee ain't ready to be nobody's daddy. I'm going to go up to Judy and tell her what a lying two-timing scoundrel he is! If she marries him anyway, she's a fool!"

"I-I ain't sure he's the one. There was two other boys . . ."

I almost choked on some air. "Two other boys what?"

"That I was with around the same time." Fiona's voice was so low, I could barely hear her.

This was the first time in my life that I wanted to slap Fiona. "What was you thinking?"

"Well, Ernest Lee thought I was you and so did them other boys. I was having too much fun to stop. Besides, if it wasn't for you, I wouldn't have got involved with your boyfriend in the first place."

"I guess it was my fault you was with them other boys too, huh?"

"I didn't say that," Fiona said with a pout.

"Good God. Them boys must really think I'm some kind of hoochie-coochie woman."

"But you always been on the wild side, so what else could they think?"

"That's true. Who was them other two boys?"

"Johnny Bridgeman and Chucky Wright."

"I seen Johnny at the market two days ago. He was with his girlfriend, but he was still looking at me like I was a prize-winning pie. I ain't spoke to him since ninth grade. He even licked his lips and winked at me. Now I know why."

"I was going to tell you. Him and Chucky promised me that they wouldn't tell nobody they'd been with me. Well, with you, I meant to say."

"That ain't the point. If they ever say something offensive to me, I'm going to punch them in the nose." I huffed out a disgusted breath and went on. "Well, at least there is a bright side; being pregnant means Mama won't whup you when you tell her."

"I know she won't. But I don't want to disappoint her."

I put my arm around my sister and patted her back. "Everything is going to be all right. I'll help you raise the baby. That way, he or she will have two mamas. They'll be the most spoiled baby in town."

There was a strange look on Fiona's face, one I had never seen before. Her eyes was staring straight ahead and her jaw twitched involuntarily. "Say something, girl. You scaring me."

"Leona, I can't tell Mama I'm fixing to have a baby."

"W-what? If you don't, she'll figure it out on her own when your belly swells up."

Fiona shook her head. "It ain't going to."

My jaw dropped so low it was a wonder it didn't touch my bosom. "I know you ain't thinking about killing it before it's born! You remember that Mitchell woman who tried to get rid of her baby by drinking some bleach?" Earline Mitchell was the only woman I had ever heard of who tried to kill a baby before it was born. The man who had got her pregnant left town a week after she told him she was expecting his baby. She got so mad, she didn't want nothing in her house that would remind her of him so she burned up everything he had left behind. Nobody was surprised when she tried to get rid of the baby. After she drunk the bleach, she lost the baby. But she also lost so much blood, she died before her brother could get her to the clinic. The thought of losing my sister the same way was more than I could stand. "Fiona, please don't get rid of that baby."

"I ain't."

"Well, you'll have to tell Mama something. You can't just start getting big in the belly and not expect her to ask why!"

"There ain't but one thing for us to do . . ."

"*Us?*"

"You can switch places with me and let Mama think you fixing to have a baby. She's been expecting that to happen for years anyway."

I was stunned at what Fiona was asking me to do. "I really would like to help you but—"

Fiona cut me off and said with her teeth clenched, "But what?"

"But I don't know if I can do something as serious as pretending I'm pregnant." I screwed up my lips and shuddered. "Jeez!"

"Think about Mama. We need to let her keep thinking she's been so blessed to have a daughter as . . . uh . . . virtuous as me. We can't let her down. Please do this for me. I swear to God, I will do whatever I can to make this up to you."

"All right, then. Give me your ribbon."

Chapter 7
Fiona

MY MONTHLY WAS SUPPOSED TO COME LAST WEEK. I WAS SO REG-
ular, that when it didn't, I knew why. I had planned to go to
Ernest Lee the first chance I got and tell him he got me pregnant. But now that I knew about him and the Davis girl, I decided not to. I prayed that Leona wouldn't change her mind
about helping me. Especially since she was part of the reason I
had got myself into such a mess!

Leona decided to tell Mama the next day. "You have to be
with me when I tell her," she told me while we was in our room
getting dressed for breakfast. Mama was in the backyard chopping firewood for the potbellied stove in our living room.

I shook my head. "Uh-uh. I'll stay in the bedroom. You go by
yourself. I don't want her to think I knew about it." I was standing by the door while Leona was sitting on the bed putting on
her shoes.

"What do we do after the baby gets here?" she asked, popping
up off the bed and standing in front of me with her hands on
her hips. "You thought about that? I don't want to spend the rest
of my life pretending to be somebody's mama." She wrung her
hands and paced in front of me for a few moments. "I-I don't
know about this, Fiona. Anything could go wrong. You could get
drunk and let the truth slip out."

I stomped my foot and gave her a cold look. "I don't get

drunk enough to do something like that. You trying to tell me you don't really want to help me?"

She shook her head. "No, I ain't. But I . . . I should think about it some more before we—"

I cut her off. "I wish I was dead, dead, dead!" I screamed as I flailed my arms. And then I threw myself onto the bed and buried my face into the pillow and cried like a baby. I abruptly stopped and sat up. "I wish I would go to sleep and never wake up!"

Leona sat down next to me and put her arm around my shoulder. "Hush your mouth! Life is a gift. You need to live as long as you can and enjoy it." She spent the next five minutes trying to calm me down, but I became even more delirious. I was still whooping and hollering when Mama stormed our room with a switch in her hand. I abruptly stopped crying and sat up.

"What's all the ruckus up in here? Why is it taking y'all so long to get to the breakfast table? I didn't stand over that hot stove to cook them grits and bacon for my health!" Mama boomed. She looked at me and then she shot Leona a sharp look. "What did you do to your sister?"

Before she could answer, I wiped tears off my face and blurted out, "Leona didn't do nothing to me."

"You ain't crying for nothing," Mama said as she wagged a fresh switch in Leona's direction. And then she came up to me and retied my ribbon. It had loosened up while I was having my fit and was dangling off the side of my head. "Y'all need to make sure these ribbons is always on tight enough so they won't fall off." When she finished, she narrowed her eyes and asked again what Leona had done to make me cry.

"Mama, I'm crying *for* Leona," I mumbled. Leona's eyes got big and stared at me like I was speaking gibberish.

Mama looked at me with a puzzled expression on her face, and then she looked at Leona. "Why would your sister be crying for you?"

I didn't let her answer. "She done finally got herself pregnant. Just like you said she would. I'm crying because I feel so bad for her . . . and you."

There was a terrified look on Leona's face. I was glad I couldn't read her mind because I didn't want to know what she was thinking about me at the moment.

Mama yelped and covered her mouth with her hand and swayed from side to side for a few seconds. And then she straightened up and walked over to Leona's side of the bed. "Shame on you, Leona Dunbar! I knew it! I knew this was bound to happen if you kept sneaking out and guzzling that moonshine with them buck-wild friends of yours. I'm going to make sure Ernest Lee marries you before you start to show!" Mama moaned for a few seconds and rubbed her head with both hands. "Mighty Moses! I tried my best to raise y'all to be fine Christian girls! I failed!"

"You didn't fail, Mama," Leona insisted. "I did."

Mama took several deep breaths before she managed to talk in a normal tone of voice. "Fiona, it pleases my soul to know I didn't fail with you." And then Mama turned back to Leona with a scowl on her face that would have shook up the devil. "Girl, why can't you be more like your sister?"

Leona dropped her head and didn't say nothing.

"Oh, that Ernest Lee! I knew he was too good to be true," Mama blasted.

Before Leona could put the blame on Ernest Lee—and I thought that would be the smartest thing to do—words shot out of my mouth like shotgun pellets. "She ain't sure it was him, Mama. She was with two other boys."

I couldn't decide if Mama was madder than she was disappointed. I couldn't think of nothing to say that would make her feel better. While I was trying to decide what to say next, she folded her arms and shook her head. "Just what I thought. Good googly moogly. Leona, you was cheating on Ernest Lee?"

"He was cheating too," I yelled. "And he's fixing to marry Judy Davis. He got her pregnant!"

There was a wild-eyed look on Mama's face as she covered her heart with her hand. "Lord, what is the world coming to. Young-

'uns ain't got no respect for God's laws. Who was them other two boys? I'm going to visit their folks as soon I can."

"Um . . . they was from Mobile. I met them at one of Nadine's parties," Leona lied.

"What's their names? Who is their people?"

"Mama, I'd been drinking. All I remember is that they was from Mobile."

"Leona didn't mean to get in trouble," I eased in. I gently poked her side with my elbow. "Did you?"

"No, I didn't. I'm sorry, Mama," she said in a meek tone. I was glad she didn't raise her voice too high because that would have made Mama even madder.

Mama stared at Leona and shook her head some more. "And to think you made it all the way to the eleventh grade. You can't go to that schoolhouse with a big belly. You'll have to drop out."

"I wasn't planning on going back when school starts up next month anyway," Leona announced.

The next thing I knew, Mama plopped down on the bed and wrapped her arms around Leona. "It'll be all right, sugar. I'll help you raise the baby. Maybe it's a good thing Ernest Lee probably ain't the daddy. Besides him being involved with another girl, his mama told me at church last Sunday that he's got a itching to join the army before the end of this year."

Hearing this piece of news surprised and disappointed me. Leona's face was so tight, I knew she was as mad as a wet hen at Ernest Lee because he hadn't told her nothing about his plans. I was mad too. I hoped Leona would get the chance to cuss him out before he got married or shipped off by the army to a foreign country. If I seen him before he left, I was going to give him a piece of my mind too. A sneaky, nasty puppy like him wasn't good enough to marry into our family.

Mama came over to me and put one arm around my shoulder. "I know it won't be long before you find a husband. In the meantime, you can help me and Leona take care of her baby when it gets here."

I felt a little better by the time Mama left our room. But as soon as she closed the door, I started crying again. "Leona, I can't believe I got you into such a mess." Her response made me feel so much better.

"Well, don't worry about nothing. As of now, you are me and I am you."

Chapter 8

Leona

I DIDN'T KNOW HOW ON EARTH FIONA WAS GOING TO BE ABLE TO carry a baby to full term. And it was also going to be hard for her to behave like she was me full-time without slipping up. We looked exactly alike, but in so many ways, we was as different as day and night. I wore a lot of makeup and clothes Mama said only fast women wore, like low-cut blouses, skimpy dresses, and tight britches. But she didn't try to stop me. I figured that by now, she knew I was going to do what I wanted to do.

I was one of the best dancers in town, so a lot of boys asked me to dance at parties. Fiona was so clumsy on the dance floor, you would have thought her feet was on backwards. I'd have to make sure she avoided dancing when she went out. I was also concerned about how somebody who was quiet and mild-mannered around folks would remember to be loud and defiant like me. We had never had no trouble fooling nobody before, but them other times was never for more than a few hours at a pop. This pregnancy ruse was going to be the biggest challenge of our lives. I didn't want my sister to suffer no more than she was already, so I wasn't going to back out.

Within days after Mama found out I was pregnant, Fiona was playing me almost as well as I played myself. What I didn't like was the way Mama kept getting in her face telling her how embarrassed she was going to be when our church family found out about her condition. I had to keep reminding myself that

Fiona was only pretending to be me, and all the abuse Mama
was throwing at her hit me just as hard. Each time she praised
Fiona and tore me down, my stomach twisted up, and I looked
at her like she was crazy. Now I was taking the heat for myself
and Fiona. I was so sick of being put down I was itching to let
Mama know what a fraud Fiona was behind her back. But there
was no way I could ever do that. Exposing my twin would be one
of the biggest mistakes I ever made in my life. We was too close
and needed each other so much, I wasn't about to risk ruining
our relationship. The only thing I could do was set my feelings
aside and continue to listen to Mama's angry words.

"Leona, I hope that you will come to your senses by the time
that baby gets here and act like the Christian I raised you to be.
If Fiona can toe the line, you ought to be able to do it. And since
you don't even know who the daddy of that baby is, we can't go
up to him and his family and ask them to help support it! How
could you do this to our family, girl?"

"I . . . I guess I wasn't thinking right," Fiona stammered. She
was hunched on the couch, looking like she was about to fall
apart. Mama was walking back and forth with her arms folded. I
was in the chair facing Fiona. Every time our eyes met, she
looked away.

"You don't never think right! All your life you been skipping
school, staying out way longer than I tell you to, and drinking
like a whale. If you continue to run amok and have babies, by
the time you reach thirty—if you live that long—your life ain't
going to be worth a plugged nickel. I can't imagine what kind of
man will want to marry you someday."

It rained hard that night. The lightning and thunder was so
bad, me and Fiona couldn't get to sleep. It must have been
around midnight when Mama came into our room, wringing
her hands. "I don't like the way the wind is rattling them windows. Y'all get up and let's slide the bed to the side of the room
in case the wind blows out the windows again." Me and Fiona
tumbled to the floor at the same time.

Our bed was small, but it was heavy. It took all three of us to push it to the other side of the room. When I seen the distressed look on Fiona's face, I held my breath. I didn't know what I would have done if she'd pulled a muscle or done something that would harm the baby. I knew two ladies who had lost their babies because they'd done things they shouldn't have. "That's close enough," I panted.

"We got a few more inches to go," Mama insisted as she adjusted the stocking cap she always slept in.

After we had scooted the bed closer to the wall, Mama still wasn't satisfied. "I don't think this is going to work. Y'all come get in my bed." When we was little, Fiona would run into Mama's room and get in the bed with her every time we had a bad storm. This was the first time I'd slept in the same bed with Mama since we was babies. And it was the first time she held me in her arms until I went to sleep. Having her show me so much affection almost made me cry, especially since she thought she was giving it to Fiona.

I was glad August was almost over. It had been one of the most miserable months in my life. Mama fussed up a storm every day now. It bothered me, but it was even worse for Fiona. She cried herself to sleep every night. I hugged her and tried to comfort her as much as I could before we went to sleep. But as hard as I tried to stay composed, I eventually snapped anyway. "Hush up, girl! You making this harder than it needs to be!"

Fiona sucked her teeth and snorted so loud she sounded like a bull. "What's that supposed to mean? I thought you wanted to help me."

I didn't let Fiona's sulking get to me. I had to say what was on my mind. "I am 'helping' you. It's just that it's going to be hard for us to keep this lie going until the baby is born."

"Leona, we done come this far. The worst part is over and that was telling Mama."

"That's true." I blew out a long, tired sigh. "Don't worry. I'll do my part so that you'll continue to smell like a rose as far as Mama is concerned. She already thinks I'm a hoochie-coochie woman. Someday I hope I can make her as proud of me as she is of you. You being such a 'good girl' is the one thing that always puts a smile on her face."

"I like Mama and everybody thinking I'm so good. But it ain't easy living a double life."

"You don't have to tell me that. I'm living a double life too."

"Maybe it's time for me to let Mama know I ain't what she thinks I am . . ."

My jaw dropped and I sat up ramrod straight. "What good would that do? Telling Mama that you are a bigger hoochie-coochie woman than I am, and have been for years, would kill her. She and everybody else knows how worldly I am. They all been expecting me to get pregnant. If Mama found out how we tried to pull off such a hoax, she would blame me."

"You're probably right. Forget what I said about telling her."

I was glad I hadn't seen Ernest Lee so I could tell him off before he left to go to the army. Nadine must have told him that she'd spilled the beans about him and Judy Davis, because he was avoiding me like I had every catchy disease in the world. I wasn't going to waste no time by going to his house to confront him because I didn't want to cause a scene and upset his mama and daddy. One day I seen him walking down the sidewalk and when he spotted me, he shot across the street. When I got closer, I seen him peeping from behind a parked car. I acted like I didn't see him and went on about my business. I had much more important things to be concerned about than his two-timing self. I needed to focus on Fiona's pregnancy.

It wouldn't be long before we'd be unable to hide Fiona's condition. So far, we hadn't told nobody and it was a good thing we hadn't. Something was about to happen that we didn't see coming. The last week in August, Mama was sure we didn't have to worry about another storm for a while. So she had us help her move our bed back to the middle of the room just before we turned in for the night. After we had gone to sleep, a few hours later Fiona woke up screaming. Mama stormed into the room. "What's the matter now, gal?"

I didn't know, so all I could do was wait for Fiona to tell us why she was screaming. "M-my stomach feels like it's about to bust open!" She threw back the bedcovers and we all yelped. The bed was soaked in blood.

"Lord, Leona! Sugar, you done had a miscarriage!" Mama shrieked. "Don't you move!"

Fiona just laid there like a piece of dead wood, but I got out of the bed as fast as I could. Within minutes, Mama returned with some wet towels and a bucket. She scooped up a lump of meat that was about the size of a man's fist, and dropped it into the bucket. "This was God's will," she muttered. She didn't even try to hide her sigh of relief.

Mama took a deep breath and glared at Fiona. "Leona, this was a blessing in disguise. Now nobody ain't got to know what you done." And then Mama hugged her and patted her back. "It's going to be all right now, sugar pie. I want y'all to know that I can't wait to have some grandchildren. But this wasn't the right time or circumstances."

Chapter 9
Fiona

I DIDN'T KNOW OF ANY GIRL OR WOMAN WHO DIDN'T LOVE CHILdren. Before Daddy died, I used to believe that God blessed the men and women He loved the most with the most children. The majority of the families in our neighborhood had at least half a dozen. One family had fifteen and another seventeen. As hard as times was, them families was happy. When they got low on food and money, the church chipped in and helped them out. Because my parents had only two children, I thought God didn't like us that much. When I was a little girl, every night when I said my prayers, I asked Him to bless me with a heap of kids. I felt disappointed and scared when I realized I was pregnant. But in a twisted way, I was also a little happy. Mama had been a real old woman when she had us. I figured that if I got started while I was still in my teens, there would be a good chance that God would bless me with at least eight babies. To know that my first one didn't even make it out of my womb alive tore me up inside. I hadn't felt so much sadness since Daddy died.

Right after my miscarriage, I laid in the bed as stiff as a plank. I scratched my head and realized my blue ribbon had loosened up and was dangling off the side of my head like a noose. I retied it as tight as I could. I couldn't wait to switch back to myself so I could wear my red ribbon.

Mama left the room with the bucket and came back about ten minutes later. This time she was holding the big metal washtub that we bathed in and used to wash some of our laundry in. She set the tub down and darted back out the room, panting like a dog. She returned a few moments later with the bucket filled to the brim with water and poured it into the tub. The water was so hot, steam was swirling up from it. "Leona, get out of that bed so I can clean you off."

"Yes, ma'am." I swung my feet to the floor and stood up in front of the tub.

"What did you do with that . . . uh . . . baby?" Leona asked in a meek tone. "Was it a boy or a girl?

Mama looked at her like she'd lost her mind. And maybe she had. What girl in her right mind would make out like she was pregnant? Maybe I'd lost my mind too for thinking we could pull off such a hoax. Mama reared back on her legs and scrunched up her face. "There wasn't no baby, Fiona. It wasn't nothing but a lump of flesh so it don't count. I took care of it and neither one of y'all need to know nothing else about it."

"Did you give it a name and bury it?" I asked in a weak tone. My heart was beating so hard, I was scared it would bust open.

Mama gave me a blank stare. "Didn't I just say that wasn't no baby, Fiona? And why are you so interested in what I did with it? Did you know about all them boys your sister was messing around with?"

"Uh-uh," Leona replied in a voice just above a whisper.

The tension was too much for me. Every time Mama asked Leona a question, I almost answered. This was the first time I regretted us ever switching identities. I was getting so confused, I could barely contain myself. But we was doing good so far, and I didn't want to blow it. I swallowed hard and repeated in my head several times, *I am Leona.*

Mama looked at Leona with her eyes squinted. "Sure, you didn't know." Then she turned back to me and added, "I don't know what's going to become of you. Whoever them boys was you was messing around with, I don't want nary one of them dogs in my house no more. And that includes Ernest Lee. By the way, his mama told me yesterday that girl he was supposed to marry changed her mind. The army done already shipped him off to one of them out-of-state bases. So we won't see his tail no time soon. But if I hear about you meeting up with them other two scalawags, I'm going to get a switch and whup your behind."

I felt so bad for my sister. But like always, getting scolded didn't seem to bother her. And when Mama mentioned that Ernest Lee's fiancée had changed her mind, Leona got a self-satisfied look on her face. All of a sudden, Mama dipped a washrag into the tub of water, and then she slid a bar of lye soap back and forth until the rag was full of foam. "Fiona, while I'm washing this girl up, you go yonder to the chifforobe and get some clean bloomers and a fresh gown for her." Leona skittered across the floor like a scared mouse.

Mama scrubbed so hard between my legs; it was painful. I scrunched up my face and held my breath, but I didn't let out nary a yelp. After she finished, she looked from me to Leona and said in a weary tone, "Now y'all get to sleep." She left the room with the washtub, fussing under her breath the whole time.

Our mama had had a hard life, but she was strong and smart. She'd took real good care of us after Daddy died. But she didn't have a close relationship with our kinfolks. I figured that was one of the reasons she doted on us so much. I would have loved to have a big extended family like most of our friends. Mama didn't tell us too much about her family. Whatever was keeping them at a distance, it had to be too painful for her to share. She'd had a uncle in Lexington that she'd been close to, but he died before Daddy. Only two of her five siblings was still alive and they lived in Mobile where Mama had been born. They was both older. Her brother was a sickly man who had been bedridden since me and Leona was babies. Mama's sister and her family, a husband that walked with two canes, and two daughters that was old enough to be our mother, hadn't visited us since Daddy died. We'd only been to visit them three times and each time they had acted like our presence annoyed them.

Mama told us that our grandparents on both sides had been

born into slavery and had lived very sad lives. They all died before me and Leona was born. That was the thing about having kids as late in age as Daddy and Mama had. The grandparents are usually on their way out by the time some of the grandkids come into the world. Daddy had a few other kinfolks that he'd been close to, but none of them cared much about having a relationship with Mama and me and Leona. One of his cousins and her husband lived in Lexington. They worked for very rich white folks and lived in a big, beautiful house two doors down from one of the doctors who ran the colored clinic. They was so uppity, they didn't have much to do with us. They had only been to our house twice and the one time that we'd attempted to pay them a visit, ten minutes after we got there, they suddenly "remembered" they had someplace else to go and had to leave right away. When we bumped into their two grown daughters in public, you would have thought we was rank strangers. They spoke, but that was all.

One thing about Mama, and me and Leona, was that we had a lot of pride. If somebody didn't want to be bothered with us, we didn't want to be bothered with them. Me and Leona had stopped mentioning the names of our "distant" kinfolks in front of Mama because the subject was painful to her. We didn't want to make her feel no worse, which was the reason I acted so goody-goody in front of her. I knew that if she ever found out what I was really like, it would break her heart in two.

Me and Leona traded ribbons as soon as we got up in the morning. We decided that it was safe enough for us to switch back. When we went to the kitchen to eat the grits, eggs, and bacon Mama had set on the table, Mama flopped down in the chair across from Leona. She stared at her for a few moments before she reached across the table and grabbed her hand. "Baby, I don't like being hard on you. But it's my job to take care of y'all and try and keep y'all out of trouble. Now, I forgive you for what you done. But please promise me you won't let this happen again."

"I won't, Mama," Leona said in a real low tone.

"How do you feel?"

"My stomach still feels strange, but it don't hurt. I'm fine."

"Maybe I should take off work and take you to the clinic so a doctor can check you out," Mama said.

That was the last thing I wanted Mama to do. I could tell Leona felt the same way. Her eyes suddenly got as big as saucers, and she held up her hand. "No, don't take me to the clinic, Mama! I hate that place. Seeing all them sick people there makes me depressed. I'm as strong as a bull." Leona sprung up out of her chair and twirled around. "See, I ain't even wobbly or nothing."

The more Leona tried to convince Mama that she didn't need to go see a doctor, the worse I felt. My head was spinning, my stomach was churning, and my thighs felt like jelly. I had some mild pain in my stomach, and my coochie still felt like somebody had slid a burning match up in it.

"Sit down, Leona," Mama said waving her back to her chair. "After you finish eating, I want you to go lay on the couch. Don't you leave this house today." Mama turned to me with a softer look on her face and said in a softer tone, "Sugar, would you do me a favor and stay in the house with your sister until I come home from work?"

"Yes, ma'am."

Mama stood up and headed to her bedroom on the other side of the kitchen. Me and Leona looked at each other and shrugged. Mama came back with a pill bottle in her hand. "Take two of these," she said to Leona as she twisted the lid off the bottle.

"I don't need no pills," Leona insisted.

"Gal, if you don't take these pills, I'm going to pry your mouth open and push them down your throat myself. And if I have to do that, I'm going to get a switch and teach you a lesson you won't never forget!"

"All right, Mama." Leona swallowed the pills and finished eating her breakfast. After that, we went on about our business like nothing had happened.

Chapter 10
Fiona

*I*T DIDN'T TAKE LONG FOR THINGS TO GET BACK TO NORMAL AT OUR house. School had started back up and Leona was still threatening to drop out. But every time she mentioned doing that, Mama told her if she did, she had to find herself a job so she wouldn't have enough time on her hands to go out and get into trouble again.

By the time October rolled around, I was antsy. Leona was too, so she had started jumping out the window again at night to go meet up with her drinking buddies. She came home with moonshine on her breath two or three times a week.

When she was too tipsy to hoist herself off the ground to climb through the window, she had to come through the front door. One of them particular nights, she slammed the door shut so hard, one of Mama's pictures of Jesus fell off the living-room wall. The commotion woke me and Mama up and we ran into the living room at the same time.

"Oops," was all Leona said before she staggered to our bedroom.

That was one of the few nights Mama didn't bother to send Leona to the yard to get a fresh switch so she could give her a whupping. "I'm so tired of trying to beat some sense into that girl's hard head," Mama said in one of the weariest tones I'd ever heard her use. "It don't do no good."

"What took you so long to realize that, Mama?" I teased.

Mama had a switch in her hand, but she didn't even bother to whup Leona this time. She just shook her head and laughed. "I've known for years that whuppings don't have no effect on girls as wild as your sister." Mama let out a mighty sigh and hauled off and hugged me. "Thank God, I got a angel like you. I guess the seed y'all came from had some defects. When it split in two, you came from the good part and Leona came from the bad."

I didn't say nothing to that, but it made me sad to know that Mama thought she had gave birth to a damaged child. The truth was, I was just as "damaged" as Leona, even more so.

Some of the nights that Leona didn't go out, when she went to sleep, I put on some of her makeup and clothes and climbed out the bedroom window and went out as her. The closest party-time place was Nadine's house. Her current boyfriend helped one of the local moonshiners operate his still. He also helped deliver moonshine to folks who couldn't come pick it up, so he always had access to Nadine who depended on him to bring drinks to her get-togethers. Every time I posed as Leona, I had a ball.

Because of my pregnancy fiasco, I had decided that I wouldn't let a boy get into my bloomers no more. I didn't care how cute he was. As much as I liked sex, I could wait until I found a husband—which would be this year, I hoped. But if I got weak and had sex again before I got married and ended up pregnant a second time, I knew that Leona would switch places with me again in a heartbeat.

I had become so restless with my life. It wasn't easy being me. Acting like a shy goody-goody when the real me was everything but that was becoming harder and harder to keep up. But I was determined not to let Mama down. I knew that once I got married and had my own house, I could set my own rules and behave any way I wanted, so long as I didn't go buck-wild. The only thing I was concerned about was leaving Leona with Mama.

All I had to do was find me a God-fearing man with a good job. He had to be strong, but obedient because I wanted to run the show in my house. All of my friend-girls wanted to marry cute men, but Mama had instilled in us that security was the most important thing in a marriage. Good looks was a option, because a handsome face didn't pay bills. I didn't want to marry no baboon, though. If I could marry a man with reasonably good looks so my kids wouldn't be pug-ugly, I'd be happy.

Jobs was scarce for everybody, but white folks had more choices, so they didn't have to rely on farmwork the way we did. Mama had to work on farms when she was young, but when she started working in nice houses for rich white families, she began to look down on field workers.

Mama didn't want me and Leona to do farm labor, but we was too young to clean houses and do other things the rich ladies wanted done. So she didn't make too much of a fuss when we told her we wanted to work on the farms like a lot of our friends.

There was a heap of cotton and sugarcane fields in and around Lexington, so when in season there was a lot of work for us. Some of the kids who worked on farms had to give most of the money they made to their folks to help out with the household bills. Mama let us spend the money we made on anything we wanted.

When I found out that one of our best friends was going to get married this month, I wanted to buy a real cute blouse to wear to her wedding. The cotton and sugarcane season was almost over and none of the farmers we approached wanted to hire new workers so late in the game. So we wouldn't be able to work on the farms again until cotton and sugarcane was back in season next year.

Me and Leona found other ways to make spending money. We did some babysitting and we ran errands for some of our grown neighbors, but we didn't make but a dollar or two here and there. One cheap woman never paid us more than a quarter each time we looked after her five unruly kids. The blouse I wanted to wear to the wedding was on sale for ninety-nine cents. I was forty cents short and the wedding was only three weeks away. Leona couldn't lend me the money because she needed hers to buy makeup and whatnot. I had tried to borrow it from a few of our friends, but they was as bad off as we was.

I was determined to get that blouse. There was going to be a lot of cute boys at the wedding and most of them had decent jobs. If I could snatch one up, the next wedding I went to could be mine.

On the first Saturday in November, I left the house right after I'd finished my chores. Because of the segregation laws, public transportation wasn't available in the colored neighborhoods. I had to walk all the way to our main downtown street where most of the businesses was located. The Ashberry Street Dress Store sat between a flower shop and a fabric store. Neither one of the two clerks seen me when I walked through the door. They was busy helping other customers. When I seen the blouse I wanted, I glanced around to make sure nobody was looking. Several other white customers was giving me suspicious looks, so I knew I had to work fast. I took the blouse off the rack and was about to stuff it into a crude-looking purse I'd made out of a crocus sack. The next thing I knew, a tall, pale-faced woman with eyes like a owl came up to me.

"What do you think you're doing, gal?" she asked as she shook her fist in my face.

"Oh! Nothing, Miss Lady."

"Can you read?"

"Yes, ma'am."

"Then you must have seen that sign in the window. It's front and center so you can't miss it. It clearly states the days and hours you colored people are allowed to shop in this establishment."

"Oh. Um . . . I was in a hurry and I didn't see it. I'll come back some other time." I gave the woman a tight smile and turned to leave. She grabbed my arm.

"You ain't going no place, you thief! You are going to stay here until the sheriff arrives."

I took the blouse out of my purse and handed it to her. "There! I didn't steal it, so I ain't no thief," I protested. I tried to leave again.

"I said, you're staying here until Sheriff Bodine arrives. The only place you're going today is jail." If she hadn't started poking my chest with her finger, I might not have sucker punched her in the jaw. She howled like a she-wolf when she hit the floor. The other clerk and two of the other customers chased me, but them old ladies wasn't fast enough to catch me. I didn't stop running until I got home.

Because I'd got away, I thought that was the end of the situation. But Leona knew something was up as soon as I joined her in our bedroom wringing my hands and breathing hard. She was stretched out in the bed reading one of the magazines the lady Mama worked for passed on to her. Mama was in the kitchen cooking supper.

"What's the matter with you?" Leona asked. "Somebody chasing after you?"

She sat there and listened with a blank expression on her face when I told her what had happened. "Well, I wouldn't worry about it if I was you. The saleswoman don't know your name or where you live, and besides we all look alike to white folks." Leona laughed, but I had a feeling she was worried.

Hearing that made me feel much better. By the time Mama put the food on the table, I had almost forgot about what I'd done.

Chapter 11
Leona

I NEVER THOUGHT THAT FIONA WOULD ATTEMPT TO STEAL SOME-thing, especially at a store owned by white folks. And I certainly never expected her to *hit* a white woman. As bad as things was in the South, colored folks was only human and could only take so much. I recalled the day in that store years ago when Mama hit a white woman who had kicked me. I still got chills when I thought about what could have happened if somebody had stopped us from running out of that store in time. I was glad Fiona had got away from that dress store woman, because if she'd been arrested and hauled off to jail, Mama would have had a fit. Fiona's image in Mama's mind was so pristine, I hoped it stayed that way. I wanted my mama to be happy as long as she could be. I was what I was. I didn't think I could change enough to be more like Fiona to please Mama.

We had almost finished eating supper. It had been a few hours since Fiona told me about the ruckus at the dress shop. There was nothing left on my plate but a pile of chicken bones and a few corn bread crumbs. Half of the food Fiona had put on her plate was still there. "What's wrong with that food, girl?" Mama asked her.

Fiona fidgeted in her chair before she said in a meek voice, "Nothing."

"And how come you so quiet this evening?"

"I . . . I ain't got nothing to say, Mama," Fiona replied.

"Fiona, can I have them gizzards you ain't even touched?" I asked.

Before she could answer, our living-room door flew open. We never locked our front door, and our back door didn't even have a lock. Everybody knew that. There was no reason for nobody to bust into our house. We lived in a safe neighborhood. The worst crimes we had to deal with was folks stealing vegetables from somebody's backyard garden, kids throwing balls and accidentally breaking windows, and the brawls at the houses run by the moonshiners. I had never known of anybody to break into a house in our part of town. "What in the world—" Mama didn't even finish her sentence. We all stood up at the same time.

Before we could make it to the living room, Sheriff Bodine and two of his deputies stormed into our kitchen. They was all pointing guns at us!

"Don't nobody move! Hands in the air!" the sheriff roared as he wagged his gun.

I was scared, but I ignored Sheriff Bodine's order. I didn't raise my hands, but Mama and Fiona did. I moved away from the table with my arms folded. The deputies pointed their guns in my direction. I couldn't believe the look of fear on Fiona's face. I thought she was going to faint like the time when a lizard crawled up her leg.

"What's the problem, sir?" Mama asked in a meek tone, with a smile. Her hands was still in the air. Despite guns pointing at us, she was able to stay calm. Lexington was the kind of small country town where almost everybody knew the same people or was connected in some way. Our family on Daddy's side had been owned by Sheriff Bodine's family during slavery days. I lost count of the horror stories Daddy used to tell us that his folks had told him about them days. But when Lincoln freed the slaves, some of Daddy's relatives chose to stay on the plantation they'd grew up on and work for the Bodine family. The main reason was because they had nowhere to go, no money, and there was mobs of angry white men who tracked down freed slaves and killed them. Mama had took care of Sheriff Bodine's grandmother until she died at the age of ninety-five, ten years ago. Mama didn't like the sheriff, and like every other colored person in town, she avoided him as much as possible. When she did have to deal with him, she was always humble and calm. Even today with his gun pointed at her head. "It's been a while since I seen you, Sheriff. I hope you and your family are doing good." I couldn't believe there was still a smile on Mama's face.

"Never mind all that, Mavis! This ain't no social call!" I didn't know how old our sheriff was, but he had deep lines on his pie-shaped face, stringy gray and brown hair, and a humongous belly. There was coffee and tobacco stains on the front of his shirt and his pants looked like they was two sizes too small.

Every colored person in Lexington agreed that Sheriff Bodine was as racist as he was mean. He had shot and killed several men over the years, colored and white.

"D-did one of us break the law?" Mama asked. She was no longer smiling, but she was still speaking in the same meek tone. I was glad she and Fiona wasn't still holding their hands up in the air.

"You're damn right! One of your look-alike gals went up into the Ashberry Street Dress Shop and caused a ruckus and a woman was almost killed." The sheriff sucked in a deep breath and added, "A *white* woman!"

"What?" Mama's mouth dropped open and she stumbled a few feet back. She didn't even look at Fiona. She looked straight at me. "How do you know it was one of my daughters?"

"One of the customers that witnessed the incident works as a checkout cashier at the store where you and your daughters buy groceries. She recognized her, but she didn't know which one it was."

Before I could say anything, Fiona started boo-hooing and wringing her hands. I knew what I had to do. "I did it! I did it! I'm the one that tried to steal a blouse. Me and the saleslady got into a scuffle, and I had to sock her so I could get away." I paused and took a deep breath. "I'm sorry."

Mama gasped so loud, you could have heard her a block away. "Leona, you tried to steal something? Didn't I raise you not to steal nothing?"

"From a white woman on a day when niggers ain't even allowed to shop in that place!" Sheriff Bodine pointed out.

"I . . . I forgot what day it was," I stuttered. "I just wanted that blouse, and I didn't have enough money to buy it."

"I could have made you another blouse," Mama whimpered.

"I didn't want no homemade blouse this time," I whined. "I . . . I wanted a brand-new one."

"All right, boys, cuff her up," Sheriff Bodine said to his scowling deputies. The tallest one stalked up to me. He grabbed my arm and twirled me around. As hot as it was, them handcuffs felt as cold as ice.

"Girl, what was you thinking?" Mama wanted to know.

"Um . . . I ain't been thinking straight lately. Ever since I caught the nasty-woman's disease . . ." I explained. Everybody in the room looked petrified. The deputy who had just cuffed me backed several feet away from me first. A split second later, Sheriff Bodine and the other deputy moved a few steps away from me too. Nothing disgusted some folks like a infected body part between a person's legs. I didn't like making such a vile claim, but if I was going to jail, I didn't want none of them nasty white devils to do nothing to me. I was still a virgin and I wanted to stay one until I was ready to have relations with somebody. When it came to sex, the Jim Crow laws didn't stop the white men who wanted to have their way with colored women. It was no secret that the sheriff and his deputies took advantage of some of the colored women they locked up. Two women that we knew had half-white babies to prove it.

"You got the clap?" Sheriff Bodine asked with his face screwed up.

"Leona Dunbar, you ought to be ashamed of yourself! You ain't but sixteen!" Mama hollered. I couldn't tell who looked the most disgusted: Mama, the sheriff, or the deputies. There was a blank expression on Fiona's face, so I couldn't tell what she was thinking. Mama had been telling me and her for years that only the most wretched and loose women caught diseases in their private parts.

I sucked in a deep breath and went on. "I just realized I had the clap this morning, so it's real fresh and catchy right now . . ."

"Sheriff Bodine, can I scrape up the money and go pay for the blouse?" Mama asked with her voice trembling. Now she was wringing her hands too.

"Forget about that blouse! We got a white woman that nearly lost her life," Sheriff Bodine barked. "That's what you need to be concerned about, Mavis." The sheriff nodded toward the door. "Boys, let's get this nasty heifer into the squad car."

Mama and Fiona watched in horror and disbelief as they jostled me out the door and loaded me into the backseat of the squad car. The deputy got in the backseat with me, and sat as close as he could to the door on his side.

Now that I didn't have to worry about nobody sexually abusing me in jail, there was still a chance the sheriff would have his deputies beat me. Roughing up colored folks was something some white folks did for sport. Almost every colored person I knew who had been arrested came home from jail with black eyes, busted lips, and other injuries.

The sheriff's office was on the other side of town, which was a several-minute drive from our neighborhood. Sheriff Bodine was so anxious to get my "diseased" self out of his car, he drove so fast, we got there in two minutes.

Chapter 12

Fiona

*A*FTER THE SHERIFF'S CAR DROVE OFF, I WAS SO NERVOUS, I COULD barely keep myself from getting hysterical. I never thought I'd see the day that the law would drag my sister away in handcuffs for something I did. I was going to pray twice as hard before I went to bed. And I was going to do everything in my power for the rest of my life to make this up to Leona.

Me and Mama left the doorway and flopped down on the couch like sacks of flour. Mama sucked in her breath and looked at me with her eyes narrowed. "Did you know about Leona?"

"You mean about her going to steal that blouse or her having the nasty woman's disease?"

"Both!"

"No, ma'am. She don't tell me too much of her business," I whimpered.

"I didn't think so. I declare, that girl is going to send me to the crazy house!" I had never seen Mama look so stupefied. She grimaced and shook her head like she was trying to shake something out of it. "When they turn that gal loose, I'm going to whup her tail like she stole my pocketbook!" So many switches had been plucked from our trees, I was surprised we still had any left. "It was bad enough she got herself pregnant, now this."

"Maybe you should make her read the Bible more," I suggested. My stomach was churning. Not only was I afraid of what could happen to Leona in that jail cell, I was feeling so guilty I had to force myself not to blurt out the truth to Mama. But even as distressed as I was, I knew that if I did, all hell would break loose. "How long do you think they'll keep her locked up?"

"I don't know. Let's get dressed and go talk to the sheriff and find out."

We walked to the jailhouse as fast as our legs could carry us. Mama was a old woman, but she was still as spry and energetic as a teenager. She was walking so fast, I had to skip a few times to keep up with her. One of the good things about the backbreaking work Mama had done all her life was that it kept her body in good condition. Her legs was thick, sturdy, and even though she was a stout woman, her fat wasn't flabby like other women her age. She got more exercise in a day than some of her friends got in a week. It was a cold, dreary day, but the weather didn't bother me. What was happening to Leona had me so hot, I had to fan my face. "Mama, what if we get there too late?"

"Too late for what?"

"You know how they usually beat up the colored prisoners as soon as they get them to the jailhouse. Remember that man they beat to death last year?"

Mama turned and gave me a worried look, but she didn't stop walking. "That fool had raped a white girl. If they hadn't killed him in the jail, a lynch mob would have busted in and took him out and finished him off. You know the rules in the South. When we break them rules, the white folks break us." She snorted and cleared her throat. "But with Leona only being a child, they might not be too rough on her."

"I don't think these people care nothing about age. The boy they lynched two years ago was only thirteen," I reminded.

"He had raped a white girl too."

We stopped walking when we got in front of the small drab-looking building where the jails was at. The windows was so dusty, you couldn't even see through them.

Mama looked all right, but my knees felt like they was going to buckle as we made our way through the front door. A middle-aged, sharp-featured white woman sitting at the front desk looked up and smiled at us. We didn't give her a chance to ask what we wanted. "We need to see the sheriff," Mama said. The woman nodded, stood up, and opened a door off to the side behind her desk. Sheriff Bodine was sitting at a big metal desk fiddling with his hat. From the frown on his face, he was not happy to see us. Most of the time when a colored person went to the jailhouse, it was to be locked up. "What in the world are y'all doing here?" he boomed. He laid his hat down on the desk next to a half-eaten pickle and stood up and put his hands on his hips.

"We came to see if you could let us know when Leona was going to court?"

He laughed and slapped the side of his hefty thigh. "Court? What gave y'all the notion that she was going to court?"

"Well, ain't that where everybody else goes when they commit a crime?" I blurted out.

"Listen here, my jail is the closest that gal is going to get to a courtroom!"

Me and Mama looked at each other and blinked. "What do you mean?" Mama asked in a strong tone. "Ain't a judge supposed to decide what punishment she'll get?"

"I done talked to Judge Smoot already. He decided it'd be too costly and disruptive to try the gal and send her to the work camp. But she ain't getting off scot-free. The judge wants to teach her a lesson she'll never forget. I suggested we keep her in my jail for two months. Him being the son of a preacher, he's a compassionate man. He told me to keep her for a month and a day."

"That long?!" me and Mama shrieked at the same time.

"But she didn't even get out the store with the blouse," I pointed out.

"I took that under consideration and dropped the attempted theft charge. But she still has to be punished for assaulting a white woman," Sheriff Bodine said with a smirk. "Now you two wenches get the hell out of here before I throw y'all in jail with her."

"Can we see her, sir?" Mama pleaded.

"Naw! I'm too busy right now to keep a eye on y'all!"

"When can we see her?" Mama asked.

"Come back tomorrow. Any more questions?"

"Uh, just one. Will you give her something clean to wear each day?"

Sheriff Bodine looked at Mama like she'd just stepped on his foot. "Look, lady, this ain't no resort hotel. I'll get her a jumper, or a duster, or something to cover up in when I get a chance to go to the work camp to get one. But she won't get a fresh frock every day. They dispense them items only once a week."

"All right, then. We'll come back tomorrow, and I'll bring her some fresh clothes," Mama said.

Chapter 13
Leona

I DIDN'T THINK THAT WHITE FOLKS COULD TREAT US NO WORSE THAN they did until I got to jail. Like everything else, our rinky-dink local jailhouse was segregated too. Behind Sheriff Bodine's cluttered office was a dark, musty-smelling hall that led to three small cells. There was one for white women, one for white men, and at the end of the hall was one that colored men and women had to share if they was in jail at the same time. All three looked spooky. Mold clung to the walls like cheap wallpaper and the tiny windows had bars.

There was bunk beds with sheets, pillows, and blankets in the white folks' cells. My cell had a naked mattress on a metal bed frame, backed up against the wall. A woman was curled up on it like a unborn baby, snoring like a moose. She was facing the wall, but I could tell from her thick gray hair that she was a older woman. She didn't move or say nothing when I was ushered in. There was just enough room on the mattress for me to sit next to her calloused bare feet. I cleared my throat when I eased down, but the woman still didn't move or say nothing. She smelled like she hadn't washed herself up in weeks.

"Gal, you behave yourself and act like a citizen and we'll get along just fine," Sheriff Bodine told me as he slammed the door shut and locked it. Before he went back to his office he muttered, "Breakfast is at eight a.m. sharp. You'll get a lunch snack around noon, and then you won't eat again until suppertime, which is usually five or six. You'll only get water with each meal."

"Yes, sir. Uh, do I get a blanket to cover up with when I get ready to go to sleep? It gets cold at night this time of year." I should have known I was asking a dumb question. The woman on the bed didn't have no blanket.

"Blanket?"

"Yes, sir. Like the man in the first cell."

Sheriff Bodine guffawed long and loud. What I'd said was not the least bit funny to me. I thought it was a reasonable question to ask, even for a colored prisoner. "I guess you want an eider-down pillow to boot. The sooner you darkies realize what life is about, the better off y'all will be. That's a white man in that cell!"

"Oh," I mumbled. The sheriff laughed again before he spun around and strolled back to his office.

There was so many different colored stains on the mattress, I couldn't tell where one ended and another started. And the mattress smelled like pee. I was surprised I didn't see no bed-bugs or roaches or rats.

My stomach knotted up as I looked around the room. I got up to see what was in the two buckets sitting on the floor in front of the window. One was supposed to be a toilet because there was a roll of toilet paper sitting next to it. The other bucket was a little bigger. I figured it was supposed to be used to wash up in be-cause there was a half-used bar of lye soap on the floor next to it, and a stiff rag. I whirled around when I heard the door being unlocked. It was Sheriff Bodine. He was holding what looked like a rubber mat about half the size of a blanket. "Two of y'all can't sleep on that mattress so you'll have to use the floor. It's a mite hard. You'll be more comfortable on this here mat." He dropped it to the floor. "The slop jar will be emptied and rinsed out every other day. Don't get greedy with the toilet paper. We don't have much left for this month. If we run out before you get released, you'll have to wipe your hind parts off with butcher block paper. Any questions?"

I shook my head, which was throbbing like somebody had clobbered it.

Sheriff Bodine left without saying another word.

I sat next to the woman's feet until it got dark. And then I laid down on the rubber mat.

Mama came Sunday morning to bring me some fresh underwear and a smock. Sheriff Bodine told her she could only stay a few minutes. "I hate this place! It's worse than a neglected outhouse!" I complained.

Mama gave me a hopeless look. "Jail ain't supposed to be pleasant, sugar. If it was, folks would run amok. Just be happy that the sheriff is going to keep you here for your whole sentence. That prison work camp is way too far and me and Fiona would have a hard time getting folks with trucks or cars to bring us out there to see you."

"Is he keeping me here because I'm just a young kid?"

Mama gave me a weary look and shook her head. "Sugar, you may be a 'young kid' now. But something like this will make you grow up real fast. I don't think they decided not to send you to the work camp because of your age. They take colored girls even younger than you—and white ones—to that wretched place. I know this is bad and sleeping on a rubber pallet floor ain't no picnic, but it could be worse."

I swallowed hard and looked around the cell. "Tell me about it. But I wonder why they decided to let me do my time in the local jail?"

"Well, I guess you can thank me for that. I told the sheriff you didn't have a lick of sense, even when you ain't got the clap."

I didn't see no reason to tell Mama that I wasn't infected, or that I had never even had sex. "Thank you, Mama."

"Sheriff Bodine told me he still remembers all the good work I did for his family back in the old days, and how much his whole family liked me. He even admitted that his elderly mama would wring his neck if he didn't give you special treatment. Be thankful you won't have to wear one of them mammy-made prison frocks they make the other females wear."

When Mama left, I stretched out on the mat, and somehow, I managed to go to sleep.

Chapter 14
Fiona

MAMA HAD LEFT THE HOUSE BEFORE I GOT OUT OF BED THIS morning. She was gone so long, I got worried. I couldn't sit down for more than a few minutes at a time. I paced around the living room for a while, then I went into the kitchen and my bedroom and done the same thing. As crazy as white folks was, I had every reason to be concerned about my mama. All kinds of thoughts was floating around inside my head. As humble as Mama was around white folks, she did have a temper. But I only seen her lose control when Leona did something _____
I never thought Mama would forget her "place" w____
white folks, but I couldn't ignore the fact that ____
her place when it came to her children.

I had been up for a hour and Mama still had____
was sitting on the living-room couch, still so fra____
my nails down to the quick. I almost jumped ____
when somebody knocked on the front door jus____
ran to answer it, but I was scared that it was some____
tell me Sheriff Bodine had done something to____
relieved when I opened the door and seen ____
Leona's friends standing there. Bonnie Sue Jo____
months older than us. She had been our best ____
we was toddlers.

"Oh, it's only you," I muttered as she pranc____
Bonnie Sue rolled her neck and put her hands ____

"Well! Thanks for making me feel welcome," she huffed. She shot me a hot look before she flopped down on the couch and crossed her bony legs. Even though me and Leona was still just teenagers, our bodies was well developed. Poor Bonnie Sue looked like a bag of bones next to us. If somebody had a contest for plain Janes, she would win first place. She had small beady black eyes, a nose that was too big for her face, and a overbite that was so profound, it looked like her teeth was going to fly out every time she opened her mouth. Her short hair was so brittle she usually kept it hid up under a scarf, like the blue plaid one she had on now. Bonnie Sue had one saving grace that was indisputable: a high-yellow skin tone. To some colored folks, light skin was one of God's greatest blessings. But Bonnie Sue was still insecure about her looks. That was the reason me and Leona often assured her that she *was* attractive. We'd been building up her self-esteem for years and now she finally carried herself as though she was as eye-catching as a swan.

"I came over to see why y'all wasn't at the morning service," Bonnie Sue explained. This was the first Sunday in more than five years that me and Mama had missed church. I couldn't remember the last time Leona went. "Reverend Sweeney preached up a storm. He asked me where y'all was at because he was concerned too."

"Bonnie Sue, you know I appreciate your concern. The thing is, we got a big mess on our hands."

Her mouth dropped open and stayed that way until I finished telling her what was going on. The only thing I didn't tell her was that I was the one who had caused the ruckus at the dress store. As close as she was to us, me and Leona didn't even want her to know that we often switched identities.

"My Lord. What was Leona thinking? Can I go see her? Me and her is supposed to get together next Friday and plan my wedding reception."

"You better get somebody else to help you plan it. She's going to be in jail for a few more weeks."

Before Bonnie Sue could speak again, Mama stumbled in the

door. I could tell that she had been walking fast, or maybe even running. Sweat was all over her face, and she was breathing hard and fanning her face with her purse.

"Where you been?" I asked with my heart beating a mile a minute. "I was worried sick."

"You ain't got to waste up no worries for me. Worry about your sister. I went to take her some fresh clothes," Mama replied in a weary tone.

"How is she doing?" I helped Mama to the wobbly-legged wooden chair facing the couch.

She let out a loud breath and shook her head before she answered. "Well, at least they didn't put their hands on her." She paused and gave me a hopeful look. "At least not yet. She's in good spirits for somebody in a mess as bad as the one she done got herself in." Mama laid her purse on the coffee table and fanned her face with her hand before she gazed at Bonnie Sue. "You knew she was planning on stealing that blouse to wear to your wedding," she accused.

"N-no, ma'am! I-I didn't know nothing about it, Sister Mavis!" Bonnie Sue leaped up from the couch and flailed her arms a couple of times. I couldn't tell which one of us was the most distressed. "I'm just as stupefied as you and Fiona to hear that Leona is the stealing type. Can I go see her?"

"Yeah, but not today. That fool sheriff is in a foul mood. For now, I think only family should go. Fiona, she told me to tell you to come see her today."

I gulped and glanced from Mama to Bonnie Sue. "Bonnie Sue can't go with me? I have to go by myself?"

"Didn't you just hear me say that the sheriff is in a foul mood and only family should go for now? Get a move on so you can get down to that jailhouse and back before Sheriff Bodine changes his mind."

"All right, then," I mumbled. Bonnie Sue came up to me and gave me a hug.

"Ask the sheriff when I can come see her. Then me and you can go together," Bonnie Sue said as she patted my back. "I'll be praying for both of y'all. If the sheriff would let me trade places with Leona, I'd do it in a heartbeat."

Them words made me feel warm all over. "Bless your soul." I had to stop talking and hold my breath before I got too emotional. Most folks went their whole lives never knowing what it was like to have a God-fearing, considerate, unselfish friend like Bonnie Sue. I didn't know what we'd do without her. I loved her almost as much as I loved Leona.

Just as I was about to walk out the door, Mama trotted across the floor and got in front of me. "Just a minute, gal! When you get to that jailhouse, remember to stay in your place," she said as she wagged her finger in front of my face. "Don't do or say nothing that'll rile Sheriff Bodine. If he arrests you, they'll have to lock me up next because I ain't going to let that cracker destroy my family. I will kill him dead first!"

Mama's grim words and the thought of her going to prison for killing a white man chilled me to my core. Except for the whuppings, she was the most nonviolent person I knew.

"I'll be as meek as a lamb."

"I know you will, sugar," she said in a much calmer tone. "You ain't nothing like your sister."

It seemed like every chance Mama got, she threw in a dig against Leona. So that Mama would rest in peace, I decided that when she was on her deathbed, I would tell her what I was really like.

Chapter 15
Fiona

I TOOK MY TIME WALKING TO THE JAILHOUSE. WHEN I GOT THERE, Sheriff Bodine was sitting at his desk leafing through a magazine with a woman in a bathing suit on the cover. He gave me the same mean look he'd gave me when he came to the house to arrest Leona yesterday. "What do you want?" he growled.

"I . . . I was hoping I could see m-my sister today, sir," I stuttered. "I won't stay but a little while."

"You damn right, you won't stay but 'a little while.'" He glared at me and chanted, "Niggers, niggers, niggers!" He wobbled up out of his seat, grabbed a big round metal ring with some keys on it off his desk, and headed out of the room. "Follow me!" He didn't say nothing when we got to Leona's cell. He just opened the door and waved me in.

I almost screamed when I seen the woeful look on my sister's face. She was sitting on the floor with her back up against the wall. Her cellmate was laying on a naked mattress facing the wall snoring like a big moose.

"Fiona, I'm so glad to see you! You all right?" Leona was always more concerned about me than she was herself. She scrambled up off the floor and ran up to me and hugged my neck so hard she almost choked the breath out of me. She let me go when I started squirming and coughing. "I didn't mean to get carried away," she apologized as she brushed some lint off the sleeve of my blouse. And then she smiled. "When you see Bonnie Sue, tell her why I got arrested, but don't tell her what really happened."

"You know I wouldn't do that. She came to the house this morning. I told her the same story I'm going to tell everybody else." I glanced at the floor for a few seconds. When I looked back up at Leona, my eyes was flooded with tears. "I declare, I am so sorry about all this," I told her, choking on a sob.

"Now don't you start crying. I feel bad enough." She chuckled and wiped tears off my cheeks. "I'm doing all right. Mama brought me some clean clothes this morning."

"Good." I glanced at the buckets. "Is one of them buckets what you have to wash up in?"

"Yeah. The other one is supposed to be a slop jar."

I shuddered and grimaced so hard my face felt as tight as a drum. "Will you and the lady on the bed have to do your business in the same bucket?"

"Sheriff didn't say, but I got a feeling we will."

"Blood of Jesus!" I squeezed my nostrils together with the tips of my fingers for a few seconds. "I can't even organize my brain to process something that nasty. I hope they empty that bucket every time one of y'all uses it."

"They'll only empty it every other day."

I sucked in so much air, my throat hurt. "I couldn't survive one hour in this place," I admitted as I glared at the toilet/bucket like it was a bomb about to go off any second.

"I know you couldn't. That's why I'm the one in here."

I didn't want to spend too much time discussing the reason Leona was in jail, so I decided to shift the conversation. "Bonnie Sue said folks at church was wondering how come me and Mama wasn't there this morning."

"They'll find out soon enough."

"I know." It was hard for me to act normal, knowing what I knew. "Um . . . Sheriff said I could only stay a little while—"

Before I could finish my sentence, Sheriff Bodine unlocked the cell door and snatched it open. "Time's up! Get a move on!"

"But sir, I just got here," I protested.

"I don't know what a little while means to you people, but you done been in here as long as I will allow," he barked.

"Go on back home, Fiona. I'll be okay," Leona assured me in a strong tone, which I knew she was faking.

"What time can we come get her on the day you release her, Sheriff Bodine, sir?"

He looked away, snorted, and scratched his chin. Something told me that the sneaky way he was acting meant bad news. "Y'all can come anytime you feel like. So long as her fine's been paid . . ."

You could have knocked me over with a rose petal. "What fine?" me and Leona asked at the same time.

"You didn't say nothing about no fine, sir!" I pointed out.

Sheriff Bodine folded his arms and glared at me. "Gal, don't you never holler at *me* again! Do you want me to teach you how to show respect to a white man?"

"No, sir," I said in a tone so low I could barely hear myself.

"I know you people ain't too smart, but did y'all think there would be no consequences for this crime?"

"I thought being arrested and put in jail for a month and a day was the only consequence?" Leona hollered.

Sheriff Bodine screwed up his thin lips like she had bit him. "Dagnabbit! You are just as uppity as your sister!" Spit flew out of his mouth and onto my face as he wagged his finger at me. "Don't you never raise your voice to a white man! You want me to add the charge of sassing a peace officer to your case? I'd have to tack on at least another week to your sentence."

"I'm sorry," Leona whimpered.

"How much is the fine?" I asked in the lowest tone I could.

"Three dollars."

Them words went into my ears like nails. "*Three dollars?* We ain't got that kind of money laying around," I said.

"Well, you'd better come up with 'that kind of money' to settle this issue. And it's got to be paid by tomorrow. Now git!" Sheriff Bodine stomped his foot and pointed to the door.

My feet felt as heavy as cement as I walked back toward the street that led to our neighborhood. Sheriff Bodine's words was ringing in my ears so loud, I could barely think straight.

If I hadn't been able to come up with ninety-nine cents in two weeks to get that blouse, how was I going to come up with three dollars by tomorrow? But I planned to get that money, and I didn't care what I had to do to get it.

I was glad Mama was gone when I got back to our house. I didn't know how long she'd be gone, so I didn't have no time to waste. I could only think of one way to get three dollars by tomorrow. It was so unspeakable it hadn't even crossed my mind to do it to get the money for the blouse. It was no secret that there was some older men in our neighborhood who paid money to females to give them some pleasure.

Bonnie Sue and some of the other girls we knew visited them old men to get money for the movies or to buy other things. Leona thought it was disgusting. I told her I felt the same way. But I didn't realize how quick I would change my tune until Sheriff Bodine told me about that fine. The thought of Leona spending a day longer in that jail cell than what Sheriff Bodine had originally sentenced her to turned my stomach.

I had to spring into action fast. I put on some of Leona's makeup and a hot pink, low-cut blouse that a hard-living older woman had gave her for babysitting. She wore it when she went out with her party-time friends. It was her favorite piece of clothing because according to her, "It protects the property but don't spoil the view." I stuffed one of my plain high-necked blouses and a damp washrag into my purse so I could duck behind a bush and wash off the makeup and change blouses before I went back home. I prayed I wouldn't run into nobody who knew me. But on Sunday, most of the people I knew would still be in church after Bonnie Sue left, or would have returned by this time.

The oldest one of them frisky men was a widower in his eighties who lived with his grandson and family one street over from us. He walked with a cane and was half-blind, so there wasn't much he could still do with a female. Everybody said he paid good money for whatever pleasure he could get. Girls usually went to his house during the week when his family was at work and he was in the house alone. Since he rarely went to church with his family, I was surprised when he didn't answer the door. I didn't want to waste no more time because I thought if I did, I might change my mind. I trotted down the same street where another nasty old man lived in a brown-shingled house.

Jake Hickey was in his late forties. He lived by hisself and rarely went to church, so I figured he'd be home. His wife had left him years ago and he wasn't close to the few other relatives he had in Lexington, so they rarely visited him. Even though he was old, folks said he still had a robust "love" life. He made good money working at the sawmill and he was generous, so he was real popular with women. Prostitutes who worked at the sporting houses loved him so much, they made house calls.

Before I could even knock on Jake's door, he opened it. "I thought I heard somebody walk up on my porch. Hello, you sweet young thing you!" The smile on his moon-shaped face was so wide, it looked like somebody had carved it with a knife. Jake looked older than his real age because most of his thick curly hair was gray. He wasn't much taller than me—and I was only five feet three—and he was as fat as a hog. If all that wasn't bad enough, four of his front teeth was missing and the ones he had left was jagged and brown because he occasionally chewed tobacco.

"I thought you'd like to have some company for a little while," I cooed as he led me into his living room.

"Every day," he said with a chuckle.

"Women like you a lot. And it ain't no wonder. You dress sporty and you got all that curly hair . . ."

Jake raked his fingers through his hair and puffed out his chest and bragged, "Shoot! You should have seen what a dandy I was before my hair started turning gray." For him to be such a wreck, he had the prettiest brown eyes. They looked so out of place on his face. "How come you ain't in church?"

"I didn't feel like going. Um . . . can we move things along? I have to get back home and mop the kitchen."

"Hmmm. I don't like to be rushed, but I wasn't expecting no company this time of day and I got things to do myself. So have a seat and tell me something good."

The inside of his house was gloomy. His mismatched furniture was shabby, the floors looked like they hadn't been swept and mopped in weeks, and old newspapers and magazines was strewn about all over the place. I forced myself to smile as we flopped down on his lumpy green couch at the same time. He let out a groan and a low-level fart at the same time. I acted like I didn't hear or smell it. "You look real nice today," I commented. His plaid shirt looked like he had just took it out of a box from a men's clothing store. The blade of a screwdriver poked from the pocket of his black corduroy pants.

Like us and almost everybody else, Jake had a potbellied stove in the middle of his living room floor. There was a big pile of wood behind the stove. A metal chair faced the couch and his coffee table was a crate that some yams had been shipped in. When he touched my jaw with one of his thick ashy fingers, I cringed. I had to get this episode over with as soon as possible before I got sick. "Um . . . we can have a little fun if you want to."

"Sounds good to me." He sucked his teeth and grinned. "I'm expecting a visit from one of my regular lady friends later on this evening. But when she gets here, I ain't going to answer my door. I'm tired of fooling around with them dried-up hags I been messing with since my wife took off. They ain't worth the dollar they charge me nohow. Besides, I done wore them out, so I could use a fresh piece of tail now and then!" He was as excited as a butcher's dog. "I declare, you cuter than a baby possum. Which one of Sister Dunbar's twin girls is you?"

"I'm . . . Leona."

Chapter 16
Fiona

"Leona, Leona, Leona. That's such a pretty name and it's right fitting for a girl like you." Jake smiled again and caressed his three chins. "I remember when you was a itty-bitty girl. You was a spitfire if ever there was one. When you was around ten, you kicked that old hound dog I owned at the time."

"He bit me." That dog's teeth prints had stayed on Leona's leg for a whole week.

"Well, you didn't have to kick him so hard. He was never the same again. He walked with a limp until he died two months later."

"I'm sorry I kicked your dog, Mr. Jake. Mama gave me a whupping for doing that."

"I'm the one who told her to chastise you! Now let's talk about something more pleasant." Jake rubbed his hands together and looked at me like I was laid out on a silver platter. "I hope your twin sister comes to see me soon. Women is what keeps me in shape, so I spend as much time with y'all as possible. Bonnie Sue said she'd drop by to give me a tune-up before her wedding. She needs a little more money to pay for some of the food they going to serve at the reception."

"What day is she supposed to come?" I knew I had to work fast. I didn't want Bonnie Sue or none of our other friends to know what I was up to. Mama had said we shouldn't tell folks about Leona right away, so it could take a day or two before somebody told Jake that the real Leona was in jail.

"I don't know, but let's forget about her. I got you here now, so I don't want to discuss none of them other gals," Jake growled.

"Um . . . I need new shoes to wear to Bonnie Sue's wedding. I hope you can give me three dollars to buy a pair."

"Eoww! That's a hell of a lot of money to pay for a little fun. Some of them gals that work in the sporting houses don't make that in a day."

"I know, but that's how much I need."

Jake scratched the top of his head. "Hmmm. Three dollars. That's a lot of money for some shoes." He glanced at the shabby brown moccasins on my feet. "What's wrong with the ones you got on now? You wore them to that Simpson gal's wedding a few weeks ago."

"Ain't nothing wrong with these. But they don't match the dress I'm going to wear."

"Damn! That's still a heap of money to spend on one pair of shoes. I could buy several pair myself for that kind of money."

"I know it's a lot of money, but I want to have enough left over to buy Bonnie Sue a nice wedding gift."

"I'm sure she'll appreciate whatever you give her. I'm giving her some potholders somebody gave me that I never used." He gazed at my bosom and a bigger smile crossed his face. "Oomph! The more I look at you, the cuter you get." He rubbed and squeezed my knee.

"W-what all do I have to do for three dollars?"

Jake shrugged. "You tell me."

"No, you tell me."

"I just got me a piece of tail last night, so I'm pretty well satisfied in that area for now. But I ran out of them nerve pills my doctor gave me, so I could still use something that'll help me relax. You good with your hands?"

"Yes, sir. My boyfriend says I am." I breathed a sigh of relief. "Will you give me three dollars just for a hand job?"

Jake frowned. "I usually pay only fifty cents for that. Since this is the first time you paid me a visit, and you one of the prettiest gals around here, I'll let you off easy. I'll only give you three bucks if what you do contents me." He paused and wagged his finger in my face. "But the next time you pay me a visit, I don't care what you do for me, I ain't paying more than fifty cents. Do you hear me?"

"Yes, sir." I would have agreed to anything Jake asked me to, and I hoped that I'd never have to visit this beast again. But I would if I had to. "Give me my money first." He reached into his pants pocket and pulled out a small wad of bills and peeled off three ones. I snatched the money, folded it, and slid it down into my sock. "You ain't going to tell nobody about me coming over here, right? If my boyfriend and my mama was to find out, they'll preach my funeral."

Jake shrugged his shoulders and snickered. "I don't kiss and tell. Now come on and let's get this show on the road."

I held my breath and followed Jake to his bedroom. He got out of his clothes so fast it made my head spin. I got out of mine real fast too because I wanted to do the deed as quick as possible. It hurt my eyes to look at his naked body. He was covered in black and gray hair from his chest on down. His pecker looked like a short snake with one eye. I shuddered when I touched it.

I guess I wasn't good enough with my hands, because after I'd stroked him for about five minutes, he told me to sit on his face. I gasped so hard I was surprised I didn't swallow my tongue. What the hell—when did men come up with *that*? I wondered. I had been with a heap of boys, but nary one had ever asked me to do something so outlandish. I had never even heard of such a thing. And it sounded downright vile. "And then what?" I asked, praying that afterwards he wouldn't ask me if he could sit on *my* face. There was no way I was going to go that far. I'd rather rob a bank to get the money to pay Leona's fine.

"And then I'll be content. Now get on it so I can take a nap."

All I had to do was straddle his face and sit, he did the rest. It only took ten minutes to satisfy him, and it wasn't as disgusting as I thought it would be. When it was over, he immediately dozed off. I scrambled off the bed, hurried back into my clothes, and bolted out the back door. All I could think about now was that I had the money to pay Leona's fine. I had already came up with a lie to tell Mama if she found out about the fine. I was going to tell her that I'd paid it with the money I had been saving up all year to spend on this year's Christmas presents.

There was a dirt road behind Jake's house that was lined with trees. As soon as I spotted a tree wide enough for me to hide behind, I fished the damp rag out of my purse and scrubbed the makeup off my face. After I changed blouses, I walked as fast as I could all the way the jailhouse.

Chapter 17
Leona

BEFORE I COULD GET TOO MISERABLE, SHERIFF BODINE CAME back to my cell. His hat was on sideways and a unlit corncob pipe was sticking from the corner of his mouth. He unlocked the door and announced in a cheerful tone, "You got a visitor. Your look-alike sister." Fiona stood behind him with a blank expression on her face. "She paid your fine, so you'll be let out on time—unless you do something that'll cost you more time." He laughed.

Sheriff Bodine waved Fiona into my cell. He slammed the door shut and shuffled back down the hallway. She rushed in and sat down next to me on the grimy pad on the floor. "I'm so glad to see you," I told her as I squeezed her hand.

"I know he ain't going to let me stay long, so we need to talk fast." Fiona stopped talking and stared at the woman on the bed. "What did that lady do?"

"I don't know. She ain't said a word since I got here. She been sleeping the whole time."

"It don't look like she's moved at all since I was here the first time. She been sleeping that long?"

I nodded. "She ain't moved a muscle."

Fiona gave the woman a pitying look and then she gave me the same kind. "I am so sorry I got you into this mess."

"It ain't your fault. I didn't have to say I was the one that hit that white woman."

"But you did it because of me."

"Let's not even discuss that part no more. What's done is done. Being locked up ain't *too* bad. I can do my time standing on my head if I have to." I laughed. Fiona cracked a weak smile. "How is Mama holding up?"

"Well, not so good, I guess. She's been reading the Bible a lot and I heard her crying in her room last night. She wasn't at home when I left."

"I done let her down again."

"No, you didn't. *I* let her down again."

"Where did you get the money to pay my fine?"

Fiona looked at the floor and cleared her throat. "I got it from Jake Hickey."

"My Lord! That nasty puppy? Please tell me he *loaned* it to you."

"Something like that." Fiona didn't have to admit it. Because from the woebegone look on her face, I knew what she had done.

"You let that old goat *pester* you?" The look of disgust on her face was as serious as the one on mine.

Fiona nodded. "I didn't have no choice. I didn't want Mama to have to spend her money on your fine. But you ain't got to worry, I didn't have to do nothing too nasty."

"Oh? What did you have to do?"

Fiona looked like she was in pain when she told me what she'd done. I had to slap my ear because I couldn't believe what I was hearing. The thought of my "prim and proper" sister sitting on that old man's face sent shivers up and down my spine. I didn't know much about sex, but I'd never heard of something as vile as a man wanting a female to sit on his face! I groaned and shook my head. "When did human beings come up with something like that? That ain't even in the Bible and Scripture even tell us about men messing around with animals! What is the world coming to? And with Jake's front teeth missing, that must have felt like sitting on the sharp edge of a rake."

"That's about what it felt like." Fiona shivered and shook her head. "Forget about it. If I talk about it anymore, I'm going to be sick." Before we could continue, I heard keys jangling, so I looked toward the door. Sheriff Bodine had returned already.

"Time's up!" he boomed as he unlocked the door.

The wife of the white man in the first cell had been visiting him for over a hour and was still there. It took all of my strength not to point that out to the sheriff. The last thing I wanted him to do was remind me that I was colored and didn't have the same privileges as white folks. Me and Fiona stood up and hugged before she left.

I slept a little better that night, but I didn't know if I could spend the rest of my sentence sleeping on that hard floor without going crazy. It was so cold when I woke up Monday morning at dawn, I was shivering. I could hear folks talking and when I rubbed my eyes and looked across the room, I seen the sheriff and one of his deputies hovering over the woman on the mattress. Sheriff Bodine looked over at me. "Well, darlin', you got the bed all to yourself now," he said with a grin. And then he adjusted his hat and told his deputy, "Go round up one of them colored undertakers and tell him I said to get his tail over here with his hearse lickety-split."

I was relieved when the sheriff and his deputy left. I was too scared to get close to the dead woman, so I stayed on the floor. I had leg cramps, a backache, and my head was aching in the front, back, and on both sides.

I stayed on the floor until Sheriff Bodine came back about thirty minutes later. His two deputies, the woman who sat at the desk in front of his office, and two colored men was with him. I recognized them as the Fuller Brothers, Ned and Percy. They was only in their early forties, but they had been undertaking for about five years now. I had no idea exactly how many folks lived in Lexington. I suspected there was at least nine or ten thousand at the time, but only about two or three thousand was colored, if that many. That wasn't a lot of folks, but with all the sickly ones, accidents, and lynchings, the colored undertakers had steady business.

When they turned the woman over to put her on a stretcher, I stood up and moved a little closer. I almost collapsed when I seen who she was: the mama of one of my used-to-be boyfriends.

After they hauled the woman away, I got up and brushed off the mattress. There was a big damp spot in the middle, so I covered it with the rubber mat before I stretched out on my side, facing the wall.

I woke up during the night when I heard keys locking the cell door. I didn't look up in time to see who had come in. But whoever it was, they had covered me with a nice blue blanket.

Chapter 18
Fiona

YESTERDAY WAS ONE OF THE WORST DAYS OF MY LIFE. I DIDN'T GET to wash between my legs until I got back home from the jailhouse. I used a whole bar of lye soap and scrubbed myself until I was almost raw. The only good thing that came out of the mess I'd created was I had learned my lesson. I would never try to steal nothing else!

When I got home from school today Mama was gone. I could tell she had come home from work because her uniform was lying on top of the clothes hamper in the bathroom. When she came home a hour later, she looked so worn out and sad, I didn't know what to say to her.

"Where you been? You look like something the cat dragged in," I said as she stumbled into the living room. I rushed up to her and took her by the arm and led her to the couch.

"I went to see Reverend Sweeney. He prayed with me and he did a laying on of hands until my body felt rejuvenated. He told me to come back if things get worse. Then he'll round up the most powerful warriors in his congregation so we can organize a prayer chain."

"Why would he have to do all of that? I thought only the real sick or dying folks got that kind of special treatment." Me and Mama sat down on the couch. She laid her purse on the coffee table and kicked off her shoes. Her rolled-up stockings had slid halfway down her legs.

"What's wrong with you, gal? Leona's is a world of trouble, and anything could happen to her in that place. Reverend Sweeney's wife just happens to work for the family of that woman she attacked in the dress store. That woman is married to a straight-up brute who is known for busting heads."

I got even more worried. "Oh," was all I could say at first. "I'm glad you went to see Reverend Sweeney."

"I know we can count on him to make a bad situation better, so we should be nice to him. As soon as I feel better, I'm going to ask if he wants me to do some babysitting or cooking and cleaning for him and his wife in my spare time."

"I wouldn't bring all that up if I was you. You going to work yourself to death. Besides, I would rather have you spend your spare time with us. And as much as I like the good reverend, we don't want to make it look like we groveling to him. So don't you go up to him for nothing else except to praise his spiritual ability."

"You are so right," Mama agreed. She sounded so tired, I couldn't believe a woman with a burden already as heavy as hers was thinking about adding to it.

Me and Mama got on our knees and prayed for Leona for ten minutes straight before we went to bed. She said we'd do it again in the morning before I went to school.

There was only one school in Lexington for colored kids. It was a used-to-be church. We had shabby, outdated books, and had to sit on pews instead of at desks. But we had some good teachers, so most of us learned a lot. I read everything I could get my hands on, in and out of school. Some of the families Mama worked for gave her all kinds of magazines and books. Leona didn't like school and wouldn't crack open a book unless she had to. She played hooky a lot to go fishing or just to hang out with Bonnie Sue or some of the other hardheaded kids.

Some of our friends only went to school long enough to learn the basics, like reading, writing, and arithmetic. One reason was because their parents had told them that everything else they needed to know was in the Bible. Half of the ones that stayed longer had to drop out eventually to go to work and help their family pay bills. Me and Leona was going to graduate next year. I planned on staying until then, but I had a feeling Leona wouldn't.

I had a hard time concentrating on schoolwork Tuesday morning. I couldn't stop thinking about Leona. I was glad Bonnie Sue was still in school, and occupied the pew behind me. When we got out for the day, me and her walked home together like we often did.

"How is Leona doing?" she asked as we strolled along the dirt road that led to my street. She lived with her family four blocks from us on the same street.

"All right, I guess. She was in pretty good spirits for a girl in her predicament."

"It's a shame she tried to steal that blouse to wear to my wedding and won't even be out of jail in time to come." Bonnie Sue shook her head and hugged her schoolbooks closer to her flat bosom. "Do you think Sheriff Bodine will let me visit her now?"

"I don't know. But I hope you'll at least try to see her. You're her best friend, so I know a visit from you would mean a lot to her."

Bonnie Sue gave me a thoughtful look. "I love Leona as much as I love my own blood sister. She is so pretty and so good to me."

I didn't like the dreamy-eyed look on Bonnie Sue's face. And then she said something that made me uncomfortable. "Since y'all look exactly alike, I feel the same way about you."

"Well, you know me and Leona care about you as much as you do about us," I replied. I was glad she changed the subject and started talking about her upcoming wedding until we reached my house.

Me and Mama didn't talk much during supper, like we usually did. But I was sure that the same thing on my mind was on hers: Leona sitting in that cold jail cell. After she chewed and swallowed a huge chunk of the fried chicken leg in her hand, she said in a dry tone, "Mighty Moses. I'm so worried about Leona.

She's already got a ungodly attitude. There ain't no telling how going to jail is going to affect her."

"I don't see how it's going to change her personality, if that's what you mean." I reached for another biscuit. I was glad I still had enough of a appetite to eat.

Mama gave me a blank stare before she continued. "What if she was to get caught stealing again? She might even rob a bank next."

"Mama, have you ever heard of a colored person in this town robbing a bank?"

"No, but there is a first time for everything. I never thought she'd try to steal a blouse. All she had to do was tell me what it looked like, and I could have made the same one for her."

"Mama, you been making most of our clothes since we was born. It's nice to have something store-bought for a change."

"If I had known what she done before the sheriff told me, I would have whupped her until I got tired!"

I rolled my eyes. "You would have been wasting your time like always. Leona is going to do whatever she wants. I know that and you should too by now."

"She's like her daddy," Mama said with her voice cracking. "Clyde was a good man, but he didn't have much common sense. I used to warn him all the time that his behavior was going to land him in a world of trouble. He never knew it, but every time he snuck into one of them moonshiners' houses to get alcohol, somebody that was there would tell me. I always let it slide because his good habits outweighed his bad ones. But every time he left the house, I balled up inside because I was scared he might not come back home alive."

"I hope you don't think that about Leona."

"I wish I could say I didn't." Mama blinked several times before she continued. "Y'all was born during a storm that was so bad, it scared the midwife to death. Folks told me that was a bad omen. Since then, I been worried about something bad happening to you or Leona."

"What could be worse than Leona getting pregnant and going to jail in the same year? I'm sure that's what the bad omen meant."

Mama shook her head. "If it means something else, I hope it don't happen while I'm still alive. I wouldn't be able to live if something worse was to happen to you or her."

Chapter 19

Leona

I WAS FEELING EVEN MORE MISERABLE BY TUESDAY EVENING. EVEN though my dead cellmate had never said nothing to me, just seeing her laying on the mattress had made being in the cell a little easier to stand. I missed her and felt lonelier than ever.

The lady who sat at the desk out front brought my evening meal on a dented metal tray. My daily menu was grits, a biscuit, one slice of bacon, and a cup of water for breakfast; a baloney sandwich for lunch and another cup of water; and for supper I got two baloney sandwiches and a Dr Pepper. When Mama came this evening to bring me some fresh clothes, she asked what they was feeding me. She was horrified when I told her. "Is that what they going to give you every day for your whole sentence?" she asked with her jaw twitching.

"So they tell me," I answered with a shrug.

"I'll ask the sheriff on my way out if I can bring you something better from home each day."

About a hour after Mama left, Fiona and Bonnie Sue came. I had never been so glad to see them before in my life.

Fiona glanced at the mattress. "Did they turn your cellmate loose?"

"She died," I answered.

Fiona's and Bonnie Sue's mouths dropped open.

"Did they kill her?" Bonnie Sue asked with her lips quivering.

"I don't know how she died. The Fuller Brothers came and took her body to their funeral home."

"My Lord!" Fiona yelled. "I bet they poisoned her!"

"I don't think they did that. They ain't that mean," I defended.

"Humph! If these crackers can go around lynching innocent colored men, they'd do just about anything to get rid of as many of us as possible. Make sure you smell the food they give you before you eat it." Bonnie Sue reached into the bag she carried her schoolbooks in and pulled out something wrapped in a paper napkin and handed it to me. "You better eat this pig foot now so I can take the bones with me."

"All right, then. Thank you, Bonnie Sue." I unwrapped the paper and started munching on the pig foot right away.

"I'll bring you some chicken wings the next time I come," Fiona told me.

I chewed and swallowed a huge chunk of the pig foot before I went on. "Don't forget to bring some hot sauce too. Anybody ask about me at school today?"

Fiona looked at Bonnie Sue before she replied, "Nobody asked me nothing."

"Me neither. You miss so much school anyway, I guess everybody is used to only seeing you in class now and then," Bonnie Sue tossed in. And then she got real quiet as she stared at the floor and twiddled her thumbs. I couldn't ignore the distressed look on her face.

"Bonnie Sue, for a girl who's getting married this month, you sure are looking glum." I gazed at her so hard, she squirmed. "There is something you ain't telling me," I accused.

"Tell her," Fiona said as she poked Bonnie Sue in her side with her elbow. "If you don't I will."

Bonnie Sue cleared her throat before she responded in a harsh tone. "I ain't got no fiancé no more. I didn't want to tell you until you got out. You got enough misery on your hands right now."

"Say what?" I yelled. Bonnie Sue's upcoming wedding had kept everybody buzzing since she got engaged four months ago. She had been bragging so much since then, people was sick of hearing about it. She was so bold she'd even told folks what gifts to buy her. But I was almost as happy about her getting married as she was.

Fiona finished telling me the reason the wedding had been called off. "That ass-clown let his folks talk him out of it! They told him he wasn't mature enough, but everybody knows the real reason is that they don't like Bonnie Sue," she snarled. "If somebody busted up my wedding plans, I'd want to kill them dead."

"That crossed my mind," Bonnie Sue hissed. "When he came to the house last night and told me we was through, I wanted to cut his throat! He couldn't even answer me when I asked him how come he waited so long to tell me." Bonnie Sue looked at me with a woebegone expression on her face. "To think that you tried to steal a blouse to wear to the ceremony and ended up in this hellhole."

"And it's a damn shame!" Fiona screamed.

"Shhh! Don't be talking that loud," I said in the lowest tone I could manage. "Do you want Sheriff Bodine to come in here and accuse you of disturbing the peace?"

"I'm sorry," Fiona whispered.

"Bonnie Sue, I'm sorry to hear things didn't work out. I guess it's all for the best. You'll get a better man the next time," I said.

"I know I will." Bonnie Sue cracked a smile.

"I guess by now everybody in town knows I'm in jail," I threw in.

"Sure enough. There was even two lines in the newspaper yesterday: 'Colored girl caught stealing at the Ashberry Street Dress Store. She was arrested for attacking the store manager,'" Fiona told me. Our flimsy newspaper catered to white folks. They reported everything that went on in the white part of town. Last Friday, a hog butchering made the front page. The last time we got that much attention was a year ago when the Klan lynched two colored men at the same time. They claimed that they fit the description of two men who had beat up a white farmer who said he'd seen them raiding his sugarcane field. There was a picture in the middle of the page of them noosed up and dangling from trees like deer carcasses on the bank of Carson Lake. That was where they'd been fishing at the time they was attacked. Several members of the Klan was in the picture, grinning like they was at a shindig.

Unspeakable crimes happened so often to us, we was used to them. What made it all the more painful was the fact that we couldn't do nothing to stop that kind of activity. The law was one of our worst enemies. The last time a colored lawyer went to court and tried to defend one of us, he sassed Judge Smoot and got arrested for "disorderly conduct." He ended up at the prison work camp for three months where the guards beat him so bad, he lost one of his eyes.

"At least the newspaper didn't print your name, but everybody knows it was you," Bonnie Sue said with a pitying look on her face. "I feel responsible for what you done."

"You ain't responsible, I am," I assured her. I took the last bite of the pig foot, wrapped the bones in the napkin, and handed them to her.

Fiona dropped her head and poked out her bottom lip. She looked relieved when Sheriff Bodine marched up to the cell, clapped his hands, and boomed, "Visiting over!"

She and Bonnie Sue skittered out like mice. I didn't sleep at all that night.

Chapter 20
Leona

MAMA CAME WEDNESDAY MORNING ON HER WAY TO WORK TO bring me a clean dress, a fresh pair of bloomers, and a bowl of the neckbone casserole left over from the supper she'd cooked Tuesday evening. Sheriff Bodine took a spoon and scooped out as much of the casserole he wanted and dumped it into a cracked saucer before he let her give the rest to me.

Mama stumbled into the cell looking like she hadn't slept in days. "The sheriff said I can only stay long enough to drop off things," she said with her voice trembling. I could tell from the way her jaw was twitching that she was mad. My heart skipped a beat when I thought about how she had hit that white woman who had kicked me when I was a little girl. What if she got mad enough to attack Sheriff Bodine or one of his deputies? I knew that her goose would be cooked, and there was no telling what would happen to me.

Mama looked behind her to make sure Sheriff Bodine had gone back to his office before she pulled out something wrapped in a brown paper bag. I felt relieved when she smiled. "That greedy hog had the nerve to tell me to bring some hush puppies the next time I come. If I wasn't a godly woman, before I wrapped him up some of my hush puppies, I'd swish them around in my slop jar before I took it to the outhouse to empty." Mama laughed. I did too and it felt good.

The days seemed twice as long as they really was. Halfway into my sentence, the front-desk lady brought me my usual breakfast one morning. I was surprised to see a piece of peanut brittle sitting next to my grits. She set the tray on the bed and then handed me two movie magazines. "I thought you might like something to read to help pass the time. And everybody likes peanut brittle." She smiled for a split second.

One thing I had learned was that there was different levels of racism. There was the Klan and other hateful people who was mean and evil to the bone. They would torture and kill a newborn colored baby if they could get their hands on one. Then there was all the nice white folks that my mama and so many of her friends and neighbors worked for. A few of them treated us better than some colored folks did. The lady Mama worked for now was so nice sometimes she drove Mama home in her car. She was generous too. She gave Mama some real nice clothes that her kids no longer wanted, and fancy food left over from parties, such as steak and lobster (caviar didn't go over too well with us but Mama brought it home anyway). When we was real young, during the summer when we was out of school, Mama's boss lady would let her bring us to work with her so Mama wouldn't have to pay a babysitter.

I had even changed my opinion about Sheriff Bodine. Yesterday when he was making his rounds, he peeped into my cell and actually smiled. "You been behaving real nice and I do appreciate that. I ain't had to beat you or hold back one of your meals like I usually do with other colored prisoners. Continue to behave while you're in here. When I turn you aloose, stop stealing and brutalizing white women, and you won't see me again, or whoever takes over after I leave office. You hear?"

"Yes, sir."

"I hear you like to read."

"Uh-huh."

He stared at me for a few seconds, but he didn't say nothing else.

When I woke up the next morning, there was a stack of old detective magazines sitting at the foot of the mattress.

Five days before Thanksgiving, the front-desk lady unlocked

my cell door and flung it open. It was lunchtime but she wasn't carrying the tray with my food on it. My heart started racing because I had no idea what she was up to. "Get up. You can go home." Her gruff tone surprised me. She had been so nice to me lately. Since the first time she'd brought me peanut brittle, she'd brought me other treats, including a slice of cake left over from her nephew's birthday party.

I sat up ramrod straight on the mattress. "But my sentence ain't even up, ma'am. I got more than a week to go."

"You being let out early due to good behavior. Sheriff Bodine said to turn you aloose at straight-up twelve noon today. Now you best skedaddle before I lock this door back and tell Sheriff Bodine you disobeyed me. He left early this morning to go spend the holiday with his sister and her family in Montgomery. If you're still here when he returns, he ain't going to be too happy."

I still didn't know this woman's name. "Um . . . Ma'am, thank you for that peanut brittle and cake and for letting me read your magazines."

"Please try to stay out of trouble. We don't like having to chastise you people. But some of y'all are so hardheaded! The law says that we have to keep y'all in line as much as we can."

I couldn't believe what I said next. But I was willing to say anything that would make my situation less painful. "I agree with you, ma'am. We got some hard heads."

I grabbed my dirty clothes and sprinted out of that cell so fast, you would have thought a mean dog was chasing me. I ran all the way home.

When I walked through our front door panting like a bull, Mama and Fiona looked at me like I was a ghost. They busted out crying at the same time. "Did you break out of jail?" Fiona sniffled. She and Mama raced up to me and hugged my neck. Fiona kissed my face all over like she was a puppy.

"Lord help us! Girl, what's going on?" Mama asked as she moved a step back and glanced toward the window.

"The lady who works at the jailhouse said Sheriff Bodine told her to let me out today because of my good behavior," I explained.

"You sure she was telling the truth? That heifer might have decided to set you up and claim you broke aloose so they can punish you even worse."

"Mama, I didn't have no choice. She told me that if I was still there when Sheriff Bodine got back from visiting his family, he'd be mad. You taught us not to argue with white folks so I didn't."

"Mighty Moses." Mama wrapped her arm around my waist and led me to my room and gently pushed me down on the bed. Fiona was right behind her. "Leona, you sit here while Fiona heats some water to put in the washtub. You smell mighty ripe."

After I washed up and put on some fresh clothes, I joined Mama and Fiona at the kitchen table where they had been shelling crowder peas. I was glad they had finished because I wasn't in the mood to shell no peas. And I didn't want to talk about jail, or me trying to steal that blouse, so I started off with a safer subject. "It's a shame about Bonnie Sue's fiancé breaking up with her."

"Maybe that bust-up was God's way of letting Bonnie Sue know that that fool wasn't the right man for her," Mama suggested.

"It would have been nice if he had broke off things with her before she made all them wedding plans," I said.

"True. And you wouldn't have had no reason to go and try to steal that blouse," Mama pointed out.

"Mama, please don't start on that. I don't want to talk about that no more today," I whined.

I was glad Fiona changed the subject before Mama could say anything else. "When are you coming back to school?"

I shook my head. "I ain't going back."

Mama raised her eyebrows, tightened her jaw, and glared at me like she did when she caught me sneaking back into the house after I'd been out drinking. "Oh? And what do you plan on doing? One of them fools you know ask to marry you so they can take care of you?"

"No. I ain't ready to get married," I replied.

Mama put her hands on her hips and gave me a hot look. "Then you going to get a job. You done shamed this family enough and I ain't going to stand for no more. Folks at church and all over the neighborhood look at me and Fiona with pity because of what you done. I don't want nobody to think I can't handle my family business by letting you run even wilder than you been doing all your life."

"I'll start looking for a job today," I said.

"You ain't going no place today except to the clinic. I'm marching you over there so they can take care of that nasty-woman's disease you got."

"You don't have to do that. I ain't got no disease," I chuckled. There was no way I could let Mama take me to the clinic. If one of the doctors examined me, they would know I'd never been pregnant and that I was still a virgin. I didn't want to think about what Mama would say if they told her that. How would I explain the miscarried baby she'd disposed of? Fiona looked like she was about to float out the window.

"She just said that so she wouldn't get raped or nothing in jail," Fiona tossed in.

Mama's look and voice got softer. "Is that true, Leona?"

"Yes, ma'am. I ain't never had no disease."

Mama smiled. "All right, then. Welcome home, baby."

Chapter 21

Fiona

LEONA DECIDED TO GO TO BED ABOUT A HOUR AFTER MAMA. AS soon as we got into our room and closed the door, I hugged her. "What was that for?" she asked.

"For you looking out for me as much as you do. I appreciate how you got out of letting Mama take you to the clinic."

"Yeah, that was a close call." Leona sucked in a real long, loud breath as she looked around the room. "I never realized how nice this place was until I seen the inside of a cell."

"Um . . . I'm glad it wasn't too bad," I said as I slid off my shoes.

"I didn't say it wasn't bad. It was hellish and I hope I never see the inside of another one for as long as I live." Her voice cracked, but she kept talking. "I don't think I could have survived if they had sent me to the work camp."

"Well, it's all over now, so let's try and forget about it," I said in a shaky voice. I wanted to talk about a few other things, but as soon as Leona's head hit her pillow, she was out like a light.

Mama had to work on Thanksgiving Day, so we all got up early before her boss picked her up so we could cook the feast we'd enjoy later in the day.

Mama was so tired when she got home a few minutes after 6 p.m., she looked like she'd been pulling a plow. "Them white folks was eating like pigs at a hog trough. I thought they would never stop sending me in and out of that kitchen to get this or that." Mama laughed. "Y'all didn't have to wait for me to eat," she gently said as she gazed at all the food still covered and sitting on top of the stove. "Let's give thanks to the Lord for all His blessings and then we'll enjoy this good food."

It was the saddest holiday we ever had. And it was all because of what I had done. I promised myself and the Lord that I would try hard to stay out of trouble and focus more on school and what was happening in the world.

There was so much going on with the rest of the world, it was hard to keep up with which country was doing what. I had never even heard of some of them places. But Mama still made us listen to the news on the radio and read the newspaper.

Life was different in little southern towns like ours. Some things moved slow, other things moved fast. Like Leona. When she got a notion in her to do something, she didn't waste no time. Because she couldn't live by Mama's rules, the Monday after Thanksgiving, she got up early, skipped breakfast, and went out to look for a job.

Me and Mama was in the kitchen getting supper ready when Leona flew into the house that evening at half past 6 p.m. I could tell from her super-wide-open eyes and the smile on her face that she had a big announcement to make. "I got a job, y'all!" I hadn't seen my sister look so happy since last Christmas morning when one of her presents from Mama was some spray bottles of French smell-goods.

I looked at her with my mouth hanging open. "You got a job already? Where at?"

"Nadine told me that if I didn't find nothing today, to come by her work before I came back home. I went over there a little while ago and her boss hired me on the spot!" Leona had to stop talking to catch her breath. "It's a full-time job and the work is year-round."

"You got a job at that *disgusting* chicken factory? Yuck!" Of all the unpleasant jobs there was for poor folks like us, plucking dead chickens was one of the worst. All of the slaughterhouses

was located on the edge of town away from where folks lived because the stench coming from each one of them places was unholy. Even if you rode through that vicinity in a car with the
windows rolled up, you could still smell the dead hogs, cows,
and chickens. Nadine claimed that after her first few weeks at
the chicken factory, the unpleasant things no longer bothered
her. Maybe not. But I knew several other people who had been
working at that ghoulish place for more than twenty years and
they still hadn't got used to the smell, or the blood and guts. "I
never thought I'd see the day this girl would be so desperate for
work," I commented. "I'd rather shovel shit. Oops!" I didn't
waste no time backtracking. Mama didn't allow nobody to cuss
in her house. "Sorry. That word slipped out." She let it slide this
time, which was something she didn't do too often. I was still
waiting to hear what else Leona had to say.

Before she could respond, Mama did something she didn't
do too often: She defended Leona. But it was still a put-down in
a way. "It's honest work, and at least 'this girl' will be making
enough money to buy what she wants instead of trying to steal
it." The more she talked, the harsher her tone got. "And maybe
now she won't have so much extra time on her hands to be
messing around with so many boys and get pregnant again, or
risk catching the nasty-woman's disease."

Leona dropped her head and muttered, "You ain't got to
worry about me no more, Mama."

Leona had to be at work at the crack of dawn, so she was gone
by the time I got up to get ready for school the next morning.
She was in a good mood the rest of the week, and so was Mama.
I believed that things could only get better for our family.

The following Sunday evening after church, we was all sitting
at the kitchen table, getting ready to eat supper. Mama had just
finished frying two chickens that Leona had brought from the
factory on Friday. One of the rules at the factory was that the
employees, white and colored, could take home one free
chicken a week. They had to pay a dime for each additional
chicken. But Leona told us Nadine told her that most of the

folks who had been working there for years took home as many extra chickens as they could sneak out. I couldn't believe that the folks who owned the factory wasn't smart enough to figure that out, especially when almost nobody ever paid for a second chicken in a week.

As measly as Leona's paycheck was, I was surprised she hadn't stole one of the two chickens she'd brought home this week. I didn't have no problem with somebody stealing what they couldn't afford. With times being so hopeless, doing something desperate like stealing seemed normal to me. So long as nobody got hurt. Every time I thought about that blouse I'd tried to steal, I got mad because I hadn't been able to make off with it. But I was so sorry that woman I'd tussled with got hurt. I even prayed for her.

Chapter 22
Fiona

*B*Y THE MIDDLE OF DECEMBER, BONNIE SUE HAD LATCHED ONTO a new boyfriend. She said the same thing about him that she'd said about the last two: "He's everything I want in a man." Clayton Frost wasn't really new; she'd dated him off and on last year. She'd dumped him after only a month because she thought she could do better. I prayed that things would work out for him and her this time because I wanted my dearest friend to be happy.

Clayton was almost old enough to be Bonnie Sue's daddy, and he had a good job working as a porter for the railroad company. He was also from a very devout Christian family. Unfortunately, he wasn't much to look at. He was lanky like Bonnie Sue and he had a horsey face, thick dingy teeth, and bald spots all over his head. Bonnie Sue wasn't no bathing beauty, so nobody expected her to land a man who looked like a film star nohow.

"I hope Clayton don't disappoint Bonnie Sue like that other fool did," Leona said. It was the week before Christmas. Mama had dragged me and Leona to a holiday program at the church right after we'd ate supper this evening. We'd just got in bed.

"I hope he don't neither." And then out of nowhere, she asked, "How many boys are you sneaking around with these days?" Leona rarely mentioned my behavior to me. And since she didn't, I figured it didn't bother her that I had Mama and so many other folks fooled because I acted so virtuous in front of them. I wasn't a bad person, I just wanted to have fun. But I didn't want a reputation that went along with being a fast girl like Leona had.

"Well, I done had a lot of fun these past few years. But I'm ready to settle down while I'm still young and cute enough to get a good husband," I replied.

"Pffftt." Leona rolled her eyes at me. "Sixteen ain't old. You need to finish school before you start thinking about marriage. Mama is proud of you, don't let her down."

"She thinks I should get married soon too."

"What? You don't even have a boyfriend. As far as she knows, you ain't never even had a serious boyfriend."

"True, and you better not never blow the whistle on me," I warned.

"As long as we been alive, when have I ever done that?"

"I just want to make sure you don't start. Anyway, you know Jubal Crockett, the mechanic who runs the garage? I been seeing him."

I was so impressed, my heart started beating real fast. "Well! He's a good egg. I'm surprised he's still single."

" 'Good egg' my foot. The man is a *golden* egg if ever there was one."

Jubal had spent a few years in the army. He'd saved his money and when he got out last year, he put a down payment on his house and took over the only colored-owned garage in Lexington. He was from a wonderful family and he attended church on a regular basis. His mama and our mama had been best friends for over ten years. They was part of a group of women who did a lot of charity work for the church. They all had sewing machines and knitting tools, so they made things like quilts, blankets, pillowcases, and whatnot that went to needy families. The charity women also did the cooking for the church events that involved food. If all of that wasn't enough, they also volunteered to do everything else for folks who needed any kind of assistance. I told Mama that when I finished school, I'd start helping with the charity work. It made me feel good to know that I could make somebody's life more enjoyable. But right now, my main goal was to land a husband.

"Mama told me Jubal would make a good husband," I added.

Leona snickered. "Ain't he pushing thirty?"

"He's twenty-six. He just got back yesterday from visiting his elderly auntie in Atlanta for a week. He took me and Mama to the movies while you was locked up."

"That was nice of him. But Mama can barely read. When did she get interested in watching silent movies?"

"I know she don't like movies where she can't hear the folks talking, and I don't care for reading off the screen neither. I dozed off a couple of times and missed some important parts of the movie. But it was Jubal's idea to go so we went. He's taking me out to supper at a restaurant next week. I almost got him in the bag."

"Girl, if I was you, I'd tie that bag up real tight so he won't get out." We laughed. "So Mama really wants you to marry him?"

"Sure enough. She's the one who said I'd make him a good wife. And she said it right in front of him." I sighed. "Mama also said she didn't care that he wasn't the best-looking man in town. She didn't say that in front of him, though."

"He's better looking than some of them other fools you used to sneak around with," Leona pointed out. Jubal Crocket was right handsome to me. He had a nice lean body, piercing black eyes with the kind of long lashes you normally see on a female, and a smile that wouldn't quit.

"He told me that if things continued to go well between us, he'd like to marry me when I finish school."

I told Bonnie Sue what Jubal said the next day when we was walking home from school. She exploded like a bomb. "He wants to wait until you finish school? Baw! Girl, that's more than a year away. Don't you let that juicy turkey dangle that long. You know what my used-to-be fiancé did to me!"

"Maybe he wasn't the man for you after all."

Bonnie Sue shot me a sharp look. "Well, maybe Jubal ain't the man for you after all neither. My used-to-be and Jubal is friends.

They go fishing all the time. You know what they say; monkey see, monkey do. He could talk Jubal into not marrying you."

Bonnie Sue's words hit me like a sledgehammer. "He's the one who wants to wait until I finish school. And I did want enough time to plan a nice big wedding and reception."

"Pffftt!" Bonnie Sue gave me a dismissive wave. "Piss on that! You seen how taking my time to plan a big wedding backfired. It gave my used-to-be's family enough time to make him change his mind. Don't give Jubal time to back out."

"But he really wants me to finish school first."

"You can be married and still go to school until you graduate, but I doubt if you'd want to stay in school. You'll be too busy fixing up that lovely house and cooking up meals fit for a king for him every day. Do you know how many other women would be eyeballing him while you was wasting time planning a big wedding? Remember that woman at church who wears that reddish wig-hat? Her fiancé's used-to-be did so much plotting, she lured him back into her arms two days before his wedding!"

I gave Bonnie Sue a thoughtful look. She was more worldly than I was, so I was convinced she knew what she was talking about. "Do you know a way I could get Jubal to marry me sooner?"

"Yup! Use the oldest trick in the book. It's right up there with a hoodoo love hex. Tell him what I should have told that fool who dumped me: You think you fixing to have his baby."

"Huh? I don't think I'm pregnant."

Bonnie Sue shook her head and gave me a hopeless look. "How many times have you done the big nasty with him?"

I looked at Bonnie Sue like she was crazy. "You know how much I like sex. He ain't no spark plug in bed, but we done it a heap of times."

"Well, it don't take but one time for a girl to get pregnant."

"What do I tell him when he finds out I ain't?"

"That's why you tell him you *think* you're pregnant. He couldn't argue with that if you ain't because you didn't say you was definitely pregnant."

I forgot all about having the big fancy wedding I'd wanted to have ever since I was a little girl. The day after my conversation with Bonnie Sue, I dropped out of school. That evening I went up to Jubal in tears and told him I thought I was pregnant. He didn't protest when I told him I had dropped out of school because I didn't want to bring shame on my family or his so he had to marry me right away. And he did.

Reverend Logan Sweeney married us in Mama's living room on Christmas Day with only a dozen family and close friends present. I'd picked that date because it was the most important day in the year to me and everybody I knew. Jubal would never have no excuse if he forgot our anniversary. And I'd picked that date because I didn't want to waste another day and give him a chance to slip through my fingers.

Jubal lived in a well-kept, two-bedroom house with a huge backyard and lovely furniture in each room. There was a large, cast-iron potbellied stove in the middle of his living room floor. It was much bigger than the one in Mama's house, so it heated up every room at the same time. He kept a huge stack of firewood right next to it. The Ford he drove was almost paid for. His garage was just a few blocks from our house, but he usually drove to work each day. He had already taught me how to drive, so he said he'd leave the car at home for me to use when I had errands to run or shopping to do. Mama and everybody else I was close to lived within walking distance. "I want to do everything I can to make sure you stay happy," Jubal told me on our wedding night. We had just got into the bed where I planned to sleep until I decided I wanted a fancier one.

I glanced around the large bedroom. I loved the lacy white curtains at the window that his widowed mama Reba had made. "You off to a good start," I told Jubal.

He was such a dud in bed, I got more pleasure out of washing dishes. But I figured he'd get better over time, or that I'd lose interest in sex and concentrate on the other things that went along with being a married woman, such as the children I hoped to have and my church activities.

I was concerned about more important things than sex. I missed school, but I didn't regret dropping out. Jubal tried to talk me into going back, because he'd had to drop out in ninth grade to work before he joined the military. Mama tried to talk me into going back too because she and Daddy hadn't even finished elementary school. I thought about it for a minute, but I decided not to return.

Leona moved out in January, three days into the new year. The run-down rooming house where she was going to rent a room was only one block over from where me and Jubal lived. She carted some of her belongings to her new home in one of his wheelbarrows. I walked along with her, holding a box that contained some of her clothes and other items. I couldn't remember the last time we had been so happy at the same time.

"Ooh wee. I believe 1918 is going to be a good year for everybody," Leona blurted out. She was so giddy it was hard to believe she'd been through so much since last year.

"I'm sure it will be," I agreed. "A heap of folks' lives will be changed forever." My words would come back to haunt me in a few months.

Chapter 23
Leona

THAT STUPID WAR IN EUROPE WAS STILL RAGING AND SEVERAL boys I grew up with had died in it. In the meantime, things was looking up for me. I was so excited about having my own place I couldn't stop grinning. It wasn't the kind of place I wanted, but it was all I could afford. Mama called it a dump. "I wouldn't let a pig I didn't like live in such a place!" she blasted when she seen it. I just laughed and brushed her off, because it was her rules and whuppings that had forced me to move out of her house.

The rooming house I had moved into was old and rickety and the last strong tornado we'd had blew away one side of the front porch banister. The old couple who owned the house was in their seventies and didn't believe in repairing nothing. Cardboard had been covering two of the front windows as far back as I could remember. My second-floor room was half the size of the smallest room in Fiona's new house. There was a rollaway bed with nothing on it, but I'd brought my own linen. After sleeping on a naked mattress in jail, I wasn't about to do the same thing in a place where I had to pay a dollar a week to live. There was nothing else in the room except a kerosene lamp sitting on the floor. But the humped-over, gray-haired old woman who ran the place was very nice. "I can knock a dollar off your rent every month if you hand scrub the kitchen floor once a week," Sister Bernice (she never told me her last name) told me the day she agreed to let me have the room. Me and Fiona had just set my stuff on the bed.

"Okay," I replied.

"What about meals?" Fiona asked.

Sister Bernice folded her flabby arms and started talking in a low steady tone, like she was reading from a magazine. "I don't cook for nobody but me and my husband. You can use the stove, keep food in the icebox, and you better clean up whatever mess you make. I know how your mama likes to cook, so I'm sure you can still eat a few meals at her house when you don't feel like cooking, or if I'm using the stove. There is a stack of old newspapers and a pile of dried-out corncobs on the floor by the back door. You can use them to wipe yourself off with when you have to use the outhouse. You can borrow one of my buckets to haul water from the well. I got a extra pitcher and a couple of glasses I'll let you use. Invite company to visit you as often as you like, so long as they don't make too much noise or kill nobody. My husband is a nervous man and can't tolerate no ruckus." Sister Bernice had said such a mouthful, she had to stop and catch her breath. Before she started up again, she sucked her yellow teeth and blinked. "Do you hear me, Leona?"

"I hear you, ma'am."

"Good! So long as you pay your rent on time, you can stay here for the rest of your life if you want to."

As soon as Sister Bernice left the room, Fiona looked at me and shook her head. "I can't let you live in a dump like this! Me and Jubal got a spare room that's three times as big as this one." Fiona waved her hands in the air.

"I don't want to move in with you and Jubal. I want a place of my own." I cleared my throat and looked around the room. It was so gloomy I wouldn't have been surprised to find out it was haunted. There was a small window facing the bed, but the only thing I could see outside was the colored cemetery across the road. Sister Bernice and her husband's bedroom, living room, and kitchen was on the first floor.

There was a frail, homely middle-aged widower in the room next to mine and he was not friendly at all. I'd spoke to him twice, and each time he'd ignored me. I decided I wouldn't speak to him no more unless he spoke to me first. A frumpy old maid with a cat occupied the room across the hall. She'd gave me a slop jar so I wouldn't have to use the outhouse when I had to do my business. The other two rooms on the second floor was vacant and I was not surprised. This was one spooky place. But I was going to make the best of it until I could afford to move into a better location.

Me and my landlady got along so good, I enjoyed living in that dingy little room because she made me feel so welcome. When she had leftovers from her supper, she gave them to me. She told me I could come down and listen to the radio with her and her husband anytime I wanted to. When I paid my rent, I felt so grown-up!

I loved having a full-time job, but it was the stuff of night-mares. The inside of the large factory building I worked at was noisy with the machinery clicking and clanking and chickens clucking up a storm from the time I got in, until the time I went home. At the trough where I worked, there was hundreds of dead chickens dangling from the low ceiling that we had to grab with both hands and drop onto a slow-moving conveyor belt. The assembly line had about thirty workers, white folks at the front, colored folks at the back. A scowling, barrel-shaped white foreman made sure we didn't lollygag by repeatedly yelling threats like, "If y'all want to keep working here, don't let them chickens slow down and pile up!" After the plucking, the col-ored workers had to cut open the chickens with butcher knives and snatch out the guts with bare hands. And then the chickens got stacked up in metal tubs and carried to the front of the line where the white workers washed them with hoses and prepared them for the stores and restaurants.

Each day when I got home from work, I was so tired I felt like I had been working on a chain gang. But I was still glad to have a full-time job.

After I had settled into my new home, the weeks seemed to go by faster. Fiona had told me back in January that a lot of folks' lives would change in 1918. She'd made a accurate prediction.

This would be one of the worst years in the history of the world. A deadly virus broke out in February and all hell broke loose. Folks was dying by the millions. Not just in America, but all over the planet. Every time we picked up the news-paper or listened to a news report on the radio, it would be the main story of the day. It seemed like the kind of catastrophe you'd read about in the Bible. Some folks thought that because human beings had been acting like fools for so long, God decided it was time to show His wrath again.

None of the hospitals that I knew of in the South treated colored folks. The virus roared through our neighborhoods like a tornado and we had to fend for ourselves. Most of the little country towns like Lexington had a clinic run by colored folks. The ones who lived in a town that didn't have a clinic had to find a way to get to a town that did.

Our little one-horse clinic couldn't handle all the people coming in with symptoms. Folks was actually dying in the lobby while they was waiting to see a doctor. Trucks was hauling dead bodies away stacked on top of each other like bales of hay. The two color-owned funeral homes in Lexington was organizing funerals back-to-back, seven days a week. Jubal's younger sister, Hattie, was one of the first people we knew who died from the virus. She was engaged to be married at the time. Before they could bury her, her fiancé and three other folks we knew caught the virus and died. Jubal's only other sibling, a older brother who lived in Atlanta, died a month after his sister.

Mama was beside herself, especially because Fiona was expecting her first baby in September this year. As it turned out, she really was pregnant when she told Jubal she thought she was last year in December. . . . But this mysterious new health issue had everybody worried. Every time me or Fiona had symptoms of the virus, like a sniffle or a cough that lasted more than a few seconds, Mama got nervous and made us take pills and drink ginger tea. Then she'd make us read the Bible. "I don't know what I'd do if I lost one of y'all. Lexington would never be the same to me."

"Maybe we should leave Alabama and head north," I suggested. Me, Mama, and Fiona was sitting in Mama's living room. It was Easter Sunday and we'd just come home from church.

Mama glared at me. "Stop talking about moving. This is our home. But now that you done got grown, you can save up your money and go wherever you want to go."

One reason it wouldn't have been easy for me to move to another state was because I worried about leaving Fiona to cope on her own. Even though she had a husband now and she was close to Mama, I still felt responsible for protecting her. I'd promised her when we was little kids that I would, and that was a promise I intended to keep. Especially since she still had some of the same desires she'd had when we was younger.

When Mama left the living room to go into the kitchen to get some cider, Fiona said, "Girl, if you don't sneak me some moonshine soon, I'm going to go crazy. I ain't had a nip since I got married. Shoot!"

I glanced toward the kitchen to make sure Mama wasn't lurking nearby, and then I looked at Fiona with my eyes narrowed. "Now you look here, gal. Don't you even think about drinking until after you give birth. Moonshine could harm your baby! And what if Jubal was to find out?" My brother-in-law was one of the most moralistic men I knew. He didn't cuss, fool around with other women (as far as I knew), didn't disrespect nobody, and he didn't drink. His daddy, one of his aunts, and two of his cousins had drunk themselves to death. When Jubal was still in his teens, he had promised his mama and God that he would never drink, or even allow alcohol in his house when he got grown.

"Pffftt!" She waved her hand and rolled her eyes. "Aw shuck it! I just want a few sips. I know a lot of girls that drank while they was pregnant, and their babies turned out fine. And don't worry about Jubal. He ain't the nosy type. And even if he was, that man is so dense, I could tell him white is black and he'd believe me. Please, Leona. I done almost forgot what it feels like to have a buzz." Fiona had a desperate look on her face and that usually made me give in.

I rubbed the back of my neck and blew out a loud sigh. "All right, then. I got half a jar left at my place that I brought home from the party I went to last weekend. I'll bring you something tomorrow morning before I go to work. If Jubal finds out you been drinking, you better not tell him I gave it to you."

Fiona went from whining like a puppy to chirping like a bird within a split second. "I won't. Praise the Lord."

As unpleasant as my job was, I never complained like some of my coworkers did. I even went in when I didn't feel well because when I didn't work, I didn't get paid. I was glad Bonnie Sue came over almost every evening to help me pluck chicken feathers out of my hair and wipe blood off my clothes. "With a job like yours, I'm surprised you still eat chicken," she said one evening in August, two months after me and Fiona had turned seventeen.

"I ain't never going to stop eating chicken," I vowed. In addition to chicken cooked every way possible, I lived on baloney sandwiches, fruit, and whatever I could pilfer from Mama's icebox on the days I had supper with her. I ate with Fiona and Jubal at least once a week. Bonnie Sue brought me snacks from her house every time she came. I didn't have to use Sister Bernice's kitchen too often.

This evening when Bonnie Sue came over, she brought me some fried chicken wings wrapped in butcher block paper. I grinned and licked my lips. "I can't wait to start smacking on them wings."

Bonnie Sue gave me a confused look and gazed at the chicken wings I'd set on top of the small wooden crate I used for a coffee table. Me and her was sitting on the edge of the bed. "If you that anxious, why ain't you chomping on them wings already then?"

"Oh, didn't I tell you? I'm having company later this evening. I want to make sure I got something here to eat in case he gets hungry."

"He? Is this *he* anybody I know?" For some reason, Bonnie Sue's jaw started twitching. I'd noticed this reaction another time when I mentioned a man. I didn't think much of it then, and I didn't think much of it now.

"It's Darnell Winthrop. He's that well-built, dark-skinned man with the cute slanty brown eyes. Don't you remember I danced with him several times at Nadine Fisher's birthday party last month? You even said he danced like a chicken." I laughed, Bonnie Sue didn't laugh, and her jaw was twitching even harder. "He's been over here a few times. And I went to his house a few times on my way home from work." I had to pause because my heart started beating real fast. That's what happened every time I thought about Darnell. He'd showed up at my place last night. When things got hot, I didn't even try to stop him when he pulled my bloomers down while we was cuddling on my bed.

My first experience with sex wasn't what I had expected. It wasn't as unpleasant as Fiona, Bonnie Sue, and several other females had told me it had been for them. Aside from the few drops of messy blood on my sheets, I'd enjoyed it. Fiona was the only other person I had told that I had finally done the deed. Her biggest concern was that I'd get pregnant and cause Mama more distress. "Well, if I do get pregnant, I'll tell Darnell we have to get married. That should take care of Mama," I assured her.

I tried to focus on Darnell as much as I could, but every now and then I thought about Ernest Lee because my relationship with him had ended on such a bad note. Nadine told me that the Davis girl he had planned to marry told him the baby he thought was his was by another man. Before he left to join the army, she moved to Montgomery to live with her baby's father and his grandmother. Ernest Lee came home from the war last month with both of his legs missing. Even though he had got another girl pregnant—or thought he had—and was going to marry her, and then he had the nerve to take off without even telling me good-bye, I still felt so sorry for him. Fiona didn't feel the same way. "I'm sorry he lost his legs. But after the way he left our house after eating up so much of our food the last time he came to see you, and never looked back, I ain't sorry that Davis girl had another man the whole time."

I wasn't upset with Fiona because of the way she felt, but I didn't have no hard feelings toward Ernest Lee. He didn't feel that way about me, though. The first time I seen one of his brother's hauling him down our street in a wheelbarrow, I could barely hold back my tears. I tried to talk to him and console him, but he'd scrunched up his face and waved me away. Three days later, his mama told me that one of their cousins, who happened to be a nurse, had come from Pennsylvania with her husband in their truck. They moved Ernest Lee back to Philadelphia to live with them so that the nurse could give him in-home care. I wrote him a letter in Pennsylvania and told him that I still cared about him and wished him all the best. I never heard from him.

Chapter 24
Fiona

*T*HE NEXT FEW WEEKS WENT BY FAST. THE VIRUS HAD EASED UP and folks wasn't as scared and careful no more. But in late September it flared up again. This time with a vengeance. Ten members of our church family caught it in the same week, three died. Me and Mama and Leona hadn't had no symptoms and I had gave birth to a healthy baby boy earlier this month.

Bonnie Sue's mama caught it the first week in October and died five days later. We all prayed for Bonnie Sue and assured her that it was God's will. Before that week was over, her daddy caught it and he died three days later. Bonnie Sue was devastated. She had only two siblings. She'd had two younger brothers who had died when they was babies. Her twenty-one-year-old brother was in the army, stationed somewhere in Europe. Bonnie Sue and her sister, who was a year older than her, had to move in with their uncle, a sickly old man who could barely get around. He was glad to take his nieces in. Bonnie Sue was so eager to please that old man, she did things most young girls never thought about doing, like going hunting and fishing with him. At the time, she wasn't interested in cooking, cleaning, and sewing, the way a real woman (like me) was supposed to be. She devoted the rest of her free time to watching her uncle repair things.

Before we knew it, Bonnie Sue was as handy with a wrench and hammer and other tools as her uncle was. I lost count of the number of times she'd unclogged Mama's kitchen sink with a wire coat hanger.

But the main thing Bonnie Sue liked was to tinker around with her uncle under the hood of his temperamental old jalopy. He had a knack for fixing cars, so he taught Bonnie a lot of the basics. There was a few times when he had problems with his old jalopy and was too sick to take care of it. Bonnie Sue surprised him, and everybody else, by correcting them problems. She wasn't as good as a trained mechanic, but she believed that what she had learned would benefit her a lot.

Unfortunately, most folks didn't trust a young girl to work on their cars, but some thought it was "cute" that Bonnie Sue had such a strong interest in manly activities. Other folks thought it was ungodly for a woman to do men's work. But the folks who couldn't afford to go to Jubal's garage, which was the only one available to colored folks, reluctantly brought their vehicles to Bonnie Sue. They didn't pay her much, but to her some money was better than none.

Things was going pretty good for Bonnie Sue for a while. She missed her parents, and every time their names came up, she would start crying. "I used to have such a big family," she sobbed. Me and Leona assured her that she would always have us. That made her feel better.

As if poor Bonnie Sue hadn't lost enough, her beloved uncle suddenly died. She was devastated again. The uncle and his wife didn't have no kids. She didn't like them and didn't want to take care of two teenagers who had been dumped into her lap. Three days after the uncle's funeral, the aunt packed up and hopped on a train and moved to Detroit and left Bonnie Sue and her sister to fend for themselves. Bonnie Sue's brother was still stationed in Europe. He'd promised her and her sister that he'd save his money so that when he got discharged, he'd find a place for them to live. But he had more than a year to go before he completed his commitment.

A week after the aunt took off, Bonnie Sue's sister attempted to rob a bank to get money for her and Bonnie Sue to live on. She got caught in the act so they didn't even have a trial. They immediately sent her to prison where she would be for the next forty years. Now that Bonnie Sue was completely alone and couldn't pay the rent or utility bills, the landlord told her she had to move within seven days. Everybody we knew vowed they would do all they could to help her. Me and Leona and some of our friends took food to her, and we took turns spending nights in the house with her to keep her company until the grown folks could figure out what to do.

Things went from bad to worse for Bonnie Sue. Two weeks after her sister got shipped off to prison, her brother lost his life in a military accident. The man who owned the house she lived in felt so bad for her, he told her she could stay on in the house for two months, rent-free. After that, she had to move out or find somebody to pay the rent. Mama and five other members of our church family immediately offered to let Bonnie Sue move in with them. She chose Mama's house because it seemed like the most logical choice. She'd already spent a heap of nights sleeping over with me and Leona in our old bedroom, which was now her bedroom. She had relatives in other states, but none of them wanted to take in a teenager.

Now that Bonnie Sue wouldn't be moving in with her brother, Mama told her she could stay with her as long as she needed to.

Unfortunately, it didn't take long for things to get sour between Bonnie Sue and Mama. Halfway into the first week, Bonnie Sue complained to me and Leona that even though she was grateful, she didn't think she'd be able to live by Mama's rules too much longer. Two older married couples from church whose kids was grown and on their own offered to her take in. But when they told her up front that they had just as many rules as Mama, she knew she couldn't live with them either. One of the couples told Bonnie Sue they had a backyard shed she could stay in. It was nothing but a glorified doghouse. When the couple told Bonnie Sue she could live in it rent-free and do as she pleased, she packed her stuff to go live in a "doghouse."

As soon as Leona heard where Bonnie Sue had moved to, she was horrified. "I can't let my best friend be treated like a dog. I'm going to go get Bonnie Sue and let her move in with me," she declared. Before Mama could talk some sense into her,

Leona went to that shed with a wheelbarrow and took Bonnie Sue and her stuff to that dreary rooming house.

Mama warned Leona that she was taking on a big responsibility, but Leona had never took advice from her. "If I needed a place to stay and Bonnie Sue was living in a rabbit hole, I know she would make room for me. Letting her move in with me is the least I can do for the best friend I ever had in my life," Leona replied. I was at Mama's house when that conversation took place, but I stayed out of it. The last thing I wanted one of them to suggest was that I let Bonnie Sue move in with me and Jubal. We had more than enough room, and I liked her, but I wasn't going to risk messing up my marriage if I didn't have to. Besides, Mama had warned me and Leona that no married woman should tempt her husband by moving a single woman into her house. Especially one who had a reputation for being a loose-booty like Bonnie Sue.

The rollaway bed in Leona's room was small. But she and Bonnie Sue was so petite, both of them could fit in it without falling off, especially if one slept at the top and the other one slept at the foot.

The day after Bonnie Sue moved in, Leona came to my house looking so tired, you would have thought she'd been pulling a buggy. "You look like hell," I told her.

She heaved out a long loud sigh. "I feel like it too. Sleeping in a rollaway bed with another girl ain't no picnic. Last night, Bonnie Sue's feet was in my face, and mine was in hers," she griped. "I didn't get much sleep."

"Make a pallet and let her sleep on the floor," I suggested.

"Pfffttt! Girl, I ain't about to let that poor girl sleep on that cold, hard floor. My bed is big enough for the both of us if we position ourselves better."

"How about if y'all sleep face-to-face or back-to-back. That's how me and you slept for years when we still lived with Mama. Except . . ."

"Except what?"

"Well, sleeping that way with another woman who ain't got

your blood would be like sleeping with a man." I cocked my head to the side and gave Leona a knowing smile. "Except you won't get the usual enjoyments. If you know what I mean."

Leona huffed out a disgusted sigh and glared at me. "You still just a nasty buzzard," she scolded. "How can you keep a straight face and compare my love life with a man to my relationship with Bonnie Sue?" Me and Leona busted out laughing at the same time.

Years later I would recall this conversation and realize it had sparked something that I never seen coming.

Chapter 25

Leona

I WAS GLAD 1918 HAD ALMOST ENDED.

The virus that had took so many lives was still going around, but it had been a while since anybody I knew caught it and died.

I wasn't looking forward to Christmas this year. It was going to be real sad for me. The family that Mama worked for was going to spend that whole week in Jamaica and they wanted her to go with them to look after the grandparents and grandchildren. Mama jumped at the chance to see a part of the world she would never have been able to afford to go to on her own.

Fiona and Jubal and their little boy, Lamar, was going to spend the holiday in Atlanta with some of his relatives. Clayton had to work so Bonnie Sue wouldn't be spending the holiday with him. Me and her stayed at Mama's house while she was away. I baked a coon that one of Mama's friends had brought to her after one of his hunting trips, Bonnie Sue made a few side dishes, and we invited Nadine and a few of our other friends over to celebrate with us. I ended up enjoying the day more than I thought I would.

The war that had been going on for more than four years had ended last month, praise the Lord. But most of the colored folks I knew didn't care one way or the other about no war because things was still bad for us in America.

I went to church with Mama on New Year's Eve for a celebration they had every year. Reverend Sweeney preached for a hour straight, the choir sung eight songs in a row, and then the entire congregation bowed down and prayed for fifteen minutes. After that, everybody went into the dining area to enjoy a feast that Mama and some of the other sisters had prepared that was fit for a king.

I had decided to go to church this year because I needed a break from Bonnie Sue. With her snuggled up behind me in that rollaway bed, she literally breathed down my neck every night. I didn't tell her I was going to church until I had got dressed and was almost ready to leave. I didn't want her to have time to get ready and go with me. "Just make sure you bring me a plate when you come home," she said as I was about to walk out the door.

I was beginning to feel uncomfortable in my own residence. There was even times when I felt like it was Bonnie Sue's room and I was the visitor. One reason was because her presence interfered with me and Darnell spending time alone. Even though Fiona had gave me a small stool that Bonnie Sue could have sat on, she would plop down onto the bed and conversate with me and Darnell anyway. We looked like three fools sitting side by side on that rollaway bed—with Bonnie Sue in the middle.

I regretted telling her to make herself at home right after she moved in because that was exactly what she did. She had dropped out of school back in November, and she hadn't been able to find a job, so I gave her a "allowance" each week when I got paid. It was never more than fifty cents, because the church was also helping support her.

Bonnie Sue eventually began to seem more like a mama or a maid to me. She'd do my laundry and sweep and mop the floor. When me and Darnell wanted to make love, we had to do it at his house after his folks went to bed. The only thing that kept me from pulling my hair out was that when Clayton was in town for a day or two from one of his train runs, he kept Bonnie Sue occupied.

"Do you think Clayton is ever going to ask you to marry him?" I asked Bonnie Sue the second week in January. The stress of living with her all this time had began to put a strain on our friendship and I didn't like that. She was still my best friend, and I didn't want that to change. But something had to change or I was going to lose my mind.

"If he don't, I'll propose to him. The only thing is, he don't want us to live with his mama. So we probably won't get married until he done saved up enough for us to get our own place right off the bat. I'm glad I can stay with you until then." Bonnie Sue sniffed. "But I don't care how long I have to wait for him to make his move. I'd be glad to stay on here with you for another few years if I have to." Them words sent a chill up my spine.

Things was going good between me and Darnell. I'd only been going with him for five months but I knew him well enough to know I wanted to have a future with him. I was praying for a marriage proposal sometime this year. One evening in February, he came to my place a couple of hours after I'd got home from work. Bonnie Sue had gone to the market to pick up a few things. I was glad she wasn't home, so I could spend a little time alone with Darnell. "I wasn't expecting you but come on in and make yourself at home." I sat down on the bed and expected him to sit down too. He didn't. He stood in front of me, folded his arms, and gave me a weak smile.

"I didn't come to stay," he said in a somber tone. There was a expression on his face that distressed me to say the least. It was the same kind of grim look I seen on the faces of pallbearers each time I attended a funeral. That should have told me something was wrong. My first thought was that he wanted to be with another woman.

"Darnell, what's the matter? Did somebody die?"

He shook his head.

"Ain't you going to sit down?" I asked.

He shook his head again. It was a few seconds before he said anything. "You know my brother moved to California two years ago?" Darnell didn't give me time to reply. "Him and his wife just opened up a little store in their neighborhood. They want me to come work for them. I can help keep the shelves stocked, the orders up-to-date and whatnot."

"Well, I know you told him you couldn't take the job. Why

would you leave a good job working for the lumber company to go be a stockboy?"

"A job is a job, Leona. Colored folks ain't got too many choices, even in a modernized place like California."

"I know we ain't got a lot of choices, but why take two steps back if you don't have to?"

"I don't see it that way. I'm taking the job, Leona."

"What about me?"

"What about you?"

"That's what I want to know. If you done already decided to take the job, did you come over here to tell me good-bye?"

"I came to ask you to go with me."

"You want us to get married?" My heart felt like it was flipping and flopping. I wanted to leap off the bed and hug Darnell as hard as I could. I decided to stay composed until he finished saying everything he had to say.

"I ain't ready to get married," he said real quick.

Now my heart felt like it had froze in place. All kinds of thoughts started swimming around in my head. Moving to the other side of the country didn't appeal to me, and leaving the only family I had was unthinkable. What if I went and Darnell decided he didn't want me with him after all? I'd have to come back home and find another job and place to live. And I'd have to find another man. "When did your brother ask you to come work for him?"

"Two weeks ago."

"And you just now telling me?" I gave him the most exasperated look I could manage. But he was gazing at the floor, so he didn't see it until he looked back up.

"You ain't got to give me the evil eye. I'm sorry. I should have told you before now. Anyway, I told him that I needed time to think about it. Well, I done thought about it long enough. The South ain't no place for colored folks. These peckerwoods down here is going to keep us under their thumbs forever."

"I know how to deal with white folks," I insisted. "They don't give me no trouble."

"Oh yeah? What about that old woman in that dress store that had you arrested?"

I huffed out a loud breath. "That wasn't that white lady's fault. I went to jail because I broke the law."

Darnell gave me a dismissive wave. "Whatever you say." He snorted and gave me a pleading look. "Leona, do you want to go with me or not?"

I hunched my shoulders and blinked. "I need to think about it for a while. And I need to discuss it with my mama and my sister. I'll let you know by next week."

"Well, I'm leaving day after tomorrow. You got until then to make up your mind. I'll even pay for your train ticket."

I didn't like for nobody to put pressure on me about nothing. As much as I cared about Darnell, I looked him in the eye and said, "I ain't going with you."

He looked so surprised you would have thought I'd slapped him. "Is that it? You want to break things off just like that?"

"Ain't that what you doing if I don't go?"

"I thought you said you'd think about it. You got a day and a half."

"I just thought about it." I didn't want to hug him or kiss him one last time. I walked over to the door and opened it. "Bye, Darnell. I wish you all the luck in the world."

He held up his hand. "Wait a minute now. We need to talk about this some more—"

I cut him off. "You said you done made up your mind to go. I told you I wasn't going with you. So there ain't nothing else to talk about." I opened the door even wider. "Bye."

He didn't say nothing else before he shuffled out the door.

Chapter 26
Fiona

I FELT SO BAD FOR LEONA. MAMA AND EVERYBODY ELSE DID TOO. Darnell had been the perfect man for her. The only person who didn't seem to be bothered about them breaking up was Bonnie Sue. "I'm glad he's out of the way," she told me. "Now me and Leona can have our privacy back." That was the last thing I wanted to hear from her. She had wore out her welcome at Leona's place ten times over, but I knew Leona would never tell her to move out.

I was glad Bonnie Sue had a skill that was always in demand. She still occasionally worked on neighbors' and church members' cars so she wouldn't have to depend on Leona for money. She had even asked Jubal to let her work at the garage when things was real busy. But my husband wasn't no fool. He was not about to upset his regular customers by having a young girl with no serious training work on their cars. If he had even thought about hiring her, I would have chewed his head off. But being the kindhearted soul he was, what he did was give her the names of a few folks with car trouble and told her she could contact them on her own.

The folks Jubal steered Bonnie Sue to was the ones real low on money, but they needed transportation to get to work and around town. It would be easier for them to take a chance and let Bonnie Sue work on their cars and pay her way much less than what they would have scraped up to pay Jubal. This worked for Bonnie Sue because she made a few dollars here and there, and the cash-strapped folks kept their jalopies running.

The prayer chain that the church had started, and me and Leona's prayers to help Bonnie Sue find a husband finally got answered in March: Clayton Frost asked her to marry him. I danced a jig when Leona told me.

The ceremony was in Clayton's mama's living room the last Saturday in March. I was almost as happy as Bonnie Sue was on her wedding day, and I knew Leona was too. She'd spent two days cooking food for the reception. Mama had even cooked a huge ham and made some potato salad. There was only about thirty guests, but enough food for twice as many. The way some of the folks was piling food onto their plates, you would have thought they'd come just to eat. A few stragglers didn't come in time for the wedding, but they came in time to eat.

After Bonnie Sue had roamed around the room and hugged and shook hands with everybody, she pranced over to where me and Leona was standing by the doorway. "Leona, I'm so happy, but I'm going to miss living with you. I felt more at home at your place than I ever felt when I was living with my family," Bonnie Sue gushed. "Fiona, I hope you didn't get jealous about me spending more time with Leona than I spent with you. Me and you grew apart and me and Leona grew even closer when she took me in. But the three of us will always be best friends."

"I'm glad you feel that way." I smiled and patted Bonnie Sue's shoulder. "I hope you and Clayton will have a long happy marriage."

"I hope we will." Bonnie Sue paused and looked straight into Leona's eyes and told her, "If things don't work out with me and Clayton, I'll move back in with you and stay for the rest of my life, praise the Lord."

"Yeah," Leona mumbled. She looked like she had just bit into a sour crab apple.

Before Bonnie Sue could say anything else, Clayton stumbled up to Leona with a wall-to-wall smile on his face. He was a caring, hard-working, godly man and everybody liked him. He was so humble and mild-mannered, anybody could control and manipulate him. He was definitely the type of man for a pushy, needy oddball like Bonnie Sue. "Leona, I can't thank you enough for being so nice to my bride in her time of need," he said as he wiped sweat off his smooth dark brown face. "She told me that you was the salt of the earth and then some. I want you to know that you will always be welcome in our home. If you ever want to move out of that sleazy *dump* you live in now, we'd be glad to accommodate you. My mama's pantry is bigger than that room you live in, and it's already got a rollaway bed in it."

I couldn't imagine a independent woman like Leona moving in with a clinging vine like Bonnie Sue, her husband and mother-in-law, not to mention a bunch of Clayton's other random kinfolks. I had to turn my head and hold my breath to keep from laughing. I was not surprised to see Leona close her mouth so tight, it looked like she had one lip. She smiled and said, "Thank you, Clayton. I'm pleased to hear that. I'm glad I was able to help Bonnie Sue out. But I'm saving up to get a better place."

"I hope you'll get married soon so you can know true bliss." Clayton kissed the tips of his fingers and got as giddy as a fox in a henhouse. "The only thing I would give up what I got now for is a early entrance into heaven."

Me and Leona laughed. "Well, I'm sure they got a spot reserved for you up there, so you ain't got to worry about going before your time," Leona told him.

"I hope not. God is so good to me." Clayton raised his hands and looked up toward the sky. "I feel His presence right now as we speak. He knows I'll be happy down here on earth with the angel He let me borrow." When Clayton lowered his gaze, there was tears in his eyes. Even though he had already made some profound statements, he went on and on about what a prize Bonnie Sue was.

I was tempted to ask him if he believed she was so perfect, why had it took him so long to marry her? Leona was so polite, she stood there with a smile still on her face. I didn't know how much longer I could listen to this lovestruck man. I had to force myself not to scream when Clayton said he wouldn't trade Bonnie Sue for five women. I was relieved when I noticed a girl across the room that I hadn't seen in a while. She had got married two years ago and moved to Mobile. I was so glad to see her, I excused myself and scurried over to the other side of the room to talk to her.

While me and my used-to-be friend-girl was yakking away about the good old days, I seen Jake go up to Leona. My heart skipped a beat. I had been avoiding him since that day I'd visited him to get the money to pay Leona's fine. I was glad I'd confessed everything to her so she had been avoiding him too. Ducking folks you didn't want to see was not easy. All the colored folks had to shop and eat at the same places, so everything we done was real limited. If one of us happened to be at the market and seen Jake, we'd ease out the door or hide behind something. The last time I seen him was at a funeral two months ago. He didn't see me when I walked into the church. I'd sat on a pew in the back and was one of the first ones to leave. I hadn't seen Jake again until today. I walked as fast as I could to get close enough to hear what he was fixing to say to Leona, but not close enough for him to see me. "I declare, Sister Leona. You looking as cute as ever. Um . . . when you get a chance, come by my house."

"For what?" she asked with a confused expression on her face. She seemed completely surprised that Jake would invite her to his house. I knew Leona couldn't have forgot what I told her about me frolicking with him to get money to pay her jail fine.

Jake chuckled. "Well, my arthritis keeps flaring up and I can't keep my house as clean as I like it. If you could come and help me do a little light housework, I sure would appreciate it. I'll pay you whatever you want."

I didn't realize Mama was standing behind me until I heard her voice. She started talking fast in a real excited tone. "Brother

Jake, Leona ain't the best housekeeper in the world. If you seen her room at that place she lives at you'd know what I mean. I been cleaning houses, cooking, and doing household chores most of my life, so you'd be better off by hiring a experienced woman like me. I sure could use the money. One of the families I been working for is fixing to move to Birmingham next week. I need to find something else to make up for that loss. When can I come see your house? I work for the Skinner family every Monday, Tuesday, and Wednesday. I'm only available every other day except Sunday. I don't work for nobody but the Lord on the Sabbath."

There was a blank expression on Jake's face, so I knew he was not too interested in a old straitlaced woman like Mama working for him. He tried to act like he was, though. "Um . . . next Saturday would be a good time for us to talk—if I ain't found nobody by then. I got a couple of other ladies lined up," Jake said in a dry tone. "Come around noon. I should be home from fishing by then."

"Good," Mama said before she made her way through the crowd. "I'll see you then."

After I had mingled with some other guests for the next fifteen minutes, Jubal came up to me, shaking his head. "What's wrong with you?" I asked. "You ready to leave?"

His tie looked like it was too tight. I reached over and loosened it while he was talking. "I been on my feet all day, so I need to go home and soak my corns."

"Hush up! We don't want to be the first ones to leave."

"All right, then. But I can't wait to get up out of here." Jubal looked around and shook his head again. "I swear to God, I ain't never been around such boring folks in my life. Jake Hickey damn near talked my ear off complaining about how he can't find a new wife."

"Humph. Maybe that ass-clown is messing around with the wrong women," I huffed.

"That's what I think. I didn't tell him that because I didn't want to make him feel no worse. I told him to pray and ask God to send him a wife," Jubal whispered. "And guess what? He had the nerve to tell me he wouldn't mind waking up every morning in bed lying next to Leona."

I choked on some air and Jubal clapped me on the back. "He can forget about her. You know how picky she is. Besides, she wouldn't have nothing to do with a geezer like him. Especially after she done been with a strapping young buck like Darnell."

"I know your sister got high expectations when it comes to men, but that's her business. Oh well. At least she got her ever-present friend-girl Bonnie Sue to fall back on so she ain't got to worry about being lonely. I don't think even Bonnie Sue being married now is going to make her cut back on her visits. She is hopelessly attached to Leona."

"Tell me about it. Too attached, in my book. You probably ain't noticed it, but Bonnie Sue done walked up to Leona twice in the last ten minutes and hugged her neck."

"So what? Other than a funeral, a wedding reception, and a sporting house, the only other place where folks are expected to get real affectionate and do a lot of hugging."

"That's true. But I ain't never seen the bride go up to one of the female guests and kiss her the way I seen Bonnie Sue try to do to Leona a little while ago. She ought to be saving her kisses for Clayton."

Jubal rolled his eyes. "There ain't nothing wrong with a woman kissing a close female friend. And there ain't no two women up in here no closer than Bonnie Sue and Leona."

I put my hands on my hips and glared at Jubal. "Bonnie Sue—and no other woman—will never be closer to Leona than I am."

"I know that, but you know what I mean. The bottom line is, some women like to kiss their lady friends on the jaw in certain situations."

"Bonnie Sue didn't try to kiss Leona on the jaw," I pointed out.

Jubal gave me a confused look. "Where did she try to kiss her at?"

"On the lips," I answered with my own lips screwed up like a coin purse.

"Hmmm." Jubal rubbed his chin and a concerned look crossed his face. "Well, drinking too much alcohol will make folks do things they wouldn't normally do. Don't worry about Bonnie Sue's behavior."

I was going to worry about Bonnie Sue's behavior. Somebody needed to.

Chapter 27
Leona

MY RENTED ROOM HAD BEGUN TO MAKE ME FEEL LIKE I WAS LIV-
ing in a barrel. Bonnie Sue had struck gold. Her new home was
not as nice as Fiona's, but I would still love to live in such a
place. The living room was big. At one end there was a blue
couch with two matching chairs facing it. The coffee table and
both end tables had doilies on them, and sitting at the end of
the living room was one thing very few colored folks owned: a
piano. There was all kinds of colorful knickknacks in other parts
of the house. When nobody was looking, I ducked down a hallway and peeped into the first bedroom. Compared to the room
Bonnie Sue had shared with me, this place probably seemed like
a palace to her. I was slightly jealous. But I was still happy for her.
If she and Fiona could make out so good, I knew there was a
chance that I would too someday.

I was one of the few females who had come to the wedding
without a man. The only other manless women was Mama, a few
other old ladies, and one of the girls that threw a lot of parties I
went to. She was pregnant and her man was in the army, so she
had a good excuse to come alone. Even Jubal's mama, Reba,
had come with a man. Sister Reba was a good-hearted, well-liked
woman who was just as overweight as most of the other women
her age. She dressed nice and wore makeup. Unfortunately, she
looked like Jubal in a wig-hat. But she still had a good man who
adored her.

"Why you looking so glum all of a sudden?" Fiona asked.

"I asked two of the men that always pick me to dance with at parties to come to the wedding with me and they both turned me down. And then they show up here with other girls. My self-esteem is lower than a snake's belly."

Before Fiona could say anything else, a tall man a year or two older than me with hazel eyes and skin the color of a walnut strutted up to Clayton. He almost took my breath away. "Who is that good-looking man in the blue suit talking to Clayton?" I asked.

Fiona squinted her eyes and looked over at the man I was talking about. "He's one of Clayton's friends who lives in Branson. I declare, he is a fine specimen of a man, if I do say so myself. Look at them juicy lips."

"Hmmm. Maybe I should spend more time over there." Branson was the next town over. It was only a little bigger than Lexington, and they had more stores that allowed colored people to shop in more days and hours.

"His name is Boaz Gibson. I wonder what his mama was thinking to give him a name like *Boaz*. That sounds like something that would come out of the mouth of a person with the croup." Fiona laughed. I didn't.

I gave her a hot look. "Maybe his mama was thinking the same thing Jubal's mama was when she named him." We laughed and then Fiona leaned closer to my ear and whispered, "I wouldn't care if his name was Peter Rabbit, I'd sit on his face in a heartbeat."

I was no prude, but I didn't like to hear females—especially my own twin sister—talk about sex in such a lewd way. "You hush your mouth, you nasty buzzard. And you got Mama and so many other folks thinking you are so prim and proper. Besides, you have a husband, and you need to forget about what you done with Jake to get the money to pay my jail fine." I cleared my throat. "Speak of that devil, he's coming this way."

Fiona didn't say nothing else. She just spun around and skittered to the other side of the room. I cringed when Jake stopped in front of me. "Leona, Leona, Leona." He leaned closer to me and whispered, "You and your sister is the best-looking women up in this place. I ain't never seen so many hoot owls at the same time—and that Bonnie Sue is the head hooter." He laughed. I gritted my teeth. He snorted and went on. "The man Clayton hired to come play the piano is running late. When he gets here, I expect you to dance with me."

"Let's wait until we see what kind of music he'll be playing."

Jake grinned with his raggedy teeth looking like pieces of broke glass, and looked me up and down. I was glad I didn't have on one of my low-cut blouses, especially the one Fiona had wore to his house the day she'd sat on his face. I excused myself before he could say anything else and rushed to the opposite side of the room. That was where the tables with all the food was. Before I could fix myself a plate, Bonnie Sue came up to me.

"What all did Jake say to you just now?" she asked.

"There was nothing coming out of his mouth but gibberish."

"I figured that. He's such a oaf around women, that's about all he can spew. No wonder he ain't got no steady woman."

I looked across the room where Clayton was still talking to the handsome man in the blue suit. "What's up with that man Clayton is talking to? I ain't met him yet."

"Clayton and Boaz have been friends for years."

"Is he a porter too?"

"Humph! That lummox ain't smart enough to be no porter. And he looks sneaky to me. I don't like him, and I told Clayton so."

One thing I didn't like about my best friend was that she didn't hesitate to mean-mouth somebody if they rubbed her the wrong way. And it seemed like every man I showed any interest in did just that. "Why do you think he looks sneaky?"

"I've heard things about him that ain't too Christian-like . . ."

"Well, I don't know the man, so whatever he does ain't no business of mine."

"Why are you asking about that snake in the grass?"

I hunched my shoulders. "No reason. I was just curious. I don't care if he is sneaky, he's one of the best-looking men here."

"Good looks is all he's got going for him. When he was in the army, they sent him to highfalutin places like France and Italy. You would think that mingling with white folks on that level would have made him more sophisticated and ambitious, like it did Clayton. But it didn't. Boaz comes back to America and settles for a job as a *field hand*!" Bonnie Sue spit out them last two words like they was vomit.

"What's wrong with that? Me and Fiona worked on farms when we was kids. And you even went with us a few times to pick cotton."

"Us working on farms when we was kids was one thing. But eventually anybody with a smidgeon of ambition moves on to something better."

"Like you did?" I didn't even try to hide the sarcasm in my tone.

"Exactly. I messed around with boys who picked cotton, but I didn't marry one. I married way up. A train porter is a job with a lot of prestige and Clayton loves his work. That's the only place where white folks call him 'sir.' If that ain't a big enough feather in my cap, he makes more than enough money for us to be comfortable. By splitting the rent with his mama, we'll be able to save up and get us a nice house before too long." We was silent for a few seconds. I was more than ready to end this conversation. But before I could walk away, Bonnie Sue took another potshot at Boaz. "Other than his good looks, I don't know what Boaz's wife sees in him . . ." The tail end of her sentence disappointed me.

"He's married?"

"Yup. She couldn't come because she sprained her ankle, or something like that. At least that's what Boaz told us. He probably didn't even tell her about the wedding so he could come here alone and flirt with other women."

It was hard to believe that a woman who had just married the man of her dreams was still able to be so mean-spirited. "He's that type, huh?"

Bonnie Sue snickered. "Let me tell you: The only difference

between him and that mangy hound dog in the backyard is a tail and four legs. And that ain't all. He is *real* particular about the type of woman he goes after."

I didn't like the smug look on Bonnie Sue's face. She had told me more about Boaz than I wanted to know. But I still didn't walk away. "What kind of woman is that?"

She moved closer to me and practically whispered in my ear. "Clayton told me that when they was in the army, Boaz made a fool of hisself chasing them white women in Europe. He knows better than to even *look* too long at one over here. He'd get lynched faster than them redneck peckerwoods could say 'Somebody get a rope.'" Bonnie Sue huffed out a disgusted sigh and shook her head. "But he got as close to a cracker woman over here as he could by marrying a redbone. His wife is practically white."

"Most colored men like light-skinned colored women. Mama said that's been going over ever since colored folks was brought to America."

"And that's the truth. I know folks think Clayton married me because I'm a redbone. I don't care if it's true. He's a good man and I'm a good woman, so we both did good." Bonnie Sue puffed out her chest and continued. "By the way, you look pretty good for a woman the color of cinnamon. And you got good hair and a nice shape. That's enough for you to land a good man. A good example of what I'm saying is your very own twin sister. Fiona hit the jackpot when she snatched up Jubal, and she ain't a redbone. If *she* can get a man like him, you'll be able to get one just as good sooner or later."

"Yeah. Sooner or later."

The piano player finally showed up. He started right off banging out some lively tunes. And it was the kind I enjoyed dancing to, but not today. When I seen Jake scanning the room, I ducked into the kitchen and slunk out the back door and went back to my dreary rooming house.

Chapter 28
Fiona

*B*EING PREGNANT WAS NOT EASY FOR ME. WITH THE BACKACHES, nausea, water retention, swole up ankles I had to deal with, it was hard for me to take care of the cooking and cleaning, but I did—and I never complained to Jubal.

The Monday after Bonnie Sue's wedding, Mama got a job working for a retired doctor named Virgil Brown. Her employer who was moving to Birmingham had recommended her to him. His family owned a lot of property and other members of the Brown family was involved in law and politics. Before the war between the North and the South, Dr. Brown's family operated one of the biggest plantations in the county. A lot of the slaves they'd owned was still alive. Some lived near us and belonged to our church. People claimed that one of the reasons the doctor was so nice to colored folks was because he felt guilty about the whole slavery thing. Me and Leona couldn't have been happier that Mama had landed such a good job. Not just because she'd be working full-time for one of the most prominent and powerful families in Lexington, but because she wouldn't have to consider doing no work for Jake now—or keep going to her other miserable part-time job. That was one less thing we had to worry about.

I had never seen Dr. Brown's house, but the way Mama described it, you would have thought it was a palace. "I never knew white folks could spend so much money! I hear that the doctor gives his wife so much, she shops up a storm every week. Every piece of furniture in each room looks like they paid hundreds of dollars for it. The doctor has a new-looking Ford sitting in the driveway and there's a great big shiny LaSalle sitting next to it for his wife!" A sad look crossed Mama's face. "Lord, I wish your daddy had taught me how to drive before he passed."

"What for? We couldn't afford no car back then," I pointed out.

"I know, but I like to dream," Mama said as she gazed at me with misty eyes. "At least one of my dreams came true. You married one of the most eligible colored men in town, and he owns a car and done already taught you how to drive. Ain't you proud of yourself?"

I sighed before I replied. "Yeah."

I was glad I had landed a good husband. But I was sorry it had to be a man as dull as Jubal. Other than church, his mama's house, fishing, and work, he didn't care about where I wanted to go, like the movies or a nice restaurant. He took me out every now and then, but only after I'd complained and badgered him enough.

Our son Lamar was old enough to walk and talk before Jubal took us to Mobile to a real nice restaurant for the first time. As soon as we got back home that evening, Jubal got out of his good clothes, put on some overhauls, and went to the garage. Lamar loved spending time with his daddy so much, he followed him around like a puppy. So if I didn't go to Jubal's mama's house with him and all the other boring places he went to, I'd be in the house by myself.

I had turned twenty-two a month ago, and I missed going out to have a good time. But I couldn't sneak out at night posing as Leona like I did when we was teenagers. I had too many other things on my plate, and I couldn't come home with moonshine on my breath. My life would never be the same and I was all right with that. But I thought about asking Leona to switch places with me every now and then so I could go out and kick up my heels. I didn't have the nerve to do that yet, though.

I was restless but I was thankful that I lived in such a nice house, and being a mother made me glow each time I looked at my son. I would have liked looking at him even more if he'd looked more like me and less like Jubal. I never knew such boring men existed! I cared for Jubal, but I didn't love him. Mama had told me and Leona when we was younger that love was optional in a marriage. And even then it only took shape over time. When and if that happened in my case, I prayed that I'd still be young enough to enjoy being in love. I loved being married, but I wished it was to a man who excited me the way my boyfriends did when I was still single.

"Mama, Jubal is about to drive me crazy," I complained.

Me and her was sitting at my kitchen table knitting new items for the church to give to needy folks that Saturday afternoon in July. I loved to sew and knit, so this was one activity that helped keep me from getting bored during the day. To get out of the house, I ran errands and did chores for some of the elderly folks on my street. I even went in the backyard and chopped firewood when I didn't have nothing better to do.

Mama sucked her teeth and gazed at me for a few seconds before she said anything. "Already? What terrible thing is he doing to make you feel like that?"

"He ain't doing nothing terrible. It's just that . . . well, he ain't fun like the boys that used to come to our house when I was younger."

Mama looked confused. "Huh? Other than a few boys from church that used to come around the house to eat supper with us, do a few chores for me, and play checkers with you and Leona, what 'fun' boys are you talking about? You didn't have no serious boyfriends before Jubal. Leona was the one dropping her bloomers for every Tom, Dick, and Harry in town. All it got her was pregnant."

"That's true. I . . . I didn't get slap-happy with boys the way she did. But I . . . um, I . . . but Ernest Lee used to make me and Leona laugh with his lame jokes. And Tyrone Peterson, who used to come help us chop wood, was good company to sit on our couch and listen to the radio with. That's what I meant about them being fun."

"Gal, is that what you expect from a husband? You didn't marry none of them silly boys you used to know. And even if you had, being married to one would be a whole different ball of wax than them games teenagers play. A boy or a man can be frivolous when they are just friends with a female. Once he becomes a husband, you get to see the real deal. If you had married any one of them boys you used to know, behind closed doors they could get on your nerves ten times worse than Jubal. You need to stop making such a fuss about him before you run him off. If you do, half the young women in this town would snatch him up so fast, it'd make your head spin clean off your neck. Pass me the green yarn."

I gave Mama a thoughtful look as I handed her a fresh roll of yarn. "You still don't ever want to get married again?"

Mama chuckled. "Married? Me? It's way too late for that. This is 1923 and women ain't as dependent on men like we was back in the old days."

"I don't care what year this is. And it ain't never too late for nothing, unless you die."

"Well, that ain't the only reason. Why would you think I'd ever want to get married again? I got everything I wanted. Besides, you have to work at a marriage. I'm too busy to be fussing and fighting and looking after another man. Your daddy gave me such a run for my money, I ain't got no steam left."

"You wanted me to get married. And I know you want Leona to settle down with a husband someday."

Mama glanced toward the wall for a few seconds. "I told Leona at Bonnie Sue's wedding all them years ago, that if she wants to get married someday, she will. I just pray that she'll find a man like Jubal."

I snickered. "If he don't get the spirit, I might take off and then she can have him."

Mama laughed long and loud. "Leona ain't never going to be like you. She's still like a fart in a windstorm. Jubal wouldn't put up with her for ten minutes. But she'll find the right man and it'll be real soon," Mama insisted. "She ain't but twenty-two, so she still got a lot of time."

The next time Mama told me Leona would get married "real soon" was at our *thirty-third* birthday party. At the time, Leona hadn't had a boyfriend in two years.

PART TWO

1934–1938

Chapter 29

Leona

*T*IME WAS GOING BY QUICKLY AND SO MUCH WAS HAPPENING, I HAD a hard time keeping track of everything. I was approaching middle age and I was still floundering about in my personal life and that saddened me. But I was proud of the fact that I had almost stopped drinking and I only went to a party every now and then. Mama had warned me when I was a teenager that fast living was not good for the body. She was right because I no longer had the energy to keep doing it.

Mama was almost eighty, but she bragged about all the steam she had left. "I ain't going to slow down and go sit on the porch until God lets me know it's time," she vowed. All of her friends had retired years ago, but she wanted to keep working. Dr. Brown had died five years ago, and that sweet old man had remembered Mama in his will. He'd left her two thousand dollars! And his family wanted her to continue working for them until she decided to retire.

Eight years ago, I moved from that dreary rooming house and into a house I loved the minute I seen it. It wasn't much to look at on the outside. The gray shingles made it look drab, but I had fixed it up so nice inside, I loved having company. My new address was only a few minutes' walk from Mama's and Fiona's.

The married couple who had lived in the house before me had suddenly decided to move to Canada, where some of their family had already fled to. Some folks could only deal with segregation and the brutal way the racists treated us for so long. Anyway, the couple sold what they could out of the house, but they let me have everything in the kitchen, even the dishes and pots and pans. Fiona made me some curtains, Jubal and one of his friends painted the walls, and Mama used part of the money she'd inherited from Dr. Brown and bought me bedroom furniture and everything else I needed. I was so giddy I could bust.

I only had one bedroom, a living room large enough for me to entertain a few friends when I felt like it, and I even had a inside toilet! I had got so used to—and sick of—relieving myself in outhouses and slop jars, this was such a blessing.

I'd only had serious relationships with three other men since Darnell moved to California almost fifteen years ago, and only one had asked me to marry him. Me and Wally Townes had been together for a year before I realized he was probably my last shot at landing a husband with a decent job. Like Fiona's and Bonnie's men, Wally was a older man. He was thirteen years older than me. I didn't worry too much about the age difference or the fact that he didn't look like no film star. He had a nose that was too pointy and long for a colored man and his lips was so thin, kissing him was like kissing the edge of a spoon. I overlooked them things because Wally was a good man for me to grow old with. He was in the church, was from a nice family, he had a great personality, and a good job. I was a little concerned about his line of work, though. He helped make caskets at a facility across the state line in Meridian, Mississippi. But it didn't bother Wally.

"The best thing about my job is that there will *always* be a need for caskets," he told me one night after we'd come home from the movies.

I had just admitted to him that I was so superstitious, anything associated with death and funerals gave me the heebie-jeebies.

"Wally, I'm glad you enjoy your work. I can say the same thing about my job. Folks will never stop eating chicken." We laughed.

Things was getting worse instead of better as far as jobs went, so I planned to stay on at the chicken factory for as long as they let me, or as long as I could stand it.

Everything was going good for everybody. Bonnie Sue and Clayton still lived with his mama along with their three teenage sons, a displaced one-eyed elderly uncle on his mama's side, and two cousins whose wives had kicked them out of their own houses.

Bonnie Sue had been griping for the past ten years about not having her own home by now. Clayton's main excuse was that with three kids to feed, they couldn't afford to move. Another excuse was that his elderly mama needed him to help take care of her. His daddy had took off when he was still in high school, and his three older siblings lived in other states so they couldn't help the mama out much.

Poor Bonnie Sue. It seemed like life was never going to stop beating her down. She didn't put up too much of a argument with Clayton because there was other advantages for them to stay on in his mama's house. The old woman doted on the grand-kids, so Bonnie Sue didn't have to do too much for them. That allowed her to still spend a unbelievable amount of time breathing down my neck.

Nadine had got married again and divorced two years ago, but she still liked to give parties. When I had extra money to buy moonshine and snacks, I had parties at my house, and Bonnie Sue was always available to help me host them. "I'm glad Clayton's mama is around to look after the kids. That way I don't feel too guilty about spending hours on end at your house, Leona. Even when you don't have a party going on."

As hard as it was to believe, Bonnie Sue was still like a shadow to me. No matter who I was involved with, she didn't let that stop her from coming over several times a week. The men in my life tolerated her, but they all complained about her constant presence. When her mother-in-law wasn't able to look after the kids, she dragged them to my house with her. And every now and then when Clayton was home for a few days from his train runs, she brought him along too. "I declare, Leona. I love coming to your house. It's such a nice change from ours with Mama moaning and groaning about every little ache and pain, and my kids acting like wild animals. I wish I could spend more time with you too," Clayton told me during one of the times he'd tagged along with Bonnie Sue. Now that he was deep into middle age, he was forgetful, slovenly, and every time I seen him, he had dark circles around his eyes.

I looked upside his head, which was almost completely gray now, and told him, "I'm glad you feel that way. I like to make my friends happy."

One thing that hadn't changed over the years was Bonnie Sue's resentment toward my men friends. I could always count on her to remind me that every man was a dog in some way, especially the ones in my life. "I don't even trust my husband and he's the cream of the crop. He's only a low-level dog, though. If I was a cat and walked past one of your men, he'd bark up a storm and chase me up a tree."

Me and Bonnie Sue was sitting on my couch, three days after Christmas. "The rest of us women can't all be as lucky as you," I said as I rolled my eyes. As much as I liked Clayton, he was a clumsy oaf that I would have never gave the time of day if he'd approached me before him and Bonnie Sue got together.

Bonnie Sue's constant mean-mouthing of my men annoyed me, but I still took it all in stride. One reason was because some of her comments was so funny, I couldn't stop myself from laughing. "I can't wait to see how much you'll be laughing when she runs Wally off," Fiona said.

I didn't have to wait long, and Bonnie Sue didn't run Wally off. On New Year's Eve, he asked me to marry him. He died the first day in the new year in a car wreck on the way to Carson Lake to do some fishing with some of his friends. He'd lost control of his car and smashed head-on into a tree. Him and all three of his passengers died.

Jubal had worked on Wally's car two days before the accident and said it was in tip-top condition. After he had it towed to his garage to try and figure out what went wrong, he hinted that it looked like somebody had tampered with the brakes. One of the men passengers had been fooling around with several married women and some of the angry husbands had been threatening him for weeks. Everybody knew about the fishing trip, so we assumed one of them husbands had finally done him in.

I had planned to go with Wally and his friends on that fishing trip so we could celebrate our engagement. Two hours before he was supposed to pick me up, Bonnie Sue stormed into my house howling like a teething baby. Between sobs, she told me that she'd had a nightmare the night before. In it, the ghosts of the loved ones she'd lost invited her to join them. I had never seen her so hysterical. She'd begged me to let her stay with me until she calmed down. Clayton was on a train run, and the rest of the folks who lived in the house told her to stop overreacting and to "get a grip." Well, I couldn't turn my back on Bonnie Sue in such a desperate time of need. I used my neighbor's phone to call Wally to let him know that I had a crisis to attend to and couldn't go to the lake. He wanted to cancel his plans, but I told him to go on without me, and that we'd celebrate our engagement later.

It took me a while to calm Bonnie Sue down. While she was still at my house, feeling much better now, Fiona came over to tell me about the car wreck that Wally had died in. Bonnie Sue was just as stunned as I was. I got hysterical and she and Fiona had to console me. "You cheated death, girl," Bonnie Sue pointed out as she rubbed my back. "I saved your life by coming over here."

I was so grateful to still be alive, I promised myself that I'd always be there for Bonnie Sue.

Despite all the heartaches I'd endured, I loved my life. I had so much to be thankful for, especially my family. My nephew, Lamar, was the kind of son I hoped to have some day. He was a good boy because he'd racked up some serious whuppings along the way that had helped keep him on the straight and narrow. All he cared about now was his family, school, church, and girls. I spent a lot of my free time with Lamar.

The days we couldn't go fishing or blackberry picking, he would come to my house, and we'd play checkers or dominoes

for hours. For some reason, he had never liked Bonnie Sue.
When he was a baby, he'd scream bloody murder every time she
tried to pick him up. The older he got, the more he disliked her.
Finally, one day when he was twelve I went up to him and asked
why he didn't like Bonnie Sue. There was a frightened look on
his face when he told me, "Every time she comes around, I get
real sad; the same way I do when I'm at somebody's funeral.
She's the only person my dog barks at." His comments spooked
me so much, I never told Fiona or anybody else what he'd said.

Time didn't change Lamar's feelings about Bonnie Sue. He
was in high school now and she still made him uncomfortable,
so he avoided her as much as he could for the next year or so.

He was going to graduate next month in June so him and his
friends was busy planning all the things they wanted to do to celebrate, but he still found time to visit me. Me and him was playing checkers when I heard footsteps on my front porch. I had a
feeling it was Bonnie Sue, but I ran to the window to see who it
was anyway. I shuddered when I opened the curtains. "Um . . .
it's Bonnie Sue," I announced.

Lamar cringed. When she came in, he hugged her neck like
he always did and then he politely excused hisself and eased out
the door. "I declare, that boy is getting so handsome," Bonnie
Sue squealed as she plopped down on my couch. "If I was a
young girl, I'd be all over him. It's a shame he's still so shy
around me. Oh, well. I'm so loud I scare a lot of young kids."
Bonnie Sue looked toward the kitchen and sniffed. "Give me
one of them tea cakes I smell."

Chapter 30
Leona

THE ONLY THING I DIDN'T LIKE TOO MUCH ABOUT THE HOUSE I'D moved into was that it was closer to where Bonnie Sue lived. Now she only had to walk a block and a half to get to me. But even if I had moved ten miles away, she'd still come over several times a week, if not more. I was so used to her presence; it didn't even faze me when she complained about something that didn't suit her. "My Lord, Leona! It seems like every time I come over here all you got to snack on is stale tea cakes and pig feet. The next time I come, I'm going to bring some sugarcane or peanut brittle."

"I declare, *Miss Ann.*" As soon as them words left my mouth, Bonnie Sue's face scrunched up like a snake had bit her. No jab ruffled a colored female's feathers quicker and harder than being called Miss Ann, which was a mean-mouth comparison to uppity white women who thought their butts didn't stink. "I'm sorry. But you have to remember that I ain't got no husband with a good job like yours who makes enough money to buy fancy snacks. I'm just a low-paid, single woman struggling to get from one payday to the next."

"I know you can barely pay rent and eat, but you don't need to overreact and low-rate me like that. I didn't mean no harm," Bonnie Sue whined. "Yeah, I got a husband who makes a good living. But marriage ain't all it's cracked up to be. You better enjoy being single and free as a bird as long as you can . . ."

I was sick and tired of getting mixed messages from everybody about married life. One day folks would be asking when I was going to get married and settle down and start having babies. The next time I seen the same folks, they would tell me how lucky I was to still be single. At the end of the day, I didn't care what nobody said. I didn't want to spend the rest of my life alone.

Mama was still working for Dr. Brown's family, and they was real generous to her. When she had to take off to go to the clinic, or she didn't feel good, they still paid her regular pay— and they gave her cash bonuses at random. Me and Fiona was very happy that she was still able to take good care of herself and live on her own.

Despite Fiona being a busy housewife and mother, and me working long hours, we spent as much time together as possible. Our thirty-fourth birthday was coming next week, and Bonnie Sue was going to pay to have a telephone installed in my house. I couldn't have been happier if she had planned to give me gold. I was tired of running next door every time I needed to call up somebody.

When I went to visit Fiona and told her about the gift Bonnie Sue was going to give me, she wasn't too happy about it. She even sounded mad. "Leona, I think it's a mistake for you to accept a gift like that from a *unhinged* woman like Bonnie Sue. If you want a telephone, I'll pay for it."

"I already told Bonnie Sue to set up the appointment for the installer to come out. You and Jubal can use that money for something else." They had already got Mama a telephone and they helped her with her bills.

"Now Bonnie Sue will be calling you day and night when she can't visit in person. That don't bother you?"

I shrugged. "Well, we been friends with her since we was little kids. I can't push her out of my life this late in the game."

"All right now. I hope you won't have to regret them words someday."

It had been six months since Wally died, but I still missed him so much I didn't even want to start up with another new man anytime soon. It seemed like each time I got with one I cared enough about to go to bed with ended in a disaster.

Another thing that hadn't changed over the years was me and Fiona switching places. We only did it every now and then, though. Like in March when she didn't want to spend five days with her mother-in-law in Atlanta to attend her niece's wedding, I went in her place. Fiona stayed at my house and went to work at the chicken factory. Because I was between boyfriends, she didn't have to worry about keeping up the ruse with a man. I'd actually had a good time in Atlanta. I couldn't wait to get back home and tell Fiona about the big wedding reception and the nice restaurants Jubal's cousins had took me to. "I hope you want me to fill in for you again on another big trip," I told her the day I got back to Lexington.

"Don't worry. I'm sure I'll need you to do it some more in the future. And anytime you don't feel like going to your chicken plucking job, let me know and I'll go in your place. You can stay at my house and lay around reading magazines, cooking pies and cakes, and making clothes and whatnot for the church folks, or listening to the radio all day." We laughed.

"Sounds good to me," I said.

Most of the friend-girls that I used to hang out with when I was younger had got married. One had been married and divorced twice and was engaged to get married again. Me and Nadine Fisher was still close and we visited each other a couple of times a week. But Bonnie Sue still visited me several times a week, sometimes twice in the same day. Fiona was more than a little concerned about her frequent visits. "If you had a welcome mat, Bonnie Sue would have wore a hole in it fifty times over by now. I passed by your house on my way to choir practice last night and she was perched on your front porch steps. When I left church two hours later to go home, Bonnie Sue was still sitting in the same spot! If you had a man, he could take you out so you wouldn't have to be bothered with her so much."

"Having Wally around hadn't made no difference. There was

times when he would take me out and she would insist on staying at my house until we got back. One time she even followed us to a restaurant, parked right in front so we could see her, and she sat in her car until Wally went outside and told her to come eat with us."

"My God! That woman is worse than I thought. Wally was too nice for his own good to put up with her antics. You need a tougher man. Now, take Otto Brewster. One reason he's been working for Jubal so long is because he knows how not to let the customers walk all over him and try to get work done on credit. If he was your man, he'd tell Bonnie Sue in a nice way to stop bringing her high-yellow tail around so much. Speaking of Otto, Jubal said that he told him he'd sure like to get to know you better. If it's all right with you, I'll invite you and him to supper and let nature take its course."

I looked at Fiona like she'd lost her mind. "You know I don't like men shorter than me. Besides, Otto ain't nowhere near my type." Otto was a divorced man in his middle forties with beautiful caramel-colored skin, but his nose looked like a meatball and his bushy mustache was lopsided.

From the look on Fiona's face, I could tell she was exasperated. "You ain't got to marry him. Just let him take you out now and then. He's got a car, a decent house, and he's generous with his money. Think of all the movies and restaurants he'd treat you to. Then Bonnie Sue would have to find somebody else to be a pest to."

"I don't really think of Bonnie Sue as a pest. She's like family, and almost every family I know got at least one bothersome relative. Why are you harping about all the time she spends at my house anyway? You been doing a lot of that lately."

"Because her sitting on your front steps waiting for you to get home ain't normal. There ain't nothing normal about her behavior, period. I think it's downright unnatural."

"When Bonnie Sue moved in with me after she lost her family, we slept in the same bed. When we was kids and she slept over at Mama's house, me, you, and her slept in the same bed. We did the same thing when we slept over at her house. Did you think that wasn't unnatural?"

"Leona, Bonnie Sue is obsessed with you," Fiona said in a firm tone.

I laughed and wagged my finger in Fiona's face. "First you said she wasn't normal. Then you said she was unnatural, now you say she's obsessed. Make up your mind and decide which one it is."

"All three."

Chapter 31
Fiona

I STILL LIKED TO KEEP UP WITH WHAT WAS GOING ON WITH THE REST of the world. Listening to the radio that Jubal bought me for my birthday this year was one of my favorite pastimes. Not only did I listen to the news and gospel programs, I loved listening to dramas like *Little Orphan Annie,* and *Burns and Allen.* But my favorite was *Amos 'n' Andy* because it was about colored folks from the Deep South—even though it was white men playing the roles of colored men.

With Jubal at work and Lamar out with one of his girlfriends or fishing buddies most of each day, I had a lot of time on my hands during the day. Mama and my mother-in-law, Reba, dropped in at least twice a week, and I enjoyed their company. But there was times when some of the things they said depressed me.

"They been talking on the radio about that crazy white man over there in Germany named Hitler," Mama said. Me and her and Reba was sitting at my kitchen table drinking tea. "He's going to stir up a worldwide mess and drag America in."

"Oh yeah. I read about that buffoon in the newspaper. He is trying to stir up things," Reba said. "As if that first war President Woodrow Wilson got us into with them Germans didn't kill and hurt enough people. Two of my nephews died in that war."

"I ball up inside every time I hear about one of our colored men joining the service," Mama said in a weary tone. "Fiona, I don't care what you and Jubal have to do to keep Lamar from getting involved. Hog-tie him and lock him in the pantry if you have to."

Lamar hadn't said nothing to me about joining the military since he'd finished high school back in June, and I didn't want to bring it up to him. He had a girlfriend, but he had told me more than once he didn't want to get tied down with a wife and children too soon. Since Mama and Reba had brought up him joining the military, I decided to feel him out when he got home from visiting his girlfriend this evening.

He was sitting on the couch munching on a tea cake when I eased down next to him. "We'll be eating supper soon. I don't want you to ruin your appetite." I straightened the collar on his shirt. He looked so much like his daddy, if he had been older they could have almost passed for twins.

"Aw, Mama," he muttered with a groan. "Stop treating me like a baby."

"I don't care how old you get; you will always be my baby." Me and Jubal had wanted several children, but I hadn't been able to get pregnant since I had Lamar. I had accepted the fact that one child was all God thought I deserved, or that He was punishing me for that pregnancy fiasco me and Leona went through when we was sixteen. "I'm going to take care of you as long as I can."

Lamar laughed. "You might have a problem with my wife."

I sucked in a deep breath and reared back. "You thinking about marrying that Mason girl you been seeing?"

He shook his head. "Naw. She's fooling around with two other boys. I want to marry a virtuous woman like you."

I exhaled and crossed my legs. "I'm glad to hear that. Do you know what you want to do now that you ain't got to worry about school? I thought it would be nice for you to go work for your daddy."

"I don't want to end up like Daddy."

His reply made me flinch. Jubal was as dull as a butter knife, but other than that, he was perfect. "What a mean thing to say about your own daddy! Do you know how many colored men would love to be in his shoes?"

"I realize that, but I ain't one of them men."

"Well, Mr. Big Shot, what do you want to do with your life, work in a sugarcane field or pick cotton?"

"No, that ain't what I want to do neither. I . . . um . . . I got a itching to join the army. I'll probably sign up next week."

I gasped so hard my bosom felt like somebody had sat down on it. "The army?" I was scared to death to think about my only child ducking and diving from all the bombs and bullets. "Why would you all of a sudden want to do that?"

"Mama, it ain't 'all of a sudden.' I started thinking about it before I even made it to high school. The only reason I didn't join right after I graduated was because Daddy told me to take my time and ease into the subject with you. So since you brought up what I wanted to do with my life, I figured this was a good time to tell you."

I had to blink hard to hold back the tears that was threatening to ooze from my eyes. "I'm proud to have a son who wants to do such a noble thing for his country. The military is a good choice, but it ain't no paradise."

"I know it ain't. Especially for colored men. I done heard all kinds of bad things about the army from some of the men that went. But they all said they was glad they went because they got paid and they got to travel all over the world at the government's expense."

I sighed. "Remember what I told you about Bonnie Sue's brother dying while he was in the army, stationed in Europe?"

"Yeah, I remember you telling me about that. He got drunk with a bunch of other soldiers and fell off a bridge in Paris, France."

"See what I mean? Anything could happen to you in the military."

"Anything could happen to a person no matter where they are at. Remember the man who fell off a ride at the county fair last year and busted his head open? And what about the five colored men the Klan lynched last year? Anything that could happen to me in the military couldn't be no worse than getting lynched. At least that's one thing I won't have to worry about happening to me in Europe."

I wobbled up off the couch and took a deep breath. Lamar seemed more interested in finishing his tea cake than listening to me. "Can you open a jar of them green peppers you canned to eat with the collard greens you cooked for supper?"

"I will, son."

Before I could make it to the kitchen, Jubal walked through the front door. As usual, he was covered in grimy mess, and he smelled like oil. After he greeted Lamar, he followed me into the kitchen. "Ain't you going to give me some sugar?" he asked.

"Did you know your son was planning on joining the army next week?"

"Good!" He rubbed his hands together. "They'll make a real man out of him."

"You ain't worried about him getting killed? Them foreign countries they send soldiers to is dangerous."

Jubal gave me a serious look. "So is Alabama. Now don't you start fussing about that! The boy is grown."

"We'll have to pray he'll be all right," I said in a meek tone. I knew it wouldn't do me no good to make a fuss about Lamar planning to join the service, and I couldn't stop him. I decided to drop the subject. I had to agree with Lamar and Jubal, my son was in just as much danger in Alabama as he would be in one of them foreign countries.

"Well, do I get some sugar or not?" Jubal asked. I turned my face so he could kiss my jaw. The way he swooned, you would have thought we'd just had sex. And that was the last thing on my mind. He had got so dull and routine, he couldn't turn me on with a monkey wrench. We hadn't had sex in three months. Last night when he tugged at my bloomers and breathed on the back of my neck, I gritted my teeth and pushed him away. "What's wrong, Fiona? My hands too cold?" he'd asked.

"Um . . . I been having headaches, mostly at night. Sometimes they get so bad, I get dizzy and have to take a pill. After they go away, I can't remember a lot of things that happened."

"My God. Well, if they get any worse, I'm going to take you to the clinic and let a doctor look at you. I would hate for you to forget you had something cooking on the stove and burn down the house."

Me and Leona had cooked up my headache "loss of memory" ruse when she went to Atlanta with my mother-in-law in my place back in March. We thought it would be a good excuse for her to use if somebody mentioned something that she didn't know about. Her loss of memory ruse was as good as mine. If somebody asked me about something while I was posing as her that I didn't know about, I would blame it on blackouts caused by alcohol. My headaches was also a great way for me to avoid having sex with Jubal.

"I already went to the clinic last week," I lied. "Dr. Underwood couldn't find nothing wrong with me. He said it could be because I had so much on my mind."

"What all do you have on your mind? You ain't got no job you have to go to. Our boy don't never cause us no trouble. Your mama and mine are in good health. You and me are in good health." Jubal paused and let out a loud sigh. "Is it something Leona is up to?"

I rolled over so I could face him. "I do worry about her. I mean, no woman, colored or white, wants to be a old maid."

"I got news for you, sugar. A unmarried woman her age is a old maid in every country on this planet."

Chapter 32
Leona

I DIDN'T KNOW WHAT I WAS GOING TO DO WITH MYSELF FOR THE holidays this year. Lamar had decided to spend it with some girl he'd met who lived near the base he was stationed at. Mama was going to spend it in Mobile with one of her close friends who used to live in Lexington. Fiona and Jubal was going to drive to Atlanta and celebrate with the same relatives I'd met over there the week I'd posed as her. His mama was going along with them. "You welcome to come with us," Fiona told me two days before Thanksgiving. "I hate to think of you spending the holiday by yourself."

"Bonnie Sue invited me to come eat with her and Clayton and his folks, but I told her I don't mind staying home alone. Besides, I got a lot of things to do around the house that I been putting off."

The Saturday after Thanksgiving, I stayed in bed for several hours after I had woke up. The only reason I got up then was because my telephone rang. I rolled out of bed and trotted to the kitchen to answer it. It was Fiona. "What took you so long to answer?"

"I was still in bed." I yawned.

"Girl, it's half past noon. You must have went out last night and drunk like a fish."

"No, I didn't. You may not have noticed, but I don't drink half as much as I used to. I had company last night."

"I don't even need to ask who it was, but I'll take a wild guess: Bonnie Sue."

"Yeah. She wanted to get out of the house for a little while."

"I declare, I'm going to ask Otto to take you to a movie or something. You are wasting away with Bonnie Sue, and I'm worried about you. I been thinking about calling her over here so we could have a talk. We ain't kids no more and we need to move in different directions. Bonnie Sue don't get that. It's time for somebody to say something to her before it's too late."

"Too late for what?"

"Too late to turn her around. She acts like she's your shadow or something. You really need to listen to me on this one. Something ain't right with that woman. I'm beginning to think that she's got a few loose screws in her head."

"We been friends with 'that woman' all our lives. I don't want you to upset her. I don't think she's got any loose screws, but I do believe she's real fragile. Upsetting her by getting in her face could make her go to pieces. Do you want her to end up in the crazy house? And don't you dare send Otto over here! I can do so much better than him."

"Then why don't you? Listen, you ain't in no position to be so choosy these days. I feel so sorry for you."

"Thanks a lot," I said in the most sarcastic tone I could manage. The last thing I wanted was pity, especially from my own twin. I decided the best thing to do was lighten up the conversation. "Um . . . if I change my mind about Otto, I'll let you know."

I was glad Fiona changed the subject. "You want to go the market with me today? Cow tongues went on sale today. I'll come pick you up."

"That's all right. I'm going to get up in a few minutes and take Jubal some of them chicken wings I smothered yesterday. He told me that the next time I cooked some to bring him a mess."

"Good. Be my guest. The less I have to cook for him, the better. But you know Otto will be at the garage . . ."

"I don't care. I'm only going to drop off them wings and come right back home."

Jubal had a clipboard in his hand and was busy talking to a customer, so I set the bowl on a table against the wall. I didn't want to interrupt him, so I just waved and started back toward the door. He smiled and waved back. On my way back out, I walked as fast as I could to get out of talking to Otto. He was working on something under the hood of a car and hadn't seen me come in.

Just as I approached the door to go out, coming in was the last person I expected to bump into at Jubal's garage: Clayton's friend Boaz. It had been more than fifteen years since I'd first seen him at Bonnie Sue's wedding. He had some gray hair and a few lines on his face, but he was still as handsome as ever. "Excuse me, sister. Ain't you Bonnie Sue's friend-girl with a twin sister?" he said.

"Have we met before?" I knew who he was the minute I seen him, but I didn't see no reason to let him know that. If anything, I thought it would benefit me more to act aloof. I still enjoyed getting attention from a handsome man, even if he was married. Ten years ago when I got attention from one, it made me feel special. Now when I got it, I felt like there was still hope for me to have one of my own someday.

"We might have and we might not have. I don't know which twin you are. I was introduced to one of y'all at Bonnie Sue and Clayton's wedding." He paused and looked around. Jubal was still conversating with the same customer. Otto peeked from under the hood of the car he was working on. I didn't even make eye contact with him. "I'm Boaz Gibson, a lifelong friend of Clayton's. You must be the twin married to Jubal." He glanced toward Jubal.

"No, I'm the other one."

"Aahh, yes. You're Leona. Um . . . who did you marry? Whoever he is, he's a very lucky man to have such a beautiful wife."

Boaz's words threw me for a big loop. My face got so hot, I wanted to crawl up under one of them cars waiting to be worked on. No man had ever made me feel so shy. He was wasting his time by being so forward with me. I had never fooled around with a married man, and never would. I was so proud of myself for having such a strict rule, I puffed out my chest. "I ain't married."

He looked surprised. "But you have been married before, right?"

I shook my head. "I came close, but my fiancé died in a car wreck shortly after we got engaged."

"I'm sorry to hear that." He shifted his weight from one foot to the other. "I came to check on my car. I dropped it off last week, but Jubal had to order the part it needed."

"I came over here today to bring him some lunch. He likes the way I cook chicken wings."

Boaz stopped shifting his weight and started scratching his head. That made me think he was as uncomfortable as I was. "Well, it was nice seeing you again." He started to walk away. Before I could make my feet move, he turned around and came back up to me. "You want to get together sometime?"

I gave him a sideways look. "I don't think your wife would like that." I swallowed hard and glanced toward Otto. He seen me looking at him and ducked his head back up under the hood. "How is she doing?"

A woeful look suddenly covered Boaz's face like a mask. "She died six months ago giving birth. The baby died too. It had took us twenty years to make that baby and . . ." He hunched his shoulders and stopped talking.

"I'm so sorry. Bonnie Sue didn't tell me that."

"She didn't know. Clayton didn't know neither until recently. Me and my wife had moved to Houston about ten years ago so we could help take care of her daddy. He was real sick at the time. After he passed, we decided to stay over there. I got a job working on a fishing boat. The pay was good for a while, but then things slowed down. So, with my wife gone, I didn't have no reason to stay in Houston. I moved back to Alabama last month."

"Do you live in Lexington?"

"No, I moved back to Branson where I was raised. A heap of

my kinfolks still live there. But I spend a lot of time over here with Clayton when he's on a break from his train runs, and I got a couple other friends over here that I go fishing with. I even bought another car this year. It's old and ugly as the one I had before, but it gets me where I need to go."

I was getting nervous. There was something about this man that excited me. "I guess I'll be getting on home." I looked up at the sky, which was dark gray. "It looks like it might rain and I can't remember if I closed my windows or not. It was nice seeing you."

"Well, do you want to get together sometime?" he asked again.

I coughed to clear my throat and reluctantly answered, "Yeah, that would be nice."

I suddenly felt so comfortable talking to Boaz, I didn't want to leave. Conversating with him seemed like the most natural thing in the world. As it turned out, we had a lot in common. He liked to listen to the radio, eat out, and dance. We talked about church and a few things going on in the world. All this time, I could hear Otto in the background mumbling to Jubal. And every time I glanced at him from the corner of my eye, he had a puppy dog expression on his face.

"It's getting a little chilly out here."

"You want to borrow my jacket?" he offered.

"No, that's okay. Um . . . do you have a telephone?"

"No. Buying the car set me back so it'll be a while before I can afford a telephone. Do you mind giving me your address?"

Neither one of us had a pencil. I didn't want to ask Jubal for one because I didn't want to make Otto feel even more slighted. "I got a good memory so you can just tell me. You want me to come over tonight?"

I shook my head. "Tomorrow or another evening would be better. Any time after six p.m." As anxious as I was to entertain Boaz at my house, I decided to play it cool and hold him off a day or two. The last thing I wanted him to know was how anxious I was to get to know him.

After I told him my address, he hugged my neck and went to check on his car.

As I was about to leave again, Otto hollered, "Wait up, Leona."

I groaned, but I waited as he trotted up to me. "What is it?" I asked.

"Did Fiona tell you I wanted to take you out?" he panted. I had only been close up to Otto a few times. He was a little better-looking than I thought, but he still didn't interest me. There was food stains on the front of his shirt and breadcrumbs in his lop-sided mustache.

"Um . . . I think she did mention something about that."

"Well, when do you want to go somewhere? We can go to that seafood place I heard you like. After that, we can go to the movies."

"I'm sorry. I'm going to be real busy with somebody else in the next few weeks," I said, hoping it was true.

Otto snorted and glanced toward Boaz. I was glad he had his back turned so he couldn't see me talking to Otto. "I see. Well, when you ain't too busy with 'somebody else,' call me or come see me. You know where I live."

"I'll do that." If something developed between me and Boaz, I wouldn't have to worry about being approached by men like Otto—at least for as long as Boaz stayed with me.

I rushed home feeling warm all over. I got a chill as soon as I got to my block. Bonnie Sue was sitting on my front porch steps waiting for me, just like a spider.

Chapter 33

Leona

"WHERE YOU BEEN, LEONA?"

It had never bothered me when Bonnie Sue grilled me about my whereabouts. But this time it did, especially since she'd used such a gruff tone. "I promised Jubal I'd bring him some chicken wings to eat for lunch, *Mama*," I said with a smirk.

"You ain't got to make fun of me," Bonnie Sue said with her bottom lip poked out like a pouty baby. "I was just asking you a simple question."

"And I was just giving you a simple answer," I said firmly. "Nobody but my mama uses that tone with me."

"I'm sorry. You was at the garage all this time? When I didn't see you inside, I said to myself, 'It ain't like Leona, to be gone over a hour during the day on a Saturday.' I was getting sick from worrying."

My eyebrows shot up. "How do you know I was gone over a hour?"

"Because that's how long I been waiting. I went into your house and sat for a while, and even mopped your kitchen."

"My goodness, Bonnie Sue. I'm a grown woman and can come and go as I please. That's why I moved out of Mama's house."

Bonnie Sue held up both hands. "Calm down now, sugar. I didn't mean no harm. I ain't trying to get into your business. But since I know you so well and didn't see you, I got scared."

She lunged at me and wrapped her arms around my neck. "I'm glad you didn't get hit by a bus or nothing. Anyway, I was at loose ends, so I thought I'd come keep you company for a few hours. You got anything to drink? I sure could use a nip."

I pried her arms from around my neck, opened the door, and motioned for her to sit on the couch. She didn't waste no time kicking off her shoes and propping her feet up on my coffee table. "I had to get out of that house. Them kids and Clayton's mama was driving me up the wall."

"How are the kids?" I stood in the middle of my living-room floor. Bonnie Sue's presence was slightly annoying today, so I wasn't ready to sit too close to her yet.

She closed her eyes and shook her head. "Mighty Moses! My plate is overflowing. All three got colds, but they still eat like pigs at a hog trough. I had to cook two pots of grits this morning. You don't know how lucky you are you ain't got no kids."

"I don't think 'lucky' is the right word. I'd like to think that I'm just late getting started. Mama was old enough to be a grandmother when she had me and Fiona," I said with a sigh. I firmly believed that kids was God's biggest blessing. I was still praying that He would eventually bless me with some—whether I had a husband or not. I loved Bonnie Sue's kids almost as much as I loved my nephew. I kept my opinions to myself, but there was a heap of times I wanted to ask Bonnie Sue how come she spent less time with her kids and more with me. I didn't see the point in asking that question this late in the game, though. And as hard as I tried not to think about what Fiona had said about Bonnie Sue's "obsession" with me, I couldn't get it off my mind.

Bonnie Sue rolled her eyes and said with a huff, "Whatever you say." She paused long enough to let out a cackle that sounded like it was coming from a crow. And then she suddenly softened her tone. "You got anything to drink?"

"Not much. I want to save it for tomorrow."

"Oh? Why do we have to wait until then to drink it?"

I sat down on the arm of my couch. "I might have company in the next day or so."

Bonnie Sue rolled her eyes again. "Here we go again. You and your fly-by-night boyfriends. Whoever this frog-prince is, I hope it ain't that liver-lipped man with the receding hairline you danced with at that new moonshiner's party a couple of weeks ago."

I chuckled and shook my head. "Marvin was a real nice man."

Bonnie Sue's eyes got big. "I bet Marvin's girlfriend in Mobile thinks he is too."

"Well, it ain't him. And I didn't like him enough to invite him to my house anyway. I ran into Boaz at the garage. It's him."

Bonnie Sue looked like I'd tossed a dead bird into her lap. She took her feet off the coffee table and sat up ramrod straight. "You must be kidding, girl."

I shook my head. "How come you never told me him and his wife had moved to Houston, and that she'd died giving birth?"

"I don't tell you everything going on with Clayton's friends. Especially a mangy dog like Boaz."

"He seems like a very nice man. Why would you call him that?"

Bonnie Sue's voice got louder. "Because that's what he is. He got women coming out of his ear—make that *both* ears."

"Oh? He gave me the impression that he ain't involved with nobody right now."

"What do you expect from a wolf in sheep's clothing?"

I gave Bonnie Sue a weary look. "I ain't never had a boyfriend that you liked. Not even Wally and he was the sweetest man I ever met."

"Wally wasn't too bad; I didn't mean mouth him that much. But all of them others you took up with was scoundrels."

I stood up and waved my hands in the air. "I declare, you are beginning to sound like one of the frustrated old women around here who sit on their front porches and complain about everybody and everything. I wouldn't be surprised if you refuse

to come to my wedding—when I do get married." I laughed.
Bonnie Sue didn't.

She narrowed her eyes and told me, "I don't want to see you
get hurt by no man. I've known Boaz for a long time so I know a
lot about him. I don't know if you want to hear some of it,
though . . ."

"I do want to hear it."

Bonnie Sue took a deep breath, sat up straighter, and started
speaking in such a serious tone, it scared me. "Clayton told me
about all the women he fooled around with before his wife died.
And it's no wonder. He can't help hisself. From what Clayton
said, Boaz sounds like a man who been in heat all his life, hop-
ping from one woman's bed to another, like a grasshopper.
He'll keep you in bed so long and often, you'll feel like a invalid.
On top of that, he'll sweet-talk you out of some of your hard-
earned cash, and then he'll take off and leave you in the dust.
I'm telling you, that man will make a fool out of you. Just like he
done all the other women he was with before he got married. I
seen him do it . . ."

What Bonnie Sue had just said was almost funny, but I managed not to laugh. I gave her the most serious look I could manage under the circumstances. "I don't plan on getting too
involved with him too soon. I just want somebody to come over
and keep me company a couple of times a week, and maybe take
me to a restaurant and a movie."

"Ain't that what I been doing for all these years? You can always call me when you want some company or somebody to go
out with."

I'd known Bonnie Sue all my life but I suddenly realized I did-
n't know her as well as I thought I did. I appreciated all the attention she gave me, and I knew she'd still be there for me, no
matter what. But her devotion had turned into something I did-
n't understand or want. "Bonnie Sue, I love you to death and
I'm trying to see things from your point of view, but I'm having
a hard time doing that." I jabbed my chest with my finger and
said in the most gentle way I could, "I'm a woman and I want the

same things other women want. You, Fiona, and almost all of our friend-girls got husbands. Some done had two or three. I don't want to grow old alone. Don't you want me to experience at least one marriage?"

"Yes, I do. And if you ever find the *right* man, I'll be the first person to congratulate you. But I'm telling you, that man ain't Boaz."

Chapter 34

Fiona

Yesterday when Leona got home from Jubal's garage, she called and told me she'd run into Boaz Gibson there. "He seems like such a nice man," she'd gushed. There was times when my poor sister sounded as giddy as a teenager. I believed there was still plenty of fish in the sea, but it was a shame that a good-looking woman in her middle thirties like her was still floundering around so bad, she couldn't hook one.

"I got the impression that he was a nice man when I met him at Bonnie Sue's wedding, but things change over the years, especially men," I replied. "Don't get your hopes up too high about him. He could end up being the husband from hell."

"Husband?" Leona laughed long and loud. "My Lord, girl! I ain't even been on a first date with the man. How did you get from that to him marrying me?"

"Well, I advise you not to beat around the bush. You need to pick his brain and find out what his intentions are as soon as possible. Time is running out."

"You make it sound like I got one foot in the grave. I'm in good health and I feel fine, but do you know something I don't know?"

"You got a heap of years left. But Mama ain't. She keeps complaining to me about you still being single and how she worries about you growing old alone. She said she done asked God to answer one more of her prayers before He calls her to heaven: a husband for you."

As much as I appreciated having a good husband, I was tired of acting like I was the happiest woman in town. It had got to the point where Jubal got on my nerves so bad, I couldn't go on too much longer without doing something about it. I knew it wouldn't do no good to sit him down and tell him how I felt. What would I say to him anyway? Men like him had the impression that as long as a woman had what I had, I didn't have nothing to complain about. He was so wrong. Last week I read a article in the newspaper that shook me up like churned milk. It was about the wife of one of the richest, most beloved white businessmen in Mobile. She had a beautiful house, a nice car, and a closet full of frocks. They was newlyweds, so they hadn't had time to have children. With all the blessings she had, she took one of her husband's hunting rifles one morning while he was at work and blew her brains out. She'd left a note that said something about how unhappy she was with her husband. She was a Catholic and divorce was out of the question, so killing herself was the only way out for her. I didn't care how bad things got for me with Jubal, they'd never be bad enough for me to do something that ghastly. The worst thing I'd ever do was get me a spare man . . .

I let Jubal make love to me last night. For the most part, all I'd done was lay there and gaze at the ceiling, and moan and groan at what I thought was the appropriate times. He was so routine and predictable now, I didn't get no satisfaction at all. We didn't even get naked when we went at it, and our sessions was so tame we didn't even wrinkle up the bedcovers. Back in the old days when I was messing around with Ernest Lee and them other boys, they'd do such a thorough job, the bedcovers would be balled up at the foot of the bed, or on the floor. The times we did it in a cornfield or on the ground in the woods, there'd be broke cornstalks and matted grass all over the place when we finished. I tried not to think about all the passion I'd enjoyed before I got married.

I got up this morning in such a foul mood, I thought it would ease my frustration if I talked to Leona. I called her up when she got home from work and told her what was on my mind. Her response didn't surprise me. "Why don't you talk to Jubal and tell him how you feel?"

"I can't do that! Telling him he don't satisfy me in bed would make him feel like less than a man."

Leona took her time responding. "Have you ever thought that the reason he is the way he is, is because of you?"

I couldn't believe what I was hearing. There was nothing wrong with me! I should have known that a woman with a love life as dismal as Leona's would miss the point and say something crazy. "I do everything a woman is supposed to do in bed with her man."

"So you say." She paused and cleared her throat. The conversation wasn't going the way I thought it would. She was making me feel like I was less than a woman! But I was interested in hearing what else she had to say. She coughed and went on. "A few weeks ago, there was a woman at work who complained about her husband's performance all the time. Come to find out, all she did in bed was lie there and holler. Finally, me and Nadine advised her to be more creative. After all, sex is a two-way-street."

"What did y'all tell her to do in bed?"

"We couldn't tell her what to do. We ain't sex coaches. She had to decide that on her own. You should too. You'd be surprised at what you can come up with by using your imagination. Whatever my coworker did worked, because now she brags about all the fun she's having in bed with her husband."

"Humph! I never had to be 'creative' and use my imagination with my boyfriends before I got married. They did all the work. And they was so good, I didn't need to do nothing extra. Even Ernest Lee knew how to make a woman feel good."

"My advice is for you to *tell* Jubal what you want him to do."

"Huh?"

"If you don't even give him a hint that something ain't working, he probably thinks you're having as much fun as he is."

"Um . . . I'll consider what you just said. But before I do anything, I'll see what Reverend Sweeney has to say. He's a expert on everything."

"Good! You should have asked him for advice in the first place."

I shuddered when I thought about how Jubal would react if I'd tried to do something out of left field, like sit on his face. The way Jake had carried on when I done it to him, I thought any man would enjoy it. I knew that I'd never attempt a episode like that with a man as straitlaced at Jubal. Besides, that trick might be fun for him, but not me.

Sex wasn't the only problem in my marriage. There was other things about Jubal that bothered me. He didn't have much interest in the things I liked to do. Every time he took me to the movies, he went to sleep. The last time he dozed off ten minutes after the movie had started. We was the only colored folks there that evening and like always, we had to sit up in the balcony. He snored so loud, the white folks in the seats on the first floor complained to the manager. I almost died of embarrassment when one of the ushers came and told us that if he didn't pipe down we'd have to leave. He stayed awake for about fifteen minutes and the next thing I knew, he was buzzing like a moose again. I didn't even wait for the usher to come back. I shook Jubal awake and we left halfway into the movie. He didn't like to take long leisurely walks, listen to the dramas on the radio, or eat out as much as I did. I was getting frantic.

I was glad Leona agreed that it'd be a good idea for me to set up some meetings with Reverend Sweeney. He could give me some spiritual guidance that might help me either accept things the way they was, or get Jubal to see things from my point of view and agree to work with me on a solution.

I decided to approach my preacher the following Sunday after the morning service. While Jubal and Mama was roaming around hugging members of our church family, I rushed up to Reverend Sweeney as soon as he was by hisself. I went to church every Sunday unless I was sick. I got tired of hearing the same old stuff and seeing the same people each week, but there was one thing that helped me get through them sermons without going to sleep or sneaking out the door: Reverend Logan Sweeney.

When me and Leona was still in elementary school, Mama made us go to Sunday school every week. Reverend Sweeney had taught the kids in our age group. He had just finished high school and was working at a lumber camp lifting heavy logs all day long, so he had muscles all over his body. I loved to look at them strong features on his copper-colored face. I fantasized about raking my fingers through his thick jet-black hair. My heart still skipped a beat every time I looked at him. Whenever I got close up on him, my face got hot and my knees almost buckled. I was ashamed of myself for having lustful thoughts about a man of the cloth, but I couldn't help it.

"Ahh, Sister Fiona, it's so good to see you," he greeted with a wall-to-wall smile on his face. "I hope you enjoyed Thanksgiving. The Lord has been so bountiful to you and Jubal."

"Uh . . . yeah. And we count our blessings every day," I replied. When I gazed into his brown, almond-shaped eyes, I almost forgot he was a man of God—and a married one at that. I wondered what it would be like to wallow around in bed with such a fine specimen of a man. I shook my head to get rid of the wicked thoughts floating around in it. I didn't want to waste time ogling him or making small talk, so I got straight to the point. "Reverend Sweeney, can I make a appointment to have a private conversation with you as soon as possible?"

"Yes, you may. Your mama mentioned that you might want to help organize our Christmas program." He had a nice deep voice too. When he slid his tongue across his juicy bottom lip, I tingled all over. "But you can talk to anybody on the committee about that."

"I can help with the program, but that ain't what I need to talk to you about."

Reverend Sweeney's smile disappeared and the look on his face got so serious, I almost changed my mind about meeting in private with him. He cleared his throat and gently touched my shoulder. "Well now, Sister Fiona. What can I do for you?"

"I need some spiritual guidance real bad. I'd like to meet with you for half a hour or longer once a week, until I feel fully restored. If Satan don't interfere and slow things down, three or four weeks should be long enough."

"I see. Well, what is causing your problem?"

I looked around to make sure nobody was close enough to hear me before I answered. "It's way too complicated for me to go into now. I'd rather tell you everything when me and you are alone."

He drew in a loud breath and clasped my hand and squeezed it. "All right, then. When would you like to start the sessions? You know I work five days a week as a houseman for Judge Smoot's family. So I'm only available on weekday evenings and some Saturdays. My wife serves supper promptly at six p.m., so it would have to be after that. What's the best time for you to come to the church?"

"I'd rather meet at my house."

"Oh? Is there a particular reason why?"

"I'd feel more comfortable there. Somebody is always lurking around the church."

"That's true. Well, I can come to your house."

"Good. Jubal gets home around six every weekday evening and I never know when he's going to go someplace else. I don't want him to know about this yet. He usually goes to his garage for a little while every Saturday after breakfast and then he goes fishing for a few hours."

"Why don't we get the ball rolling next Saturday. I'll be at your house around noon. If you change your mind or need to reschedule, let me know right away."

"I . . . will." I had to rush away from him because my crotch was starting to itch.

Chapter 35
Leona

WHEN I OPENED MY DOOR AROUND SEVEN P.M. THE SUNDAY AFTER Thanksgiving, I got the surprise of my life. Boaz was standing there holding a bouquet of flowers. I almost busted out crying. He was the first man to bring me flowers. I was glad I was able to stay composed. The last thing I wanted to do was act like a babbling idiot and make him so uncomfortable, he'd end the relationship before it even got started—if that was what he had in mind. As bad as my luck had been in the romance department, I didn't want to flatter myself by assuming he was interested in a long-term relationship with me.

"You didn't have to bring me no flowers," I said as I waved him to my couch.

"Well, I ain't met a woman yet who didn't like a nice mess of flowers to set on her coffee table." He handed me the flowers and kissed me on my jaw at the same time. The touch of his lips sent a shiver up my spine. He took off his jacket and laid it on the arm of the couch. His shirt had short sleeves so I could see how muscular his arms was. I was pleased to see that he didn't have a potbelly like so many other men his age.

"Have a seat while I go get something to put the flowers in." I spun around and headed to the kitchen. Since nobody had ever brought me flowers, I didn't own a vase. I put them in one of the tall canning jars I usually drank moonshine out of. When I went back into the living room and set the flowers on my coffee table, I looked at Boaz and grinned. "I know it looks tacky to put these lovely flowers in a canning jar, but one of my clumsy friends broke my vase," I said.

"I don't think it's tacky at all. You'll laugh your head off when you see my place. I store my flour and meal in old coffee cans." We laughed.

"So, do you want something to drink? I like to keep a small supply of moonshine in the house."

"I stopped drinking right after I got out of the army. It makes a person feel good, but in the long run, it ain't worth the long-term problems it causes."

"That's right. I mainly keep it around for my guests, but I take a nip every now and then. My radio has pretty decent reception this late in the day, so we can listen to a comedy show or some hillbillies playing banjos and blowing on harmonicas."

Boaz laughed and waved his hand. "My radio only gets one station no matter what time of day or night, so all I can listen to at my house is them hillbillies. They sound pretty good." He laughed some more.

I had never felt so comfortable and weak in the knees with a man before. I'd loved Darnell and Wally, but neither one of them ever made me feel the way Boaz did. My stomach was fluttering like a dozen butterflies was flying around in it. He was so charming and easy on the eyes, but if he had been butt-ugly, he still would have impressed me. The way he looked at me with them hazel eyes almost made me freeze solid where I stood. I had to get a grip before I made a complete fool of myself. I sniffed and cleared my throat. "You hungry?"

"Ummm . . . I wouldn't mind gnawing on something."

"I got some of them chicken wings left over from yesterday. Since I get free chickens, I always have a mess on hand."

"You still pluck chickens for a living?"

I raised my eyebrows. "How did you know about my job?"

"Clayton told me, and your sister mentioned it right after I met her."

My eyebrows was still raised and now they was twitching. "Why was you asking about me back then when you still had a wife?"

"I wasn't asking about you. Well, I did ask Bonnie Sue what

you was like after I'd found out you was a twin. She told me all you cared about was drinking and going to parties."

His last comment ruffled my feathers. It was bad enough Bonnie Sue said so many unflattering things about the men in my life, but I didn't like her saying unflattering things about me to them—especially behind my back. "Is that all she told you about me?"

"I didn't ask her to tell me nothing about your personal life, so I was annoyed when she took it upon herself to do so. She was laughing when she spewed all them comments, but I didn't think none of it was funny. I don't like to repeat ugly gossip, so I won't tell you everything she said."

I shook my head and chuckled. "That woman just loves to gossip. I think it's what keeps her ticking."

"You ain't mad at her?"

I waved my hand. "Pffftt! No, I ain't mad. She is the best friend I ever had and always speaks her mind. She wasn't being mean. She was just being honest. That's one thing I look for in a true friend: honesty. Bonnie Sue has been honest and loyal to me since we was kids. I'm lucky to have her as a best friend."

Boaz gave me a dry look and rubbed the back of his head. "Everybody should have a friend like you. I ain't perfect and I'd be lying if I said I ain't never told a lie. But I will say that I treat women with nothing but respect. Even *fishwives* like Bonnie Sue."

I didn't like what he'd called Bonnie Sue, but I could understand why he thought of her like that. He wasn't the only one. Not a single one of the men I'd been involved with liked her. But they always treated her with respect. Despite the harsh demeanor Bonnie Sue showed sometimes, she was a good-hearted, caring woman. "I'm glad you feel that way about her because my relationship with her is very important, so I need her in my life."

"Yeah. Good friends are real important." His tone was so weak, I knew he was saying one thing and thinking another.

"After the tragic life she's had, it's a wonder she ain't lost her mind."

"Uh, let's forget about Bonnie Sue for the rest of the night. Would you like some seafood?" I was so happy Boaz changed the subject.

"Every day!" I hollered. I used a loud tone because it helped clear my mind. I didn't want to think about or discuss Bonnie Sue no more tonight. "We only have one colored-owned seafood restaurant in Lexington so we can go any day of the week. Otherwise, if we went to a white restaurant we'd have to go in and leave through the kitchen door and order our food to go."

Boaz scrunched up his face and shook his head. "I stopped going to white restaurants after one of my white coworkers told me that the folks in some of them kitchens put spit or something else as vile in food that colored folks order."

I blew out a disgusted breath and shook my head. "Let's talk about something else." I was glad he nodded and smiled. "So, what kind of work do you do?" I asked.

"Well, I been working on farms since I was twelve. I had to drop out of school that year to help out at home."

"I didn't finish school neither. And I want you to know up front that I had a little run-in with the law."

"Oh? What did you do?"

I told him about the incident at the dress store and my stint in jail. I felt like a straight-up hypocrite after making such a big deal about honesty. But there was no way I'd ever tell anybody that I'd took the fall for Fiona, and I would never ever tell anybody that we'd been switching places all our lives.

"You ain't the first one to try and steal something. When I was a kid, I used to lift candy every time I went into our main grocery store. I'm glad I came to my senses before I got caught. It's too dangerous to swipe stuff, especially from white stores. Listen, if we want to get a good table, we'd better leave for the restaurant now. I hope you don't mind walking them eight blocks. Jubal is still working on my car."

"I don't mind at all. The bus that comes to this part of town stops running at six p.m., so I have to do a lot of walking anyway."

The moment we walked out my front door, I seen Bonnie Sue prancing toward my house. When she spotted us she did a double take and stopped at the foot of my steps with her hands on her hips.

"Oh no, not *her*," Boaz griped.

"Where y'all going all dressed up like circus clowns?" she asked, looking from me to Boaz with a amused expression on her face. I had on a red cotton dress, my good green coat, and a silver cap that Fiona had knitted for my birthday. Boaz had on a off-white suit, a green jacket, and a white hat with a brown feather hanging off the side. I thought we both looked very sharp. If anybody looked like a clown, it was Bonnie Sue. She had on a loud orange jumper, a lime-green jacket, and a flowered scarf I wouldn't even sleep in.

"Um . . . we was just going over to that fish place to eat supper," I answered.

"Ain't that a coincidence! I came over here to see if you wanted to go there with me this evening. I'll treat you," she chirped. "You too, Boaz."

Before I could say anything else, Boaz held up his hand. "Not this time, sister-woman," he said in a harsh tone. Bonnie Sue took a short, quick breath before she reared her head back and looked at him like she wanted to bite his nose off.

"Maybe me and you can go one evening next week, Bonnie Sue," I said as fast as I could get the words out.

"Yeah, let's do that," she mumbled in a low squeaky tone I'd never heard her use. "I'll see y'all later." She whirled around and started walking back down the street so fast, by the time we made it to the corner, she was out of sight.

Bonnie Sue's name didn't come up no more that night, but she was on my mind. One thing me and her had promised each other when we was teenagers was that we would never put a man before our friendship. I didn't feel so strong about that promise now . . .

Chapter 36
Fiona

LEONA HAD BEEN KEEPING COMPANY WITH BOAZ FOR ALMOST A month. I hadn't seen her as happy as she was now since we was kids.

I was surprised she had agreed to bring him to my house to share our Christmas supper. I didn't tell Mama he was coming, or that Leona was seeing a new man, until Mama got to the house. "Who is this man Leona is bringing to eat with us?" she asked as she helped me set the plates and food on the table. Jubal was in the backyard chopping firewood.

"You didn't know Leona had a new boyfriend?"

Mama huffed out a impatient sigh. "I'm the last person your sister would discuss her love life with these days. With her track record, I'm surprised she's still trying to find somebody to settle down with."

"Mama, Leona wants the same thing every woman wants: a husband, a home, and a family."

"You think I don't know that. But if she ain't found all that by now, her chances of getting it at her age ain't likely."

I shook a spoon in Mama's face. "You was older than she is now when you married Daddy," I reminded.

"That was different. I would even call it a fluke. Before I met Clyde, my luck with men was real weak." Mama sniffed and looked at the table. "I hope this man she's bringing got good table manners."

"I don't think you need to worry about that."

We kept talking as we set all the side dishes onto the table. "I hope this new man is one of Jubal's friends. I'd ball up if she was to latch onto one of them fools she messes around with at them wild parties."

"He knows Jubal, but I wouldn't say they was friends."

Mama folded her arms and stared at me. "You mean she done finally agreed to keep company with Otto?"

I clapped my hands and laughed. "He's the last man Leona would keep company with. Her new friend lives in Branson, but he's a good friend of Clayton's so he comes over here quite a bit."

"Well, I hope this one works out for her. The poor little thing. Maybe God will answer my last prayer after all." Mama took the huge ham off the counter and set it on the table next to the golden-brown baked turkey. The stuffing looked so scrumptious, she dug out a sample with the tip of her finger and gobbled it up before she went on. "If he's a friend of Clayton's and he knows Jubal, I know he can't be no lowlife. Next to Reverend Sweeney, Clayton and Jubal are two of the most honorable colored men we got. What line of work is Leona's new friend in?"

"He makes good money. And Leona said he likes to spend it treating her to movies, taking her to restaurants, bringing her flowers, and whatnot."

Mama covered her mouth with her hand before she spoke again, "Oh, Lord. If he ain't a undertaker or one of the doctors at the clinic and got money to throw around like that, he's a moonshiner! I knew that as much time as she spends around them ungodly creatures, she'd eventually get involved with one. I hope he's sober when he gets here."

"He ain't a undertaker, a doctor, or a moonshiner. And Leona says he don't even drink."

Mama looked surprised. "Oh? I ain't never knew her to keep company with a man who didn't drink. And if he's making good money, he must have a fancy job working for one of them high-falutin white families. Is he a driver or a butler?"

"Um . . . no. He's a field hand."

The way Mama scrunched up her face, you would have thought I'd told her Boaz was a bank robber. "A field hand? Well, I guess that's the best Leona can do now. What do he do when the crops ain't in season?"

"A bunch of things. He drives for the man who owns the farm he works on, and he does handyman chores for the same man and some of his kinfolks."

Mama let out a weary sigh and shook her head. "I hope she don't get serious about this man."

"Why not? You been praying for her to get married."

"Yes, I have. But I never prayed for her to end up with a field hand. Oh, your poor daddy must be rolling over in his grave."

"Mama, you stop that. Give the man a chance. You better be nice to him and don't ask him no questions that'll make him feel bad about being just a field hand."

"Hush up. I know how to act, even in the most trying situations." Mama sighed again and set a huge bowl of potato salad onto the table. The way she cooked and ate, it was a wonder she wasn't as big as a horse. She was slightly overweight, though. "I declare, Otto don't sound so bad now. At least he's got a honorable job."

Leona ended up coming to supper by herself because Boaz's car wouldn't start when he got ready to leave his house. So it was just me, Jubal, Mama, and Leona. Jubal's mama was spending the holiday in Mobile with her boyfriend's family.

During supper, we talked about things related to church and the world. I was surprised Mama didn't mention Boaz. While Jubal was in the bathroom and Mama was in the kitchen putting the leftovers away, I joined Leona on the living-room couch and told her everything Mama had said about Boaz. "Pffftt," she replied with a neck roll and a giggle. "I'm not going to worry about nothing Mama said. I really like this man. And I know that once she gets to know him, she will too. If she don't, I'm still going to see him."

"So, how is he?"

"What do you mean?"

I stared at Leona from the corner of my eye. "You know what I'm talking about."

Leona gazed at me for several seconds before her eyes got big. "He's a world-beater," she whispered. We giggled like school-girls up to no good. "Speaking of sex, what's up with your counseling sessions with Reverend Sweeney?"

I glared at Leona and pressed my fingers against my lips. "Shh! I don't want Mama to hear you use the word 'sex' in the same breath with a preacher's name." I waited a few moments to make sure Mama wasn't lurking nearby. "He's coming over again Monday evening after he eats supper."

"Won't Jubal be home by then?"

"Not this Monday. He's going straight from the garage to take his mama to see her godson in Hartville. That's such a long drive, they plan to check into a motel and spend the night."

I looked forward to my sessions with Reverend Sweeney. I'd only had four, but he said I didn't sound as desperate as I did when he first started counseling me.

The Monday after Christmas, I was looking out my front window when Reverend Sweeney pulled up and parked.

It wasn't easy discussing my sex life with somebody other than Leona—especially my preacher. But I continued to do so. No matter what I told Reverend Sweeney, he quoted something from the Bible and told me to keep praying. I almost laughed the time I told him Jubal sweated too much when he was on top of me. Reverend Sweeney told me to keep a towel nearby so I could wipe him off. And then there was the time I told him Jubal finished way too soon. Reverend Sweeney told me to stop in the middle of the episode and go into the bathroom and stay a few minutes. That way Jubal would fizzle out and have to start all over again. I hadn't tried none of my preacher's techniques because I hadn't let Jubal pester me since I'd started my counseling sessions. I didn't want to tell my preacher that, though.

But I did plan to do everything he told me to do the next time me and Jubal had a intimate encounter.

I opened the door as Reverend Sweeney walked up onto the porch and strolled in. I was already grinning. "Good evening, Reverend Sweeney. Have a seat."

"Bless you, Sister Fiona." He sat down on the couch and set his Bible on the coffee table. I sat down close to him and crossed my legs. When I noticed how glassy his eyes got when he looked at my legs, I uncrossed them. "Well now! You seem very chipper these days. I am pleased to see that you've made so much progress."

I was disappointed to hear him say that. I looked forward to his visits, and going to church wasn't as boring as it used to be. I actually enjoyed listening to his long-winded, repetitious sermons now, and looking at his pretty eyes. "Does that mean you don't think I need no more spiritual guidance?" I crossed my legs again. He looked at them again, but only for a split second this time.

"What do you think? Has your intimate relationship with Jubal improved to your satisfaction?"

"Uh . . . it's improved, but not enough to suit me. So, if you don't mind, can you continue giving me spiritual guidance until I feel more confident? I'd hate to stop seeing you too soon and have a relapse. Then I'd have to start all over again . . ."

"I see. Well, I'd like to keep counseling you for as long as you need me to. My job is very important. One of the most crucial aspects of my commitment to God is to act as a conduit so I can keep you connected to Him. If you feel I haven't completed my task, I have no choice but to continue seeing you."

"The last time me and you was together, I told you I enjoyed being kissed on the lips, but that Jubal only gives me a peck on my jaw these days."

"Hmmm. That's a shame. A juicy woman like you should have her lips kissed on a regular basis."

"That would content me just fine." I didn't mean to close my eyes and swoon, but I did. When I opened my eyes, I was surprised to see Reverend Sweeney gazing at me like I was something good to eat.

"Then let it be," he said in a low tone. The next thing I knew, he hauled off and kissed me, and I didn't try to stop him. When he stuck his tongue in my mouth and slid his hand up under my dress and tugged my bloomers, I didn't try to stop him from doing that neither.

Chapter 37
Leona

BONNIE SUE KNEW JUST ABOUT EVERYBODY'S BUSINESS. SHE WAS the one who told me about Boaz and a woman who occasionally worked at one of the sporting houses in Lexington. "You sure about that?" I asked her. It was three days before New Year's Day.

"As sure as I'm sitting here on this couch with you," she replied. "I heard he was seen sashaying out of that sporting house the day after he took you to supper at the seafood place last month."

I gave Bonnie Sue a curious look. "Who told you that?"

"I don't want to mention no names because if folks found out I blabbed, they would stop telling me stuff."

"Thanks for telling me. I guess I need to get to know Boaz better before I get too committed. I done lived too long to let a man make a fool out of me."

"I feel the same way. Don't forget what I told you Clayton told me about him cheating on his wife." Bonnie Sue bobbed her head like a rooster. "I hope I ain't depressing you."

"Um . . . no, you ain't."

"You look like you just swallowed a nail."

The thought of my man going at it with floozies made my blood run cold, especially floozies who pleasured men for money in a sporting house. There was only two such places in Lexington operated by colored folks. Both was run by rough older women who only cared about pleasing their regular white customers and making money. As unspeakable as it was to work as a prostitute, more and more women I'd grown up with—even a few married ones—went to bed with men for money because they couldn't find other work. Even my own twin had turned a trick. But that was different . . .

Bonnie Sue returned the following night. This time she wasn't alone. Sedella Freeman was with her. Sedella was a heavyset, jolly-looking woman in her late thirties. I used to attend her frequent parties before she got married and had to slow down. Now she only entertained during holidays and on special occasions.

As soon as I gave each one a glass filled with moonshine, they immediately started guzzling. It loosened their lips because within seconds after the first pull, Sedella started repeating some of the same stuff about Boaz that Bonnie Sue had already told me. "I hope you believe us," Sedella said. She was known to be a docile woman who always went with the flow, so I took everything that came out of her mouth with a grain of salt. But she sounded so convincing and concerned. "We women have to look out for one another." The whole time she was talking, Bonnie Sue was beaming and nodding and egging her on. They was sitting on the couch, I was in the chair facing them.

"We are just looking out for you, Leona," Bonnie Sue said.

I felt so let down by Boaz. "Hush up! Y'all don't need to tell me nothing else. I done heard enough," I insisted.

Bonnie Sue continued anyway. "If I was you, I'd drop him like a bad habit. Don't be a fool and keep letting him take advantage of you."

"I ain't going to be a fool for no man. The next time I see him, I'll let him know what I heard!" I fumed.

A scared look crossed Bonnie Sue's face. "You going to tell him who told you?" she wanted to know.

"You better not. He's violent too so there ain't no telling what a brute like him would do to us!" Sedella added with her voice trembling.

"Y'all ain't got to worry about me telling him who told me." I stood up and stretched my arms above my head and yawned. "I need some time by myself so I can think about everything now. Y'all have a blessed evening."

Sedella and Bonnie Sue reluctantly got up and left.

Boaz came over about a hour after Bonnie Sue and Sedella left. Everything they had told me was still ringing in my ears. "You seem jumpy tonight. Is anything wrong?" he asked. He was sitting on the couch. I was in the chair facing him.

"Why do you ask that?"

"Well, for one thing, I'm sitting on the couch and you sitting in that chair. Is there some reason you don't want to sit next to me?"

I took a long breath and then I let the words roll off my tongue, loud and clear. "I heard some unpleasant things about you . . ."

Boaz looked like he was about to laugh. I guess he didn't because I was looking so serious. He cleared his throat and asked, "What did you hear?"

I exhaled and the words oozed out of my mouth in one breath. "Do you fool around with prostitutes and a bunch of other women?"

Boaz looked at me like I had turned green. He gasped so hard it made me gasp. This time he did laugh. And then he clenched his teeth before he asked, "Who told you that?"

"Never mind who told me," I snarled. "Is it true?"

Words shot out of Boaz's mouth like bullets. "No, it ain't true! I ain't never even been near no prostitutes!"

"What about other women?"

"Leona, I'm a man. Of course I've been with other women."

"Even when you was married? Even while you been seeing me?"

"I never cheated on my wife and I ain't been with no other woman since I started courting you." Boaz paused and gave me a hot look. "If you believe all that foolishness and don't trust me, maybe we should end things now."

"I just want you to tell me the truth."

"I did." He heaved out a loud breath and stood up. "I'm a honest man."

"So you say," I hissed.

There was a exasperated look on his face. "You been drinking," he accused.

"I ain't drunk nothing today."

"Then I don't know what's wrong with you. I think the best thing I can do right now is leave."

I stood up too and stabbed him in the chest with my finger. "And don't come back unless you decide to tell me the truth."

Boaz looked at me and shook his head. The next thing I knew, he shuffled over to the door and walked out. Just like that! I couldn't believe how fast he had given up on our relationship. I had expected him to either deny or admit everything, apologize, and then ask me to forgive him. I thought it would be interesting to see him grovel and beg me for another chance to prove how much he loved me. Now he was gone!

I looked out the window and watched until Boaz's raggedy old Buick was out of sight. Two minutes later, Bonnie Sue called me up. "I just seen Boaz's car pass by my house just now. Did he come see you tonight?"

"Yeah. I confronted him and he denied everything."

"What did you expect him to do? What are you going to say the next time he comes over?"

"There won't be no next time."

"You broke up with him?"

"Something like that. I told him not to come back unless he could tell me the truth."

"He won't be coming back then, praise the Lord. He wouldn't know the truth if it jumped up and bit him on his butt. I know you like him and enjoy his company, but if you had decided to keep seeing him anyway, it would have been like you moving into a burning house. I hope you don't blame me and Sedella for y'all breaking up. We was just trying to help."

Chapter 38
Fiona

TODAY HAD BEEN REAL BUSY FOR ME. I GOT UP RIGHT AFTER JUBAL left to go to the garage and started working on the drapes that I had volunteered to make for the church windows. It was going to be a big job because our church had a lot of windows, and the ones in the front was real big. Mama and Reba had picked out the fabric, but Jubal had paid for it.

I worked straight through for four hours before I decided to call it quits for the day. I didn't have no deadline, but when I said I'd do something, I liked to get it done as quick as possible and move on to something else.

Leona had called me up last night just before I went to bed. I could tell right away from her weak voice that something was wrong. She told me that she'd just broke up with Boaz and would come talk to me about it when she was ready. It didn't take long. She stopped by the house on her way home from work on Thursday. I was not surprised when she told me all the things Bonnie Sue and Sedella had told her about Boaz.

"You believed everything they told you?" I asked.

"Why would they lie to me?" Leona was sitting at my kitchen table, tapping her fingers on the top. I was at the counter chopping the celery and carrots that I was going to put in the stew I was making for supper.

I put my knife down and looked at her with my eyes narrowed. "Do you mean to tell me you stopped seeing a man you really like just because a couple of gossips mean-mouthed him? Did it ever cross your mind that they was telling you all that mess because they was jealous?"

"That did cross my mind when I thought more about it. But Bonnie Sue and Sedella are both happily married. Why would they be jealous of me?"

"Leona, I can't answer that. But they was repeating stuff they heard. I can't believe you'd give up on a man because of hearsay without getting some proof."

"I would have but he didn't give me a chance. Once I confronted him, he took off. He didn't even try that hard to convince me it was all lies."

"Well, maybe you shouldn't have said nothing to him about it right away. If you had kept seeing him for another few weeks, he would have slipped up in some way and then you'd have something to go by."

"You're right. Well, it's too late now. I refuse to hunt him down so I can talk to him. But I still think he gave up on me too quick. That's enough to make me wonder just how bad he wanted to be with me. I couldn't believe how fast he jumped the gun!" I was pleased to hear Leona laugh. "Oh, well. I guess I'm back at square one, huh? I know one thing, I don't care what man tries to court me next. I'm going to feed him with a long-handled spoon."

"I keep telling you to give Otto a chance. He's been eye-balling you since his wife left him five years ago. He's got a job making decent money and he owns a house that's almost as nice as ours. A heap of women would be glad to call him their man."

"Not this woman."

"Oh, well. I'm just trying to help."

"Do me a favor and don't try to help me no more. And if you don't mind, I'd rather talk about something else." Leona didn't give me time to come up with a different subject; she did it.

"When was the last time you got a letter from Lamar?"

"I got one last week. He says that the routine is real rigid, but he's glad he joined the service. They'll be shipping him off to

Europe next month. He is really looking forward to being in a place where colored men can eat, drink, and have fun anywhere they want without having to worry about keeping their distance from white folks. He even bragged about how much fun him and the colored soldiers plan on having with them white gals over there."

"I'm happy he's happy. I'll write him in the next day or so." Leona stopped talking and looked around. "Shouldn't Jubal be home by now?"

"Him and Otto had to go to Mobile this evening to pick up some car parts. He probably won't be home for another couple of hours." I seen Leona's face tighten when I mentioned Otto's name again, so I wasn't surprised that she steered the conversation in a new direction.

"How come you all dressed up in one of your cutest dresses? You usually drag around the house in a robe this time of evening, especially when Jubal ain't home."

"Huh? Oh! I felt like dolling up for a change. I do it sometimes when I'm in the house alone."

Leona wiggled her nose. "And you wearing one of your rose-scented smell-goods that you only wear to church and weddings, and when y'all go out. You going somewhere?"

I glanced at the door and started folding and unfolding my arms. "I ain't going nowhere."

Leona gave me a sideways look. "Are you up to no good? If so, you know you don't have to hide nothing from me. There ain't never been no secrets between us."

"You hush up! I ain't up to no good," I protested. As much as I loved and trusted my twin, I was at the age now where I didn't want her to know all of my business. I knew she wouldn't judge me, but there was a thing or two that I wanted to keep to myself that might have embarrassed me if I told her. I glanced at the door again.

Leona cocked her head to the side and looked me up and down. "Your hair looks like you just pressed and curled it . . ."

"I did. Like I said, sometimes when I'm by myself, I like to get dolled up. It makes me feel good about myself. Especially after sitting in the house for hours on end at my sewing machine or with my hands full of knitting items."

Leona sighed and gave me a tight smile. "I bought some new face powder and rouge last Saturday when I went shopping. Maybe I'll go home and doll myself up. It'll probably make me feel better. I might even take a notion and visit Nadine or one of the moonshiners' houses. Some dancing and a drink or two might be just what I need. I'll call you tomorrow evening."

I was glad when Leona decided to leave. Five minutes after she let herself out the door, Reverend Sweeney let hisself in. I darted across the floor and wrapped my arms around him. "When I walked up on your porch and heard Leona's voice a few minutes ago, I got back in my car and parked one street over. I been peeping round a tree all this time. I thought she'd never leave," he told me.

"I'm sorry, sugar. She knows you been coming to the house to counsel me, so don't worry about her." We bypassed the couch and went straight into my bedroom, holding hands like teenagers. He flopped down on the bed and pulled me into his lap. We kissed hard, but too quick for me. "Do that again and longer this time."

I never shut my bedroom door when I was doing my business with the reverend. I needed to be able to hear if somebody walked up on the porch. Nobody I knew locked their doors, so some folks never knocked when they went to visit somebody; they just let themselves in. I kept my bedroom closet door open in case I had to usher Reverend Sweeney into it before somebody made it to my bedroom. "Fiona, since I been counseling you, you seem like a new woman. I hope my visits are making you feel better about your marriage."

"Bless your soul. I am a new woman. I ain't as bored and antsy no more. I got the spirit back into me so deep, I feel like I been reborn."

"Well, that's what rebirth is all about. Some folks don't know the God I know. The mysterious ways Scripture says that He works in, is only mysterious to the ones who ain't reached divinity like me."

"What do you mean?'

"The Bible is not meant to be taken literally. A good preacher can read between the lines. I knew that the way God wanted me to get your life back on track was to restore your physical needs, which would restore your equilibrium to its original state. The devil's got a itching to drive as many God-fearing women, and men, off the deep end by denying them pleasures of the flesh."

"Even with people they ain't married to?"

"Yup. See, marriage is a misleading word. What it really means is the coming together of two like-minded people."

"Then I shouldn't feel guilty about cheating on Jubal, huh?"

"Pffftt!" Reverend Sweeney gave me a dismissive wave. "Why should you feel guilty about a spiritual mission? I sure don't and I been helping restore women's equilibrium for years."

Knowing that I wasn't the first woman he'd "helped" didn't really surprise me. I'd been hearing rumors about him messing around for years, but people gossiped and lied so much, I took it all with a grain of salt. But his last statement gave me a jolt. I'd convinced myself that I was special to him. Well, he still made me feel special (and satisfied). So I decided that since I was "feeding the cow," I was going to "milk the cow" until it ran dry.

"I hope I don't sound too nosy, but I'm going to ask anyway. What other women are you giving spiritual guidance to besides me?"

I knew I shouldn't have asked that question when Reverend Sweeney frowned, something I had only seen him do at church when he was condemning Satan. "It don't matter." When a smile crossed his face, I breathed a sigh of relief. I didn't want to upset him enough so that he would stop counseling me before I felt fully restored. "Why do you need to know?"

"Because I wouldn't want you to mention my name to none of them. All hell would break loose if Jubal ever found out about me and you, not to mention my mama. She thinks I can't do nothing wrong."

"Well, that's true in regard to the bedroom. You ain't done nothing 'wrong' yet." Reverend Sweeney kissed my forehead. "You are a very satisfying woman. I could wallow around in bed with you seven days a week. But to answer your question, you're the only woman I'm counseling right now." He held a finger up to my face. "And you ain't got to worry about me mentioning your name to nobody. I don't kiss and tell. I will never tell nobody about us. One thing I want you to know is that I'm a one-woman man, in a sense. I won't get together with another woman until I've satisfied all of your needs."

I gave Reverend Sweeney a thoughtful look. I knew our relationship couldn't go on forever. I knew I'd have to start weaning myself soon. "Hmmm. It's a good thing I got you to give me a heap of pleasure before you have to move on to the next poor soul. From now on, when I'm with Jubal and things ain't going too good, all I'll have to do is pretend it's you I'm in bed with. I know that'll get me to the finish line."

I never seen a man look so self-satisfied. "Praise the Lord." Reverend Sweeney stretched out in the bed and pulled me on top of him. "Do you want to take off them bloomers yourself, or do I have to do it?"

I giggled. "I ain't going to take them off, so I guess you'll have to do it." The next thing I knew, he flipped me over onto my back and ripped my bloomers off with his *teeth*. I giggled harder and louder before I whispered in his ear, "Take your time. Jubal won't be home for hours. I want to savor every second of your visit." I giggled some more when he climbed on top of me.

Chapter 39
Leona

*I*COULDN'T STOP THINKING ABOUT HOW JUMPY FIONA HAD BEHAVED when I stopped by her house this evening. And she seemed anxious to get rid of me. I wasn't going to get worked up over that, though. What my sister did was her business—unless she dragged me into it.

Sedella was having a New Year's Eve party and she'd invited me the day after Christmas. I told her I'd think about it. She had recently got a telephone installed, so she called me for the first time on New Year's Eve to invite me again. "I got musicians coming all the way from Mobile," she gushed. "And a few folks from Mobile and Branson are coming. They'll all probably bring a friend or two, so my party will be a humdinger."

"I'm tempted, but I'm going to stay home this year."

"All right, then. You must be one of the best dancers I know, so the men will be disappointed if you don't come." Sedella sounded disappointed, but I was not going to change my mind. "Well then, who do you plan to ring in the New Year with?"

"Me, myself, and I."

"You still got Boaz on your mind, ain't you?"

I sighed. "Sedella, I ain't never cared about a man like I did him. He was one of a kind."

"He sure was. But you done the right thing by dropping him. You wouldn't believe how mad Bonnie Sue would get when his name came up. She even said she hated him so much that she wished he'd fall off a truck and die, or that some maniac would kill him."

A chill went up my spine, but I ignored it. I let out a dry laugh. "I wouldn't worry about that. Bonnie Sue likes to run her mouth, but she would never hurt a fly. That was just her emotions talking. I'm the closest friend-girl she ever had, so I ain't surprised she feels the way she do."

I knew Bonnie Sue was still bitter about the way fate had treated her by taking away so many of her loved ones. But I couldn't believe that a woman who'd had so much death in her life would seriously wish it on somebody else.

On New Year's Day, which was a Friday, a man named Quincy Blackburn Jr. came to my house around 5 p.m. Me and him often ended up at some of the same parties and I'd danced with him a lot. But he'd never showed no romantic interest in me. It was just as well because he wasn't my type. And he was married. "What are you doing here?" I asked as soon as I opened the door and motioned for him to come in. Before answering me, he plopped down onto my couch. I stood in the middle of the floor with my hands on my hips.

"I thought you'd be at Sedella's party last night. I was hoping to see you."

I shrugged. "She invited me, but I decided to stay home." I tilted my head and narrowed my eyes. "Does your wife know where you at?"

Quincy dropped his head. "She took off last month while I was at work. I knew she wasn't happy, so I wasn't surprised. She left a note stuck to the kitchen wall and told me she never wanted to see me again. She didn't say where she was going, but I heard from one of her sisters that she was in New York." When Quincy looked back up at me, I could see tears in his eyes. He sniffed and rubbed his nose. He was a tall, slender man in his middle forties, but his cute coffee-colored baby face made him look much younger. I wondered what made his wife leave a prize like him, but I didn't care enough to ask.

"Oh. I hadn't heard about your wife."

His voice cracked when he spoke again. "You mean Bonnie Sue or one of them other gossips ain't told you?"

I shook my head. "Um . . . I was fixing to put away my laundry. After I do that, I might go visit my mama. You ain't told me why you came to my house."

Quincy cleared his throat and scratched the side of his head. "I heard you had broke up with Boaz and I didn't want to wait until somebody else snatched you up. I decided to strike while the iron is hot."

I thought his last comment was corny and a waste of his time as well as mine. "You asking me for a date?" I asked dumbly.

"You ain't deaf."

I laughed, which was something I hadn't done much of since I gave Boaz his walking papers. I shook my head. "I thought I'd take a break from dating for a while. But we can still be friends. I'm sure I'll be seeing you at another party soon. I like dancing with you."

"All right, then. Can I give you my telephone number in case you want me to come back before I run into you at a party?"

I shrugged. "Yeah, you can give it to me."

"You going to call me up?"

I pursed my lips and gave Quincy a dry look. "I might and I might not." And then I winked at him.

He grinned. "That's good enough for me."

I tore a piece of paper off a grocery store bag I'd left on my coffee table and wrote down his number. He left right after that.

I wondered if it would be worth my time to start up a relationship with Quincy, even a casual one. When Fiona came over half a hour after he'd left, I told her about him. We conversated while I washed a few dishes. Fiona sat at my kitchen table, finishing up a tea cake I'd left on a saucer.

"Quincy would make you a nice boyfriend," she said as she dabbed crumbs off her chin. "But I would think long and hard before getting too involved with him. Nadine told me at church this morning that his wife is already calling folks back here from New York to tell them she wish she hadn't left him."

I laid the dishrag on the counter and sat down in the chair across from Fiona. "Oh? Is that a fact? Well, I don't like him enough to get that serious. If I do decide to see him, I'll let him know that from the get-go. Besides, I don't think I could be happy with another woman's leftovers."

Fiona looked at me like I had turned blue. "Girl, unless you meet a male angel that fell from the sky, *every* man is some woman's leftovers."

I gave her a thoughtful look. "You're right. I didn't think before I spoke." I laughed. "So, how was the New Year's Day celebration at church today?"

"It was wonderful." A dreamy-eyed look crossed Fiona's face as she rubbed her bosom. "I can't wait to go back."

I was confused because she'd been complaining about how boring and routine church had become over the years. "What's going on over there now to make you swoon like that?"

"Huh? I ain't swooning. The reason I enjoyed today's service so much is because Reverend Sweeney preached like he ain't never preached before. Ten women got the spirit and shouted so hard their floppy hats, eyeglasses, and shoes went flying everywhere."

"Is that so? Maybe I'll go to church next Sunday." I gave Fiona a tight smile and said something I had never said about a man of God. "A man as handsome as Reverend Logan Sweeney ought to be served on a silver platter. The older he gets, the more scrumptious he looks, right?"

"Uh . . . right."

Fiona suddenly changed the subject and started talking about the drapes she was making for the church, some new recipes somebody had gave her, and a bunch of other mundane things. My boredom level had rose so high since Fiona walked in the door, I was glad when she left.

Monday evening when I got off work, I decided to go pick up a few groceries. The holidays was over so the market wouldn't be too crowded. Even though the buses provided service to the colored part of town now, I still liked to walk to certain places. The weather was chilly so by the time I got halfway to the market, which was eight blocks from my house, I wished I had got on the bus.

I was a block away from the market when I seen something that made me stop dead in my tracks: Boaz. Him and a real pretty woman with light skin and long brown hair was walking out of the market. Each one was holding a large bag of groceries. I hid behind a tree so they wouldn't see me. I was not surprised to see that rascal hadn't wasted no time replacing me. And the female he was with was young enough to be his daughter.

I changed my mind about picking up some groceries and headed back to my house with my jaws twitching. When I got home, before I even took off my scarf and jacket, I dialed Quincy's number. He didn't answer, but I planned to keep calling until I reached him.

As if on cue, Bonnie Sue let herself in and headed to the couch where I had already stretched out with one of my mail-order catalogues. After she greeted me with a wave and a grin, I sat up so she could sit down. "Did you go out New Year's Eve?" she asked.

"No."

"That's a damn shame. I had a ball. Clayton invited a bunch of folks over who work for the railroad company too. I was going to invite you until Clayton told me Boaz was going to be there."

"I probably wouldn't have come anyway. I went to enough parties during the year, so I decided to stay home this New Year's Eve and get some rest."

"Tell me about it. You need to keep resting because you still look tired to me." Bonnie Sue glanced around. "Do you want me to do anything around the house? Laundry, ironing?"

"I got my laundry and ironing caught up. And I spent the day mopping and dusting."

"How about some supper then? What do you have in your ice-box that wouldn't take too long for me to cook?" Bonnie Sue's concern and her comforting tone was so uplifting.

"You don't have to do that, Bonnie Sue. I'm fine. I might be going out to eat later this evening."

Her demeanor changed in a split second. "Oh? With who?" she asked in a loud, gruff tone.

She just blinked when I told her about Quincy. "But I ain't about to jump into another serious relationship anytime soon. I just thought I'd go out with him a few times."

"Well, he ain't as big a dog as Boaz. But you're right not to want to get serious with him. It's just a matter of time before his wife comes back."

I exhaled. "I know you don't like Boaz, but I really cared about that man. And I am sorry things didn't work out with me and him. I think he would have made me a good husband."

Bonnie Sue reared back and looked at me like I was speaking Greek. "Pfftt! Girl, Boaz would never marry a woman like you . . ."

"What's that supposed to mean? He liked me enough to date me."

"That's because he wanted some poontang."

"Well, he's a healthy man so that don't surprise me. But why do you think he would never marry a woman like me?"

Bonnie Sue dropped her head and then she gave me a look that made me feel like I had been whupped with a ugly stick. "I didn't want to tell you, but I heard him talking to Clayton one day when they didn't know I was in the next room."

"Did Boaz say something mean about me?"

Bonnie Sue nodded. "I didn't hear the whole conversation, but he said you was a sweet piece of tail, but he wanted to marry a woman young enough to give him some children."

"I'm still in my thirties! I got a heap of years left to have chil-dren."

"I declare, some women's baby-making days have ended by the time they reach our age. And another thing, I told you he likes redbones. He would never marry a woman who is darker than a paper bag like you." Bonnie Sue paused and looked at me from the corner of her eye. "The bottom line is, he was using you for your body."

"It don't matter now." I scratched the side of my aching head. "But I will tell you one thing, I used his body as much as he used mine and it sure felt good." I laughed and that felt good too.

Chapter 40
Leona

I CALLED QUINCY'S NUMBER AGAIN RIGHT AFTER BONNIE SUE'S hour-long visit and this time he answered. "This is Leona. Do you want to come over and have supper with me this evening? I'm cooking pig ears, collard greens, corn, yams, and hot-water corn bread." I was talking so fast, I had to pause and catch my breath. "I got a new checkerboard so we can play a few games after we eat."

"Hmmm. I could sure go for some pig ears." He smacked his lips "That's my favorite delicacy. And I love checkers. What time do you want me to be there and do you want me to bring something?"

"You can come around seven and you don't have to bring nothing." I was not too excited about Quincy coming, but I didn't want to go out and I just wanted somebody to kill time with tonight.

Quincy arrived right on time. Within seconds after he walked through my front door, he started groping me. "You stop that!" I scolded as I pushed him away. "You came to eat supper and play checkers."

"I did. But I thought we'd start with dessert," he growled. He plopped down on the couch and looked at me like I was a slice of cake.

I didn't want to sit close enough for him to reach me, so I sat in the chair across from him. But he sprung up and came at me again. This time he had his lips puckered and was unbuckling his belt. "Quincy, I don't know what you had in mind, but if it's what I think it is, you came to the wrong place."

He stood back on his legs and gave me the harshest look a man ever gave me. "Look, lady. I used to run around with Ernest Lee back when he was fooling around with you. He told me you was as hot as cayenne pepper, so don't be playing like a prissy little virgin now—especially at your age. And I know how buck-wild you used to get with Wally before he died in that car wreck."

"Ernest Lee was my boyfriend." I never thought that Fiona's fooling around with Ernest Lee would come back to haunt me. "Me and Wally was engaged to be married. What I done with them ain't got nothing—"

He cut me off. "You can't invite me over here and not expect to show me a good time."

I threw up my hands and headed for the kitchen. "I think it would be better for you to leave." He followed so close behind me, I could feel his hot breath on the back of my neck.

Before I knew what he was doing, he grabbed me by my shoulders and spun me around to face him. "Do you think I came over here just for some pig ears and greens and to play checkers?"

"That was the idea. Now you take your hands off me." I pried his hands off my shoulders and shook my finger in his face. "Get out of here before somebody gets hurt."

"I'll leave, but I ain't going no place until I get what I came for. You can't tease a man and get away with it, BITCH!"

The last time a man called me such a disrespectful name, I bounced a brick off his head. I was a lot younger and in better shape when that happened, but I was still feisty enough to defend myself. I didn't have no bricks handy this time, so I had to use one of the frying pans I'd set on the counter. I batted the side of Quincy's head so hard, the handle broke.

He screamed bloody murder and stumbled back until he hit the wall so hard a calendar I had tacked on it fell.

"Woman, what's the matter with you? You just tried to kill

me!" Blood was sliding down his face and a large ugly black-and-purple bruise had formed where I'd hit him.

"The next time you call me out my name, I ain't going to *try* to kill. I will kill you. Now you get your tail up out of my house!"

He rebuckled his belt and gave me such a hot look I could almost feel his heat. "You lucky I am a God-fearing man. If I wasn't, I'd beat the dog shit out of you."

I grabbed another frying pan and started moving toward him. He scrambled to the door so fast, he almost fell.

I immediately called up Fiona and told her what had happened. "If I was you, I'd give up on men for a while." We chuckled.

I didn't go straight home after work on Tuesday. I went back to the market to pick up the groceries that I had meant to buy yesterday when I seen Boaz with that young pretty girl. I was horrified when I bumped into him in the produce section. He seen me this time so I couldn't hide. "Hello, Leona," he said in that husky voice of his.

"Hello," I muttered, barely moving my lips.

"It's good to see you again. You're looking well."

"You too." I looked around. "You come here by yourself today?"

"Yeah. The last time I came here was because my niece dragged me along to help her pick out a good chicken to cook for her fiancé's supper. They just moved over here from Branson last week because he got hired at the turpentine mill. Anyway, I forgot to get something, so here I am again." He chuckled. "Too bad me and you ain't still together. I could have had you give me one of them chickens you bring home from work to give to my niece."

"Yeah, you could have." I shifted my weight from one foot to the other.

"I ain't going to hold you up. I just came to pick up some onions to go with the supper my niece is cooking for my birthday this evening." He held up a bag of yellow onions.

"Today's your birthday?"

"Yup. Thirty-nine years young, and I don't care who knows it."

"That ain't old. I'll be thirty-six in June."

"You don't look a day over twenty-five. It was nice seeing you."

Boaz gently patted my shoulder and turned to leave. "Wait! Before you go, I need to ask you something."

He gave me a puzzled look and hunched his shoulders. "Ask me."

"Did you ever tell anybody I was too old for you?"

His eyes got big and he looked at me like I'd lost my mind. "Excuse me?"

"And is it true that you will only marry a light-skinned woman?"

The way Boaz was staring at me with such disbelief on his face, I wished I could disappear into thin air. I felt like a complete fool for asking him such odd questions. "Who told you that?"

"It don't matter now. I'm just curious."

"I ain't never said you was too old for me, or that I would only marry a light-skinned woman. I don't know who is feeding you all this mess, but whoever it is, you need to cut them out of your life. Just tell me this, was it the same person who told you they seen me with a prostitute and that I cheated on my wife?"

"Like I said, it don't matter."

"All right, then. If this person or persons mean-mouths me again, tell them I said go to hell. Now you have a blessed day." Boaz whirled around and rushed to go pay for his onions without looking back.

I got what I came for and went home, feeling lower than a worm's belly.

Bonnie Sue was sitting on my living-room couch when I walked in the house. Before I could even say anything she leaped up and followed me into the kitchen. "Guess what, Leona?"

"I'm scared to ask," I said as I set my groceries on the counter.

"Quincy's wife came back to town yesterday. He picked her up at the train station. Clayton told me that he unloaded so many suitcases for her, it's plain as day that she came back to stay. See there. Ain't you glad you didn't get too involved with Quincy?"

I shook my head. "I wouldn't have got too involved with him, so I don't care that his wife is back." I told Bonnie Sue about the altercation I'd had with Quincy.

"Too bad that frying pan broke. Now you got to go out and buy a new one."

I decided not to mention running into Boaz at the market. For the first time in years, I didn't want Bonnie Sue to leave so soon. "You want to spend the night?"

"Not tonight. Clayton is taking me to the movies." She glanced at the clock on my kitchen wall. "Look at the time. I better run."

When my telephone rang, I figured it was either Mama or Fiona. I hadn't talked to Mama since New Year's Day and I had promised to bring her a chicken this week. When I heard Boaz's voice, my knees almost buckled. "Leona, I just wanted to say a few more things."

"Where you at?" I asked.

"I'm still at my niece's house."

"Oh. So, what's the couple of more things you want to say?"

"I really care about you and I'm sorry things didn't work out. If I ever do get married, I'd be proud to have a woman like you. Of all the women I ever met, I enjoyed your company the most. I wish you all the best and I hope we can still be friends."

"Yeah, we can still be friends."

"That's all I wanted to say. Bye."

He hung up before I could say another word.

Chapter 41
Fiona

*R*EVEREND SWEENEY WAS DOING SO MUCH FOR MY MORALE, I thought about him day and night. When we started up, he was only supposed to come see me once a week. Now he came two or three times a week, once he came twice in the same day! But the first few months in the year was his busiest. He had evening and weekend meetings with the deacons, the charity committee that I was on, and he had to approve so many things that the congregation had come up with. He had his wife and kids to spend time with too, and I admired him for not neglecting that responsibility. I didn't expect to see him as often as I wanted to until things slowed down for him.

But just being in his presence pacified me when he couldn't come see me. So, after church on the last Sunday in January, I joined the rest of the folks who had lined up to thank Reverend Sweeney for such a beautiful service. I tried my best not to get too close to Mama or Jubal. From the corner of my eye, I seen him talking to Otto and the woman he had recently started courting. But the man in front of me had let Mama cut the line to be closer to me. "Fiona, you and Jubal want to come have supper with me this evening? I'm cooking spoon bread, turnip greens, pig feet, potato salad, and peach cobbler," she said with a wide smile on her face and her eyes shining like new pennies.

"My mouth is watering, but no thanks."

Her eyebrows rose up. "Y'all got something better to do?"

"Jubal is leaving church early so he can go to Mobile and visit one of his army buddies that had a mild stroke a few days ago. He don't want to do that hour-long drive back home at night, so he's going to get a motel room and stay over. And I feel one of my headaches coming on, so I'd better go home and take a pill and lay down." I scrunched up my face and rubbed the back of my head.

"All right, sugar. I hope you feel better. Call me if you need me."

"I will, Mama. I'm sorry you have to eat all that good food alone."

"Oh, I ain't going to eat alone. Reverend Sweeney will be joining me. I asked him before the service started today. Bless his heart. I'm so glad you asked him to give you some one-on-one spiritual guidance. He'll straighten you out."

I had told Mama about my meetings the same time I told Jubal, which was the second week after Reverend Sweeney's first visit. They knew I'd been down in the dumps lately, so they was very supportive. Jubal even volunteered to attend a few sessions with me, if I wanted him to. I told him I didn't. I wasn't embarrassed or ashamed for people to know that my marriage needed a little boost. It was no secret that a heap of our church family often turned to our preacher when they needed a spiritual shot in the arm.

"Um . . . if I feel better by the time you serve supper, I might swing by there."

"I hope you can make it, baby. I'm sure the good reverend would enjoy your company. And so will Sister Sweeney."

I gulped. Zula Mae Sweeney was a ordinary-looking little woman who was as meek and quiet as a mouse. I couldn't for the life of me figure out what made a hot-natured man like Reverend Logan Sweeney marry her. But she was the kind of wife every man wanted. She treated him like he was gold-plated and had gave him five beautiful children. I turned around and seen Zula Mae standing by the wall conversating with Jake Hickey. I couldn't imagine what that nasty buzzard was saying to make her laugh so much. I was glad the line was moving fast. I wanted to get out of Dodge before Zula Mae came up to me. I had never been involved with another woman's husband before, and I didn't like being "the other woman." Especially when I had to be around the wife every time I went to church, and at the market or some other place that we both shopped at. I had been able to avoid her since I started fooling around with her husband so far. Just seeing her today made me nervous. What if she caught up with me before I could escape? Would I say or do something that would make her suspicious of me? I wondered. My face burned just thinking about such a thing happening. I scolded myself for having such thoughts. There was no way I'd go to Mama's house for supper and be around Sister Sweeney, grinning in her face. "All right, then, Mama. If I don't make it, save me some of that spoon bread and I'll send Jubal to get it," I muttered.

Mama said a few words to Reverend Sweeney, hugged his neck, and told him what time to come for supper.

By the time I got up to him, my knees felt like jelly. "Happy Sunday, Sister Fiona. Bless your heart. Your presence is always a pleasure," Reverend Sweeney said as he grabbed my hand and squeezed it. Just looking into his sexy eyes and feeling his hand on mine made my coochie itch. He must have been reading my mind because he winked at me.

The woman behind me was a few feet away, so I thought it was safe enough for me to whisper to him, "Can you come see me after you leave my mama's house this evening?"

"You betcha! I'll be there with bells on," he whispered back. And then he spoke in his normal tone of voice. "Sister Fiona, I hope to see you again before I leave for my six-week retreat in Montgomery."

I froze. I couldn't believe my ears! What retreat? This was news to me. The thought of not seeing Reverend Sweeney for six weeks almost made my knees buckle. I tried to play it off. "Yes, the retreat. I hope to see you before you leave too."

When I got home, I started pacing around the living room like a tiger in a cage. Every few seconds I looked at the clock on the wall. It was almost eight o'clock when Reverend Sweeney showed up. "Get in here!" I ordered as I pulled him into the house by his hand. "What's this I hear about you going away for a six-week long retreat?"

"I was going to tell you the next time we got together. It just came up a couple of days ago. Deacon Hancock will be filling in until I return. It's been more than two years since I visited Montgomery, and even longer since I participated in a retreat." He shook his head and swooned as if the Lord hisself had suddenly appeared. "It'll be a monumental refreshment for my ever-evolving spiritual leadership. One thing my relationship with God has taught me is that every preacher, no matter how long he's been preaching, is a work in progress. I'll still be learning how to spread the Lord's message until the day I die."

"Yeah, yeah," I said in a dry tone. "When are you leaving?"

"I'll be riding with Brother Sibley so I'm not sure what day he wants to leave."

"Will you be able to see me before you leave? I . . . I was making such good progress, several people have commented on how mellow I am these days. I'd hate to disrupt my counseling now and backslide to square one. If that was to happen, I'd have to start the sessions all over again . . ."

"Sister Fiona, you done made so much progress, you will never fall back that far. Even if I don't counsel you for six months." He gave me a quick peck on my cheek and rubbed his hands together. "I declare, my back is still aching from the last time I seen you!" There was a sheepish grin on his face as he nodded toward my bedroom. "We got time to do a little business? I'm hotter than a six-shooter."

I felt a little better about him going away for all them weeks, knowing that his desire for me hadn't waned. I just hoped he'd still have it when he returned. "Yeah. Jubal plans to spend the night in Mobile. What about your wife? Is she still at Mama's house?"

"Pffftt! Don't worry about Zula Mae."

"Look, I know she's got a blind eye, but I do worry about her getting suspicious."

"She ain't got just 'a blind eye.' She's blind in one eye and can't see out the other. She sees what I tell her to see and will do whatever I tell her to do."

"Did you take her home?"

"Yup. I got socks and shirts for her to mend, and she needs to be there to look after them kids."

"Oh. She seems like such a good wife."

"She is. I'm lucky to have a saintly, obedient woman like her. I can do anything I want and not have to worry about her snooping into my business."

For the first time, I felt a little guilty about what I was doing with Zula Mae's husband. I promised myself that when our relationship ended, I'd never get involved with another married man, or a preacher. I didn't feel guilty for long. When Reverend Sweeney put his arm around my shoulder and ushered me to my bedroom, I giggled and groped him all the way.

Chapter 42

Leona

I HAD CALLED FIONA A COUPLE OF TIMES SINCE OUR LAST CONVERSATION, but she hadn't answered her phone. She had told me that Jubal was going to go to Mobile to visit a sick friend today and wouldn't come back until sometime on Monday. I called her house again a few minutes before 9 p.m., nobody answered the telephone. When I called again a hour later, she answered. "Hello," she chirped, sounding like she didn't have a care in the world.

"I been calling and calling. Where was you?"

"Uh . . . I been running around doing all kinds of stuff. Jubal forgot to chop some firewood before he left, so I had to do that. That took quite a while because I ain't too handy with a ax. I was in church all morning and part of the afternoon."

"Oh. Well, how was church?"

"Same old, same old. You wouldn't believe some of the outfits I seen today. Loud-colored, floor-length dresses, hats that looked like the lard can lids, and blouses covered in flowers, stripes, and great big polka dots."

"That don't sound no different from any other Sunday. Well, I hope you enjoyed Reverend Sweeney's sermon."

"I did. He works better on me than a tonic."

"I feel the same way," was all I said. And then I turned the conversation into a different direction. "I been thinking that maybe

I should consider leaving Alabama and move to a place where nobody knows me."

Fiona gulped. "Say what? You can't do that!"

I was as nonchalant as I could be. "I can do whatever I want."

"What about me? We belong to the same package. If you was to leave here, you'd be leaving half of yourself behind. Why would you want to move and start all over in a strange place where you don't know nobody?"

"Because life in Lexington, Alabama, ain't working for me. I got a despicable job and all of my relationships with men fizzle out. The Klan and other racists are lynching our boys and men, left and right. The law don't protect us and will abuse us as quick as the Klan! If this is all I have to look forward to for the rest of my life, why would I want to continue living here?"

"Don't blame the place, Leona."

"What should I blame?"

"One thing Mama always told us is that you can't run away from your problems. They'll be waiting for you no matter where you go."

"Not everything. If I moved to a state in the North, I wouldn't have to deal with segregation. Before I leave this earth, I'd like to know what it's like to eat, live, and shop anywhere I want. If I was a man, I'd join the military and beg them to ship me to Europe where I can do them things."

"Segregation is all we know, but things have changed a little so we don't have to deal with peckerwoods as much as we used to. We got a few restaurants and other businesses of our own, and our neighborhoods are clean and safe. Segregation is the law down here, but it's a unspoken law up North. Jubal got some cousins that moved to Detroit and Boston. They told him that some of the white businesses up there always find underhanded ways not to serve colored folks. So you wouldn't be getting away from Jim Crow rules by moving to the North."

"It still ain't as bad as the white businesses down here. At least I'd be able to get medical assistance at a full-service hospital if I needed it. And if I move to a big city where they got more colored men, I'd have a better chance of finding a husband. I want to see what it's like to have a nice home and a husband and some children. I'd be a fool to think now that I'd get to have that if I stayed in this hick town. The eligible colored men here want to marry real young women. The last four weddings I went to, the men was in their mid or late thirties. They all married teenagers. The last bride was only *fourteen*."

"Well, there are some men here old enough that you'd be a young woman to them. Remember Larry Wheeler, the widower man who works in the kitchen at the Fourth Street Café?"

"Fiona, I'm scandalized! That man's got one foot and a big toe in the grave. His *granddaughter* is old enough to be our mama. I'd rather settle for a slimy devil like Jake Hickey. At least he's still got some gas in his tank. I ain't ready to give up sex just yet."

"Don't make no plans to leave here anytime soon. We need to talk about this a heap more. Think about Mama. If you was to take off, she'd worry about you day and night for the rest of her life. I'll pray for you and you need to pray harder yourself. With God's help, you'll eventually get what you want."

"That's easy for you to say. You got married, moved into a lovely house, and gave birth to a wonderful son, all while you was still in your teens. I'm getting close to middle age and I ain't got nary one of them things. I know Jubal is as dull as a butter knife and you want more excitement in your life, but if I could, I'd trade places with you."

I heard Fiona suck in a deep breath. "You would?"

"In a heartbeat."

She took her time responding. "Hmmm. I think I might know of a way to kill two birds with one stone. It'll benefit us both."

"Whatever it is, you need to tell me and fast. We—I—ain't getting no younger."

"Can you come over? I don't want to discuss it over the telephone."

Fiona was breathing so hard on her end I didn't know what to think. "Look, if you cooking up something that ain't legal and *I* could end up in jail again, leave me out of it."

"Humph! After that dress store thing, I been a law-abiding woman. So what could I be cooking up illegal?"

"There ain't no telling."

"Hush up. What I got up my sleeve is the perfect solution to both our problems. Get over here as fast as you can. I want to discuss this while Jubal ain't in the house."

Chapter 43

Fiona

FIVE MINUTES AFTER I GOT OFF THE TELEPHONE WITH LEONA, I PUT on my nightgown and plopped down on the couch. I picked up a catalogue to kill time until she arrived. I was so anxious to tell her what was on my mind, I could barely sit still. When I heard the door open, I thought it was her. It was Jubal.

I leaped up and folded my arms. "What you doing here?" I hollered.

He gave me a confused look. "I live here," he replied with a smirk.

"I thought you was going to visit your friend in Mobile."

"I did. Right after I got to his house, he took a turn for the worse and slipped into a coma. I drove him and his wife to the clinic so she could have him admitted."

"Oh. Well, I hope he gets better. There is some smothered chicken and pinto beans in the icebox."

"I ain't hungry. I picked up some baloney and crackers on my way home." Jubal dropped his jacket onto the back of the couch before he eased down and took off his heavy black clodhoppers.

"Don't you leave them clodhoppers, dropping all that clumped-up dirt onto my clean floor. I just swept."

"Baby, I'm tired. I'll clean up the dirt before I go to bed," he whined.

I pointed toward the kitchen. "Take them shoes out to the backyard and scrape the bottoms real good. Take a bucket and a rag with you so you can spit-clean them."

"What's the matter with you? I leave my shoes in this same spot all the time."

"I got company coming in a few minutes."

Jubal sat up straighter. "Oh? Who?"

"Leona is on her way."

"Leona? Pfftt!" He gave me a dismissive wave and snickered. "Woman, the way you carrying on, I thought maybe Reverend Sweeney or one of the deacons was coming. Leona ain't 'company' in this house."

"She is to me so you take them shoes and go in the backyard and clean them. Now git!"

"All right, then. It's a good thing for you that I'm too tired to fuss." He laughed. He was such a jovial man, he usually laughed when I fussed at him.

I was a lucky woman. I thanked the Lord every day for sending Jubal to me. He had the kind of patience I'd only read about in the Bible. In all the years we had been together, he had never said or done nothing the least bit mean to me or Lamar. Not even the time Lamar borrowed the car without his permission and went joyriding with some of his friends and hit a deer. Jubal was so happy that none of the kids got hurt, he didn't even scold Lamar. I knew my limitations with him, so there was a few things I did that I never let him know about. Slipping money to Leona when she needed it was one. And I shuddered when I thought about what he'd do if he ever found out about me and Reverend Sweeney. "Jubal, I really appreciate you. When God created you, he threw away the mold. You are one of a kind and I feel so blessed to be your wife."

He looked at me with so much love and admiration in his eyes, I should have kissed him all over. I didn't because I didn't want to tamper with his ego. It was at a adequate level, so I never had to worry about him behaving cocky and throwing his weight around. Shoot. I stroked his ego enough just by being a good wife. "I feel the same way about you, sugar." I could see that he was getting uncomfortable because he was blinking and scratching the side of his head, and not looking me in the eye. I figured he felt that way because I rarely praised him. "While I'm in the backyard, I'll chop some more firewood, so I'll be out there for a while."

"Okay, sugar pie." A few minutes later, Leona stumbled through the door. "What took you so long?" We sat down on the couch.

"Bonnie Sue and Sedella was at the house. Sedella's husband called to tell her one of her sisters was raiding her icebox and he couldn't get her to stop, so she took off. Bonnie Sue stayed but by then I was so impatient, I just told her I had somewhere to go."

"Did you tell her where you was going?"

"No. If she knew I was coming over here she probably would have followed me."

I heard the kitchen door open and slam shut. "Don't say nothing that'll make Jubal want to stick around. If you do, he'll sit here and talk your head off," I warned.

After Jubal and Leona greeted each other, he gave me a weary look. "Fiona, I'm more tired than I thought. And that lamp wouldn't stay lit, so I couldn't see what I was doing out there in the dark. I'll clean off my shoes and chop some wood before I go to work tomorrow morning. I'm going to take a quick washup and get in bed. Good night, y'all."

"Good night, Jubal," me and Leona said at the same time.

We didn't say nothing else until we heard the water running in the bathroom. "So, what's so important?" Leona asked in a low tone.

I scooted close up to her and whispered, "It's been a while since we switched."

She nodded. "So? The way things have been going since the last time we did, we ain't had no reason to. Why? Is there something coming up you want me to stand in for?" Leona suddenly got real giddy. There was a smile on her face that stretched from one side to the other. "I hope it's another trip to Atlanta with your mother-in-law. When I went in your place that time for a whole week, I enjoyed it so much, I would love to do it again."

I scooted even closer to her. "No, it ain't that. It's something much better. Um . . . you keep saying you would like to know what it's like to live in a lovely house like mine, right?"

Leona looked confused. "Right. But you know I been working on that for years and ain't no closer. That's why I told you I might leave Alabama."

"Well, I can't stop you from doing that, if it's really what you want to do. But in the meantime, I could help you enjoy life more here for a little while."

"So far you ain't making no sense. If you have a plan that can make us both happy, spit it out now."

I took a real deep breath before I went on. "I really miss the single life. Ain't nothing like being able to come and go as I please, go out and drink and have a good time and not have to deal with a stick-in-the-mud husband like Jubal." When the water in the bathroom stopped running, I stopped talking and shook my head at Leona. I waited until I heard Jubal walk into the bedroom, which he was still sleeping in alone. "How would you like to be me and come live in my house for a while?"

"Huh? W-what are you talking about?"

Leona looked so dazed and puzzled, I didn't want to keep her in suspense. "If we switch places, I'll get to be a single woman again and you'll *finally* know what it's like to be a married woman." I waved my hand. "Just look at this beautiful room. This can be all yours."

Leona chuckled and I didn't like that because I was dead serious. "My Lord. Are you sure you want to do something that risky?" she asked as she chuckled again.

"I am. Now, do you want to do it or not?"

"Well, me being you and living in your house sounds like fun, but if I do it, I'd have to go at it with Jubal."

I shook my head and gave her a dismissive wave. "Pffftt! I told you we only have sex every few weeks. Sometimes months. I gave him a dose last night, so he's content for at least another five or six weeks."

"I don't know if I'd feel safe sleeping under the same roof with a man who thinks I'm his wife. I know Jubal is mild-mannered and all, but he's still a man. He might get frisky one night, come into the other bedroom, and try to have his way with me. What would I do?"

"Well, you could tell him you got one of my world-beating headaches. No! I got a better idea. I ain't met a man yet that didn't get squeamish when a woman told him she was on her monthly. And you know Jubal hates the sight of blood."

Leona bit her bottom lip and glanced toward the bedroom where Jubal was at. "Do you have to talk so loud?"

"Don't worry. He can't hear us. That man is so dense, when he falls asleep, he wouldn't know if the house was on fire."

"Maybe so, but I think we should go to my house to finish discussing this."

"Then you'll do it?"

"I don't know yet. I need to know all the details. How long a switch are we talking about?"

"A month."

Leona reared back and looked at me with her mouth hanging open. "A whole month? You must be kidding! How am I going to live in your house for that long and come home from work with them chicken feathers stuck all over me and Jubal not get suspicious?"

I rolled my eyes and gave Leona a hot look. "Turn on your brain and pay attention to what I'm saying. I'm going to be you. I'll be the one going to that loathsome job of yours, coming home with feathers on me."

Leona suddenly looked very interested. "Hmmm. That sweetens the pot." She glanced toward the bedroom. "I still think we should go to my house to finish this discussion." We leaped up from the couch at the same time and headed to the door.

Chapter 44

Leona

ME AND FIONA RUSHED OVER TO MY HOUSE. WHEN WE GOT there, we picked up the conversation where we'd left off at her house. "I been praying to God for something to happen so I could take a break from that damn chicken factory. I never thought it would be something like me moving into your house and you going to my job for a month!" I squealed. We was in the kitchen. Fiona was sitting at the table. I was too anxious to sit so I stood in front of the counter.

"I'm offering you the chance of a lifetime. Let's go to the living room where we can be more comfortable," she told me.

"I better stay close to the window so I can see Bonnie Sue walk up on the porch in case she wanders back over here."

Fiona rolled her eyes. "Speaking of Bonnie Sue, wouldn't it be nice for you to take a break from her?"

I laughed. "I got a lot more patience than you. How would you deal with her daily visits and not go crazy?"

"I know how pesky she is. But I could stand her for a month."

I sighed and gave Fiona a thoughtful look. "This sounds real sweet, but it's kind of serious, so maybe we should take a few days and think it through some more."

"If you're having second thoughts, forget I suggested it."

I held up my hand. I could see that Fiona was getting frustrated, but I didn't care. She was asking me to take part in the biggest hoax we ever pulled. "Hold on, now. I didn't say I didn't want to do it."

"Then say what you want to do so we can get started."

"I just want to make sure this is something you really want to do."

"If I wasn't sure, I wouldn't have brought it up in the first place. For the last time, do you want to switch or not?"

I was getting weaker by the second. "I guess if I'm going to do it, this would be the perfect time. I ain't involved with no man right now, so we wouldn't have to be concerned about keeping the wool over one's eyes. But could you stand to pluck chickens for a whole month? You got a short fuse. I don't want you to go up in that place and say something stupid to one of my bosses and make me lose my job."

"Girl, please! That's the last thing you'll have to worry about. I know how important it is for you to keep your job. I'll be on my best behavior. Besides, I done it for a whole week that time you went to Atlanta with my mother-in-law in my place. As disgusting as it was, plucking chickens was a small price to pay not to go to Atlanta and deal with Jubal's family."

I gave Fiona a hopeless look. "Is the man really that bad?"

"Yup."

"Then why don't you get a divorce and find one you'll enjoy being married to?"

"What's wrong with you, Leona? I ain't no baby chick no more. Do you know how many teenage girls are sashaying around Lexington looking for men like Jubal to marry? As soon as word got out that I'd left him, them young hussies, and a few old ones, would swoop down on him like buzzards." Fiona let out a long, loud breath. "Think about it. This might be your only chance to see what it's like to live like a queen."

I looked at her and sniffed. "You'll have to remember to put on face powder, rouge, and lipstick every time you leave my house. You won't have to wear much when you go to work, just a little rouge and lipstick. There's so much steam in that place, it makes face powder melt and slide like mud."

"I know that." Fiona stood up and came up to me and placed her hands on my shoulders. "This will be the only time I make this offer. So, you in or out?"

"I'm in. When do you want to start it off?"

Fiona giggled. "Tonight is as good a time as any, I guess. Now go scrub off your makeup and I'll put some on in case Bonnie Sue or somebody else shows up before I go to bed. When you leave, I'm going to get in bed. I'll put out all the lamps so if Bonnie Sue comes back, she'll think I'm sleeping and go back home."

I shook my head. "That never stopped her. She'll just let herself in, light a lamp, and wake you up."

"I declare! Maybe it's finally time for you to start locking your doors."

"You know folks around here always leave their doors unlocked in case somebody needs to get in their house and check on them. I don't want none of my neighbors to think that I done suddenly got snooty by locking them out. Besides, I locked my doors one time and Bonnie Sue pried open my kitchen window and crawled in."

Fiona froze and stared at me with a frightened look on her face. "Good God! Didn't that scare you?"

I laughed. "Why would it? You have to remember that after all the misery Bonnie Sue's been through, it wouldn't be fitting for nobody to expect her brain to still be intact."

"What I don't understand is why she wants to spend so much time around you when she's got so many other friends."

"It's got to be because they don't pity her the way I do."

Fiona cocked her head and said, "You're right. I'll try to remember everything you just said when she starts to get on my nerves."

I clapped my hands once. "Okay. Is there anything particular going on in your life that I don't know about?"

"You kidding? You know everything there is to know about me, and vice versa. How else would we have fooled folks so many times for so many years?"

"We don't know *everything* going on in each other's lives. There's bound to be little things we forgot. I'm talking about things like doctor appointments and church commitments.

Where you at with the robes you been working on for the choir? I can't sew as good as you so that could be a problem."

"I ain't got no appointments at the clinic and you don't need to do nothing with them robes. I told Mama to let the committee know that I'm going to take a break and finish them next month. See, I thought of everything."

"That was smart of you to think ahead before I even agreed to go along with this."

"Leona, don't forget that our brains came from the same batter."

"I can't argue with that. All right now." I looked at the calendar on my wall next to my telephone. "A month from today will be February twenty-eight. That's a Sunday. We'll be talking on a regular basis all month to keep each other up-to-date. Did we forget anything?"

"You ain't got no appointments I need to know about?"

"Nope."

"Then get up out of here and go enjoy your new home. Oh! Don't forget, I sleep in Lamar's old room. If you was to crawl into the bed with Jubal, he'd probably have a heart attack." We laughed long and loud.

Chapter 45

Leona

I WAS NERVOUS WHEN I GOT BACK TO FIONA'S HOUSE. BUT I WAS also excited. I looked around her living room and smiled, thinking how nice it was going to be to call this place my own for a whole month.

I puffed out my chest and admired the living room some more before I tiptoed to the room where Jubal was sleeping. Even before I cracked open the door, I could hear him snoring. I wondered how Fiona had been able to sleep in the same bed with him making all that racket for so many years. I was glad I would be sleeping in a different room.

One thing I had to say about my brother-in-law was that he sure was a very understanding man. Either that or some of the screws inside his head had come loose. Here he was married to a woman who could barely stand to have sex with him and who had decided she wasn't even going to sleep in the same bedroom with him. Jubal was not deaf, dumb, or blind. He had to know that Fiona was not happy being married to him. His mama told him he should be with Fiona during some of the counseling sessions because it might help him get to the root of her problems. Jubal was glad Fiona was getting help, but he insisted he didn't need none because he loved being married to her. And even if he did think he needed some spiritual guidance, he was probably too proud to admit it.

I turned off all the lamps and went into my bedroom. I found a nightgown in the top drawer of the huge dresser facing the bed. I held it up and shook my head. I would never wear such a mammy-made nightie. Not only was it made out of cotton, it had a high neck and it was so long it touched the floor. I couldn't imagine why a woman would want to own such unsexy things. I owned some fairly plain nighties, but I also had several see-through skimpy ones to wear when I was in a serious relationship with a man.

After I said my prayers, I crawled up under the covers and slept like a baby.

Things hit a snag the very next morning! When I heard Jubal stirring around in the kitchen, I got up. He seemed surprised to see me standing in the doorway. "What you doing up, Fiona?"

"Um . . . I came to make you some lunch to carry to work."

His eyes got wide and he looked at me like I had cussed at him. "I don't remember the last time you made my lunch. You all right?"

I raked my fingers through my hair. "Yeah! I . . . I just thought I'd get up this morning and see if you wanted me to make your lunch."

"Baby, you can go back to bed. I got it." He turned back to the icebox. "Don't forget to go to the market today and get some more baloney and bread. I used the last of it this morning."

"I will. What do you want me to cook for supper?"

I got another wide-eyed look from him. "You done forgot what day this is? You know I been having supper with Mama every Monday for the past few weeks."

I snapped my fingers. "Oh, that's right! I had a real bad headache when I woke up this morning. As usual, it fogged up my memory . . ."

Jubal chuckled and shook his head. "Well, I better get going. I don't want Otto to get there and loaf off on my dime. You take it easy and swallow a few pills for that headache."

"All right, then. You have a nice day, sugar." When I went up to Jubal to give him a kiss, he almost jumped out of his skin.

"I declare, Fiona. You ain't yourself this morning."

That's for sure, I said to myself. "I can't kiss my own husband?"

"Every day, if I had my way. The night you decided to start sleeping in Lamar's room, you told me that we was getting too old to be smooching and carrying on like young'uns. You done forgot you said that?"

I slapped the side of my head. "Them headaches will be the end of me! I forgot I said that."

He gazed at me from the corner of his eye. "I guess them headaches is causing you to forget more and more stuff, huh?"

"I guess so," I said as I grimaced and rubbed the back of my head.

I had to talk to Fiona, but she would have already left to go to my job. The people that ran the chicken factory would only allow employees to have visitors if it was a emergency.

I was so nervous most of the day, I couldn't sit still for more than a few minutes at a time. Mama was at work so I couldn't kill time by going to visit her. I'd have to do enough of that when she retired next year anyway.

I liked Jubal's mama, but that old sister had retired last year and moved her retired boyfriend in with her. Them two was the most active old couple I knew. They fished almost every day, went to restaurants two or three times a week, church all day every Sunday, and they liked to be alone and snuggle up and listen to dramas on the radio before they went to bed. What little spare time they had left, they spent at the church helping organize events and whatnot. I didn't want to get close to a elderly couple anyway, not even for a month. The only other person I knew who was at home during the day was Bonnie Sue. I went into the kitchen and dialed her number. She answered on the first ring. "This is Fiona," I said.

"Fiona?" She sounded surprised. "You ain't called me in a while. Is anything wrong?"

"No. I just thought I'd give you a call to see how you're doing. You ain't been to my house in a while."

"Well, I don't like the looks Jubal gives me when I do. That's why I spend way more time visiting Leona. We had a ball last night!"

"Oh? What did y'all do? Other than have a few drinks," I said with a chuckle.

"We just played checkers and listened to the radio. I only had two drinks, but Leona sucked up moonshine like she'd just been let out of prison. I bet she went to work with a world-beating hangover this morning."

"Well, you know my sister." I laughed.

"I told her I'd be back over there this evening. She was a little upset when I left."

"Why was she upset?"

"That beast Boaz had the nerve to show up while she was in the bathroom. While he was waiting for her, I gave him a piece of my mind. I told him everything she probably would have told him, and I didn't mince words. He didn't even wait for her after that. That hound from hell took off like I'd scalded him."

"Leona made it clear to him that she didn't want to see him. I don't know why he showed up. I hope he don't start harassing her," I replied. It felt strange to be talking about myself like I really was Fiona.

"He won't if I can help it! I heard he got violent with one of his other girlfriends. If he even acts like he's going to manhandle Leona, I'll put something on him a doctor can't take off!"

I had never heard Bonnie Sue sound so hostile. She wouldn't even defend herself when the bullies at school messed with her. But she had changed a lot since we was kids. I didn't know what she was capable of doing these days. I was scared for Boaz. I didn't know any man who could handle a shotgun as good as Bonnie Sue could. I scolded myself for letting my thoughts run wild. "I hope it don't come to that. I'll call Leona this evening. If you see her before I talk to her, tell her I said to give me a call as soon as possible."

I couldn't believe how slow the day was going by. I even checked the clock on the living-room wall against the one in the kitchen to make sure they was both still working.

Finally, around six thirty, Fiona called me up. "Thank God it's you!" I yelled.

"What's wrong? Bonnie Sue said you needed to talk to me as soon as possible. How was last night?"

"Last night was all right. I didn't have to talk to Jubal at all until this morning. You didn't tell me you had stopped fixing his lunch. He looked at me like I was crazy when I tried to do it. And when I tried to kiss him good-bye, he almost had a heart attack he was so surprised."

"Hmmm. That's two of them little details I forgot."

"Is there any more 'little details' you forgot to tell me?"

"I can't think of none. Listen, I told you that all you need to do is blame little memory slipups on them headaches. I been falling back on that excuse so long, I almost believe it myself." Fiona laughed.

"That's what I did. How was work today?"

"As disgusting as it was that other time I done it. But you ain't got to worry. I can handle it. We was so busy today, the time went by real fast. By the way, Bonnie Sue told me that she told you Boaz came to your house last night."

"She wasn't too happy about that. She sounded like she wanted to kill him dead. But Bonnie Sue was just blowing off steam. I had no idea that man was so stubborn. I don't know why he can't take no for a answer."

"Uh . . . Leona, I been meaning to bring up something that's been on my mind a lot lately. Even more so in the last few days. I know I asked you this before, but I need to ask you again. Do you *really* believe all that stuff Bonnie Sue and Sedella told you about how they seen Boaz with other women?"

"They didn't say they seen him. They said they heard it from somebody else."

"Uh-huh. And I bet that 'somebody else' heard it from somebody else."

"Fiona, what is it you trying to say?"

"Stories grow like weeds as they make the rounds. The last

time I heard Jubal brag about the size of the same fish, by the time he stopped talking about it, it was almost as big as me."

"I know stories change from mouth to mouth. But Bonnie Sue overheard him with her own ears tell Clayton he didn't want to marry a woman as old as me."

"Maybe she heard wrong. Did you ever think that she might have just caught part of that conversation and jumped to her own conclusion?"

"I'm done with Boaz, now let's move on." I exhaled and clutched the telephone tighter. "I'm glad I don't have to cook supper for Jubal today. And that's another thing; you didn't tell me he had started eating supper with his mama every Monday."

"Dagnabbit! That's another one of them little details I forgot to mention."

Chapter 46

Fiona

*T*HE FIRST DAY OF OUR LATEST HOAX HAD FELT LIKE A BREATH OF fresh air. I was going to love being Leona this time because it would be so much longer than them other times. I got up early yesterday morning, washed up, and put on some of Leona's makeup. I didn't have to do much with my hair because we'd both been wearing our shoulder-length hair in the same style, a flip with bangs since we'd stopped wearing them silly colored ribbons Mama made us wear.

I put on one of the plain white blouses and denim britches Leona usually wore to work. I was too excited to make myself some breakfast. But I did make a jelly sandwich to eat at lunchtime.

Even going to Leona's filthy job didn't bother me. I was so giddy when I walked into that foul-smelling barn of a building this morning, a few of the other workers thought I'd been drinking and even had the nerve to sniff my breath! Nadine did it twice before we even got to our workstations. "Girl, if you ain't drunk, you must be in love," she commented.

"Don't be saying stuff like that. If somebody heard you and was to blab to the boss on me, they'll be watching me like a hawk," I scolded as I took Leona's regular spot in the colored section of the assembly line.

The following Sunday night, me and Bonnie Sue went to a house on the edge of town that belonged to a old man who had recently started selling moonshine. His shabby little house was so packed that night, I didn't even get a chance to meet the moonshiner. When somebody tapped me on the shoulder, I whirled around and almost fainted when I seen Jake Hickey's face. "Jake? I ain't seen you since last year."

"What's wrong with your memory, Leona? I bought you a drink at that house over on West Noble Street a month ago. You danced with me too."

"Huh? Oh yeah! Well, you know I was probably tipsy and had a blackout, that's why I don't remember . . ."

"Humph. You forgetting me that quick and easy could rupture my ego if I wasn't such a strong man." Jake snorted and glanced around. "When you coming to visit me again, sugar pie? I know it's been almost twenty years, but I still remember all the fun we had that day. And please don't tell me you forgot that too . . ."

"I still remember that day."

"You needed money to buy shoes to wear to Bonnie Sue's wedding. Since she didn't get married, what did you do with them three dollars?"

"I spent it on some fabric so I could help make a quilt for the church."

"I'm glad you put it to good use." Jake glanced around again and lowered his voice. "After you left my house that day, I couldn't stop grinning. You was a kid back then but I bet you done got even sweeter over the years. No wonder Boaz keeps telling folks he ain't going to stop until he gets you back. You sure know how to make a man feel good. Oomph!"

"I hope you didn't tell nobody about my visit—especially Boaz."

"Shoot! He's the last person I would tell. I don't know what the problem was between you and him, but he's the most righteous man I ever knew, praise the Lord." Jake paused and wiped sweat off his face, which had got even bigger over the years, so he had a lot of wiping to do. "When I was his age, I had to beat the gals off with a stick. Still do, every now and then," he bragged.

"What makes you think Boaz is so pious? I done heard a few things about him that wasn't very nice."

"Pfffft! Girl, who is *truly* 'pious' these days? I ain't. You sure ain't. The last and only person who could claim that position was Jesus. But Boaz is a good man regardless. Besides, you ought to know that you can't believe everything you hear. You don't want to hear some of the stuff I done heard about you . . ."

My chest tightened and a heat wave slid across my face. "Who's been talking about me, and what did they say?"

Jake gave me a dismissive wave. "You know how folks lie, so why do you care what I heard?"

"I don't really care. I'm just curious. You might as well tell me some of it because I'll hound you to death until you do."

"All right. Did you roll a passed-out man you was with in a motel and take every dime he had in his pocket?"

My chest felt even tighter. I couldn't believe anybody could tell such a bald-faced lie. If Leona had robbed somebody, she would have told me about it. But Jake was so shady, he could have been making up stuff just to get my goat. He was wretched enough to be telling lies on the Sabbath. "I ain't never stole nothing before in my life."

"Oh yeah? You done forgot about that blouse you tried to steal for Bonnie Sue's wedding?"

"I didn't know no better. I was a stupid teenager," I explained.

Jake laughed. "Girl, Boaz said the same thing about you when I told him about it. He said that the woman you are now is all he cares about. He even told me how folks been feeding you lies about him."

"I wish you and him both would stop talking about me."

"I only bump into him at that fishing creek in Branson I like to go to. And every time I do, he got this puppy-dog look on his face because he misses you so much."

I didn't even excuse myself before I shuffled across the floor to where Bonnie Sue was. I told her that I would be leaving soon because I had a headache.

"You look terrible. Did somebody say something to offend you?"

"Jake Hickey told me folks have been lying about me," I griped.

"About what?"

"Some hogwash about me robbing a man while he was passed out."

"I ain't heard nothing about that and you know I hear everything."

"Jake also told me that Boaz said he ain't going to stop trying until he gets me back."

Bonnie Sue looked mad enough to cuss out the world. "Can't that bastard get it through his thick skull that you don't want to be with him no more?"

"I guess he's going to keep trying." I laughed. "Oh, well. Maybe I'll sit down and talk to him one more time. If he's so determined to talk to me, the least I can do is listen to what he has to say." I exhaled and gave Bonnie Sue a serious look. She still looked mad enough to cuss out the world. "I don't want to talk about Boaz no more tonight. Come on, let's get out on that floor and dance."

Chapter 47

Leona

THINGS HAD GONE SO WELL THE FIRST WEEK, I COULDN'T WAIT TO see how much I would enjoy the second one. Being a housewife was more fulfilling than I ever imagined. For the first time in my life, I felt like I had a real purpose. After me and Fiona switched back, I was going to pray and try even harder to find a husband of my own. I wasn't going to settle for none of them party-going fools I knew. I wanted a righteous man like Jubal. Instead of hanging out at parties and moonshiners' houses, I'd start going to church more and socializing with a better class of friends. There was some folks at work who didn't drink much and they was real happy with their lives. They gave cookouts and had gatherings where there was very little alcohol available, and they didn't invite no rowdy people. One thing I could say about the wild life I'd been living was that I hadn't gained nothing from it.

When I got up Monday morning and walked into the kitchen, Jubal was sweeping glass off the floor. He smiled when he looked up and seen me. "Fiona, I'm sorry I was making so much noise I woke you up. This glass just slipped out of my hand."

"Leave the rest of it. I'll finish cleaning it up. I don't want you to be late for work."

"All right." He propped the broom up against the counter and wiped his hands on a dishrag. "What do you have planned for today?"

"Nothing special." I hunched my shoulders. I'm glad I remembered that Fiona had told me Jubal hadn't took her out to dinner or the movies in months. "It would be so nice to get out of the house. Now that the buses have service in the colored neighborhoods, I could ride one to the movie theater to see a matinee. Shoot. After I cook and clean up, all I do is listen to the radio or fiddle around with that new sewing machine you got me."

"What about them robes you been working on for the choir?"

"Well, that's a really big job, so I'm taking a break until the end of the month."

"I don't know why you agreed to do that in the first place. I wish you would stop letting that church committee take advantage of you."

"I don't see it that way. I promised the Lord that for Him blessing me with so much, I would give back to my community."

Jubal sighed and rubbed the back of his head and then shook it real hard. "Maybe you should check with Reverend Sweeney. He might have something else you can do for the church besides sewing and making clothes and baking pies for them bake sales every month."

"That's all right. I don't want to take on no more responsibilities."

One of the reasons I'd agreed to do the switch with Fiona was so I could spend part of the day relaxing while Jubal was at work. I wasn't about to ask Reverend Sweeney or anybody else for more work. I was happy lounging on the couch nibbling on tea cakes and whatnot, and I wanted to savor every minute I had left until the end of the month when I had to go back to being me.

Jubal called me up just before it was time for him to close up the garage and told me he was going to go fishing for a while before he came home.

Ten minutes after I got off the phone with him, I stretched back out on the couch. Before I could get comfortable, I heard footsteps on the front porch. I assumed Jubal had changed his mind. I was surprised when Reverend Sweeney let hisself in and strutted in like he was in his own house. My first thought was that Jubal had contacted him and told him to pay me a visit this evening so I would forget about movies and whatnot. I wobbled up and went up to him. "Good evening, Reverend Sweeney. Do I have a session with you this evening?"

"Yessiree!" he answered with a look on his face I'd never seen. His eyes seemed like they was staring straight through me and he was licking his lips. Before I knew what was happening, he lunged at me, wrapped his arms around my waist, and kissed me on my lips!

My body felt like it had turned into a pillar of salt. I couldn't move nothing for a few seconds except my mouth. "What in the world—why Reverend Sweeney, what's got into you?"

He leaned his head back and chuckled. "What's the matter with you? We do this all the time. Hush up and give me some sugar." He didn't give me time to reply before he kissed me again. When he leaned his head back this time, he nodded toward my bedroom. "I'm so hot, if you don't cool me off soon, I'm going to have blisters."

"I—I thought you was going to Montgomery to that retreat." One of the things Fiona had told me that I needed to know was that our preacher was going on a retreat and wouldn't be coming to her house to give her spiritual guidance sessions for several weeks. The way he was behaving now, something other than "spiritual guidance" was going on between them two!

"I was. Brother Bowles came down with some kind of bug and we had to cancel it."

"Um . . . um . . . you should leave. Jubal might be home any minute."

Reverend Sweeney shook his head. "No, he won't. I seen him at the gas station filling up his tank a little while ago. He told me he was on his way to the lake because them bass is biting like mosquitoes. You know as well as I do that when he hits that fishing bank, he won't be home for a few hours."

"Well, you still need to leave. I got the worst headache I done had in weeks." I grimaced and rubbed the side of my head. "I don't feel like having no company this evening."

"I didn't come here to be company. I came to do the Lord's work."

I was so stunned I could barely talk. A lot of the females I knew often commented on how luscious Reverend Sweeney was and how they would like to get him in a bed and have their way with him. I agreed with every one of them. But I never expected a man of the cloth to behave in such a worldly manner. That Fiona. She had some explaining to do.

"I-I don't need no counseling this evening," I insisted.

He shook his head. "I'll be the judge of that. You look tense and I'm fixing to loosen you up." He puckered his lips like he was fixing to kiss me again, but I pushed him away.

"I just told you I got one of my headaches."

"I can fix that. A laying on of hands might help get rid of that headache." Reverend Sweeney licked his lips some more. "I declare, you gave me a good working over the last time we was together. I been walking on air ever since." He hauled off and kissed me again. As good as it felt, I didn't want to get carried away until I talked to Fiona and found out what the heck was going on between her and Reverend Sweeney.

As soon as he ended the kiss, I pushed him toward the door. "I need to go take a pill and lay down. Why don't you call me up tomorrow and we can discuss a time for my next session. Besides, Mama said she might drop by on her way home from work this evening."

"I can't wait to take you back to that motel we went to last week."

Motel? My Lord! "We'll talk about that when you call me tomorrow. But like I just told you, I need to go take a pill and lay down now."

"Aw shuck it!" Reverend Sweeney scrunched up his face like a spoiled child and stomped his foot. "I guess I'll go home to my icy-cold wife and try to heat her up," he whined.

I grabbed his arm and steered him to the door. I even gave him a quick peck on his jaw. "Now you have a blessed evening."

"I don't see how I can do that!" he griped before he shuffled out the door.

I couldn't get to the telephone fast enough. I dialed the number at my house and Bonnie Sue answered. "Put my sister on the phone."

"My goodness, Fiona. You sound distressed. Is Jubal mistreating you?"

"Just let me talk to Leona."

I heard some muffled voices in the background and then Fiona came on the line. "Hello, sister-girl," she chirped.

"We need to talk!"

"Okay. I got company right now. Can I call you back later?"

"What is going on between you and Reverend Sweeney?!"

"Huh? Why?" she asked dumbly in a high-pitched tone.

"He came over here a few minutes ago and jumped on me like a flea! From what he said, you and him been getting together for quite a while—even at a motel."

Fiona took her time responding. "Dagnabbit! He told me he was going to be at a retreat for several weeks," she whispered.

"It got canceled. Something about Brother Bowles getting sick. Of *all* the things you should have told me about, your hanky-panky with our preacher should have been at the top of the list. How could you forget to tell me about you and him?"

"I'll come right over so we can discuss this some more."

"You do that." I was talking so fast; words was shooting out of my mouth like loose teeth. "I can't believe your coochie is itching so bad, you have to get it scratched by a man of God! Get your tail over here right now and don't bring Bonnie Sue."

I hung up and started pacing around the living room. I was still pacing ten minutes later when Fiona shuffled through the door with a dazed expression on her face. "I am so sorry," she said as she rushed up to me. "I didn't mean to get involved with our preacher. It just happened. One day during one of my sessions, he kissed me. One thing led to another . . ."

"I guess that's part of his spiritual guidance, huh?"

Fiona hunched her shoulders. "I guess it is." She started wringing her hands and blinking. "You know how bad things done got between me and Jubal in the bedroom."

I nodded. "Are you fooling around with anybody else? If so, you need to tell me in case they show up. I don't want to blow things up and have people figure out we switched places. That would be the biggest scandal this town ever seen."

"I ain't seeing nobody else." Fiona paused. She shifted gears so fast it made my head spin. "By the way, Boaz called again last night. I don't think he's going to let up until you listen to what he has to say."

"If he keeps pushing it, let him come over and say what he got to say. Then tell him not to come back."

"You sure you want to give up on him for good? What if he convinces me he wasn't lying about them rumors you heard about him?"

"That still won't change the fact that he gave up on me so fast first." I looked at Fiona and narrowed my eyes. "If he 'convinces' you that he wasn't lying, I hope you don't get weak and let something 'just happen' with him."

"Like what?"

"Remember Ernest Lee and how you went at it with him all of them times? I'd die if you got pregnant by Boaz. That's one thing we'd never be able to fix by switching places."

"Don't forget I only had sex with Ernest Lee because you wouldn't do it and you wasn't ready to break up with him. I did you a favor. But I won't have sex with Boaz because I know how much you care about him." Fiona stopped talking and gave me a sideways look. "If Jubal was to get frisky before we switch back, would you do it with him?"

"You told me y'all only go at it every now and then. You should be back in your place when the notion hits him again."

"That's true, but you know how unpredictable men can be. Look how Reverend Sweeney popped up out of the blue. I didn't know nothing about his retreat getting canceled. If I had, I would have put off our switch until I knew for sure that he'd be out of town."

I sighed. "To answer your question about Jubal getting frisky, no I ain't going to do nothing with him. I'll tell him I got one of them headaches you always fall back on."

"Okay. Well, I better get back to your house before Bonnie Sue and Sedella drink up everything." Fiona smoothed down the sides of the skirt she had on, one of my tightest and shortest. She was playing me to the hilt.

I looked her up and down. "You know, I didn't realize how cute I was. My makeup and frocks suit you. You look just like me."

"I always have," Fiona replied with her eyeballs rolling upward. "Listen, don't mess up things for me with Reverend Sweeney. Play sick if he comes back and stay sick until I come back home. I'll suddenly recover and play catch-up with him then."

"Fiona, you would be run out of town on a rail if you broke up his marriage."

"Oh no! It ain't nothing like that. He ain't leaving his wife for me, and I sure ain't leaving Jubal for him. We just having fun. He makes me feel special and that's what I need in my life right now. You know how miserable I been. Well, I'm doing so much better now."

"I'm glad to hear that. Well, your relationship with our preacher ain't really my business. If you are happy with him, I won't do nothing to ruin it for you. Just be careful. And I advise you to stay away from motels with him. Eventually somebody who knows you or him will see y'all going in or out and blab all over town. Poor Mama would have a cow."

"I'll be careful."

"We'll talk again soon. If you have some rowdy people at my house, make sure they don't break or steal nothing."

Chapter 48
Fiona

BY THE TIME WE WAS IN THE THIRD WEEK OF THE RUSE, I WAS HAVing so much fun, I didn't know if I'd be ready to go back home at the end of the month. Leona was enjoying herself too.

She called me when I got home from work today and told me that Reverend Sweeney hadn't come back to the house yet. But he'd called this morning to see if she felt like having company this evening. I laughed when she told me the excuse she'd used to stall him. "I told him I had a rash between my thighs and the doctor at the clinic gave me this stinky crème to slather on myself every day for three weeks."

"Mighty Moses! I hope Reverend Sweeney don't think I got the nasty-woman's disease! I ain't ready to turn him loose yet."

"He ain't got no reason to think that. I also told him that the doctor said I'd got the rash from using too much lye soap when I do laundry." Leona laughed, I didn't. "Guess what me and Jubal did last night? We went to Mobile to eat supper at a real nice restaurant and we went to the movies to see *Black Legion*, that new Humphrey Bogart movie that came out last month."

"That's nice." A lump rose in my throat. "How did you get him to do that?"

"I just asked him to take me out and he did."

"Humph. I bet he wouldn't have took me if I'd asked. The last time I did, he claimed his corns was aching too bad. But he still went fishing a hour later."

"Maybe it was the way you asked him."

"How did you ask him?"

"He did say his corns was hurting. I offered to give him a foot massage. He was kind of skittish at first, but I insisted. Oh, he really enjoyed that and didn't want me to stop. While I still had his toes in my hand, covering them with calamine lotion, I told him how pleased I was to be seen in public with a handsome man like him. While he was swooning, I asked him to take me out on the town. He said he'd be happy to."

"Well! I ain't never told him nothing like that and I ain't never even thought about massaging his feet. Eeww!" And then I softened my tone. "Maybe I should start saying stuff like that and offering to do his feet."

"Maybe you should."

"You didn't have to do nothing for him?"

"If you mean what I think you mean, no, I didn't have to do nothing like that. But we kissed a few times."

"He kissed you?"

"Actually, I kissed him first because he'd brought me some ice cream on the way home. He was surprised but he seemed to like it. When you come back, you need to show him more affection. If you don't, he might wonder why you suddenly stopped. Maybe if y'all got closer, I do believe your feelings for him would change."

"I'll think about it." As miserable as I was with Jubal, I wasn't about to let him get away. If my sister could make him feel so good, another woman could too. Maybe it was time for me to make some changes in my real life . . .

"By the way, I slept in the bed with him last night."

My jaw dropped so low I was surprised it didn't lock up. "You did? Why?"

"I was feeling so lonesome I thought it would be nice to sleep close to a man. Besides, it was chilly so he kept my back warm."

"Oh? He had to be snuggled up real close to you to keep your back warm." I couldn't remember the last time I let Jubal get that close up on me in bed. I had to remind myself that the woman he had snuggled up to was not me. And that if she hadn't got in bed with him in the first place, he never would have got that close to her. "He didn't try nothing?"

"Nope. The only thing he did was grind his teeth in my ear."

"That's him. Dull no matter what," I laughed. "You should be safe until I get back home. But if he gets a nasty notion, remember you got that headache excuse to calm him down and hold him off."

"I know. He told me this morning he prays all the time that I will start sleeping with him again every night and that last night was a hopeful sign. I told him I wasn't ready yet, but I would think about it. By me telling him that, you can decide what you want to do when you get back home. Is everything going all right at work?"

"Everything's fine on my end." I laughed again. "Girl, I'm having a ball! I didn't realize how much I missed going to parties. I didn't realize how popular you still was! I walked into that moonshiner's house on Pike Street the other night and had to beat the men off with a stick. It reminded me of the good old days when we was still living with Mama and I was sneaking out and posing as you. I was wondering if we could extend the switch a little longer."

"Why?"

"Sedella is giving a birthday party for her husband next month. I'd love to go."

"I don't mind one more week. But I don't think we should go no longer than that, I don't care how much fun you're having. I don't think I can hold Reverend Sweeney off too much longer. And I don't know how long I can sleep in the same bed with Jubal before he wants to get even closer, if you know what I mean. He's been looking at me with a hungry eye these past few days."

"Hmmm. I guess I could sleep with him for a couple of weeks after I get back home, and even let him pester me at least once during that time. And then I'll tell him his snoring drives me crazy and I'll move back to the other room."

"That's a reasonable excuse. So, what do you have planned for tonight?"

"I had a itching to go to Sedella's house, but Bonnie Sue called me up a little while ago and told me she needed to come talk to me about something important."

"Why did she call? She usually just shows up."

"I thought the same thing so I asked her. She told me she needed to make sure I'd be by myself so we could talk in private. Her voice sounded real strange."

"Hmmm. I hope Clayton ain't thinking about leaving her. Poor thing. She done already had too much misery in her life. Tell her Fiona said hi."

While I was waiting for Bonnie Sue to arrive, somebody knocked on Leona's living-room door. I knew it wasn't Bonnie Sue because she always let herself in. I trotted to the door and cracked it open just wide enough to peep out. I was shocked to see Boaz standing there holding a bunch of flowers. "What are you doing here?" I asked.

"Can I come in?"

I glanced over his shoulder before I opened the door wider. He shuffled in and handed me the flowers. "I wasn't expecting you."

"I'm sure you wasn't. I didn't call because I knew you would have told me not to come. Can we sit down?"

I shook my head and set the flowers on the coffee table. "Thank you for the flowers, but you can't stay but a few minutes. I'm expecting company any minute."

"Just let me stay long enough to say what I got to say." Boaz paused and gave me a pleading look. "Leona, I just wanted to tell you that I love you. I can't stop thinking about you. All I want is for you to give me another chance—" Before he could finish his sentence, Bonnie Sue strode in. When she seen Boaz, she looked at him like she wanted to roast him alive.

"Leona, you told me you was going to be alone so we could have a private conversation," she whined. Her jaws suddenly started twitching like she was having a spasm. "Can you call me when you ain't got company?"

Boaz gave Bonnie Sue the most exasperating look I ever seen. His handsome face suddenly looked like he'd put on a fright mask. "I was just leaving," he said as he moved real slow toward the door. Before he opened it and left, he skittered back up to me and kissed me. I was so taken aback I didn't know how to react. I just stood rooted in my spot like a tree. "I'll see you later, Leona."

As soon as Boaz left, Bonnie Sue gave me a relieved look. "I was surprised that hound from hell was here."

"So was I."

She looked at the flowers with the same hateful expression on her face that was on it when she looked at Boaz. "That mangy dog is trying every trick in the book to get you back, ain't he?"

"I guess he is. Let me put these flowers in some water and then you can tell me what you need to talk to me about." I gave Bonnie Sue a curious look. "I hope you didn't come to tell me your marriage is in trouble."

"Naw, it ain't nothing like that."

While I was standing at the sink putting water in the vase that Leona had recently bought, Bonnie Sue came up behind me and put her hands on my shoulders. I froze when she kissed the back of my neck. I set the vase on the counter and whirled around to face her. "What in the world do you—"

She cut me off so fast by pressing her finger to my lips, I got scared. "Leona, I can't go on no longer. It's time for me to tell you how I feel about you. I'm about to lose my mind."

I snatched her finger away from my lips. "Is this a joke?"

"I ain't joking. The older we get, the more I love you. I'm at a point now where if I don't let you know how I feel about you, there ain't no telling what I'll do."

I was so confused I didn't know what to say or think. The extremely glazed-over look in Bonnie Sue's eyes was enough to convince me she wasn't joking. I took a deep breath and tried to make sense of what I was hearing. "You always been like family. I . . . I love you too."

She shook her head. "I ain't talking about kinfolk kind of love. I love you the way a man loves a woman."

Chapter 49
Fiona

BONNIE SUE LOVES LEONA THE WAY A MAN LOVES A WOMAN! I COULD not believe my ears! If she had told me she was growing a tail, I couldn't have been more stupefied. I pushed her back and held up my hand. "Girl, you must be crazy!"

"I must be. I am so crazy in love with you, I got to do something about it." Tears was rolling down Bonnie Sue's cheeks.

What woman in her right mind would fall in love with another woman and admit it? Especially after Reverend Sweeney had preached that such a lifestyle was the mark of the beast. Knowing I'd been so close to Satan's influence all these years terrified me. "I don't know what you think you can do about being crazy in love with me. You done said some outlandish stuff before, but I can't beat this with a eggbeater!"

"Don't make fun of me. You make me sound like some kind of freak of nature."

I stomped my foot on the floor so hard, all the glasses in Leona's cabinet rattled. "What else could you be? You . . . you are a *mannish* woman! Maybe that's why you care more about working on cars than baking pies like a real woman is supposed to."

Bonnie Sue shook her head. "I'm a woman in love. And ain't nothing unnatural or freaky about that." She moved closer to me. I moved closer to the door in case I needed to bolt and run for help.

"Look, I don't care what you say, you ain't normal. Admit

you're a freak and try to get some help *quick*! Go see Reverend Sweeney. If you don't want your own preacher to know about you, try Reverend Wiggins. If one of them can't straighten you out, nobody can. You need to pray that you won't get no worse. My Lord!"

"I ain't no freak," Bonnie Sue insisted. "I read about women like me. They live all over the world. Especially in places like New York City."

"Humph! Everybody knows that New York City is neck and neck with Sodom and Gomorrah. This is Lexington, Alabama— God's country. What you need to do is move to a big city and find one of them women like you."

"You are the only woman I ever felt this way about, so I ain't going to live in no place you ain't at. That should mean something to you."

"The only thing it means to me is that you ain't the person I thought you was, and I don't want to be around somebody that goes against the Bible."

Bonnie Sue rolled her neck and folded her arms. "I'm going against the Bible? When did *you* get so holy?"

I held up my hand. "You hold on! This ain't about me. I ain't the one that's been living a double life." As soon as them last words left my mouth, my heart skipped a beat because I'd been living a "double life" all my life. But me and Leona switching identities was a long way from me being in love with a woman and expecting her to go along with it. "I'm a lot holier than you!"

"I never expected you to hurt my feelings in such a profound way," Bonnie Sue sobbed. She wiped snot and tears off her face with the back of her trembling hand.

"I never expected you to come up in my house and drop such a 'profound' load on me. You should have gave this situation a whole lot of thought before you actually said what you said."

"I-I did g-give it a lot of thought," Bonnie Sue stammered. "I been wrestling with Satan for years over this. That low-down, funky black dog tried to make me keep my feelings to myself so I could continue to be miserable. But I didn't let him hold me back from telling you. I thought you'd be flattered if nothing else."

"Flattered? Girl, I am repulsed!" I yelled. Bonnie Sue cried harder. I was sorry to see her so upset, but I was in such a state of disbelief, I didn't know what else to say, and I couldn't stop myself from rearing my head back and laughing. I laughed so long and hard, tears drizzled down my face. I put my hands on my hips and looked Bonnie Sue up and down. "If, and I do mean if, I was into women, do you think I'd want a headscarf-wearing frump like you?"

Bonnie Sue's eyes got big and her lips quivered. "You . . . you used to tell me I didn't look as bad as I thought I did. Now you trying to say I'm too ugly for you?"

"Look, it wouldn't matter if you looked like a film star, I wouldn't want you. I ain't never done nothing with no woman and you know it."

"I ain't never done nothing with no woman neither. Maybe I . . . I might not be all the way funny, because you are the only woman in my whole life I ever wanted to be with."

"You know being 'funny' is a sin and a crime. You could go to jail in this state if the law found out about you."

"I don't care about none of that. I would go to jail for you, and I'd even die for you."

Bonnie Sue's last words chilled me to the bone. I glanced toward the door. If she didn't leave in the next minute, I would. I'd run next door to where a man with a shotgun lived. "You scaring me."

"I don't mean to. It's just that . . . I like the way you look, the way you smell—I like everything about you."

"Then that must mean you fell in love with my twin too, huh?"

"Naw. It ain't nothing like that. Fiona is just as pretty as you, and I do like her, but she ain't my type. For one thing, she is too dull for me."

I didn't know if I was mad or amused to hear that anybody thought I was dull. I needed a break from Jubal because he was too dull. The bottom line was, I didn't like what I was hearing.

"Bonnie Sue, what did you think I was going to say when you told me all this stuff?"

"I didn't know how you would react. I was scared you wouldn't feel the same way about me. You wouldn't be happy with Boaz. I can't let you get more involved with that jackal. He don't like me and I *despise* him. If you was to marry him, our friendship would be over."

Leona wasn't even courting Boaz no more, so her marrying him was about as likely as me marrying a hound dog. "Look, I done heard enough. You need to leave NOW!" I stomped my foot again and pointed at the door. "I don't want to hear nothing else from you tonight."

"What about tomorrow? Can we discuss this some more then?"

"There ain't nothing else to discuss on this subject, tomorrow or any other day. And as long as you feel the way you do about me, I don't think you should come back over here."

The blood drained from Bonnie Sue's face and her eyelids drooped. Her scarf had slid a few inches to the side, and I seen gray hair I'd never noticed before. It seemed like she was aging right before my eyes. "Are . . . are you telling me we can't even be friends no more?" Her voice was so low and raspy, I could barely hear her.

"I don't know," I said, shaking my head as I paced the floor. "I need to think about all the stuff you said tonight." I pointed to the door again. "Good night, Bonnie Sue."

"I'm going." She sobbed some more and shuffled out my kitchen door.

I immediately locked the kitchen door, the front door, and all of the windows.

Chapter 50
Leona

AFTER ME AND JUBAL ATE THE PIG EARS AND COLLARD GREENS I
had cooked for supper, he helped me reorganize both bedroom
closets and he mopped the kitchen floor for me. I was amazed at
how sweet and agreeable my brother-in-law was. I still couldn't
figure out why Fiona thought he was so humdrum—in and out
of the bedroom. Sex with him must have been pretty bad for a
woman who had always loved it as much as she did to be avoiding it now.

Fiona had told me that folks rarely called her house after supper. So when the telephone rang a few minutes before eight, me
and Jubal gasped at the same time. "Lord, I wonder who is that
calling here? I hope nothing ain't happened to my mama!" he
hollered. There was a frantic look on his face. He sprung up out
of his chair at the kitchen table where we'd been sitting for the
past fifteen minutes playing dominoes.

"Or my mama," I wailed. I stood up and followed him over to
the telephone. "Who is it?" I asked with my heart skipping every
other beat.

"It's your sister," he said with a relieved look on his face as he
handed the phone to me.

"Leona, is everything all right?" I asked.

"We got a problem," she replied. Her voice sounded raspy, so
she'd either just done a lot of crying or a lot of laughing. "Get
over here as fast as you can."

I was so scared, my heart started beating even harder.

"Uh . . . okay. I'll be there in a few minutes. Let me get back in my clothes and shoes." I hung up and looked at Jubal. "She can't find her hot comb and wants to borrow mine. She's going out after work tomorrow and wants to look good," I lied.

"Is that what she called here for this time of night? Can't she pick it up after work? It's kind of late for you to be going out just to drop off a hot comb."

"I don't mind. I know how fussy she is when it comes to her hair."

Fiona was outside standing in front of my door when I got there. She was wringing her hands and shifting her weight from one foot to the other. "What's the matter? Did somebody find out you ain't me?" I asked as soon as I piled out of the car and rushed up to her.

"Naw, it ain't nothing like that. Come on in and sit down while I pour us a drink. You going to need one."

We went into my kitchen and she took a jar from the cabinet. "I better not drink nothing. Jubal will smell it on my breath. He thinks I came over here to bring you my hot comb. And—oh shit! I forgot to bring it." I didn't wait for Fiona to say nothing. I sprinted to the phone and dialed. "I must be losing my mind," I chuckled when Jubal answered. "I forgot to bring the hot comb."

"I know," he said in a stiff tone. "You want me to bring it?"

"Um . . . Leona said she'll leave work early tomorrow and come pick it up then. I'll be home in a few minutes." I hung up fast so Jubal wouldn't have time to say nothing else. And then I spun around to face Fiona. "What's going on?"

"Girl, you better sit down for this," she replied. "And I need to sit down myself."

We sat down at my kitchen table. She told me everything Bonnie Sue had said about being in love with me. I almost fell out of my chair! I was so stunned; I needed a drink. But I still couldn't risk having Jubal smell it on my breath.

"What do we do about her, Leona?"

"I don't know. I . . . I never expected to hear nothing like this about her!"

"I told you the way she had to be around you so much—even after she got married—was unnatural. If you had cut her out of your life when I first started warning you about her, we wouldn't be having this conversation."

All kinds of thoughts was dancing around in my head. But I still wasn't ready to give up on the woman who had been so loyal to me. "Do you think she'll come back over here before I move back home?"

Fiona narrowed her eyes. "I told that heifer not to come back. But that don't mean she won't."

I straightened up in my chair and gave Fiona a serious look. "I don't know if that was a smart thing to do yet. We need to get to the bottom of this thing. Maybe Bonnie Sue is having a breakdown."

"She asked if you and her could still be just friends, but I told her I didn't know."

"Fiona, you know your Bible, so you know God is all about forgiveness."

"That's true, but I don't think that's such a good idea in this case."

"This is a small town. Unless she goes out of her way to avoid me now, me and her will bump into each other on a regular basis. Maybe I can turn her around. If she was to renounce this foolishness, we can put it behind us and move forward. One thing I will make her promise me is that she won't *never* bring it up again."

"And you need to make her promise to stop mean-mouthing every man you get involved with. Since Boaz has been trying to get you back, she done spewed so many hateful words about him, I wouldn't be surprised if she got violent with him."

I looked at Fiona like she was talking gibberish. "You can't believe that! Bonnie Sue ain't never been violent." I threw up my hands and stood up. "I done heard enough for tonight. I better get back home before Jubal comes looking for me. Let's sleep on this and discuss it some more tomorrow. Maybe what you told Bonnie Sue gave her such a jolt, she done already came to her senses and will confine her passion to her husband."

"And maybe she won't. She might be too close to falling off the deep end for that." Fiona's words sounded so ominous, I shuddered.

When I got back to Fiona's house, I got another shock. Jubal was sitting at the kitchen table with Boaz! I couldn't feel my feet on the floor as I moved toward the table. "Um . . . how are you doing, Boaz?" I asked.

"I'm fine, Fiona. I'm sorry for coming over here so late. I'd promised Jubal that I'd pay him tonight for the last work he done on my car. I had supper with some friends a couple of blocks from here and lost track of time. I decided to come here anyway before I drove back to Branson." Boaz stopped talking and looked me up and down. "You're looking as beautiful as ever."

"Thank you," I murmured.

Jubal waved me to the chair facing Boaz. "Um . . . all . . . right," I stammered. My legs was shaking and I wanted to get out of the room as fast as I could, but I didn't have a good reason not to sit down.

"I just asked Boaz if he wanted us to talk to Leona to see if we could get her to change her mind about him," Jubal said with a wink.

I felt like slapping him. I didn't appreciate him interfering in my love life. I snorted so hard my nostrils hurt. "Um . . . that might help," I said with my eyes blinking as I stared at Boaz's handsome face.

"I know me and her ain't known each other that long, but I know your sister as well as I need to. Besides, we ain't teenagers, so we can't spend years or even months on end getting to know one another better. I want to ask her to marry me," Boaz said with his voice cracking.

I got so light-headed when I heard them words. I was surprised I didn't collapse.

"Leona needs a strong, God-fearing man like you, Boaz. Maybe you can get her to stop going to all of them parties," Jubal tossed in.

"I wouldn't try to change her. I heard about her party life and it don't bother me one bit. I might start going to some of them parties with her." Boaz laughed.

"I'm sure she'd like that," I mumbled. My stomach was churning and my heart was beating like a drum. I was so nervous, I knew that if I didn't leave the room in the next few moments, Jubal or Boaz would notice how hard my hands was shaking. "I think I'll turn in for the night." I rubbed the back of my head. "I got one of my headaches."

"Then you better take a pill before you get in the bed," Jubal ordered.

"I will. Um . . . Boaz, it was nice seeing you again."

"I told him to come over more often, whether him and Leona get back together or not. Boaz, you ought to come visit our church sometime. You'll love listening to Reverend Sweeney preach."

"I would love to do that," Boaz said. "My preacher's sermons done got so boring, I get as much sleep at church as I get at home." He laughed again.

"After church one Sunday come join us for supper. Fiona makes a mean bean pie," Jubal added. "And since you like to fish as much as I do, we can start going together."

"I'll do that too," Boaz said.

I excused myself and stumbled to the bedroom. I was going to pray that Boaz wouldn't start visiting this house until after I'd moved back home.

Chapter 51
Fiona

A WHOLE WEEK HAD GONE BY SINCE BONNIE SUE'S CONFESSION and I hadn't seen her or heard from her no more. I was conflicted because she had been such a big part of my family's life. I wondered what Leona was going to do without her. I still didn't think it was such a good idea for her to try and get Bonnie Sue to renounce her feelings. That sounded like hogwash to me!

When I got home from work Tuesday evening, I called Leona up and she answered right away. "Can you talk?" I asked.

She hesitated for a few seconds. "Yeah. Jubal's outside cleaning fish."

"You heard from Bonnie Sue?"

"No. Have you?"

"No, but Boaz called again this evening. He told me he'd visited with you and Jubal."

"I was going to tell you about that."

"Leona, I think you should at least sit down and talk to the man. He's serious."

"I know he is. He told me and Jubal that he wants to marry me."

"Mighty Moses! I didn't know the man was *that* serious. I declare, he don't sound like a man who's been fooling around with prostitutes and a bunch of other women—and saying stuff like you was too old for him. I think all that mess you heard was just rumors started by jealous females."

"And another thing—I got to go! I hear Jubal coming back in!"

I didn't know if I was more nervous about Bonnie Sue coming back or Boaz. Wednesday when I got to Leona's house after work, Bonnie Sue was sitting on the front steps. Her eyes was red and so swollen you would have thought somebody had sucker punched her. "Why did you come back here?" I asked with my hands on my hips.

"I just need to say a few more things to you."

"If you didn't come to tell me all that stuff you said was a big joke, I don't want to hear nothing else."

"Leona, can I come in?"

I reluctantly answered, "I guess. But you can't stay long. I made plans for this evening."

She followed me to the couch. I flopped down, but she stood in the middle of the floor, shifting her weight from one foot to the other.

"I'm sorry if I made you mad. If you don't want to get involved with me, that's fine. Just make out like I didn't say nothing and we'll go on like nothing happened. Can we?"

I couldn't believe that she thought we could go on like before. "That ain't going to happen. I can't do nothing about you falling in love with me, but I ain't going to lead you on no further by letting you continue to spend time with me. When you leave here this time, don't come back and don't call me. If you bump into me in public, don't say nothing. Act like I'm a stranger. I hope I'm making myself clear this time so we won't have to conversate about this again. You get the picture?"

"I got it. I won't bother you no more," Bonnie Sue replied with her teeth clenched. She retied the scarf on her head and glanced around the room. I could see she was stalling, and that agitated me even more. "Before I leave, can I have a glass of water and a pig foot if you got some laying around?" she whimpered.

"I ain't got no pig feet."

She followed me into the kitchen and I poured her a glass of water as fast as I could. She drunk it in one long pull, set the glass on the counter, and started talking again in a low voice that sounded almost like a growl. "Leona, I did so much for you."

"I know and I thank you for that. I've did a lot for you too so I think we can call it even. We had a good past, so at least we got a heap of fond memories."

All of a sudden, there was a look on her face that I would never forget. Her eyes got darker, her nostrils flared, and her jaws started twitching. This time she did growl, "*I even killed for you.*"

I couldn't have been more dumbfounded if she had told me she had a tail tucked inside her bloomers. "What?"

"I knew that if you had married Wally, I would have lost you for good. He hated me, so I knew he wouldn't stand for me to spend too much time with you."

My jaw dropped and so did my heart. "Y-you killed Wally?"

"Damn right I did! As soon as you got so goo-goo-eyed over him, I started planning to get rid of him. You know I know a lot about cars, so I knew what to tamper with under the hood that would make his brakes stop working after he'd drove a few miles. I was sorry his three friends died with him. I prayed for their souls."

Good God! I was stupefied to find out that the bogeyman I used to fret about when I was a little girl had a sister. I pointed to the kitchen door. "Get out of my house before I throw you out! I'm going to call Sheriff Zachary so he can arrest you for murdering *four* people! Your goose won't just be cooked, it'll be *incinerated* when they strap you into the electric chair and pull the switch!" I grabbed Bonnie Sue's arm and steered her toward the door.

"Turn me loose! You ain't got to manhandle me!" she yelled with spit flying out both sides of her mouth. She was dragging her feet like a unruly toddler. She suddenly snatched her arm away and wagged her finger in my face. "Don't put your hands on me, bitch!"

I gulped so hard my tongue froze for a split second. "What did you call me?"

"BITCH!"

I slapped Bonnie Sue's face so hard my hand stung and her scarf slid off her head. I pulled her by her hair to the door and pushed her out. I couldn't get to the telephone fast enough to call up Leona. I was so happy she answered on the first ring, I almost passed out. "Is Jubal around?" I panted.

"I sent him to get me a fish sandwich. Why?"

"I need to tell you something!"

"I'm listening. But calm down and stop hollering so loud."

I said in a even louder tone, "Bonnie Sue killed Wally and his friends!"

"What in the world—Wally died in a car wreck. Jubal said that somebody who had it in for one of his friends must have messed with the car to make it crash."

"Bonnie Sue done it."

"No, she didn't!"

"Yes, she did, Leona. She knows almost as much about cars as Jubal."

"I don't know who told you that, but you need to get that idea out of your head. I know Bonnie Sue scared you by claiming to be in love with me. That scared me too. But we both know that there ain't a violent bone in her body. She wouldn't even fight back when the kids at school beat her up."

"Leona, I ain't playing with you. Bonnie Sue is dangerous. *She told me herself that she killed Wally!* She hated him and she hates Boaz. All because she was afraid they'd push her out of your life. You need to get in touch with Boaz and warn him!"

Leona gasped so loud it sounded like she was standing right in front of me. "My God! I-I don't know how to get in touch with him. He ain't got no telephone and I ain't got no way to get to his house in Branson."

"When Jubal gets back, tell him you need to use the car to take me somewhere. I'll ride over to Boaz's house with you. I can—hold on, I just heard the front door slam. Let me see who it is and I'll call you back."

Before I could make it to the living room, Bonnie Sue entered the kitchen. "What are you doing back here, girl?" I boomed.

"I'm sorry. I swear to God, I won't do or say nothing else to upset you." Bonnie Sue's voice was so raspy, she didn't sound nothing like herself.

"You killed four people. I'm going to call up Sheriff Zachary so he can come and arrest you." I immediately started dialing. When Bonnie Sue knocked the telephone out of my hand, I seen fifty shades of red.

"You miserable lovestruck *bulldagging* heifer!" I slapped her face so hard, I left a handprint on her jaw. She stumbled and fell to the floor and curled up in a ball like a land slug. "Get up!" I ordered. I kicked her foot, but she just laid there crying, slobbering, and cussing. I grabbed her hand and pulled her up and tried to push her toward the door. She wouldn't budge a inch. Before I realized what was happening, she reached around me and grabbed the butcher knife that I'd left on the counter. I didn't know that I was about to utter my last words. "Bonnie Sue, you put that knife down! I ain't going to—MAMA!"

Chapter 52
Leona

I WAS IN BED WITH THE COVERS PULLED UP TO MY CHIN WHEN JUBAL came into the bedroom. I had so much on my mind, I knew it was going to be a rough night for me. One minute I thought about what Fiona told me about Bonnie Sue and how we was going to fix that dilemma. The next minute I thought about Boaz and him wanting to marry me. I didn't know which one to focus on the most. I'd probably see Bonnie Sue before I seen Boaz, so I decided it would make more sense to come up with a plan to straighten her out first. Knowing she was in love with me, I knew it would have a strong impact on our relationship. Would I ever feel comfortable when I was alone with her? I wondered. And the same went for Boaz. I couldn't do nothing with neither one of them until I resumed my real identity. Meanwhile, I would think about both cases as much as I could until I came up with the right solutions to fix each one.

After I finally dozed off, I woke back up with a sharp pain in my chest. Suddenly, I felt overwhelmed with sadness. The first thought that came to my mind was that something had happened to my mama. I tumbled out of bed and sprinted to the kitchen and dialed her number. The phone rang eight times, but I wasn't about to hang up. If she didn't answer, I'd go over to her house. "You all right?" I asked when she answered on the tenth ring.

Mama took her time responding. "Who is this?"

"Uh, it's Le—Fiona," I whimpered. I couldn't believe that as careful as me and Fiona was about not giving ourselves away, I'd almost said my real name.

"What's wrong? You sick? Jubal done left you?"

"No, nothing like that, Mama. I just had a strange feeling . . ."

"Well, you ain't got to worry about me. Except for stiff joints, heartburn, gas, and a weak bladder, I'm doing just fine. I hope that your buck-wild sister ain't finally got herself arrested again, or worse."

"I'm sure Leona is fine, Mama. You go back to sleep."

At daybreak, the telephone rang. I scrambled out of bed to answer it. It was Mama. "I went over to Sister Bea's house this morning to take her some witch hazel before I left for work. I was on my way back home when I seen the sheriff's car leaving my house."

My heart felt like it had froze. "What do you think he wanted?"

"I don't know, but I doubt if he was paying me a social visit. When did you last talk to Leona?"

"Last night. She was all right."

"Okay. Well, I'll stop by the sheriff's office on my way home this evening to see what he wanted. I seen his mama at the market last week. She admired the shawl I had on so much, she told me she wanted me to knit one for her and that she would send the yarn and everything else to me by one of her kids."

"That's probably why the sheriff was at your house."

Mama took several seconds to respond. "This early in the morning?"

"Maybe he decided to drop off that stuff on his way to work. Now, you better get to work before your boss starts to worry about you."

After I hung up, I started fixing breakfast. Jubal was in the bathroom getting ready for work when I heard a car stop in front of the house. I trotted to the living-room window and looked out. I almost swallowed my tongue when I seen Sheriff Zachary's squad car. I didn't even wait for him to get out before

I opened the door. He adjusted his hat and strode up on the front porch.

"Good morning, Sheriff Zachary," I said. I made myself sound as cheerful as I could when he shuffled in. Sheriff Zachary was as mean and racist as Sheriff Bodine had been before he got voted out of office and Sheriff Zachary got voted in. He was even fatter, homelier, and even more slovenly than Sheriff Bodine. The grim expression on his face and his empty hands told me he didn't come to bring no yarn for me to give to Mama to make his mama a shawl. "How you doing?"

"Tolerable. Just tolerable," he answered in a dry tone. He stopped in the middle of the floor, folded his arms, and the look on his face got even grimmer. "You the sister of one Leona Dunbar?"

"Yes, sir."

"Is there somebody here with you? You don't need to be by yourself when you hear what I came to tell you."

"My husband is here." Without looking away from Sheriff Zachary's icy blue eyes, I yelled, "Jubal, get in here!"

He immediately skittered into the room, with shaving cream still on half of his face. His jaw dropped when he seen the sheriff. "Hello. What's the matter, sir? Did somebody burn down my garage?"

"Not that I know of. This is much worse." Sheriff Zachary stopped talking for a moment and looked at the floor. When he looked back up, I was surprised to see tears in his eyes. Everybody knew he was in cahoots with the Ku Klux Klan. Our newspaper had run a picture of him grinning and shaking hands with a Klansman at one of their stupid rallies last year. I figured that at some point in their lives, even the worst racists had a spot in their heart that had some feeling for folks other than their own kind. I would never forget how "nice" Sheriff Bodine had been to me when I was in jail. "Leona lost her life last night. The Fuller Brothers undertaking outfit done already picked up her body and hauled her to their funeral home. Y'all need to get in touch with them."

I stumbled and almost hit the floor, but I didn't. My head was spinning so hard, I could barely see straight. I knew I wasn't supposed to raise my voice when talking to a white person, especially a peacemaker. But this was one time I overlooked them stupid-ass rules about how colored folks was supposed to behave when dealing with them. "WHAT HAPPENED?" I boomed.

My loud tone didn't bother the sheriff. He continued to gaze at me with a sympathetic look on his face. "Well, I can't go into detail, but she was murdered."

"By who?" me and Jubal said at the same time. I stumbled again. This time I fell against Jubal. He wrapped his arm around my waist and that was the only thing that kept me from hitting the floor.

Sheriff Zachary held up both his hands. "Y'all calm down and don't worry. I got the culprit locked up. I'll be bound if she ever sees the light of day again. Judge Hanley is my uncle so I'll make sure of that."

I was so flabbergasted a flea could have knocked me over. "*She?* Was it . . . Bonnie Sue Frost?"

"I'm afraid so. According to Leona's next-door neighbors on both sides, they heard bloodcurdling screams coming from her house. When they went outside to take a look-see, they seen your sister running out of her front door bleeding like a stuck pig. Her killer had already stabbed her a few times, but she chased her down the street, caught up with her, and stabbed her some more."

Tears gushed out of my eyes. I couldn't talk or move. The next thing I knew, my knees buckled and I fainted.

When I came to, I was in bed. I was in such a daze, I thought I was waking up from a bad dream. My longtime drinking buddy Nadine was sitting on the side of the bed, dabbing her eyes with a handkerchief.

"What happened?" I whimpered.

She hesitated and cleared her throat. I could tell from the grimace on her face that she was going to tell me something I didn't want to hear. "Y-you fainted when the sheriff told you . . . what happened to Leona."

I took a deep breath. "Then I wasn't dreaming."

Nadine shook her head. "Your sister is gone." Them four words felt like knives going into my ears.

"Where's Jubal?" It was a struggle, but I managed to sit up. I was aching in so many places, I didn't even bother to try and ease my discomfort.

"He's at the funeral home," Nadine said, choking on a sob. She pulled a handkerchief out of her brassiere and blew her nose into it. "Your mama and his mama went with him. Sweet Jesus! I—I don't know if I can get through this."

Nadine was trembling so hard; I grabbed her hand. She attempted to get up but I pulled her back down. "I don't know if I can neither, so I need you to be strong for me." I couldn't believe how strong I sounded. I sat up straighter. "I need to go see her."

Nadine threw her arms up in the air and waved them. "No, you don't! Your mama and Jubal said you wouldn't be able to handle it."

I tried to get out of bed, but Nadine held me in place. "Don't tell me what I can't handle! I want to see her! I want to go see where she was killed," I hollered.

"Fiona, calm down and listen to me. You don't need to see where Leona died." Nadine heaved out a long, deep breath. "Bonnie Sue stabbed her so many times, the undertakers stopped counting after thirty. And . . . and she cut her throat so deep, the neighbors said her head was hanging on by a thread. By the time I got over there, it looked like a hog had been butchered." Nadine paused and heaved out another deep breath. "I ran into Leona's house and got some towels and me and the lady next door sopped up the blood off the porch and sidewalk."

If Nadine had told me that today was the Apocalypse, I couldn't have felt no worse. "No, no, no!" I cried. "This is all my fault!"

"It ain't nobody's fault but Bonnie Sue's. Only God knows

what got into her. I suspect her mind went off-kilter when she lost so many folks in her family. Leona must have said something that triggered a flashback and she finally snapped. Now you just stay put and I'll go fix you a cup of tea. Everybody should be back soon."

Nadine left the bedroom and I laid back down. I wanted to cry some more, but I was so stunned, I couldn't squeeze out no more tears.

Chapter 53
Leona

WE DIDN'T HAVE BUT ONE HOSPITAL. THEY DIDN'T ADMIT COLored people under no circumstances. Whenever one of us had a medical emergency, we had to be hauled to the colored clinic by somebody with a car or a truck.

While I was still laying in bed, a bunch of Leona's neighbors came to the house. I found out from one that another neighbor had hog-tied Bonnie Sue with a rope that somebody had handed him. He was a great big man so he hadn't had no trouble sitting on her and holding her in place on the ground until Sheriff Zachary showed up. Like always, when colored folks called him, he took his time coming. The Fuller Brothers showed up with their hearse first.

The same neighbor who had hog-tied Bonnie Sue had hauled her onto his front porch. She had stopped kicking and screaming, but she boo-hooed until the sheriff arrived forty minutes later.

The undertakers hadn't even bothered to take Fiona to the clinic; every witness claimed that she was way too far gone. They didn't do autopsies on colored folks in our town, but it was obvious what had killed her. One of the undertakers told me and Mama that he counted fifty stab wounds in Fiona's chest. And most of them was in her heart. If I could have got my hands on Bonnie Sue before the sheriff took her away, I would have done so much damage to her, they would have needed glue to put her back together!

My anger and grief was so extreme, I didn't want to see nobody, not even Mama or Jubal. But as soon as they got back from the funeral home, they came into the room. "How you feel, sugar?" Jubal asked as he eased down on the foot of the bed.

I didn't say nothing. I just hunched my shoulders. "Can I get you something to eat or drink?" Mama asked.

"I don't want nothing," I sobbed. I sat up in bed and looked from Jubal to Mama. "I need to see my sister before they put her in the ground."

Mama shook her head. "We ain't going to let you see her."

"She don't look like herself no more, baby," Jubal added. "We want you to remember how beautiful she was in life."

I wanted to remind them that if I wanted to remember how beautiful my twin was in life, all I had to do was look in the mirror. "Does anybody know why Bonnie Sue did what she did?"

Jubal rubbed his head and went on. "She ain't talking. Sheriff Zachary was nice enough to allow Reverend Sweeney to visit her at the jailhouse so he could pray for her. He told us he tried to get her to tell him what caused the ruckus, but she wouldn't tell him."

I wasn't sure what had happened at my house last night, but I was convinced that it had something to do with Bonnie Sue confessing her feelings of love for me. I was sorry I had not got in touch with her right after Fiona told me. Maybe I could have talked some sense into her. I didn't know how I would have reacted, but I wouldn't have reacted the way Fiona did. The bottom line was if we hadn't switched, my sister would still be alive.

I wondered what my life was going to be like now. The hardest thing I had to deal with was that I couldn't tell Mama, Jubal, or nobody else that me and Fiona had switched places and that she was the one dead. The truth would only devastate Mama and as old as she was, it might have even killed her. If she found out I was really Leona and had gone along with the ruse for selfish and frivolous reasons, I didn't think she'd ever forgive me. Especially since she'd been telling me all my life that I should be more like Fiona. I had two choices: Tell folks what me and Fiona had done and go back to my old life, or pretend to be her until the day I died. I decided to be Fiona. It seemed like the most reasonable choice. I didn't want to hurt my mama no more and I didn't want everybody else—especially Jubal—to know I was a fraud.

The next couple of days went by in a blur. The day of the funeral, I had to force myself to get out of bed. Mama came to the house so me and her and Jubal could ride to the church together in Jubal's car. I wore the plainest of the three black dresses Fiona had in her closet. Mama had on a floor-length black dress, a black shawl, and a wide-brimmed hat with a black veil. Jubal hadn't had time to get his only black suit cleaned, so he wore one that was so dark blue, it almost looked black.

Our church was only three blocks from our house, but we rarely walked to it, especially if we was going to attend a funeral.

"I just knew something like this would happen someday," Mama muttered. She was sitting on the backseat with Lamar. He looked so big and strong in his uniform, but he'd cried so much he'd barely spoken since he got home from France last night. I was in front with Jubal. He had one hand on the steering wheel and his other arm was around my shoulder. "I prayed for years that Leona would stop living such a worldly life."

"I didn't think she was so worldly," Jubal said. "She was one of the most responsible, caring women I knew. I ain't surprised Boaz was planning to ask her to marry him."

"That field hand?" Mama said sharply.

"Yes, that field hand," I snapped.

"Well, if she had married him, I would have welcomed him into the family regardless of his line of work. Last month when I attended a funeral over in Branson, he was there. We had a nice little chat. He seemed like a fine man. And a godly man. I would have been proud to call him my son-in-law." Mama chuckled. "As proud as I am of you, Jubal."

"Thank you," he said.

"How come you never told Leona you had a chat with Boaz and that you had changed your tune about him?" I asked.

"How do you know I didn't?"

"She would have told me if you did."

"No, I didn't tell her. But since she had broke up with him and never wanted to see him again, I didn't think it mattered."

I felt better knowing that Mama had changed her tune about Boaz, even though I knew me and him could never be together now. I had told Mama that there was no way I could go with her and a few ladies from our church to pack up Leona's stuff and clean up her house. She understood and even told me that I was too fragile for something like that. Otto and Lamar said they'd help Jubal haul away the heavy stuff.

Our church was small and ordinary looking, and like so many of the churches in Alabama, it was Baptist. The steeple on top was a little crooked, but the front lawn always looked well-tended. For some reason, the tornadoes we had every year had never done any damage to it. Mama said it was because of divine intervention. Even though our church was plain on the outside, inside it had a homey feel to it. The walls was covered with loud-colored pictures of people from the Bible and the floor always looked like it had just been mopped. It was near the colored cemetery and that miserable rooming house I used to live at. Just being in this vicinity depressed me even more than I already was. On top of that, about a dozen crows was flying overhead. One reason this was so eerie to me was because the only time I seen a mob of them creatures flapping around in this area was when a funeral was about to take place.

We had arrived half a hour before the service was scheduled to start. Before we could make it to the front pew, dozens of people came up and hugged us and said the usual stuff folks say to a bereaved family. I grabbed Jubal's arm when I seen the grim-faced pallbearers coming in with Fiona's casket. "I . . . I don't think I'm going to make it through this," I whispered to him.

"Yes, you will, sugar," he replied in a strong tone.

I closed my eyes when I seen them open the casket. "I want to go see my sister now before I get too distressed to do it," I told Jubal. He didn't say nothing as he led me to the front of the church. The Fuller Brothers had done a good job. Fiona just looked like she was sleeping. Mama told me she had instructed them to use the same makeup she'd always wore in public. I couldn't go into my house to pick out a burial outfit. Mama couldn't neither. She had bought a new pink dress with a high-neck collar so nobody could see the slash on Fiona's neck. As a finishing touch, Mama had tied a blue ribbon on a clump of Fiona's hair after the Fuller Brothers finished what they had to do. "Leona has to have on the right-colored ribbon so God will know which twin she is," she'd said. I had busted out crying when I heard her say that.

Reverend Sweeney hadn't been back to the house after that day he'd come at me. And I hadn't expected him to until me and Fiona had switched back. Now that I was stuck in her place, I didn't know how I was going to handle him when he did return.

Every pew was filled at "my" funeral. Dozens of mourners had to stand in the back of the room and outside in the front of the church. I had no idea so many people cared about me. I couldn't wait for the service to end so I could go home and pull myself back together. Lamar was so overcome with grief, he decided to sit closer to the back with some of his friends.

After we'd returned to our pew, Mama said, "It's a shame you couldn't tame your sister down. Maybe I should have whupped her more." Even in death I was still getting mean-mouthed.

"Maybe you shouldn't have criticized her so much," I said.

"Sweet Jesus! I didn't 'criticize' her. I was only telling her that if she was more like you, she'd have a much better life. She wouldn't have got pregnant or went to jail."

Jubal's eyes got big. He knew about Leona going to jail, but this was the first time he was hearing about the pregnancy. "Who got Leona pregnant?"

"She didn't know who the daddy was," Mama said with a sniffle. "She lost the baby, so we'd never know what it looked like. Maybe then we could have figured out who the daddy was."

"Y'all hush up. Reverend Sweeney is about to start," I said.

Like he always did at every funeral, Reverend Sweeney

preached up a storm about the evils of living a worldly life. Twenty minutes into his ramblings, he said, "I prayed and prayed and prayed until I was blue in the face for Sister Leona. I wanted her to come to me for some spiritual guidance so I could turn her around!" He stopped talking long enough to mop his face with a small white towel and drink from the glass of water he'd set on top of the pulpit. "I also prayed for Sister Bonnie Sue. She's got to live with a burden that's going to wear her down to a frazzle."

As soon as Reverend Sweeney finished, I wobbled up and went into the dining area. I put a fried chicken leg, a few hush puppies, and some potato salad on a plate. I didn't have much of a appetite, but since I had only nibbled on a few biscuits in the last couple of days, I knew I had to eat something more substantial to keep up my strength.

Before I could move to another part of the room, Otto Brewster came up to me. Jubal was so distraught, he had took off from work for the whole week and had Otto running the garage. I had to admit to myself that he looked very handsome in his black suit, white shirt, and red tie. He looked so sad, I hugged him long and hard. He reared back and mopped sweat and tears off his face with a napkin. "Fiona, I declare, I miss Leona and I'm sorry I didn't try hard enough to win her over. If she'd gave me a chance, I would have made her real happy. I . . . I fell in love with her years ago," he said, with his voice cracking on a sob.

"I'm sorry she didn't give you a chance, Otto. Thank you for coming." I couldn't think of nothing else to say to him so I moved to another spot.

Lamar was so upset, he said he didn't want to be in Lexington no longer than he had to be. He had made arrangements to leave right after the funeral. I was glad he was the next person who came up to me. "Mama, even when I was a little bitty boy I knew Bonnie Sue was evil. I could feel it in my bones every time she came around. Now everybody else knows it too," he said in a raspy tone of voice.

"You was right, sugar. I just wish we could have figured that out before it was too late," I said. He hugged me and went to talk to some of his friends.

While everybody was piling food onto their plates, I stood in a corner eating by myself. Several folks came up and gave me condolences. When Reverend Sweeney strode up to me and hugged my neck, he whispered in my ear, "As soon as you done finished grieving, let me know and we can pick up where we left off."

I was so appalled at his nerve, my chest tightened. I couldn't believe that this man was thinking about sex right after he'd preached my sister's funeral! I wanted to cuss him out and let everybody know what a womanizing scoundrel he really was. But this was not the time or place to do that. "We will never pick up where we left off," I whispered back. "It's over!"

Reverend Sweeney took a short, deep breath and looked at me with his eyes narrowed. "Huh? Do you mean that?"

"You better believe it. If you ever attempt anything inappropriate with me again, I'm going to tell my husband and your wife everything. Do you hear me, preacher man?"

He looked so stunned, I could have blew him to the floor with one breath. "I hear you." He paused and started wagging his finger in my face. "Let me tell you one thing before I go, *Sister* Fiona, if you ever need spiritual guidance again, that's *all* you'll get from me. I won't waste no more of my time fiddling around with a woman who is so ungrateful after all I did to put some harmony into your lackluster marriage." He shot me a red-hot look, and then he whirled around to leave so fast he almost fell. Reverend Sweeney didn't say nothing else to me that day.

Chapter 54
Leona

*T*HE KINFOLKS ON MAMA'S AND DADDY'S SIDE WHO HAD ALWAYS avoided us showed up at my funeral. They was cordial, and me and Mama was cordial to them. A few on Daddy's side hinted that they would like to have a closer relationship with us. Mama was pleased to hear that and so was I. But I wasn't going to get too excited about it until they proved they meant it.

I didn't know Boaz was present until he came up to me in the dining area. He looked so good in his black pinstriped suit. "How are you holding up, Sister Fiona?" he asked.

I dabbed a tear from my eye and gave him a crooked smile before I answered. "I'm doing all right, I guess." I had to force myself not to think about what Fiona had told me about Bonnie Sue killing Wally and that she had probably planned to kill Boaz. I couldn't tell nobody about that stuff neither. It wouldn't have done no good, and it would have opened up a barrel full of worms. Mama and everybody else would have suspected that I knew something about why Bonnie Sue killed Fiona. I never thought I'd lose my beloved twin and my best friend at the same time. I would pray that the knowledge wouldn't eventually overwhelm me so much I'd lose my mind and end up in the crazy house. I had to be stronger than ever now and move forward for Fiona because I wanted something positive to come from this horrific tragedy.

I was so light-headed, I had to stop my mind from wandering

and return my attention to Boaz. "I'm going to miss Leona. I'll never love another woman the way I loved her," he declared in a strong tone.

"Don't say that. I'm sure you'll love again."

"Not the way I loved her. I do know that I'll never marry again now. I don't think there's another woman alive who could take her place in my heart."

Hearing him say that almost made me break down. "I-I'm sure she would have loved to hear you say that." It sickened me to know that I could never marry Boaz now.

While he was still standing next to me, Mama approached us. She had cried so much, her eyes was red and swollen, her veil and floppy hat was turned sideways, and lipstick was smeared on her teeth. "Son, I'm sorry things didn't work out between you and Leona." She sniffled as she dabbed her eyes with a white handkerchief. "I want you to know that you can still come visit with me. I cook a mean mess of collard greens. I heard from Leona that it's one of your favorite dishes."

"I will take you up on that real soon, Sister Mavis." Boaz let out a dry laugh and then he dabbed tears from his eyes. "If only I had gone to her house that night, I could have stopped Bonnie Sue, even if I'd had to kill her! If they ever let her out of prison, I won't be responsible for my actions!"

I didn't want to hear Mama's response to Boaz's outburst so I excused myself. I plowed through the crowd until I found Jubal and told him to take me home. As we was leaving, I caught a glimpse of a man squatting between two trees in front of the church. He was crying like a baby. It took me a few seconds to re-alize it was Clayton. I hadn't seen him in the church during the service, and I hadn't seen or heard from him since the last time Bonnie Sue dragged him to my house last month. I didn't know what to say to him now, so I was glad he was keeping his dis-tance. I told myself that maybe after enough time had passed, I could resume my relationship with him.

When me and Jubal went to bed that night, he immediately

pulled me into his arms and we cried together some more. I didn't sleep more than a couple of hours.

The first week was the hardest. I didn't know if I was going to be able to spend the rest of my days on earth living such a massive lie. I felt so lost, I didn't know which way to turn. Even a simple trip to the market was a challenge. I went to pick up some chicken feet and turnip greens to cook for supper the Monday after the funeral. When I got back out on the street, I was so disoriented it took me a few moments to figure out if I was supposed to go left or right.

Each day it got a little easier for me. I didn't know how I would have kept myself from going to pieces if it hadn't been for Jubal. He was still grieving just as hard as me and Mama was, and he didn't complain about the way I was walking around like one of them zombies in Haiti that I read about in a book. "Fiona, I love you and I always will. If there is anything I can do to help ease your pain, just let me know," Jubal told me on one of them nights when I couldn't sleep.

Him just being hisself was enough for me. Bless his soul. He treated me like a queen. I still couldn't help but wonder why Fiona had resented him so much.

I was still grieving two weeks after Fiona's funeral. Some days was worse than others. On one particularly bad day I was so distressed, I couldn't even get out of bed. Jubal stayed home from work and served me breakfast in bed, did the laundry I hadn't done in two weeks, and he even bathed me like I was a baby.

Jubal was the kind of man I would have liked to marry—for real. And for all intents and purposes, I was married to him.

After two more weeks had went by, I was almost my old self. I picked up a few things from the market and invited Mama to come over and have lunch with me that Saturday afternoon. After we had ate up the chicken gizzards and okra I'd fried, we went into the living room and flopped down on the couch. Mama suddenly put her arm around my shoulder, let out a loud sigh, and started to talk in a weary tone. "I wish Leona had been more like you and—"

I cut her off as fast as I could. Them was the last words I wanted to hear while I was still grieving. "Is that why you didn't love her as much as you loved me?"

Mama removed her arm from around my shoulder and looked at me like I'd lost my mind. "I declare, I didn't love you no more than I loved her!"

"Then why was you so hard on her? She told me how much it hurt her every time you told her to be more like me."

Mama sucked in a deep breath and stared at the wall before she turned back to face me. "I said it because I didn't want her to be like me."

I gave Mama a curious look. "What? Next to Reverend Sweeney's wife, you must be the most pious colored woman in Lexington."

Mama shook her head. "I am now. But when I was young, I was even wilder than Leona."

My head started throbbing on both sides. I couldn't imagine Mama being "wilder than Leona." "What do you mean?"

"I was married to another man before I met your daddy. We lived in Mobile and had three baby boys before I even turned eighteen. It didn't take long for me to realize I had gave up the single life too soon. I started hanging out with a rowdy, hard-drinking crowd. Well, one night when I staggered back into my house, my husband and the boys was gone. My in-laws wouldn't tell me where they went. Mama was so disgusted with the way I had been behaving, she was glad Eddie had run off. Years went by. I never heard from him or my boys. Finally, I moved to Lexington where nobody knew me. I joined church and started living a holy life. I promised God I would stay on the straight and narrow and I asked Him to let me see my children again. He didn't answer that prayer, but He sent me your daddy and you and Leona. I was determined to keep you and her from being the kind of floozy I'd been. That was why I was so hard on her. But it didn't do no good . . ."

You could have knocked me over with a feather. It never occurred to me that my own mama had some deep dark secrets too. I shifted in my seat and slid a few inches closer to her because tears was streaming down her face. "Mama, I am so sorry you went through that." I suddenly got so giddy I could barely contain myself. "I . . . I can't believe I got three big brothers! I sure would like to meet them and their families!" I had to stop and catch my breath. "After all these years, maybe your first husband's family ain't still mad at you. We can go to Mobile and ask them how we can get in touch with my brothers—"

Mama cut me off. "No, we can't. When I was pregnant with you and Leona, I finally got up enough nerve to go see if they'd had a change of heart. I was too late. Everybody in the family had either died or moved to places unknown."

I felt like a balloon somebody had let the air out of. For Mama's sake as well as mine, I was ready to end this conversation. "I can see how painful this is for you. You don't need to tell me nothing else about your past."

"I wish I had told Leona this before she died. Maybe she would have understood why I was so hard on her."

I sniffed and patted Mama's shoulder. "I got a feeling she knew you had a good reason to treat her the way you did." I wished I had heard Mama's confession before I took over Fiona's identity. If I had, I might not have agreed to do it, and she'd probably still be alive. But I wanted to heal now, so I wasn't going to dwell on things that couldn't be changed. "Did Daddy know you'd been married before?"

"I told him everything before we got married. He didn't tell nobody in Lexington because he didn't want them to judge me." Mama's voice got real low, even though we was alone in the house. "I don't want you to tell nobody nothing about my past neither, Fiona."

"I won't," I muttered.

"I'm glad you've always been honest with me about everything. I hope you stay this way."

"I will." Mama's strange story was on my mind so much, I didn't sleep much when I went to bed. I still didn't like the way she had treated me, but knowing why she had done it made me feel so much better. I woke up the next morning feeling more chipper than I'd felt since my twin died.

By the end of the second month after Fiona's murder, my emotions had stabilized. I felt like I was at a point where I could truly be happy despite everything that had happened. But when I seen Boaz in public, I tensed up and couldn't wait to get away from him. Each time he would mention Leona and how much he missed her. The last time I ran into him at the market he said something that really threw me for a loop. "I ain't told nobody else this, but I feel guilty about what happened to Leona."

"Oh?" was all I could say at first.

"I feel like it's my fault that she's dead."

"Oh?" I said again. My knees almost buckled and I had to cough to clear my throat before I could say something else. "I feel that way myself sometimes, but neither one of us should."

"You're right, Fiona. Guilt can really wear a person down and if it gets too bad, they might end up doing something crazy."

I sighed and shook my head. "They sure might." I still believed that it didn't make no sense for me to tell Mama and Jubal about the identity switch. Mama wouldn't tell nobody, but I couldn't be sure about Jubal. Him and his mama was so close, he'd probably end up telling her sooner or later. I also knew that if I did tell him everything, our "marriage" would be over. In the long run, if the truth ever came out, everybody that knew me would be horrified. I'd have to pack my bags and leave town because nobody would ever want to have anything else to do with me. Not only that, everybody who had loved Fiona would also denounce her as a fraud for living a double life and getting involved in such a ungodly scheme. Even though she was dead, I didn't want folks to say mean things about her. And they would have a field day if they ever found out she was the real floozy in our family, not me.

I missed going to parties and drinking at my house with my rowdy friends, but I was glad I had ended the lifestyle that had led me down such a dark path. I believed in my heart that if I hadn't made what I was doing look like so much fun, Fiona wouldn't have wanted to be in my place for a month.

We was all surprised that Bonnie Sue got sentenced to ninety-nine years in prison and not the electric chair. That's what usually happened to a colored person when they killed somebody. But some folks, me included, thought that being locked up for almost a hundred years was a life sentence and worse than being put to death in the state electric chair that everybody called Yellow Mama. Everything about prison was hellish. The warden and some of the guards treated the prisoners, colored and white, like animals. They would randomly beat them and feed them slop that wasn't fit for a hog. And when the prisoners got sick or injured, they never got medical attention until it was too late. There was no way Bonnie Sue was going to live long enough to serve out her sentence without going stone crazy.

Bonnie Sue's crime affected everybody. When Clayton's mama heard what she had done, she had a heart attack and died. Poor Clayton was so broke up, the day after Bonnie Sue got sentenced, he quit his beloved job as a train porter. Three days after that, he moved to Ohio to live with relatives who had moved up there years ago. All three of him and Bonnie Sue's sons went with him.

One night four months after the murder, Jubal didn't just hold me in his arms when we went to bed, he went the whole hog and tugged my bloomers off me. I didn't have no reason to reject him. Besides, it had been so long since I'd had sex, I was more than ready to go at it. I didn't expect to see stars like I had with Boaz. Fiona had convinced me that Jubal's performance was so pitiful, she had to force herself not to go to sleep in the middle of the act. I was stunned when it turned out that he was a better lover than Boaz!

That night was the beginning of a whole new aspect of the bizarre situation I was in. Now I had to be more affectionate toward Jubal because I wanted to keep him happy. I realized I felt the same passion for him that I'd felt for Boaz. Every evening when he came home from the garage, I met him at the door and wrapped my arms around his neck so tight, one time I almost strangled him. One thing that puzzled me was the fact that he hadn't said nothing about how much I had changed—even before Fiona's murder. She had told me a heap of times how she used to brow-beat him and make fun of him to his face. I had never said nothing unflattering or disrespectful to him since the day I moved in.

I was glad that our mothers came around so often because six months after Fiona's death, Jubal's mama went to sleep one night and never woke up. Jubal took it real hard. He was so distraught he didn't go to work for a whole week. I'd consoled him as much as I could. Three weeks later, Mama died and he had to console me. There was some kind of uproar going on at the airport in Germany where Lamar was stationed so he wasn't able to attend Mama's funeral. But everybody else who knew her came. Dr. Brown's family had been so fond of Mama that his widow and five children paid for her funeral! If that wasn't enough of a kind gesture, them and all of the grandchildren attended my sweet mama's funeral. This was the first time that white folks had ever been inside our church. They had sat on the back pews and had not gone around hugging folks, like everybody else. They took off the second the service ended. That was all right with me, though. I was surprised, but pleased, that they had come.

After the folks who had come to the house to grieve with us had gone home, me and Jubal sat across from one another at the kitchen table. "I hope nobody else dies anytime soon," I said with my voice cracking. "I never thought I'd lose my twin, my mama, and my mother-in-law all within a few months of each other."

Jubal rubbed the back of his head and exhaled. "Baby, whatever happens is God's will."

"I know, I know. I just wish me and my family could have had many more years together." I paused and chuckled. I wondered if all three of the half brothers I'd never met was still alive. But that was a subject I could never discuss with Jubal. I cleared my throat and went on. "Boy, was Leona a wild woman. I wish she had slowed down enough to please Mama."

Jubal stood up and gave me a sideways look. "She did slow down, *Leona*," he said with a wink.

Chapter 55
Leona

RIGHT AFTER JUBAL STOPPED TALKING, I FROZE. DID HE KNOW I was not his real wife? I answered my own question: no. Me and Fiona had been so careful, there was no way he could know. Or was there? I mentally counted to five and took a very deep breath. That helped because I immediately felt more relaxed. But I wouldn't get too relaxed just yet.

I took another deep breath and told myself that Jubal calling me by my real name was just a slip of the tongue. A heap of other people had accidentally called me and Fiona by each other's name over the years. But because he had winked at me, a little voice told me he knew *something*. I tried to play it off anyway. "Um . . . you called me Leona by mistake." My voice was so small and weak, I could barely hear myself. But he heard me.

"I didn't make no mistake. I called you Leona because that's your name, ain't it?" Jubal put his hands on the back of the chair in front of him and leaned forward.

I was so mortified, I wanted to crawl into a hole and pull it in after me. I dropped my head and stared at the floor for a few seconds. When I looked back up, there was a tight smile on his face.

"You know I ain't Fiona?"

Jubal nodded.

I knew that it wouldn't do me no good to deny it. But he couldn't prove I was her, and I couldn't prove I wasn't. What kind of mess had I got myself into? I asked myself. Now that I didn't have Fiona to turn to for support and guidance, I wasn't just in a pickle, I was in a pickle barrel. "W-when d-did you figure it out?" I stammered.

He sniffed and sat back down. "I didn't have to figure out nothing. I knew from the get-go."

I stared at him with my mouth gaped open like a bottomless hole. "Then how could you let me go on and—"

Jubal held up his hand. "I overheard y'all plotting and planning that night when y'all thought I was in the bed sleeping. When you insisted on going to your house to finalize everything, I waited until I heard the front door shut and I followed y'all. I hid by the side of your house and listened through that window you always left cracked open."

My whole body felt so hot, I was surprised I didn't go up in flames. My hands was shaking and so much sweat was sliding down my face, it felt like a waterfall. "All this time . . . you let me believe you thought I was Fiona? W-why?"

"I decided not to say nothing because I never thought y'all would keep the prank going for more than a couple of days. Another reason was because you treated me the way I always wanted my woman to treat me. And when you got in the bed with me . . . well, I don't want to say nothing that might sound disrespectful about Fiona, but I enjoyed making love to you more than I ever enjoyed it with her. I'm sure she told you that she only let me make love to her every now and then. I knew that the day was coming when she'd stop letting me touch her at all. I figured I'd get the loving I needed from you while the getting was good. So I decided to go along with the scheme y'all concocted."

"And our little prank got my sister killed. If you never forgive me—"

Jubal held up his hand again. "Hush up. I forgave you a long time ago."

"I'm glad you didn't say nothing while our mamas was still alive. If the busybodies in this town ever find out, they will crucify me and you both for deceiving them. Me more than you because I let my sister walk into a snake pit and she ended up dead. Can I stay here until I find another place to live? They are always hiring at the chicken factory so I know I can get a job over there. I'll work in the fields again if I have to."

"You ain't got to work and you can stay here as long as you want. I make more than enough money for us to live good for the rest of our lives," Jubal assured me.

"I can't stay here and be a burden to you. We can wait a few weeks or months, and then we'll tell everybody we decided to get a divorce. Once you become a single man again, you can marry a righteous woman. But so many members of our church family look down on divorce. I don't think there's more than two or three divorced couples in the whole church! It'd be a big transgression against God if we got divorced. Poor Reverend Sweeney—oh, poor Reverend Sweeney. You know how he goes on a tangent every time there is a scandal that involves somebody in his church. He'll be devastated." I was talking so fast; I had to stop and catch my breath.

Jubal reached across the table and took my hand in his. "Humph! He's lucky that his church family don't know about him and Fiona . . ."

I felt the blood drain from my face. "*You know about them too?*"

Jubal nodded. "I came home early from fishing one evening and heard whooping and hollering coming from the bedroom. They was going at it like wild rabbits. I listened at the door until I could figure out who Fiona was in bed with. As soon as I heard her scream out his name, I left the house."

"Did you tell Fiona what you heard?"

"No, I didn't. I been hearing rumors for years about Reverend Sweeney fooling around. I didn't believe it until I seen him coming out of that motel on Webb Street with that big-bosom sister who sings so many solos at his church. They was kissing and hugging like newlyweds. Otto recently told me that one of his cousins had a fling with the preacher last year. Reverend Sweeney never stays with the same woman too long. So I knew that once he got tired of Fiona, he'd move on to the next woman."

"Fiona told me she was bored with you in the bedroom, but I never thought she'd do something so extreme about it. I didn't know about her and Reverend Sweeney until he came over here one day for her counseling session and lunged at me. I held him off and as soon as I was able to talk to her, she told me the whole story. The only reason Fiona hadn't told me what was going on was because she thought Reverend Sweeney would be at a retreat for a few weeks. I swear I never did nothing with him."

"I know you never done nothing with that countrified *Casanova*."

"How do you know I didn't? If I could lie about some things, I could lie about others."

"That's true, but I don't think you have any reason to lie to me now."

I dropped my head and started talking in a low, meek tone. "There's something else I need to get off my chest. It's important for you to know." I paused. "Fiona wasn't the girl everybody thought she was. Even before she married you."

When I looked back up at Jubal, his face looked like it had turned to solid stone. "What do you mean? And don't hold nothing back." He abruptly let go of my hand, which was covered in so much sweat I had to pick up a dishrag laying nearby and dry it off.

I had to swallow a huge lump in my throat before I could go on. "All of them times when Mama and so many other folks thought I was a floozy, it was really Fiona posing as me."

Jubal still looked like he had turned to stone. I was surprised he was able to move his lips without the skin cracking. "Good God! And you went along with it?"

I nodded. "When we was real young, Fiona was so sickly she almost died several times. I wanted to do everything I could to make sure she had as much happiness in her life as possible because I didn't know how long God would let us have her. It made her happy to sneak out of the house at night wearing my makeup and clothes so she could go to parties and drink and have a good time. I'd appreciate it if you would keep that to yourself too. When Mama thought I was pregnant, it was really Fiona. I agreed to be her until she had her baby."

"Damn!" Jubal was staring at me with a look on his face words couldn't describe. "Anything else?" I told him about the blouse thing and how I took the blame for that. "You went to jail in Fiona's place." Jubal blinked and shook his head. "So y'all switched places a lot when y'all was growing up?"

I nodded and told him how Fiona had let me pose as her so I could play Cinderella and Sleeping Beauty in our elementary school plays.

"Mama made me and my sister go with her to see them two plays." He laughed for a few moments and then he got real serious. "I declare, I don't ever want my son to know about his mama."

"Jubal, there is something else . . ."

He didn't say nothing at first, but he looked scared. "Do I need to know what it is?"

"I know *why* Bonnie Sue killed Fiona." He sat as stiff as a board while I told him what Fiona had told me, and I didn't leave nothing out. He flinched when I got to the part about Bonnie Sue confessing that she was the one who had caused Wally's car to crash.

He held up his hand and stared at me so hard, I cringed and almost slid out of my chair. "We need to let Sheriff Zachary know what Bonnie Sue done."

I shifted in my seat and went on. "Do you think he'll waste his time investigating the deaths of four more colored folks? Bonnie Sue would probably deny it and then we'll have hurt folks for nothing."

"We can at least try to get him to look into it. If she confesses and they charge her with them murders, they'll resentence her. If we don't do nothing, she could get out some day and go on with her life like nothing happened."

I looked at Jubal like he was crazy. "Bonnie Sue is thirty-seven years old. Do you think she'll live another ninety-nine years? She didn't get the electric chair, but she got a death sentence anyway because she is going to die in prison. The state can't kill her but one time."

Jubal looked so woebegone, I was almost sorry I'd told him this additional piece of news.

"I guess you're right. Besides, I don't want Clayton and him and Bonnie Sue's kids, not to mention everybody else, to go through some more pain. What good would it do?" He sighed and took my hand in his again. "I can't believe you been carrying this load around all this time."

"I wouldn't have told you if you hadn't busted me about the . . . uh . . . other thing." I pulled my hand away from his and folded my arms. "But you don't have to worry about taking care of me no longer. All I want is to stay here until I find a job and another place to live . . ."

Jubal shook his head again. "I said you could stay here."

"But if I do, we'd have to make out like I'm Fiona for the rest of our lives!" I had to stop talking and catch my breath. "I am so sorry we played such a deceitful trick on everybody. When I get a job and save enough money, I'll move away from Lexington, and you won't never have to see me again. Mama was the last close kin I had in this town anyway," I wheezed. "I really need to get away from here. As small as this town is, me and you would bump into one another all the time and as long as I'm around, you'd never have the peace of mind you deserve."

"Leona, I have peace of mind and it's because of you. You make me very happy. I love you."

I had to force myself to say what I said next. "I love you too. It's just that living such a epic lie ain't fitting for Christians like us. If I stay, I'll go back to sleeping in the spare bedroom."

Jubal leaned back in his chair and then he started talking real slow. "If it'd make you feel better, we can drive over to Mobile or Mississippi and find a preacher to marry us."

"That wouldn't work because I'd have to use my real name for it to be legal. I'd be worried every day that somebody with relatives in Mobile or Mississippi would find out. Forget that."

"All right, then. We'll just go on like we been doing. But I want my wife to sleep in the same bed with me. I ain't going to force it, though."

"Okay." We stayed silent for a few moments. "Jubal, I am sorry you got dragged into this mess. I didn't mean to hurt you."

"You didn't hurt me none. But if you ever leave me, I will be the most hurt man in the world." He laughed. After a few seconds, I did too.

I didn't know what to say next. Jubal stood up again and held out his hand to me. "We done said all we need to say on this subject. So we ain't *never* going to bring it up again, right?"

I tried to speak but nothing came out. I managed to nod, though. Jubal smiled again, pulled me up from my seat, and led me to the bedroom. "Let's get some sleep. From now on, we'll be man and wife for real this time. That suit you?"

I still couldn't get a word out. I just smiled and nodded again.

EPILOGUE
Leona

April 1938

IT HAD BEEN A YEAR AND ALMOST TWO MONTHS SINCE BONNIE SUE murdered Fiona.

A few folks still felt sorry for her, especially because she'd lost so many loved ones herself at such a young age. I even felt a little bit of pity for her—even though she had ended part of my life. I couldn't imagine how hellish it must have been for her to be in love with a woman for so many years only to end up the way she did. All them times she was at my house—and in that rollaway bed with me when I lived at the rooming house—it must have been pure torture for her to hide her romantic feelings for me. I don't know how I would have reacted if I had really been the one she'd revealed her true feelings to. I doubt if I would have laughed at her the way Fiona told me she had done. And I wouldn't have slapped her neither. But I had to admit to myself that my friendship with Bonnie Sue would never have been the same again. And if I couldn't have turned her around, eventually I would have told her not to come back to my house.

If I broke down one day and told the world that I was really Leona and somebody told Bonnie Sue, I wondered how she would feel if she knew she had killed the wrong twin. I'd never know now. There was not a chance in hell that I would ever reveal my identity to anybody. It was a secret I'd take to my grave. And since Jubal already knew, I didn't have to be on pins and needles for the rest of my life with him. He had too much to lose, so I knew he'd never tell anybody who I really was, or the reason Bonnie Sue had killed Fiona and Wally and his friends.

As time went on, I stopped thinking about Bonnie Sue so much. But I thought about Fiona every day. I was glad our good times had outweighed the bad and that was what I focused on. I was so happy I had enough distractions to help me not think about her too much, though. The main thing in my life now was being the kind of woman I should have been in the first place.

Running around with a wild crowd didn't even appeal to me no more. When I ran into some of my used-to-be drinking buddies, I was so uncomfortable I could barely stand to talk to them for more than a minute or two. One day I went to the market and seen Nadine and Sedella shopping together. They didn't see me because I ducked behind a big barrel and peeped around it until I see them leave.

I missed Fiona so much, there was times when I had to go off by myself and grieve some more. I felt more comfortable pretending to be her now, though. One of my fears was that her friends or in-laws would say something about a past event or something else that I didn't know nothing about and I wouldn't know how to respond. There was no telling what they would think, but I doubted if they would suspect that I was posing as Fiona. Especially if I continued to use that "loss of memory headache" Fiona had used for years. I convinced myself that if Jubal hadn't been eavesdropping that night, he never would have found out I was a imposter.

A few days before Easter while I was at the market in the produce section, somebody tapped me on the shoulder. I immediately turned around. I didn't recognize the gray-haired white woman standing in front of me. My first thought was that she was a employee and was going to accuse me of stealing, so my chest tightened. "You don't remember me, do you?" she asked.

"No, ma'am?"

"I was working for Sheriff Bodine when your twin sister got arrested."

I gulped. "My Lord. I . . . I seen you when I visited her. She told me you gave her peanut brittle and movie magazines. My name is Fiona."

She nodded. "After we turned her loose, I never forgot her. She reminded me so much of my deceased daughter." The woman dabbed a tear from her eye. "I cried when I heard about her getting killed. Sheriff Bodine took it hard too. He told me that he knew she wasn't no bad kid, just a confused one, when she tried to steal that blouse. He had fond memories of your mama and all the hard work she done for the Bodine family." The woman looked around before she whispered, "He even sent flowers to Leona's funeral, but it wasn't fitting for him to sign his name on the card. I'm sure you understand. Anyway, I put his flowers with the ones I sent and I put my name on the card."

What Sheriff Bodine had done sure threw me for a loop. That was the last thing I expected to hear about a man who was affiliated with the Ku Klux Klan. "Thank you for being so nice, ma'am. God's got his eye on you."

Other white folks was staring at us, but I didn't care. The woman went on. "I'm retired, so all I do now is sit on my porch like the rest of the old folks do down here in the South."

I chuckled. "I'll be sitting on my porch someday myself—and not too far from now." We laughed.

"Well, it was nice seeing you." The woman patted my shoulder, slowly turned around, and walked off. I still didn't know her name. When I got home and told Jubal about my conversation with her, I made him promise that we would never refer to white folks, good or bad, as crackers, peckerwoods, devils, or white trash again in our house. He assured me that he wouldn't have no trouble keeping his promise.

Me and him was sitting in church on Easter Sunday when Reverend Sweeney made a comment that gave me something else to think about. "Sometimes God lets a tragedy happen to a person because He's trying to tell them something. If that person gave

Him their attention, He'd reward them with something that would enrich their lives tenfold." That sounded so strange coming from a man who was as deceitful and unfaithful as he was. But I was glad I'd heard what he said. I'd lost my twin, but the week after Easter, I found out I was pregnant!

Jubal couldn't have been more surprised or happier. "I been praying that the Lord would bless me with another child before I got too old," he said when I told him. "I can't wait to tell Lamar he will finally have the baby brother, or sister, he used to badger me and your sister about."

I smiled, but inside it felt like hot coals was burning a hole in my flesh. I had dreams every now and then that was so disturbing I'd wake up sweating. The worst one was with Fiona running down the street covered in blood trying to get back to the home she never should have left.

"I just wish . . ." I couldn't finish my sentence. Jubal finished it for me.

"You wish your twin was still with us. I wish she was too." He paused and caressed the side of my face. "Well, in a way, she is still with us."

I exhaled and nodded. "She sure enough is. Praise the Lord."

DOUBLE LIVES

Mary Monroe

ABOUT THIS GUIDE

The suggested questions that follow are included to
enhance your group's reading of this book.

DISCUSSION QUESTIONS

1. What did you think when Leona encouraged Fiona to pose as her and have sex with her pushy boyfriend so he wouldn't break up with her?

2. When Fiona became pregnant, she talked Leona into switching identities with her because she didn't want to face their pious mother's wrath. Did you think Leona would go this far to protect Fiona's "saintly" reputation?

3. When Fiona assaulted the manager at the dress store, Leona took the blame because she knew Fiona was too fragile to survive incarceration. Under the circumstances, did Leona do what was best for Fiona?

4. Did you think that switching identities would eventually lead to serious trouble for the twins?

5. When Leona took Bonnie Sue in, she gave her spending money and even let her sleep in the same bed with her. Did you think that these gestures sent the wrong message to Bonnie Sue and was part of the reason she fell in love with Leona?

6. Bonnie Sue thought she was talking to Leona when she told Fiona that she was in love with her. Fiona laughed and insulted her. If a close friend of the same sex fell in love with you, how would you react?

7. Would you end your relationship with this friend? If yes, why? If not, why?

8. Bonnie Sue killed Leona's fiancé, Wally, to get him out of Leona's life. When Leona fell in love with Boaz, did you think Bonnie Sue would kill him next?

9. Were you surprised when Bonnie Sue confessed to Fiona that she had killed Wally?

10. When Fiona attempted to call the police and turn Bonnie Sue in for killing Wally, did you think Bonnie Sue would snap and kill Fiona?

11. Bonnie Sue killed the wrong twin, but Leona decided to continue the deception permanently. She didn't think she could deal with the consequences if she told everyone about the identity switch. Did Leona make the right decision?

12. Were you surprised to learn that Fiona's husband, Jubal, had known about the identity switch from day one and had decided to go along with it because Leona treated him so much better than Fiona?

13. Leona eventually fell in love with Jubal and forgot about Boaz. She and Jubal were ecstatic when they found out they were going to be parents. Did you expect such a positive ending to this story?